DEATH'S LAST RUN

A CLARE VENGEL UNDERCOVER NOVEL

ROBIN SPANO

ECW PRESS

Published by ECW Press
2120 Queen Street East, Suite 200, Toronto, Ontario, Canada M4E 1E2
416-694-3348 / info@ecwpress.com

LIBRARY AND ARCHIVES CANADA CATALOGUING IN PUBLICATION

Spano, Robin
Death's last run / Robin Spano.

(A Clare Vengel undercover novel)

ISBN 978-1-55022-997-4
ALSO ISSUED AS: 978-1-77090-351-7 (PDF); 978-1-77090-352-4 (EPUB)

I. Title. II. Series: Spano, Robin Clare Vengel undercover novel.

PS8637.P35D43 2013   C813'.6   C2012-907521-3

Editor for the press: Emily Schultz
Cover and text design: Cyanotype
Printing: Friesens 5 4 3 2 1

The publication of *Death's Last Run* has been generously supported by the Canada Council for the Arts which last year invested $20.1 million in writing and publishing throughout Canada, and by the Ontario Arts Council, an agency of the Government of Ontario. We also acknowledge the financial support of the Government of Canada through the Canada Book Fund for our publishing activities, and the contribution of the Government of Ontario through the Ontario Book Publishing Tax Credit. The marketing of this book was made possible with the support of the Ontario Media Development Corporation.

PRINTED AND BOUND IN CANADA

SUNDAY / FEBRUARY 12

ONE
CLARE

The snowboard was still attached to her feet as the slim brunette lay sprawled, almost posed, in the Whistler mountain snow. Bright red blood spread in two pools from her wrists, sparkling in the sun like crystallized suicide. Or murder. The photo of Sacha Westlake's remains had been clawing at Clare since she'd been shown it the previous afternoon. Twenty-three years old. And dead. And Clare's job to make it make sense.

Clare stared at the chess board. She didn't care about the game, but it was better than the image in her mind. Better, too, than staring at Noah, with his shaggy hair that flopped into his face like he couldn't be bothered with anything past it.

"Check," Clare said.

Noah frowned. "It's only check until I take your queen."

"So take my queen." Clare's carry-on bag was waiting at the door. Her cab to LaGuardia would be outside Noah's Chelsea apartment in less than an hour. Her full luggage — along with her next new identity — would be handed to her at the Toronto airport before her flight to Vancouver.

"Come on, Clare. It's no fun winning when you're not playing the game." He moved his knight in to take her queen.

"I'm so sorry," Clare said, "that in addition to all the other ways I disappoint you, I'm also a dull chess opponent."

"There's nothing dull about you." Noah tugged a string of fluff from his parents' old blue sofa. He could afford his own sofa, but sticking with ugly hand-me-downs was part of the slacker image he still thought was cool at twenty-nine. "It's . . . god, you already know what my problem is. You're flying away to Whistler for who knows how long? It's a terrific assignment — I'm excited as hell for you — but I'm not looking forward to waiting at home while you're out there getting boned by some snowboard instructor who doesn't even know your real name."

"I'm all yours in real life." Clare moved her bishop to protect it from Noah's knight, pulled her feet off the floor, and hugged her legs in. Her sock had a hole in the toe. She didn't care. "But I need the freedom to jump into my job — completely. In today's case, that's Lucy Lipton, snowboarder and soul-searcher."

"*Single* snowboarder and soul-searcher."

"Yeah." Clare shrugged. "Well, snowboarder wannabe — I'm taking lessons when I get there. So, uh, we'll see about that instructor."

Noah nudged a pawn forward. "That doesn't help."

Clare took Noah's pawn with another pawn. It was probably a bad move, but she wanted the game to be over. "*You've* dated suspects when you're undercover. You do remember that's how we met?" Clare loved the memory of meeting Noah, the two of them on their separate poker tour assignments. It had been hot, fun — and kind of dangerous, until she'd learned he was also on the side of the law.

"Right," Noah said. "And you fell for me despite having a boyfriend back home. Can you see why I might be the tiniest bit insecure?"

Clare felt her chest deflate a little. She kind of saw his point.

Noah shook out two Marlboros and passed one to Clare. "You get so into your cover that you feel real attraction from behind some fake person's eyes. Then when the case is over, your feelings aren't."

On the stereo, Ella and Louis were crooning away to "Let's Call the Whole Thing Off." Clare wondered if Noah had played the album on purpose for that song.

"Noah, this is dumb. Should we break up now, before we hate each other?"

"I'll never hate you." Noah moved his bishop across to take Clare's pawn and said, "Checkmate."

"But you're not in love with me." Clare stared at the lines on the hardwood floor, waiting — wishing — for him to contradict her. "And you won't be exclusive unless I give up what makes me good at my job."

"Being a slut isn't what makes you good at your job." Noah pushed the hair out of his face, smiled crookedly across at Clare to let her know he wasn't actually calling her a slut. "You have a knack with suspects — male *and* female. They might not always like you, but you always find your way into their inner circle. Man, I can't believe you got assigned to Sacha Westlake's death."

Of course Noah wouldn't touch the real issue — which was that he'd never told Clare he anything more than liked her, though they'd been dating for nearly a year. He'd said other things, like at the beginning, he said he was *falling for* her, and later, several times actually, that he was *totally into* her. But today that wasn't enough.

Noah picked up his remote and turned the volume down on the music. "How is this even an FBI case, if Sacha died in Canada? Or are the Mounties drafting you back? Luring you with your very own horse named Northern Lights?"

"Oh, you're hilarious." Clare suppressed a grin; she didn't want him off the hook. "I'm going as FBI."

"Okay. But why?"

Clare wasn't officially supposed to tell Noah anything, but their team leader unofficially trusted them to talk freely about their assignments. So she said, "Martha Westlake doesn't think her daughter killed herself."

Noah snorted. "And let me guess — because Martha Westlake's a senator, the FBI jumps when she asks for more men on the job."

Clare nodded. "Paul Worthington is watching this case personally."

"The head of the FBI?" Noah pulled a chipped Niagara Falls ashtray from the floor and set it on the chessboard. "Shit, Clare. That's fantastic. You crack this, you can be sent anywhere you like."

Yeah, and if she messed up, she'd be sent nowhere ever again. But she gave Noah a half grin and said, "I've always wanted to see Europe. Maybe you should consider becoming exclusive with me now, in case I become a female James Bond. An international woman of mystery."

Noah leaned forward to ash his cigarette at the same time as Clare did. Their faces came within an inch of meeting. They both pulled away quickly.

"Because James Bond is such a model of fidelity," Noah said. "And you won't be sent to Europe — it would have to be somewhere the FBI operates."

"I'm going to Canada today. We don't officially operate there."

"Sure we do. We own Canada." Noah's mouth corners lifted.

Clare would take the bait some other time. She studied Noah's face, shadowed by a full day's stubble because she'd woken him up early, surprised him on her way to the airport. She wished she was on the couch beside him, nestled into his lean, strong arms. He was right, in a way, that they should fight another day. But Clare couldn't cross the floor to sit with him.

"Do you think Sacha killed herself?" she asked.

Noah nodded slowly. "I only know the case from the news. From what I've seen, yeah, it looks like suicide. She'd been living in Whistler for just over a year, waitressing at a bar without any clear career direction, even though she had a degree from NYU. On the physical side, there was no bruising, no struggle . . . I can see why the local cops are ready to close this."

"No history of self-harm, though," Clare said. "Don't people who slice their wrists to die have a history of cutting themselves?"

"There's a link. It's not absolute." Typical Noah — unwilling to commit.

"Did you know Sacha was on a sedative when she died?" Clare said.

"In her twenties in Whistler? I'd say it's not a stretch if she liked to take drugs."

"Maybe that's why she didn't fight back." Sacha was only a year younger than Clare. Clare imagined herself in Sacha's place, wanting to fight an assailant but being too doped up to struggle. It would be awful, like swimming in quicksand — or like a dream where your limbs can't move.

"I think the drugs make a better case for suicide." Noah leaned forward on the couch. "They were talking about that on CNN. There was this doctor, he said a lot of people pop pills before they kill themselves — even guys who shoot themselves or jump off bridges. Helps them take that final step."

Clare thought of the picture — the snowboard, the blood. It *looked* like suicide. And it didn't.

"Sacha's mom's popularity is way up," Noah said. "She's been completely out of the public spotlight for the past week and a half, since Sacha died. But now she's second only to Geoffrey Kearnes." Noah must have seen Clare's blank look, because he said, "Martha Westlake is running for the Republican presidential nomination."

"Oh." Clare had heard Westlake's name a lot in the media recently, but she'd assumed it was because of her daughter's death. She found it hard to follow U.S. politics — or maybe she just found it hard to care. "How can a New York senator run for the Republican nomination? I thought New York elected Democrats."

"We usually do. But . . . here, come see on my computer." Noah crossed the small room to his desk overlooking dirty, hip Eighth Avenue. He moved his mouse and the screen flickered to life. He held out his rolling desk chair, motioned for Clare to come sit in it.

Clare frowned, but she brought her cigarette and the ashtray over to Noah's desk.

Noah pulled up Martha Westlake's home page. "Westlake is moderate," he said. "Right wing, but not a total crazy. She got in by a hair when the economy took that huge nosedive. I guess that was before you moved here — you were probably still building igloos."

"That's really funny, Noah." Clare wondered when the Canadian jokes would dry up — she'd been waiting eleven months.

She looked at the face staring back at her from the computer. Martha Westlake's features weren't as fine as her daughter's, but their eyes shared an intensity, and they had the same pale white skin and dark brown hair. Clare looked sideways at Noah. "So Sacha's death helped her mom politically. Is the senator being investigated as a suspect?"

"Probably. But if Martha Westlake had murdered her daughter, she would hardly have asked the FBI to get involved."

"Sure she would. Because she can control us." Clare took a long drag of her cigarette and wondered why she'd never tried to quit. Probably because it felt so damn good, nicotine moving through her veins and relaxing the parts that were tense. "You know it's most often family members who kill."

"It's most often spouses," Noah said, "or boyfriends."

Clare laughed. "Is that meant to be menacing?"

"Yes. I'm going to kill you." Noah stubbed out his cigarette and stood behind Clare, massaging her shoulders. "I meant you'll likely soon know who Sacha was dating. The press hasn't been able to find out."

Clare clicked on a tab that opened Martha Westlake's photo gallery. Standard shots of a politician on the campaign trail: Martha eating a hot dog in a park wearing a pantsuit she must have been sweltering in, Martha smiling broadly at a baby while she touched the child's nose, Martha wearing a conservative-length pair of shorts while helping at a car wash with a banner that said *Wash for a Cure*. What struck Clare as strange: there were no photos of Sacha on the campaign trail with her mom. There was one posed studio shot of mother and daughter together. But it almost made the overall picture worse.

Clare spun her chair around to look at Noah. The massage felt great, but it wasn't solving anything. "You'd think every guy Sacha had slept with would give a teary press statement. Or maybe she wasn't a slut like me."

Noah shook his head, like he wasn't touching that. His eyes met Clare's and he looked like he'd just lost his puppy.

"Speaking of teary press statements, Sacha's best friend is my new roommate, starting tonight."

"Jana Riley?" Noah said. "She looks like a psycho. Be careful."

"She looks melodramatic," Clare acknowledged, wondering how come Noah knew so much about this case. She turned back to the computer and Googled *Jana Riley*. "I also have a job interview at the bar where Sacha worked."

"That's great." Noah's voice behind Clare was flat. "Before long, you'll be boning Sacha's boyfriend."

"Man, I hope he's hot." She clicked on a link that took her to Jana's Facebook profile. Public — surprise, surprise.

Noah sighed. "You don't get it, Clare."

"What don't I get?"

"If you want to be in a committed relationship, you don't say things like, 'I hope I get to have sex with a hot stud on this assignment.'"

"I was joking." But Clare knew he was right.

Jana's Facebook status said, *Shredding the mountain snow. Trying to fill my days with fun because Sacha was nothing if not fun. Still sad, though.* Well, at least Clare wouldn't have to wear black all the time in the apartment.

"It's not funny," Noah said. "You know how hard this is for me, playing chess with you, browsing websites with you for your last hour in New York?" He grabbed her chair and spun her back around. They locked eyes. "I want to be naked with you — not fucking you, but touching you, feeling your muscled little legs wrapped around me, running my fingers through your hair, kissing your lips, your neck, your body. Why do you think I put on romantic music as soon as you came over?" When Clare said nothing, Noah continued, "Are you even capable of falling in love? As you, I mean. Not as Lucy, or as Tiffany, or whatever cover role you're playing. It's Clare Vengel I'm trying to reach. Is she even fucking available?"

Clare couldn't speak to that, so she went back to Noah's coffee table and started setting up the chess board. She had time for one more game before her airport cab came.

But as she arranged the wooden men into their orderly lines, the image of Sacha Westlake's death shot came back to the front of Clare's mind. No matter what Noah said — or what they said on CNN — the biggest inconsistency was staring right out from that photograph.

Suicide was leaving life. Snowboarding was living it. They didn't go together. That was the killer's mistake.

"You know what, Noah? Fuck this." Clare stood up. "I'd rather stare at the blank walls of the airport gate than sit here and listen to you tell me all my flaws."

"Clare, I . . ."

"Oh, and jazz isn't romantic. It's lame. You want to get me naked, try Depeche Mode or Leonard Cohen. We've been together for a year. I can't believe you don't know that."

Clare grabbed her carry-on and slammed the door shut behind her. She'd cancel her scheduled airport car and hail a cab on the street. She had to figure out what the killer's other mistakes were. Before he — or she — killed again.

TWO
MARTHA

Martha Westlake gazed out the back window of her West Seventieth Street brownstone. A few stories up, in an apartment that backed onto Martha's courtyard from West Seventy-first, a naked, fleshy fortysomething contemplated her wardrobe options. In other windows, a retired couple drank tea with no animation and a shirtless man, maybe in his twenties, danced around his bathroom as he shaved. Her constituents. She hated them right now, probably because they were alive.

How had she failed so completely?

She had a zillion phone calls to return and her email inbox was bulging to the point of overflow, but all Martha wanted to do was sit and stare at photographs.

She opened the fourth giant album, the one where Sacha was three. There should have been twenty-three years to go through, but somewhere along the way the world had gone digital and now no one printed photos anymore.

She touched the photograph on the first page, traced her finger along Sacha in her brown plaid trench coat, marching through Central Park and looking like a tiny reporter. Martha remembered the day she'd taken the picture. One of the rare full days she had spent with her daughter. The nanny had the flu and Fraser was out of town, so Martha was stuck — she felt that way, *stuck* — looking after Sacha. Near the park entrance, she and Sacha passed a homeless man with a three-legged dog. Sacha looked up at Martha with her big brown eyes and said, "Mommy, can we bring that man home tonight? If I give him my dinner, he won't have to eat his dog's other legs." Martha had hurried Sacha along with some brusque explanation of why inviting strangers into your house was unsafe. She wished now that she'd helped Sacha take the man a sandwich.

She reached for her coffee and took a sip — lukewarm. Why could she not shed a single tear? Martha had always suspected herself of being a cold bitch; now she knew for sure. She touched the photo again and closed her eyes.

Martha's BlackBerry rang. Ted. She'd been ignoring his calls for over a week. She sighed and picked it up.

"Martha. So sorry to bother you. Kearnes is pulling tricks in Michigan."

"What kind of tricks?"

A metal snapping sound came through the phone. That would be Ted cracking his first can of Red Bull for the day. Or maybe his second, judging by the speed he was talking. "He's been making phone calls to your supporters. In particular, he's aiming to snag Hillier's endorsement."

"He can aim all he likes. Reverend Hillier and I had dinner three weeks ago. We shook hands and agreed that I have his support."

"That was before . . . Kearnes is implying that it's a good thing this happened now — Sacha's death — so the Republican Party can see your so-called true colors before making the mistake of electing you as leader. He's trying to prove that if you're taking this much time off over one death, how would you handle the presidency in wartime?"

"For Christ's sake, this is my daughter. Can't Hillier see that? Can't Kearnes?"

"Yeah, but you're not there to defend yourself."

"How do you know what Geoff Kearnes is saying on the phone, anyway? Or do I not want to know?"

"A college friend is involved in Kearnes' campaign. He and I grabbed a coffee after the all-candidates town hall meeting in Flint ..."

The meeting Martha should have been at was the implication and why Ted let his sentence trail. She eyed her photo album and wished Ted would get to the point.

"It's disgusting," Ted said. "And don't worry — voters disagree with Kearnes, if your new popularity is anything to gauge by."

Martha willed herself not to comment on the absurd stupidity of that statement.

"But ... and this is bad ... I called Hillier's office half an hour ago to make sure things are still good, that we still have his endorsement ..."

"And?"

"He took the call personally. Says he hasn't made up his mind."

Martha clenched her hand tighter around her phone. If Hillier took the call personally, it was a good sign and a bad one. It meant he was still open to backing Martha. And it meant that he wanted something.

"Kearnes is offering a cabinet post." Ted's voice was flat.

"Hillier told you that?"

"No — that's through the grapevine." Ted's code for *you don't want any more details.*

"A reliable grapevine?"

"Yes."

"Motherfucker," Martha said. "Let him go, then. Let Hillier endorse whomever he chooses."

"I wish that was an option," Ted said. "But we can't win Michigan without him."

"So we lose Michigan." Martha didn't see the big deal. There were more states.

"We can't lose Michigan, or Kearnes will have enough delegates to win the nomination."

"Officially?"

"Effectively — unless you plan on taking him in his home state. But trust me — Michigan is easier. All we need is Hillier and we should have it."

Martha tried to care — she *should* care — but she didn't. "I'm not giving a cabinet position to anyone with a religious background."

"You have to give him something. He's already out on a limb, supporting the only Republican campaigning on the separation of church and state."

"Meaning?"

"*Reverend* Hillier has a congregation to keep happy. He needs to take them something positive — something to make them understand why you as president is best for their self-interest, even if you are a heathen."

Martha snorted. "We've been through all this, Ted. Three weeks ago, my education plan and the war on drugs were enough for him. And to be frank, I don't care that much anymore. Losing Michigan — giving up this race — is looking tempting."

"Forget about it," Ted said with a nervous laugh. "Your team won't let you fall. Anyway, I called because I need your approval on a statement before we release it to the press. It's loosely aimed at Hillier, but there are others who could use their confidence in you rejuvenated. We want to talk about your grief — how Sacha's death knocked you down — and we'll focus on your bereavement as inspiring your rebirth as a stronger, more compassionate world leader."

"Rebirth? Is that in case I have one lone supporter left from the religious right?"

"Look, you have the moderates, independents, and coastal conservatives locked tight. But it doesn't hurt to use the odd bit of churchy language as a bone to throw to the evangelicals. Like it or not, we will need them eventually."

Martha smiled as she recalled Sacha, age fifteen, saying, *You know that seventy percent of Republicans don't believe in evolution? You're too smart to align yourself with these idiots. Or is it the low taxes you like? Does the Republican ethic work for you because you're rich and you want to keep it that way?*

Ted was still talking. "The idea is for Hillier and the rest of the party to see you as not only a viable candidate, but a better candidate for having gone through this turmoil and come out on top." Poor

Ted. He was a smart enough kid when he wasn't trying to prove how smart he was.

"I don't like it. A news release reeks of excuses when it's obvious to anyone with a brain why I'm not at full strength."

"We have to act, though. If we lose Michigan or Arizona, the battle will be too far uphill. Washington is yours, Alaska isn't significant, but taking Kearnes in Georgia is going to be next to impossible. Unless we can find a prostitute in his closet, or even a blow-up cocker spaniel — but so far no luck on either." Ted paused. "You still say no about bringing up the affair, right? I know it was over twenty years ago, but Kearnes was married; you weren't. We could blow him out of the race with one piece of evidence."

"Yes, I still say no." Martha's head was spinning with the rapid-fire speed of Ted's talking. Her own words felt slow and sluggish in comparison. "Arrange a lunch with Reverend Hillier. I'll tell him face to face that I still plan to win this. Was there anything else?"

"Um, the FBI has been in touch. You cleared them to talk to me, right?"

"Yes."

"They're training an undercover to send to Whistler."

Martha's head began to pound. "When do they think he'll be ready?"

"He's arriving in Whistler this evening. Um, Martha?"

"Yes?"

"I don't think it was suicide, either. Sacha was strong. She loved being alive."

Martha clicked off her phone before she could tear a strip off Ted that he didn't deserve. It wasn't Ted's fault he was twenty-six in Washington.

THREE
RICHIE

Richie Lebar leaned in the doorway between Jana's kitchen and living room. Outside the dirty window, snow was dumping on the village.

Past some other apartment buildings and houses in the Upper Village, Richie saw the Fairmont Chateau Whistler, nestled on its own at the foot of Blackcomb Mountain. Though it was at the base of the hill, that hotel was the peak for Richie. He liked to take Jana there, sit in the bar and order a bottle of Cristal and just lounge there sipping it, living the life. It showed him how far he'd come, how different he was from the rough guy he used to be. With snow cascading down upon its turrets, the hotel looked like a fairytale castle, straight out of Germany or Switzerland.

He wished Jana would hurry up and eat. He wanted to hit the slopes, feel his board glide through powder, burn off some of the nasty energy that had been eating him up for over a week.

"Sacha Westlake was no angel." Jana poked her spoon violently into her Mueslix. "How come every time someone young dies, they're suddenly an honor student with a heart of gold?"

Richie laughed, which felt good because not much was funny these days. "True, that. In high school, my friend got shot. He was an evil mofo — had his eight-year-old brother selling meth for him 'cause the kid was too young for juvie. Day after he dies, there's a picture in the paper of my friend singing in the church choir when he was, like, five years old. The headline was *Choir Boy Slain.*"

Jana lifted a spoonful of cereal from the bowl and frowned at it. She set her spoon back down. "Seriously. Sacha was awesome, but the press has to stop sticking her on this tragic pedestal. I want to tell the next reporter who calls that she was fucking her married boss and selling LSD into the States."

"Yeah, but you won't, right?" Richie flicked his tongue against the back of his mouth grill — the gold and diamonds that decorated his teeth and told the world he had money.

"Of course not. I'm not going to throw you and Chopper under the bus. Maybe I'll say the married boss part though. Let Wade squirm." Jana nudged her green-rimmed glasses up on her nose. They were cute on her. Richie wished she'd wear them out of the house sometimes.

Richie looked past Jana out the kitchen window at the heavy falling snow. First powder day since Sacha died — like the sky was trying to tell them to move on. "Are you planning to eat your cereal, or play with it until it turns to mush?"

"I'm out of Smarties. It tastes boring with just seeds and oats."

"So add bananas. But speed up."

Jana pushed back her chair and pulled a banana from the bunch on the counter. "Go without me. I feel like a lazy morning."

Richie frowned. Since Sacha's death, he didn't like to leave Jana alone. "Keep the door locked."

"Aw. Are you my big black bodyguard?"

Richie flinched. He knew she wasn't racist, but sometimes it kind of felt like Jana was dating him to piss off her parents, some kind of extended teenage rebellion. Maybe he was being oversensitive. "Is your new roommate coming today?"

"Tonight," Jana said.

"Be careful with her. Don't let this get out, but there's an under-cover coming to town. Maybe already here."

"And you think it might be my new roommate?"

"Probably not. They say it's a guy. Still . . ."

Jana glanced at him. "How do you know?"

"Norris told me. But hush. It's not for everyone's ears."

"So I can't smoke drugs with my new roommate? Man, this is going to be fun."

"You can smoke pot. But play it safe with the shit you say. No mentioning Sacha's extracurricular activities, for example."

"You mean her trips to the States with a knapsack full of acid?"

"Yeah." Richie grinned. "Things like that."

A chunk of banana splashed into Jana's bowl, sending drops of milk flying. It grossed Richie out that she didn't grab a cloth, just let the droplets land wherever.

"I should never have put that ad for a new roommate up so soon," Jana said. "Sacha's mom is paying her rent until the end of March, so it's not like I need the new girl's money."

"You should tell Sacha's mom to stop paying."

"I should, right? But she's rich. I kind of figured it didn't matter."

Richie normally found Jana's full figure attractive. He liked that she had meat he could grab and an ass that wasn't bony when he squeezed it. But this morning, she looked fat and selfish, like a cat who thought all the cream should be hers.

Jana toyed with the tiny braid in her otherwise loose long hair. "What's the undercover here for? Drugs?"

"No. He's here for Sacha."

"What? Why?"

"Her mom don't think —" Richie cringed from his own grammar. "*Doesn't* think it's suicide."

"Her mom should get a grip."

"You think Sacha killed herself?" Richie picked up his ski pants, which he'd slung over the back of a chair the night before.

"I know she killed herself — that's why I'm so mad at her. She wrote me a letter before she went up Blackcomb."

"She left a note?" Richie wondered why he didn't know this

already. Norris should have told him; things were supposed to be transparent between them. Unless Jana was making shit up again.

Jana was tearing up, which Richie wished he had more patience for. If they'd actually been best friends, it would be one thing. But that was all in Jana's fucked-up head — to Sacha, Jana had just been someone fun to party with.

"Have you shown the note to the cops?" Richie asked.

Jana shook her head. "I miss her too much to give up the last thing Sacha gave me."

Richie dropped his ski pants back over the sofa. He was starting to think there really was a note. "You have to show me."

"No. It's private."

"Jana."

Jana wrinkled her mouth. "This is about your business, isn't it? You think if you show the cops the note, the undercover will go home and you'll be able to keep selling drugs."

Richie lifted his eyebrows, meaning *Duh.*

"So this note is worth a lot of money."

"You want me to pay you for it?" Richie wanted to slug her, but kept calm. Hitting women was not in his repertoire — he'd left Scarborough behind, and all his father's ways with it. "How much?"

"I don't know. What's it worth?"

To Richie at that moment, it was worth fifty grand or so — maybe more — if the letter could send the FBI guy away. "I'll give you a thousand bucks for it."

"No shit?" Jana's eyes lit up. "I'd rather keep the letter, but cool that it's worth so much."

"We have to show the police — especially now that it's a murder investigation."

Jana laughed. "A lecture from a drug dealer about how to help the cops. Good one."

"You want your supply to dry up? That's what's gonna happen while the FBI is here. Chopper's going to stop production, too — so no more Mountain Snow."

"Fine." Jana pushed back her chair and stomped into her room. She came out with a piece of paper that she thrust into Richie's hand. "But I'm not selling it. I want this back by tonight. I've been sleeping with it under my pillow."

"A-ight," Richie said, and then kicked himself. *So ghetto.* Why did he keep slipping today? That part of him was supposed to already be dead.

FOUR
CLARE

Clare passed the final customs checkpoint at the Toronto airport. It was weird being so close to her hometown and only stopping long enough to grab a coffee and a new identity. She chewed her lip as she searched the crowd for her ex-handler, Amanda.

"Clare!" Amanda smiled broadly and approached. She was struggling with an old hockey bag that was almost the size of her tiny frame. Clare was impressed that she could carry it in heels.

"You should probably start calling me Lucy." Clare took the bag from Amanda and nearly dropped it to the floor. "Is this my luggage?"

"I know it's bulky." Amanda pointed the way to an escalator. "But Lucy is a seriously casual chick. And there's a snowboard in here. You'll have to send it as oversized luggage. I had fun shopping for your wardrobe."

"Oh, I'm so glad." Clare was trying to be polite. It was just hard. Amanda was one of those girly girls who thought a woman was incomplete without her nails done. *Seriously casual* probably meant dry cleaning was optional.

"Don't worry," Amanda said. "There's nothing pink."

They reached the top of the escalator and emerged at the

departures level. Amanda dealt with the self-serve check-in. She discreetly handed Clare her new passport before they went through domestic security.

Clare had done this before, and of course she wasn't doing anything illegal, but it always taxed her nerves, clearing security under a false name. They didn't even ask for ID at this stage — all they cared about was the boarding pass — but what if a guard sensed something off about Clare, like they were trained to do? This felt like a test, like if Clare couldn't pass security, she wouldn't pull off her new identity in the world she was about to enter. She tried not to show her relief when she had her bag again, her new phone and laptop packed back into place, and Amanda led the way to the gate for Clare's plane to Vancouver.

At the gate, Clare was pleased to see Tim Hortons — her favorite Canadian coffee chain, which she'd missed, since there was only one that she knew of in New York and it was in crappy touristy Times Square. She was even more pleased when Amanda headed for its lineup. Clare needed a caffeine injection. It was eleven a.m., and she'd been up since five so she could spend time with Noah. In retrospect, she should have slept in.

They loaded up with coffee and found a seating area with a cool view of the runways.

Amanda pulled a thick envelope from her soft leather handbag. She passed it to Clare. "I'll trade you."

Clare lifted her knapsack to her lap and pulled her passport and wallet from the front pouch. She handed it to Amanda. "This always freaks me out. Saying goodbye to my identity in some random airport or café. I always wonder, will I get my real self back?"

"I think you'll be fine. We're not going deep into Communist Russia. Do you know how to snowboard?"

"No." Clare slid her new wallet into her knapsack. It was about as ratty as her old one — maybe there was hope for her new wardrobe.

"That's fine. I've arranged a lesson for tomorrow. You don't have to be a pro on the slopes when you get there. The snowboard is a hand-me-down from Lucy's older brother. The hockey bag is from her younger brother."

"I get to ride a guy's snowboard?"

"Thought you'd like that. You'll want to get up to speed as fast as you can. Sacha loved snowboarding and her peer group spends most of their downtime on the mountain."

"I've been studying snowboarder lingo," Clare said. "On UrbanDictionary.com, and from movies and stuff. So I'll have a clue what they're talking about."

"Good work," Amanda said.

"Thanks, *boss*." Clare sounded sharper than she'd meant to. But whatever; it was true that Amanda wasn't in charge. "Sorry. I mean, I know I'm on your turf, and I'll cooperate. But I work for the FBI now."

"*Ac-tu-al-ly* . . ." Amanda let the word trail so it sounded like it had about six syllables. She tapped a slender finger against her lips, as if she was trying to break some terrible news and was secretly gleeful about it.

"Actually what?" Clare glared.

"We agreed that the FBI could send an operative, but the RCMP insists on running you jointly."

"Running me." As if Clare were a dog, or a car.

"I'm not a handler anymore, but because you and I have worked together, we all agreed that I could step into the role again. I'll report to both organizations. Your team leader in New York will have your contact info and he can call you for an update anytime. And you can contact him."

"Gee, thanks. I can talk to my boss while I'm working." Clare had to rein this in. She felt like she was visiting her parents — riled to act like a teenager all over again despite everything she'd learned in the world since leaving home.

"Come on, Clare. I'm looking forward to working together."

Clare stared into her coffee. Tim Hortons wasn't as good as she remembered it. "I've learned a lot in the past year."

"I'm sure that's true," Amanda said. "But I'm not your obstacle, despite what you seem to believe."

Clare looked out the window at the runway, wet with Toronto winter slush. In the distance, a plane took off. Half of her wished she was on it, heading back to Noah and her life in New York instead of about to jump on another plane that would take her even farther away. She was glad Amanda was traveling on a different plane so they wouldn't be seen arriving together. "So what *is* my obstacle?"

Amanda pursed her lips, as if trying to decide how much to share. Finally, she said, "You know that Inspector Norris with the Whistler RCMP wants to close the Westlake case as a suicide."

"Uh, yeah. This has all been in the news."

Amanda sighed. "If you prove Norris wrong, his credibility comes into question."

"If *I* prove him wrong? Is he going to blame me if it turns out Sacha was murdered?"

Amanda tilted her head to one side, which Clare took as a yes.

"Can I meet with him? Maybe in person I can let Norris know I'm not hostile."

"I don't think that will help."

"Why? I can be diplomatic if I have to. I told you I've learned a lot."

"I don't think he'll appreciate a twenty-four-year-old trying to placate his professional concerns."

Clare flashed a super-fake smile. "I love it when you use big words *and* belittle me all in one sentence." Okay, that wasn't a great start in the maturity direction.

"More important," Amanda said, "Inspector Norris doesn't know your name. He knows you'll be arriving — for some reason, one of my colleagues saw fit to loop him in that far — but he doesn't know who you are or where you'll be staying."

"So we're not on the same team?"

"We are . . ." Amanda frowned. "But Norris grew up in Pemberton. That's thirty minutes up the highway from Whistler. Two of his high school friends are prime suspects in this case. The decision from above is that the less he knows, the better."

Clare threw her hands in the air. "Of course the fact he's local should be a point against the man. No sense treating that as an asset. No wonder he doesn't want me here. His employers already treat him like garbage."

"It's an obstacle, Clare. Don't turn it into a roadblock. I requested you for this job because I'm impressed by your open mind."

"You requested me?"

"I think you have the right character to immerse yourself in this culture. You'll want to add a couple of traits to help you blend in — like an eco-friendly mindset and an appreciation of organic food."

"Are you asking me to be a vegetarian?"

"No." Amanda smiled. "Just, if you're picking up potato chips, grab the hippie kind, with the biodegradable packaging. And drink local craft beer rather than Bud. It's not a culture of extremists, but they do have a sensibility about preserving the environment. They love the outdoors."

"Sounds okay," Clare said.

"You'll have to watch the marijuana, though. We don't want you so stoned that you're not in control of your reactions."

"I don't smoke pot. So that won't be a problem."

Amanda frowned. "Actually, I think you *should* smoke, at least a little. It's an unconventional directive, but your new peer group smokes marijuana liberally."

"Fine," Clare said, a small grin tugging the corner of her lips. "But you can't make me inhale."

FIVE
WADE

Wade's head throbbed. It had been throbbing most mornings lately. His throat was dry and so was the water glass on the bedside table. He thought vaguely about cutting back his smoking but really, why? It wasn't like he wanted a long life.

A ray of sun pierced in from the skylight, hitting the snow on the mountain and reflecting directly into Wade's eyes. Even nature wouldn't leave him alone.

Wade recalled a distant past when he used to love waking up. It was a very distant past. Before he owned a bar. Before he was married. Maybe it was a false memory.

He shuffled out to the kitchen and was surprised to see Georgia there, also in a robe, waxed legs stretching down to her spa slippers. She looked like she was in *Perfect Housewife* magazine. Wade wanted to close the page.

"Isn't it Monday?" Wade said, meaning, *Why aren't you already at that desk in Vancouver you love so much?*

"Nope. Sunday. Would you like me to squeeze you some juice?"

Wade wrapped his arms around his wife's waist from behind. He tried to figure out how he could slip a shot of vodka into the juice without her seeing. "You squeeze the oranges; I'll squeeze you."

"Maybe not at the same time." Georgia uncoiled Wade from around her.

Wade shrugged and took a stool across the double-wide counter. The vodka was in the cupboard beside him, but he'd wait until Georgia left the room. He pulled that day's newspaper toward him, hoping — and not hoping — for a new article about Sacha.

"You still read that?" Georgia said. "I was thinking of canceling the subscription."

"I read it sometimes," Wade said. "I like that it comes to the door."

"We're leaking money."

"It's a dollar a day." Wade flipped as casually as he could to the national news section. Or would the story be in international, since Sacha was American? "Fine. Cancel the subscription."

Georgia pushed an orange half onto the machine, taking over the kitchen with noise. When she'd finished, she handed Wade a half-full glass of juice.

"I don't even rate a full glass?"

"Oranges are expensive. When we figure out what's happening with Avalanche, I'll squeeze you a full glass of juice."

"Ouch." Wade was tempted to reach for the vodka openly. But it wasn't even eight a.m. Georgia could be really judgmental about morning drinking.

"You know I don't mean to stomp on your dream. But it drives me insane that I'm making more money than ever before and I still have to pinch pennies when I'm shopping for a pair of shoes."

Wade's dream? Oh, right. She meant the bar. "I have an investor for Avalanche," Wade said. "We're getting close to a deal."

"You sure it's a real investor, not some nosy businessman who wants you to show him the books so he can open his own bar?" Georgia popped the top off the juicer and took the dirty parts to the sink.

Wade casually opened the cupboard. Georgia's back was to him. When she turned on the water, he'd have a few clear seconds easily.

He aimed for a conciliatory tone when he said, "I know the past few people I've talked to have been disappointing. But this guy's for real. I already know him."

"You do?" Georgia turned back around to face him. Her eyes moved to the open liquor cupboard door and fixed pointedly on it. "Do I know him, too?"

"Maybe. Richie Lebar. Nice guy. In his late twenties and smart. I think he'll go far."

"You mean the drug dealer. The one who looks like Jay-Z." Georgia returned to face the sink, where she started banging juicer parts around in soapy water.

In one swift movement, Wade unscrewed the vodka cap and poured a healthy two ounces into his juice glass, which was still a quarter full. Since Georgia had already seen the open cupboard door, he didn't bother shutting it when he put the bottle away.

When she'd finished washing up, Georgia walked over and took Wade's hand. "I can see why you're tempted — I know how hard you've been working to get Avalanche off the ground. But I don't want to be in business with a drug dealer."

Wade finished the juice in one gulp and set the glass on the counter. "That was good. Thanks."

"Did you add booze to your juice?"

Wade lowered his brow, trying to look baffled by the question.

Georgia shook her head. Wade remembered when he'd loved to look at her long, mussed-up hair in the morning, before she showered and made it all perfect.

"Look, Georgia, you can't treat me like I'm a five-year-old with my first lemonade stand. I'm supposed to be your partner in life."

"You think I like this role?" Georgia's eyes were tearing up.

"Of course not. I appreciate the fashion sacrifices you've made to help me launch Avalanche."

"Jesus. Have another shot." Georgia started pulling out bottles from the cupboard at random. "What would you like? Whiskey? Grand Marnier?"

"A vodka would be fine," Wade said. "It would help me deal with your irrational rage."

"*I'm* irrational?" Georgia grabbed the vodka bottle and free-poured into Wade's dirty juice glass. She stopped just before the glass was brimming over. "Here, Wade. Here's your fucking medicine. Too bad you never made it as a rock star; your alcoholism would have worked for your public image."

Wade took a sip.

Georgia's eyes bugged. "You're actually *having* that? It's not even eight in the morning."

Wade took a larger sip — more like a gulp.

"Think about it, though." Georgia's tone softened into something sad. "We close the bar, then it's just you and me, living like we used to. We can move back to the city, wander into Stanley Park and have weekends like normal people."

"Maybe have some kids."

"I'm too old to have children." Georgia shivered like a ghost had just passed through her.

"You're only thirty-six. You want to condemn us to a childless old age?" Wade said, feeling bleaker than ever. He was thirty-eight, which at the moment felt ancient.

"Jesus, Wade, do you have to be so melodramatic when life doesn't do what you want it to?"

"I'm just trying to find something to make my life worth living." Because Sacha was gone, and Wade wasn't sure anything was left.

"Now you have nothing to live for." Georgia grabbed a towel and began fiercely drying the juicer parts from the dish rack.

Shit. Wade had to get her onside, to agree to the partnership with Richie. "We used to have so much fun together. Remember Morocco?"

Georgia smiled, but it was short-lived. "We were in our twenties. We didn't know what stress was."

"I'm taking Richie's offer. It's a fair price, and he'll help pump young blood into the place."

"No."

Wade glared at Georgia. Their eyes locked in what felt to Wade like hate.

Georgia shook her head firmly. "I know I said I wouldn't exercise my signing authority. But this is a hard no. You get partners like that, you're only asking to get raped. I love you too much to see that happen."

"That's not love, Georgia. That's control."

"My name is on that lease, and I have a professional reputation to maintain. I can't have my name dragged through the mud."

"Don't you get it? The landlords are taking back the bar if I don't give them forty-five grand in two weeks. Partnering with Richie solves that — *plus* it gives the place a cash infusion to really get it pumping."

"I'm fine with closing the bar. I'm not fine being in bed with criminals."

SIX

RICHIE

Richie Lebar tapped his fur-lined boot against the police station floor. He saw a tiny tear on the suede at his toe, which annoyed him. He didn't like leaving his boots in Jana's foyer — she just threw her stuff everywhere, no regard for anything of hers or anyone else's.

Inspector Norris was taking forever to read the suicide note. His thin lips pushed in and out from his face like a goldfish in a tank, slow and stupid. Finally, the little inspector looked up. "Thank you for this. You're free to leave."

"I promised Jana I'd bring the note back." As Richie held out his hand, he wondered if maybe he should lose a few of his gold rings. Less bling might make people take him more seriously as a businessman when he became Wade's partner in the bar. On the other hand, nothing said confidence like personal style. Richie had to make sure he stayed true to his real self, even while he tweaked his image to fit into the business world.

Norris smoothed the note on the desk in front of him. "Jana's going to have to find another memento to clutch in her sleep. This is evidence."

Richie shook his head. For a cop on the criminals' payroll, Norris didn't seem to understand who was in charge. But the little cop had real control issues — probably why he became a cop — so Richie had to tread lightly, not undermine Norris in an obvious way.

"Do you have anything else with Sacha's handwriting?" Norris slid the note into a large machine that looked like it served triple duty as a copier, printer, and scanner. Maybe a fax machine, too. He pressed a couple of buttons and two pages came out. He handed one to Richie — the photocopy. "Give this to Jana. I'll log the note as her official property so when we close the case, it will belong to her. Tell her *you're welcome*. She's about eleven days too late for a thank you."

Richie's gaze wandered to the certificates on the wall, commemorating Norris' graduation from police academy and completion of various officer training. Richie was pretty sure this was why cops were always two steps behind criminals — they stopped to commemorate things while criminals just got on with business.

"How's your kid?" Richie said.

Norris' whole body seemed to relax into a smile. "Zoe was invited to play in the junior string orchestra with the Vancouver Youth Symphony."

"I take it that's a good thing." Richie couldn't help but smile back. If he ever had kids, he was taking a page out of Norris' book.

"Zoe's going to have the musical career that I never . . . that she deserves."

"Good for her," Richie said. Then he had a thought: "You loved that band, huh? Avalanche Nights?"

Norris frowned.

"Why don't you revive the group? You're all still here — you, Wade, Chopper — you're all still talented." Richie was clutching at straws maybe. But if he could get Avalanche Nights back together onstage, and especially if he got credit for it, it could be the final in he needed. His goal was clear: Richie wanted to run this town — legitimately.

"I'm not a dreamer. That part of my life is over." Norris gave a short shake of his head. "You can go now."

"Sure," Richie said. "Just give me that original note, and we're good. Pretty sure I'm not getting laid until I get it back into Jana's hands." Totally not true. Jana never stayed angry. But Richie would lay money that Norris' wife was the type to withhold sex in an argument, so he said, "You know, man to man."

"Man to man," Norris said, "does Jana not understand this is a death investigation?"

Richie shrugged. "She's messed up. Thinks she can talk to Sacha beyond the grave."

Norris shivered. "You believe in that ghost shit?"

"No," Richie said. "Not that it matters. Any faith looks like craziness to those outside it." Richie had learned that from Bob Billingsley at a success seminar in Toronto. *Never let someone shake your faith in where you're going*, Bob had said, preaching from his book, *The Religion of Success*. *People will think you're crazy — they might even call you crazy — but you'll be crazy all the way to the bank.*

"All right, so tell Jana if she gets me a second piece of Sacha's handwriting — preferably from this side of the grave — this note will be back in her hands all the sooner. If it's a match, we can close this case, put the RCMP's resources toward more productive uses."

"And send the FBI packing?"

"In a perfect world, yes." Norris scrunched up his face. He looked like he was constipated and confused about it. "Jesus, I wish the FBI would tell me who their damn undercover is."

"I know," Richie said with a smirk. "It's so unfair that they don't trust you."

"Fuck off, Lebar."

Richie grinned. "Yeah, fair. I got one more run I need to make. Tomorrow, to Seattle. Sacha was supposed to make it, but, well . . . anyway, I got it covered."

"No," Norris said. "I mean, I'd like to say yes, but we can't take any chances. You're going to have to cancel."

"Can't. The Mountain Snow is sold — meaning heavy penalties for non-delivery."

"So stall. In a perfect world, it will only take a day or two for this note to work its magic." Norris held the original suicide note and waved it briefly in the air.

Richie glanced at Norris' heavy wooden bookcase. Mostly it held police manuals and other boring-as-shit-looking hardcovers. But from a middle shelf, Zoe glanced out.

"You're doing all this for her, huh? Because a cop's salary can't finance the kind of music education you think she should have?"

Norris scowled. "With all due respect, I don't ask you your reasons for breaking the law."

"I break the law because it's what I grew up thinking I was good for. But I'm changing all that. I'm soon gonna be a legitimate businessman."

"Are you?" Norris met Richie's eye. "You're a weirdo, Lebar."

SEVEN
CLARE

"Lucy, have you seen my December *Snow Betty*?" Jana was standing in the doorless doorway between the living room and kitchen. Her thick dirty blond hair fell around her shoulders and one hand was on her hip.

"Is that a magazine?" Clare took a long sip from her bottle of amber-colored local beer. It wasn't.Bud, but it wasn't bad, either.

"Yeah. I'm not mad if you borrowed it. There's an article I need that tells you how to use a scarf or a sock as a cock ring."

Clare curled her legs up on the deep blue sofa. Her duffel bag was only half-unpacked, but that could wait. She'd been at the apartment for a couple of hours and she still had no clear read on Jana. "You might have an easier time with a scrunchie. Or a sweatband."

"Hey, good idea. You want to smoke a joint with me?"

"Sure." Clare didn't, but she had to take the in. "I haven't smoked pot in ages, so forgive me if I cough a lot. I've been dating this straight-laced dude who thinks two beers is a wild night on the town."

"Are you still dating him?"

"No. We broke up for good when I left Toronto." It was easy enough for Clare to rep this emotion — all she had to do was think of Noah. Minus the fact that she and Noah were neither broken up nor together. "God, I can't wait to get laid by someone who's actually fun."

Jana opened a small wooden box on the coffee table. She plucked out a joint that was as fat as a cigarette, if not quite as perfectly round. "You want a tourist. No drama — fun for a day or two, then they go home. Or an Australian. The town is full of them. They're here to party and they don't get attached."

"Sounds perfect. You know where I can find either of those?"

"They're everywhere. Coffee shops, bars, gondolas. Australians are easy to spot because they talk funny — they say *oy* and *no worries* and *the dingo ate my baby*." Jana's accent was actually pretty good. "Tourists are easy to spot, too — they're walking through the village in the *après* hours with lost looks on their faces. They want to hang with locals because we know where the sickest parties are. We sometimes let them — the ones who aren't too gorby."

"Oh." Clare assumed *gorby* came from GORB — Geek On Rental Board. She didn't want to ask, though — that would be gorby. "Are you local, then? You grew up around here?"

Jana shook her head. "Salt Lake City. But I've lived up here over a year. So I'm, like, more local than a weekend warrior, or even someone with a condo who only uses it for holidays."

"Right," Clare said. Sacha had lived in Whistler for around a year, too.

"But you have to be careful right now. Australians should be good, but maybe don't hang with tourists for the next week or two."

"Why not?"

"Um. I'm not supposed to say."

Clare's eyebrows shot up. "What? You can't tease me like that."

"My roommate died. My boyfriend told me not to trust any strangers for the next little while. He says he'll tell me when things are clear."

Clare wasn't sure how to react. She'd been briefed on Jana's boyfriend — a local drug dealer, Richie Lebar. She met Jana's eyes with sympathy.

"Anyway, if you see the December *Snow Betty*, let me know." Jana set down the joint without lighting it. She stood up and went to the kitchen.

Clare took a chance and followed. "I'm sorry about your room-mate. Are you okay?"

Jana opened the freezer and pulled out a tub of ice cream. "Want a sundae? I always have one before I go out partying. I use organic chocolate sauce. It gives me energy."

Clare eyed the Breyer's carton and was tempted to explain that ice cream did not give you energy — even with organic chocolate sauce. But there were too many other conversations going on, all of which were more relevant to her job. "I'm happy with beer, but thanks. Where's the party?"

"Just, around. I figured I'd start at Avalanche — I work there, so I get half-price drinks. Then I'll see what other people are up to. You want to come?"

"You don't mind?"

"No, it's cool. You know you look like Sacha?" Jana peered at Clare. "You could be her sister. Not her twin, though. Sacha was pret-tier. She had these perfect chiseled cheekbones. No offense."

"None taken." Clare was happy in her Lucy costume — no makeup, messy hair, baggy jeans and a flannel shirt. Amanda had shopped well. It was like getting paid to stay in pajamas all day.

Jana brought her sundae into the living room. Clare followed again and they sat together on the couch. Jana set down the sundae, untouched, and picked up the joint.

After Jana had inhaled a few tokes and Clare had pretended to do the same, Jana said, "I miss her like crazy. It's like half of me is gone."

"You and your roommate were close?"

"We used to talk without talking. Have you ever had a friend like that?"

Clare thought of Roberta, the way they could work together on a car engine, sometimes go hours without saying a word, just passing parts and tools to each other like they were sharing the same brain. "Yeah," Clare said.

"Except she never told me she was going to kill herself."

"Your roommate . . . um . . . she killed herself?" Clare didn't have to feign shock — there was something about hearing it through the mouth of a grieving friend that made any death feel freshly tragic. "Was she depressed?"

"No, and she wasn't a drug addict, either, which is the reason the stupid cops are trying to give." Jana took a deep draw in, held the smoke in her mouth for several seconds. "I'm surprised you haven't heard of her. Her death has been all over the news. Sacha's mom is a bigwig American senator."

Clare shook her head. "I don't watch the news much."

"Hm." Jana frowned, like she thought she was more famous than this. "Maybe in Toronto, it's not that big a story. It's on all the big American news stations. I've been interviewed by Fox News, CNN, MSNBC . . ."

"It's sad," Clare said. "I guess she was a really cool person?"

"The coolest. Anyway, the reason you have to be careful with tourists . . . oh shit, I promised I wouldn't say anything. Here, you better smoke some of this before I lose all my senses."

Clare wondered if the cliffhanger was intentional. She lifted her eyebrows in what she hoped was a conspiratorial way and said, "Oh, come on. I love gossip."

"Me, too! Okay, but this is top secret." Jana peered into Clare's eyes.

"Who would I tell? You're my only friend in town."

"Good point. There's apparently a cop in the village, like an undercover with the FBI, and Richie told me I have to watch everything I say. That's why you can't sleep with tourists right now — we don't want to give the undercover any ins. Cool?"

"I promise." Clare tried not to lose the beat as her brain raced into rapid fire. "Not a word about the undercover and I'll let you vet my hook-ups."

"Good. I mean, we'll probably spot him a mile away. We had a cop in town before. A narc. I would have known even without Richie saying anything."

"How?" Clare doubted Jana could spot a cop unless sirens were blazing, but she was curious what she thought the tells might be.

"He never inhaled."

Clare took a deep drag and made sure it went into her lungs.

"You know the one thing a cop would never do? Drop acid. Richie even agrees."

"Why not?"

"They just wouldn't. Anyway, that's why we came to Whistler. Sacha dragged me up here for the acid."

"LSD?"

Jana nodded. She fingered the jagged blue crystal that hung from her neck.

"Like, the Magical Mystery Tour drug? The one that was in style in the same decade as this wallpaper?" Clare nodded at the living room walls with their bright orange and lime green floral design.

Jana grinned. "Kind of retro, huh? I've had some crazy nights tripping to these walls."

"Seriously though, that's pretty rad. You came to Whistler because Sacha heard the drugs were good."

"Better than good. There's this tab called Mountain Snow. Purest high she'd ever had."

Clare laughed. "So because this tab is called Mountain Snow, Sacha wanted to live at a ski resort? Was she high when she made that decision?"

"No, silly. The drug is made here. Sacha tried it in New York when some guy who had just been to Whistler gave her a tab he brought home. But it wasn't available in the States. I mean *isn't*."

Score another point for Amanda — she'd been smart about landing Clare this roommate. Clare let the wasn't/isn't slide — for now. There was obviously something illegal — something more than casual pot smoking — that Sacha's friends were involved in. Or they wouldn't be so concerned that an undercover was coming to town.

"Um . . ." Clare had a zillion questions. "So you lived in New York, too?"

"Yeah, we went to college there. Sacha finished her degree a semester early, and I was just ready to get the hell away from school. I only need three courses to graduate."

"What did you study?" Clare asked, mostly to be polite, but you never knew what would be relevant.

"Hotel and tourism management. Sacha's degree was in international relations. We met at a frat party and clicked hard. There was no separating us after that. So when she said she was coming up here, even though I wasn't *quite* finished school, I thought *yeah, that's kind of perfect.* Because where better than Whistler to finish my education about tourism?"

Right. As long as she could, you know, find a way to get credit. But Clare wasn't here to be anyone's guidance counselor.

"Last time I took Mountain Snow — like, a week ago — I asked the universe to bring Sacha back into my life. The very next day, I put the ad on Craigslist for a new roommate." Jana set down the joint and grabbed Clare's hands in hers. "We have to do Mountain Snow together. How about tonight?"

Clare gulped. "I've never done acid. I'm actually kind of afraid to." That, and there was no way Amanda would let her. Because Jana was right about one thing: an undercover cop would not drop acid on assignment.

"Come on. How else will I know if you're Sacha?"

"What?"

Jana pulled the sundae bowl toward her. "I brought two spoons. You want some now, right? I always want ice cream when I smoke pot."

Clare took a spoon and dug in. The chocolate sauce and vanilla ice cream tasted amazing — cold and rich and soft against all sides of her mouth. She felt like she was biting into Wonderland. Except Alice was dead.

Clare had definitely inhaled.

MONDAY / FEBRUARY 13

EIGHT
WADE

Wade pushed the sealed white envelope marked with an N across his cheap metal desk. They were in Wade's cramped office at Avalanche — because where else would Wade be? He'd done nothing but work in the three and a half years since he'd opened this damn bar.

He had trouble releasing his hands when the envelope got to the other side. There was enough cash inside to put a big dent in Wade's problems.

These were his best friends in the world. Why couldn't he tell them the truth?

Stu Norris took the envelope. Wade watched him quiver as he slipped it into his inner jacket pocket. He wondered how Stu reconciled these envelopes with his position as police inspector — which in Whistler made him head cop in town. Was he torn between his friends and his job?

"How much is in here?" Norris asked.

"Eleven grand."

Beside Norris, Chopper leaned back on two legs of his chair, twirling his blond dreads like he didn't have a care in the world. Wade watched them, side by side, such different men — they always had been — Norris small and nervous, Chopper big and bold. And Wade somewhere in the middle, on both counts.

"It's been a good week," Chopper said. "These dudes in Seattle have been moving Mountain Snow like crazy. Keeping me up nights in my lab, but that's cool. I dig the midnight oil."

"Shame," Norris said, "that production has to stop."

Wade frowned. He met Chopper's gaze, and Chopper looked confused, too. "What are you talking about?" they said virtually in tandem. Neither of them laughed, like they normally would, at the synchronicity.

"Richie didn't tell you?" Norris shook his little head back and forth. "He was supposed to tell you both. Piece of shit drug dealer."

Chopper tumbled his chair forward so it was back on all four legs. "Relax, man. Richie's cool. Whatever this problem is, it can't be the end of the world."

"You vouch for that?" Norris said.

"Are we back to that?" Chopper held his palms face-up in the air. "I brought Richie in over a year ago. He's been nothing but lucrative for us all."

Norris wrinkled his mouth. "I don't like his attitude. Stomps into my office, tells me how to do my job. And I don't like how he looks at Zoe in her photographs."

"Please. Richie's not a pedophile."

"Not like that," Norris said. "He eyes her up like . . . collateral."

"You think he'd hurt her?" Wade asked. "I mean, if things got bad?"

"No!" Chopper shook his head vigorously, blond braids whipping back and forth. "Richie's good shit. And yes, I vouch for him. His bling is only skin deep."

"You have an extra cigarette?" Norris asked Wade.

Wade pulled two cigarettes from his pack and passed one to Norris. His ashtray was overflowing, but he didn't feel like crossing the room to the garbage bin. "Shit, Stu. This must be bad. I haven't seen you smoke in years."

Norris' small limbs trembled like he'd just had a quintuple

espresso. He clutched at the cigarette and flicked Wade's lighter a few times before he got it. He took a deep draw in and exhaled before saying, "I have to get out of here. My family belongs in a city — not in this frivolous ski town."

Chopper and Wade exchanged glances again.

"Frivolous?" Wade said.

"Zoe needs a real cello teacher, someone worthy of her talent. My wife needs an intellectual community. Do you know that her book club in Pemberton actually chose a murder mystery for last month's discussion? And I need . . ." Norris picked at his fraying cuff. "I don't know what I need. A new jacket, for starters."

Wade took a sip of coffee, which he'd laced with cherry brandy to take the chill out of his bones. It was a cold winter, difficult to keep the office warm.

Chopper said, "What's really eating you, man? You're not deep-throating that cigarette because of cellos and literature."

Norris cast his eyes around Wade's office like he didn't trust the Grateful Dead posters on the walls. "I hate my bosses."

Wade was tempted to laugh but held back. "You sound like you did when we were seventeen. Remember the first time we wanted to hit the road with Avalanche Nights?"

"Of course I remember. My parents said no, as usual. Trying to keep me boxed into life as they knew it." Wade watched Norris' fingers curl as he spoke, clenching like he wanted to form a fist. Odd that he was still so angry, twenty years after leaving home. Odd, too, that he couldn't bring himself to form that fist.

Wade turned his gaze to Chopper. "Do *you* remember? When we got to Stu's place, the truck loaded up with all our road gear, Stu came storming out of his house and said in *exactly* that voice he just used, 'I hate my parents.'"

Chopper gave Wade a sideways smile. "How the hell do you remember that?"

"I remember that whole ten years," Wade said, "from age sixteen to twenty-six, probably verbatim. God, I even loved the hangovers."

"My wife calls those the lost years," Norris said. "I tend to agree.

You and Georgia should have a child. I guarantee you'll stop pining after ten years of musical failure."

Wade wouldn't call it failure, exactly. The band had had some good reviews. They just couldn't make a living. "Did we really plan to be thirty-eight and still living within half an hour from the shit-hole where we grew up?"

"Would you guys stop trashing our home?" Chopper looked at both of them sternly. "Some people think this is the most beautiful place on Earth."

Wade took a deep breath and said, "Richie suggested reviving the band, getting together for an event here in Avalanche."

"Yeah." Norris snorted. "He said that to me, too. What's in it for Richie?"

"Come on, Norris." Chopper waved his hand in front of his face to move the cigarette smoke away. "Richie's on our side."

"So was Sacha," Norris said. "Until everything went so fucking wrong."

They were all quiet. Sacha's death had messed them all up, in very separate ways.

Chopper said, maybe to deflect tension, "I like the band revival idea. I'm game for another night onstage."

Norris shook his head and muttered, "Are you two done reminiscing? We have grown-up issues here, problems that live in the present."

"So kill the suspense, Stu. Why the hell would we have to stop production of Mountain Snow?"

"Sacha Westlake's mommy," Norris said through clenched teeth, "doesn't like my suicide verdict. She wants the FBI to come investigate. So instead of having my back, telling the Americans to stay at home because they trust their man in Whistler, the RCMP says sure, come play in our sandbox. Let's share the investigation."

"Can't you just give them what they need?" Wade didn't see the big deal. "Show the dude your files, let him poke around town until he's satisfied?"

"No, because they won't give me a name. Their man is undercover, and apparently that means keeping me in the dark, too. Me — the head cop in town."

Wade said, "You like the verdict, though, right? You think they'll come to the same conclusion."

"I don't *like* that a young girl committed suicide on my slopes. But I think that's what happened. Don't you?"

Wade nodded. Took another large gulp. He wanted to add more brandy but he didn't want Norris and Chopper to see. Not that they were judgmental like Georgia, but still.

He drained his mug and pushed some papers aside so he could see the monthly calendar that was taped to his desk. He couldn't look at that page without remembering Sacha's round little ass squished onto it after — or occasionally during — a shift. He could almost imagine that he was holding Sacha's hands, whispering words that would get her excited. She was so easy to turn on, Wade could just —

"Are you looking at the calendar for something?" Norris asked.

Wade mentally shoved Sacha off the schedule and willed his mind to focus on the dates. Two weeks took them to the end of February, when he needed to pay his landlords forty-five thousand dollars in back rent — or close the bar.

"Avalanche has two weeks to survive if I can't put together forty-five grand by March first."

Norris shot Wade a look of concern. "Things are that close to the wire?"

"Yup. Landlords gave me notice."

"Isn't it busy season?"

"Slammed every night. Which means break-even, at the extortion rent I'm being charged. Only way I've been starting to turn a profit is through my new laundry services. I've saved about twenty of the forty-five. But it's not going to stay saved — payroll alone will eat a good chunk of that. And I can't exactly ask my staff to work for free."

Norris frowned. "So if you can't survive without laundering, why not shut the doors?"

Wade wished he could answer that.

"Shit, man." Norris opened the envelope from his pocket. He

winced as he pulled out a couple of thousand and slid it across the desk to Wade. "Give it back when you can."

"Thanks." The two grand wasn't going to touch Wade's problem. "How does Zoe like her new cello?"

On most people, *ear to ear* was an expression. On Norris, because his head was so small, it was practically the literal truth. "Loves it. Man, she's going to be something."

Chopper was tilting back on his chair again. "Look, Wade, I'd give you the money. I would. But I think you'd be better off without this place."

Wade blinked hard. "Maybe. But I plan to do whatever I can to keep it."

"Why?" Norris had a hard look in his eyes, but a kind one, like he was talking to a child and trying to make a firm point. "Because we played our first gig here?"

"I still have the old risers that formed the stage that night. I use them for karaoke."

"You're living in the past," Norris said. "Don't you know it's fucking dangerous there?"

"It's not all about the past. I've been writing some new songs . . ."

"Which you could play in a new bar," Chopper said. "Owned by someone else. Is there a present-day reason why you can't close Avalanche?"

"Georgia. She makes me feel like a fuck-up. I know her parents think I am — when I nearly had to close a year and a half ago, they gave us a hundred grand of their retirement fund." Which was why his wife had signing authority, but Wade wasn't about to admit that. "And then the envelopes started not long after, and I've been slowly digging myself out — paying off taxes, suppliers, credit card loans. Once I pay this last chunk to the landlords, I can devote the rest of my income to repaying my in-laws."

"But if it's a money pit, should you maybe walk away?" Norris met Wade's eyes with sympathy, though he was clearly still on edge about the undercover. "Swallow your pride? Find another way to pay back your in-laws? Maybe something with a healthier lifestyle."

Wade looked back and forth between his two friends. Chopper full of drugged-out Zen, Norris full of rules and regulations. It was rare for them to be giving the same advice. Still . . . "And another way to launder cash for you guys and Richie? You need this place as much as I do."

"We'll figure something out," Chopper said. "It's not worth killing yourself over."

Wade tugged at his hair, felt the prick of a few hairs coming loose. Georgia had been telling him for weeks that he needed a cut but he'd been putting it off. He couldn't justify paying his Whistler stylist the hundred bucks she'd want, and neither could he bring himself to go back to that discount barber who made him look like a twelve-year-old redneck.

Wade's phone beeped with an appointment reminder. "That's my interview. A new waitress, I'm hoping."

"She new to town?" Norris was quick with the question.

"I get it," Wade said. "Everyone could be the FBI."

Wade saw Norris and Chopper out and picked up the résumé on his desk. Lucy Lipton. Two years' waitressing experience in a café in Toronto. He couldn't call the reference because the café had closed down. Typical way to fudge experience — which was a point in her favor, because the FBI would no doubt arrange for an excellent list of fake references.

Wade heard a light knock. A thin brunette pushed the door open and smiled. "Are you Wade? I'm Lucy."

"Have a seat. I've just pulled up your résumé." Wade didn't know much, but he knew this girl was no FBI agent.

Still, Norris was right. It wasn't a chance he could afford to take.

NINE
CLARE

Clare slipped into the seat opposite Wade. The chair was hard and the office was cramped and stark, but she felt groovy in her new skin. She wore loose jeans and a soft cotton shirt with a logo that said *Haters Gonna Hate*.

"What brings you to Whistler?" Wade asked.

Lucy was supposed to lack confidence. She had dropped out from life to find herself. Clare leaned forward in her chair, shoulders hunched. "I'm . . . well, is it awful to admit that I came because I need to figure some shit out?" Clare clapped a hand to her mouth. "I mean, some stuff out. I won't swear in front of your customers, don't worry."

Wade took a large gulp of coffee. "What needs figuring out?"

"My entire future. I finished university six months ago and every job I apply for makes me miserable before I walk in the door."

"I see."

Wade seemed all right. Not cute exactly — no one with a mullet could really be called cute — but like a good guy to work for. He looked like he was around forty, but he also looked tired, so maybe he was younger and just looked old.

"Does the thought of working at Avalanche make you miserable?"

Clare shook her head. "I love restaurant jobs — or anything, really, where I'm active and working with people. It's when I walk into an office and I see all the cubicles and I think I might have to punch computer keys all day and all year and maybe all my life . . . During one interview, I was so nauseous I thought I'd spew the sandwich I'd just eaten all over the guy who was interviewing me. Another time, this woman with a tight bun and a pencil skirt asked me why I wanted the job, and I was so scared of becoming like her, I told her I didn't. Sorry, I'm totally rambling."

"I'm afraid I'm not hiring now," Wade said. "I did have an opening, but a few of my part-timers have asked for more hours."

Shit. Clare had gone overboard with the insecurity. And this was the job Amanda wanted her to land — it was where Sacha had worked and it was the hub of her peer group's social action. "I'm happy with one shift a week," Clare said. "Or whatever's extra. I was hanging out here last night for a bit. I like the vibe of this place."

"You could pay your bills on one shift a week?"

"No, but . . . I have some savings. I'd rather be working, because that's a good way to meet people when you move somewhere new."

"Great." Wade groaned.

Clare wrinkled her nose. She was having trouble nailing Lucy. She closed her eyes for a moment and channeled a slacker, but a responsible one, someone she'd want to hire. She smiled and said, "Sorry. I can see how that was the wrong thing to say."

"I'm not running a community center. I have enough staff who treat their shifts like optional social engagements."

"I understand. But I'm a really hard worker. I throw my whole self into every job I have. I hate standing around. A shift goes by so much faster when you're productive." Still rambling, but hopefully in a better direction.

"Thanks, Lucy. I'll keep your résumé, and I'll call you if something comes up."

"I'll train for free," Clare said. "Then when your opening comes up, I'll be ready to slide right in."

Wade smiled at that, like he found her a little bit crazy. "Do you snowboard? Ski?"

"I skied a bit as a kid. My first snowboarding lesson is right after this interview. I'm a bit nervous — can you tell?"

"You could skip the lesson. There are already too many snowboarders in the world."

"Do you not like snowboarding?" Clare glanced around the office again, this time with cop's eyes. Wade had a desktop computer — an old model — but no laptop in sight. His cell phone on the desk looked old, too, and it wasn't a smartphone. He must be cash-poor.

"I like the sport of snowboarding just fine. What I don't like are the idiots who push in front of you in lift lines and whiz by with two inches to spare on the hill. No offense to you, but your generation has no manners."

"None taken." Clare smiled. "I agree. We're all rude assholes."

The filing cabinets were cheap metal. The posters were all of seventies bands — the Grateful Dead, the Doors, the Rolling Stones.

"And what I truly abhor is staff who call in sick — or late — on powder days."

"I can promise I'll never do that." Clare eyed the giant ashtray on the desk. She wanted a cigarette, but she couldn't afford another mistake in this interview, so she decided to wait until she was outside. She didn't like her cover roles to resemble her real life too much, but she figured this was important. She said, "I worked for my dad growing up. I know how important it is for a business owner to be able to count on their employees. And, well, if I'm trained on your computer system, I can fill in for the people who do call in sick. Or late."

Wade looked like this was hard for him, and Clare wondered what the dilemma was. Wade finally said, "Come in tonight. You can shadow an experienced waitress, and we'll take your future schedule from there."

Clare clapped her hands quickly, like she was so excited for this bar job.

TEN

RICHIE

Richie slid his finger down the screen of his phone until he found the Seattle phone number. He did the breathing exercise he'd learned at the Bob Billingsley seminar — the deep inhaling that helped you take back control in a stressful situation. He couldn't get relaxed, though. He dreaded making this call.

"Yo," came the answer.

Richie was tempted to tell his American colleague that he'd go further if he lost the street vocab. Instead he said, "We have to hold back today's delivery."

Silence from Seattle.

"You there?" Richie said. "I'm not talking holding back indefinitely. Just . . . we've hit a snag." Richie should have dealt with this a week ago, should have made this call, postponed the batch. He'd known in his heart when Sacha had died that it wasn't smart to continue taking drugs across the border, not until the investigation had officially been closed. But this new news — this goddamn FBI secret agent — it turned a routine crossing into a suicide run.

"This'll cost you," said Seattle.

"Cost me what?" Richie was prepared to pay a penalty. Of course he was. He'd demand one himself in the Seattle crew's position.

The sound of clucking teeth preceded: "How late is the shipment gonna be?"

Richie sighed. He should play this straight. There were too many variables circling around as it was. "Our transporter was murdered. We have to postpone indefinitely."

Seattle whistled. "Indefinite, huh? That could be a long time."

From his skylight, Richie could see a snowy peak. He focused on that — his goal, to be above all the bullshit, looking down from the top. *Always have your eye on the prize,* said Bob Billingsley in *The Religion of Success. If you know where you're going, you're far more likely to get there.*

"Anyway, I thought your transporter killed herself. That's what the papers say."

Richie wondered how Seattle knew that. Certainly no one had advertised that the Mountain Snow courier had been Senator Westlake's daughter. "Cops are still sniffing. We're playing safe until we know."

"Tell you what: you get me the shipment by next Monday, I'll pay half-price."

Richie's teeth clenched. "Come on, man. I wouldn't screw you this way if I was wearing your damn shoes."

"Because you don't got the muscle on your side — just some tweaked-out ski bums, who I'm guessing won't have your back when things get messy."

"Guess again." But Richie was bluffing — he had no muscle; he was at the Americans' mercy. "Anyway, I'm canceling. You want me to let you know when it's safe to deliver?"

"Hm." Seattle was quiet for a moment. Richie could picture the calculator in his head crunching numbers and spitting them out on an imaginary paper feed. "Mountain Snow is a quality product — I'd like to keep things friendly. But a supplier has to have supply, or the demand will go elsewhere. I gotta ask myself, what would Walmart do?"

"Jesus, you have to pick the least ethical company in all of America? Why don't you ask yourself, what would Microsoft do?"

"Walmart does some good charity work. You get the Snow down

here today — okay, tomorrow, because I'm feeling charitable, too — I'll give you two hundred grand, as per usual. Any later, up to a week, it's half-price. More than a week, I'm gonna have to call a default. You don't want me to call a default."

Richie willed his voice to sound reasonable — contrite even — when he said, "How about I wire you some cash as a sign of good faith? Then I'll bring the shipment down when everything's clear. Say twenty grand as a penalty — I can get that to you in an hour — and we talk again when things are cool."

Seattle snorted. "Say two million bucks as a penalty. What the shipment is worth at street value."

"Come on, be reasonable."

"All right, one million — we'll split the difference. Look, I got your product sold already. I was supposed to start filling orders today. You don't deliver, it costs me about a million in lost profit."

"Is there a human option?" Richie said. "Like, based on understanding that the world doesn't always work like clockwork?"

"Nah. We don't got a human option here at Walmart. That's a good one, though."

Richie ended the call and stared at his phone. He finally understood what Billingsley meant when he warned against rapid expansion. Mountain Snow was a phenomenal product and demand across the border had been shooting through the roof. Which was great when things were smooth, because everything was profit. But Richie had ignored one of Billingsley's tenets: *Always have a reserve fund commensurate with your level of production. Either that, or great insurance. If your factory catches on fire, you don't want the whole operation to go up in flames.*

Well, the factory was burning. And since Richie didn't have a million bucks to spare, and he didn't relish the thought of the bodily harm these Seattle guys were capable of delivering *or* of being their bitch for years while he worked off the debt, he was going to have to get those drugs across the border.

Richie stared out his window at the white peak of the mountaintop, which now looked impossibly far away.

ELEVEN
CLARE

"So there's good and there's bad." Clare kicked some gravel in the parking lot as she spoke to Amanda on the phone. "I got the job at Avalanche. But it's probably moot, because Sacha's friends know the FBI's in town."

"They what? Clare, that's not good."

Clare was tempted to respond sarcastically, but didn't have the heart. "You want me to pack up and bail?"

"Not necessarily," Amanda said. "What have these friends said specifically?"

"Jana thinks the undercover's a man."

"Good. We told Inspector Norris it was. And Senator Westlake's assistant. Only three people in each organization know your name. In the FBI, it's you, your team leader, and Paul Worthington. In the RCMP, it's my two direct bosses and me."

And Noah, Clare thought. She said, "Can we trust all those people?"

Amanda hesitated. "I trust my colleagues. You?"

"I trust Bert — my team leader."

"Not Worthington?" Clare heard the implied criticism in Amanda's voice, like Clare should automatically respect the head of the FBI because of his exalted position.

"I've never met him. Hard to know if you trust someone if you haven't looked them in the eye."

"Fair," said Amanda. "And there's obviously a leak somewhere. But I'd say the fact they think you're a man is a good case for the leak being *outside* the inner circle."

Clare had to acknowledge that was true. Unless Jana was lying.

"Where are you?" Amanda asked.

"Walking home from my job interview. On a detour through the all-day parking lot so I could talk without being overheard. Do you want me to come to your condo?"

"Go back to your apartment for now. And go to your snow-boarding lesson this afternoon as planned. This is bad, but at least you found out before they found you."

"And after the lesson?"

"Do whatever Lucy does. You're still on the case until further notice."

"Where do you think the leak is?"

"I'll make some calls. But it's a good thing that Jana confided in you. It means she doesn't think you're the agent."

"Or she thinks I am, and she's trying to warn me off the case."

Clare passed a family of four loading ski gear into their car. They looked happily exhausted after a weekend of simple recreation. Clare wondered if she was insane for wanting a job with so much subter-fuge. Simple recreation looked damn good to her.

"Leave this with me," said Amanda. "I'll look after it."

TWELVE
MARTHA

Martha allowed Fraser to hold open the door as they entered the Wall Street restaurant. The hostess led them to a table for two and left Martha and Fraser to stare across at each other. Though they'd been divorced for six years, it was still odd for Martha, seeing Fraser's pale blue eyes and knowing they weren't hers to try to look behind. Despite his tanned skin in winter, his full head of sandy hair, Fraser looked fragile. Not quite sick, but not quite healthy. Martha wanted to protect him — from what, she had no clue.

Secret Service took the closest table, which was discreetly out of earshot.

Martha had been offered the protection shortly after Sacha died, as special dispensation to see her through the nomination race — or until Sacha's case had been closed and it was clear there was no threat to Martha. She said yes, mainly to give her an extra buffer from the press. But it was almost more invasive that the men said absolutely nothing. They just watched. She couldn't even pick her nose in private.

"Sacha was having trouble, of course." Fraser lifted his white cloth napkin and unfolded it with a flourish, like a hack magician about to pull a card from up his sleeve. "I wish I could have seen that her trouble would lead to this."

Martha felt her hands and her teeth clench simultaneously. "You can't think Sacha's murder was her own fault."

"I understand that you're blaming yourself. Daisy said this would happen."

"Did she? Daisy offered you insight into how I feel about my daughter being slandered because some backwater Canadian cop can't differentiate murder from suicide?" An internal warning bell sounded, reminding Martha that ears were everywhere during an election, and disparaging rants against foreign law enforcement might not paint her in the best light.

"Daisy's a psychologist. She's trying to help."

Daisy wasn't a psychologist; she was a student at an online university. Martha said in a lower voice, "I'm not allowing those Mounties to close Sacha's murder as suicide."

"Well, what do you propose? You obviously can't use your influence to interfere with investigations."

"Of course I can." Martha wondered how she could have ever been in love with anyone so thick. She still loved him, in a stupid way. She wanted to reach across the wide table and straighten Fraser's pink silk tie. "There's no point having influence if I can't use it to protect my family."

"You wouldn't be protecting Sacha. You'd be jeopardizing what you have for what you can't have back. Wait — tell me you haven't already taken action." Fraser met her eye. "You have."

Martha lifted her eyebrows.

"You want to throw away everything you've worked for?"

"Fraser, think about it. (a) The FBI is discreet enough to keep my involvement under the public radar. (b) If my request for help does come out, the public will forgive me — maybe even applaud me — for putting my daughter ahead of my political interests. (c) If they don't forgive me, who cares? Yes, I want to be president. But I am capable of other things. (d) Sacha was your daughter, too. You should be willing to move the earth for her, not fight me for trying."

Fraser was quiet, maybe waiting for an E. He finally said, "Sacha wasn't my daughter."

Martha sipped her ice water. She hoped the Pellegrino arrived soon to settle her stomach and maybe ease the dull ache that had been living at the back of her throat for the past several days. "Maybe you weren't the best father. You didn't visit her at summer camp when she would have liked that, or give her stellar report cards more than a cursory glance. But that doesn't change that you *were* her father."

"I'm not second-guessing my parenting skills. It's a genetic impossibility. I can't have children."

"What?" Martha felt as foggy as if she'd had three Scotches. She vaguely remembered the thought crossing her mind, when she'd found out she was pregnant, that maybe it had been the other man . . . but Fraser had been so loving — so excited to start a family — she'd successfully pushed those doubts away.

The drinks arrived. Though she was not remotely hungry, Martha asked to hear the specials and said "That sounds lovely" to one of the middle options. She was pretty sure it was a salad, but it might have been a pasta. It was something with sundried tomato, which she liked.

When the waitress left, she said to Fraser, "Maybe you can't father children now. That happens to some men as they get older. But Sacha is your daughter."

"I'm missing the tube that releases my sperm into the world. I've been missing it since birth."

"But . . . I remember . . ." Martha tried to think of a less than crude way to say she'd been swallowing something all those years.

"I have ejaculate. There's no sperm in it."

"But Daisy's pregnant."

"In vitro." Fraser expanded his arms, as if to say, *It wasn't my choice.*

Martha wondered why this even mattered now. It wasn't like she and Fraser were going to hole up over Häagen-Dazs and grieve together. Ugh — the thought of ice cream made her stomach knot. She hoped whatever she'd ordered didn't have a cream-based sauce.

Fraser met Martha's eye. "Sacha was mine as far as anything important was concerned. I didn't change my will, she was welcome to stay in our apartment anytime. And I never said a word to her — I figured there was nothing that knowledge could help. But Daisy . . ."

"Right." Daisy had to know, because even an idiot could understand science that far.

"Daisy thought I should tell Sacha. She thought we were living a lie."

"Says the woman with the breast implants."

"When we found out the in vitro had taken and Daisy was pregnant, she thought, well, she thought Sacha, not being a blood relative, should back out of our family. Let the baby be our only child."

Martha simultaneously recoiled and felt her eyes bug forward. "What did *you* think, Fraser? Did you even have an opinion?"

The bread arrived. It looked bland and white. Fraser took a chunk and started buttering it.

"My opinion is moot now," he said.

"Your opinion is not even remotely moot. Someone killed Sacha. Or had her killed. You ask me, Daisy is looking like a damn good suspect. Where was Daisy eleven days ago, incidentally?"

The conversation stopped while the smooth-as-silk waitress topped up Martha's mineral water. When she'd left, Fraser said, "You can't accuse my wife of murder. Not in your position."

"Because I'm a politician, I'm supposed to not think like a mother?"

Fraser smiled. "This is why men are better suited to high-powered jobs."

"Fraser, fuck off. Don't you care who killed Sacha?"

"Sacha killed herself. It's the most horrible thing for a mother to acknowledge, I'm sure. But wake up. She wasn't happy."

Martha matched Fraser's passive smile and said, "Of course Sacha was happy. Off the beaten track, perhaps. But she would have found her way."

"She was using drugs. Hard drugs and lots of them. Daisy saw when she visited."

"Daisy visited Sacha in Whistler?" Martha stared hard, compelling Fraser's eyes to meet hers.

Fraser obliged, but with a sigh. "Yes, Daisy visited. But it was in November; not last week. They skied together."

"Sacha snowboarded. She found skis too restrictive. Remember that trip we took to Sun Valley?" Martha felt weird, like she had a fever. Her limbs felt heavy and light all at once. Like the two balloons in the Pink Floyd song. She wanted to remember every detail from every day of Sacha's life, because maybe then she could put it back together again.

"You need to get a grip."

Martha came back to reality with a thud. "Did Daisy say anything to Sacha about her lineage?"

"She says not."

"Hm." Martha would have to pay Daisy a visit. "Is she home this afternoon?"

THIRTEEN
CLARE

Clare tried for the twelfth time to get her snowboard to do what she wanted it to.

Her instructor laughed. He was probably a nice guy when he wasn't making fun of someone who couldn't understand his terrible instructions.

"Forget it." Clare bent over, released her bindings, and stepped off the board. "I can live in Whistler without knowing how to ride this thing."

The instructor shrugged. His name was something goofy, like Flippy or Flopper; Clare hadn't bothered to remember it. "Shredding's the crunchiest thing you'll ever do. Total body awesomeness. Like sex on shrooms. You just have to wait for it to click."

"Oh, is that all I have to do?" Clare narrowed her eyes through her balaclava. She wanted to rip the thing off — her head was too hot; she was sweating. But that would mean taking off her helmet and rearranging, and it was annoying enough just trying to learn how to snowboard. "Aren't you supposed to be teaching me how 'it clicks'? Or would it be easier if I just smoke a joint and try to get down the hill?"

Flipper grinned, exposing straight, white teeth that looked strange against his dry, cracked skin. "That might help, actually. I learned when I was baked. Took me one lesson and I was down."

"Are you baked now? Because the instructions you're giving me are completely unclear." Shit. Clare sounded like a prudish bitch.

"One more try," said Chipster. "You're doing well, despite your defeatist attitude. Your aggression will actually work for you, if you let it."

Clare rolled her eyes. "Didn't realize I'd signed up for Snowboarding Buddhism." She strapped her boots back into her bindings and immediately crashed to the ground.

"Get up," said Flooper.

Clare got up.

"Weight on your heels."

"Duh. Or else I would have fallen again." Clare began to slide slowly and horizontally, like Flapjack had been teaching her. She would fall again any second.

"Weight on your toes. All at once."

Clare did what was completely counter-intuitive, and listened to Flopface. Instead of falling, though, she found that she had successfully turned and was now facing up the hill.

"Weight on your heels." The guy could at least congratulate her.

Clare shifted her weight again and she was facing down the hill. Another successful turn.

"Great. Now keep doing that, but while you're moving down the hill. Back and forth. Like this." Flip took off. In a ridiculously fluid movement, he made about six turns and was a fair way down the hill. He shouted up to Clare, "Your turn!"

Clare wanted to swear at him, but she reminded herself that she was Lucy — she was supposed to be making friends, not alienating them. So she did what he said. A lot less gracefully. And with three falls along the way.

When she'd caught up with him, Chiphead grinned. "You're a snowboarder, Lucy. You can work on your style, build up speed, tighten those angles. But you've got the basics down. Whistler's gonna be your town, dude."

"Dude," Clare said. "Are you available for another lesson, say, tomorrow?"

"Oh," Flippy said. "She doesn't hate me anymore."

"I know you're not full of shit now. Your lesson kind of worked."

"Kind of, huh? Come on. We can ride the gondola up and do one run down from the top."

Clare undid her bindings and followed Flippy Floopface to the Whistler gondola.

"Hey, Chopper," the attendant said to her instructor, which was cool because Clare was ready to learn his real name. "Who's the chick?"

"Hey, man, this is Lucy. It's her first day on a board. She's cool."

"Man, you're gonna love it here," the lift attendant said. "Sorry you got stuck with Chopper, though. Sick snowboarder, but can't teach worth shit."

"She told me already." Chopper took Clare's board and ushered her into the moving gondola. "But if I can get her down this hill in one piece, she's gonna buy me a beer."

"I am?" Clare said, as the gondola doors closed behind them.

"Yeah. Hey don't take this wrong, but you look just like this dead girl."

"What?" Clare knew she looked like Sacha — same shoulder-length dark hair; same slight, wiry build.

"She died a week and a half ago. Up in the Blackcomb Glacier."

"I'm so sorry," Clare said.

The view behind Chopper was one of the most gorgeous sights Clare had ever seen. Whistler Village receding below them looked like a European fairytale town. Clare half expected a cobbler and some elves to run into the streets.

"Where's Blackcomb?" she asked.

Chopper pointed at the mountain beside theirs, with its own gondola that didn't go up quite as high.

"Are people avoiding the run where she died?"

Chopper shook his head. "That's the fucked-up thing, man. Everyone's all, this is so sad, let's have a candlelight vigil and cry together and shit. I mean not literally — we haven't done the candle thing — but Sacha's all anyone wants to talk about when they're drinking."

Good to know.

"But by daylight," Chopper said, "it's like Sacha was never even here. People are skiing and riding the glacier like it's all still fun and games."

Clare frowned. "It's a transient town, right? Do you think people are just used to other people coming and going?"

"Yeah, but Sacha never left. This town wasn't transient for her."

"Were you, um — I mean you and Sacha — had you dated or anything?"

Chopper looked past Clare, into the mountain behind her. "Nothing serious."

Clare smiled sadly. Of course she'd buy Chopper a beer. This was business.

FOURTEEN
RICHIE

Richie grooved around his all-white living room, past the sofa and club chairs, dance tunes in his ears. He was trying to pick up his mood, find a positive head space where he could get some clarity on his massive fucking problem.

Great choices he had. Take the drugs to the States, and maybe get busted. Or play safe with the law and get into indefinite debt with one of the scariest cartels in the States. What the fuck would Billingsley do?

He looked at his couch — white, leather, pristine — and remembered Sacha lounging with her feet up on the arm. Even in clean socks, there was no way Richie would have let anyone else put their feet there. Not even his mother.

He picked up his snowboard, turned the volume up on Flo Rida, and opened his door to leave. He dug this song, "Wild Ones." It made him think of Jana, always ready to go with some crazy new bedroom idea. Man, that chick made Richie's head spin.

It was raining in the village, but Chopper had texted to say it was dumping at the peak. The slopes would clear his head — whooshing down, fighting the wind and the snow, letting rap and dance music impart their wisdom through his earbuds.

Except when he was about to step out of his apartment, he didn't see an empty hallway. He saw Norris, the little inspector, standing a full head shorter than Richie in his I'm-so-important black trench coat.

Richie yanked his earbuds out, gestured for Norris to come in.

"I left Sacha's handwriting sample with your receptionist," Richie said. "I assume that's cool, since it's official police business."

"It's fine. I've faxed the sample to head office. That's not why I'm here."

Richie shut the door and remained standing in his gear. "How long for the handwriting analysis?"

"Couple days," Norris said. "Do you have a cigarette?"

Richie was getting hot in his snow clothes, but he didn't want to unzip his jacket in case Norris took that as an invitation to stay awhile. As much as he wanted to keep things on good terms with the inspector, Richie had energy to burn — he wanted at least one good run before his meeting with Chopper at the peak. "I don't smoke. I didn't think you did, either."

"The stress is making me start again. I'd buy a pack, but my wife would freak if she found it." Norris smiled sheepishly, like he was embarrassed to acknowledge he was like every other married man: whipped.

"Man, I hear you," Richie said, meeting Norris' eyes with a grin.

Norris shifted his feet, like he wanted to pace but he'd have to get past Richie to do it. Richie didn't move.

"Look, I came to see you because . . . for ten grand, I can get the name of the FBI agent."

"Ten grand?" Richie felt his eyebrows rocket sky-high. "What happened to all the cash me and Chopper have already given you?"

Norris glanced at the sofa but Richie stood firm, blocking his entrance past the alcove by the door. "We bought Zoe a cello. A Leon Bernadel, which that kid deserves, but it damn near broke our bank. I'd go to the poorhouse if it meant she could follow her dream."

"She's ten," Richie said. "Next year the only dream she'll want to follow will be an eleven-year-old boy."

"I wouldn't expect you to share an understanding of classical music."

"Hey, no disrespect, Norris, but Chopper and I pay you to protect us from prison. This ten grand is yours to pay."

"You pay me not to arrest your asses."

Richie liked that line. He wished he was recording this conversation.

"I'll talk to Chopper," Richie said, keeping his voice even despite the rage that was beginning to boil just below the surface. "If nothing else, maybe he can better explain to you how our arrangement is supposed to work."

"Don't forget which one of us will look better in court. Me in my tailored suit, you in lovely orange coveralls . . ." Norris tossed this out with a smile, but you couldn't say a thing like that without meaning it at least a little.

"Come on, man. You're threatening me?"

"Of course not. *No disrespect*, Richie. I'm just reminding you how things lie."

Richie was tempted to put Norris in his place, but the cop worked better if he thought he was the man in control.

FIFTEEN
MARTHA

The heavy apartment door opened to reveal a tall blond in gray yoga pants that she must have had painted onto her legs. Daisy's pregnancy was early — barely past the three-month safety mark — so she didn't have much of a bump. If anything, her body only looked more luscious.

"Can you nurse from silicone?" Martha said. "Or will you have to use formula?"

Daisy frowned. "Are you meeting Fraser for something? I thought he was at work."

"He probably is." Martha pushed past Daisy and left the younger woman standing with one hand on the door. "I've just left him in the financial district."

Daisy remained in the doorway. She nodded to the two Secret Service men in the hallway. "Are they coming in?"

"No," Martha said. "I've told them it's not necessary. You're not planning to kill me, correct?"

After Martha stood staring at her for a long moment, Daisy shut the door slowly and asked, "Did you, um, want a cup of tea?"

"Coffee would be better."

"Oh. Well. Fraser drinks the coffee. I'm not even sure how to work the machine. But I've just boiled the kettle."

Martha stared. No wonder things hadn't worked between her and Fraser. Clearly he'd been lusting after geniuses the whole time. "I can work the coffee machine."

Daisy's top lip curved slightly over her bottom one. She looked like she was trying to find an alternative to inviting Martha into her kitchen. After a few seconds, when apparently no inspired solution came to her, Daisy pushed through the swinging kitchen door. Martha followed.

"You must be gutted." Daisy pulled grounds down from a high shelf. Martha would have needed a stool. "About Sacha and everything."

"Yes. Fraser mentioned you were psychoanalyzing my grief."

"Um. I know I'm supposed to be an expert in psychology by now. And I have learned a lot of stuff — like did you know that our minds and our bodies are connected? For example, if you get the flu, it's probably because you're stressed, not because you've been around a virus?"

Martha wondered how Ebola patients would respond to this sage observation.

"But — and please don't tell Fraser; he's spent a fortune on these courses — I feel like the lessons never prepared me for Sacha's death. The stuff in the textbooks is too simple for all the complicated emotions floating around right now."

"That's the most intelligent thing I've ever heard you say."

"It is?" Daisy brightened, turned to face Martha, and frowned again. "Oh, you mean because you think I'm really dumb."

Martha slid the filter drawer out from the side of Fraser's coffee maker. It *was* a funny machine — it had taken Martha awhile to figure out, the first time she'd used it.

"I meant to ask, how long are you staying?"

"Is that what you asked Sacha? How long she planned to stay? In Fraser's life, that is."

"Oh." Daisy took a seat at the round wooden table that Martha had found at a Connecticut craft fair. "You want to have *this* conversation."

"I didn't come to learn about the human brain."

Daisy twirled curly blond hair around her finger. "Sacha would have been welcome in our home anytime as a guest. She could have kept her key."

"Oh good. A tiny metal key would compensate for taking away Sacha's sense of belonging."

"I didn't drive Sacha to suicide. You can't make this my fault." Daisy pulled a sparkle-covered phone from her pocket and glanced at it. "I have to meet a friend in SoHo. And I need to change clothes — I'm not pregnant enough that I can get away with bad fashion. So, um . . . I guess I'll see you out?"

Martha started the coffee machine and sat at the round table with Daisy. "You might want to cancel with your friend."

"You can't tell me to cancel my social life. You're not senator of this apartment."

"Sure I am. This apartment is in New York, no?"

Daisy's shoulders fell. "Why are you doing this?"

"Because you're the only person I know who visited Sacha in Whistler, who saw firsthand what her life was like leading up to . . ." Martha felt her words begin to falter. Stupidly, she felt closer to tears in this horrible kitchen than she had in the past eleven days. But she steeled herself. "Leading up to her death."

Daisy reached a hand toward Martha and touched her arm. "I guess that's a fair question. You want to piece together why she killed herself. But it had nothing to do with family. Sacha's life in Whistler was complicated."

"Sacha did not kill herself." Martha lifted Daisy's hand from her arm and placed it gently on the table. "But how was her life complicated?"

"I don't want to betray her friends' confidence."

Martha inhaled deeply so she didn't strangle Daisy. She could not understand the bond between her intelligent daughter and this trivial piece of fluff — and she didn't want to admit that she cared.

"These *friends* could be involved in her death. I would expect your loyalty to be with Sacha rather than with some Canadian snowboarding slackers."

Daisy pushed her chest out even further than she normally did. "No wonder Sacha never shared private details of her life with you. All you do is criticize."

Martha felt her cheeks tighten, maybe because her teeth were clenched inside them. "I want you to pretend for five seconds that you have one intelligent brain cell. Okay? Are you imagining that? I want you to use that one cell to analyze this situation: your stepdaughter is dead. You have information that might shed light onto why. Do you (a) use that information to help find her killer or do you (b) withhold the information to protect the identity of some degenerate ski bums?"

"For someone who wants information, you're sure not asking very nicely." Daisy leaned back in her chair and stuck out her chin. "I think I'm going to ask you to leave."

Ugh. Martha was tired and the coffee was starting to smell good. "Forgive me. I know I should be nicer. This is not a normal week for me."

"Yeah, but you're not normally nice to me, either." Daisy rested her hands on her tiny belly.

"Look, you're right — I've never fully forgiven you for your affair with Fraser while he was married to me."

"But you've forgiven Fraser." Sharper than she looked, this one.

"We have a child together."

"You don't, though. Isn't that why you're here?"

"Look, Daisy, this isn't about you and me. It's about what we can both do for Sacha."

"Sacha's dead. We can't do anything for her."

The coffee machine was gurgling to say it was nearly ready, and Martha sat quietly, listening to it. "Please, Daisy, tell me what my daughter was involved in."

"Why? So you can tell the FBI? Fraser called me after his lunch with you."

The table was big enough for four, but Martha felt suddenly claustrophobic. It was the same feeling she'd had earlier in the restaurant. She might be getting a fever — Daisy's head seemed cartoonishly large. She wished she'd impressed the need for silence upon Fraser — as in *please don't tell your bimbo wife about the* FBI *involvement* — but she'd thought it was obvious.

"That's top secret information, Daisy. Fraser trusts you with it, clearly. But it's vital that you don't tell a soul about the FBI being in Whistler."

Daisy smirked. "Or what?"

"Or Sacha's killer might go free."

"Oh. For a second I thought you were going to tell the truth and admit that it could ruin you politically."

"For Sacha, can we not be on the same side?"

"If I tell you what I know, will you leave? I hate being late for appointments. It stresses me out and throws off the rest of my day."

"Yes. I'll gladly go back to the ten million other things I have to do if you tell me what you know."

"Your daughter was running LSD across the British Columbia–Washington border. Now can you see why I didn't want her influencing my baby?"

Martha rolled her eyes. "There is no way Sacha would get involved in drug smuggling." And Sacha on crack would be a better influence on a baby than Daisy would sober, but Martha kept this thought to herself in order to get the rest of the information.

Daisy shrugged. "Believe what you want. She was really mad at you."

"At me?"

"She thought you were a hypocrite. Your hard line on drugs especially. She figured if the system was corrupt, she might as well profit from it."

Martha shook her head. "That's not even logical."

"Whatever. I've said what I know. You can leave now."

"I want the names of her friends. I presume you hung out with them when you visited." Martha drew out the words *hung out* very slightly, to imply that she thought of Daisy as little more than a teenage layabout.

Daisy either missed that or ignored it. "Do you think poking into this is smart? We can't bring Sacha back, but if word got out about what she was doing, it could hurt your career."

"I hope that when your child is born, you realize how stupid that sounds. There is no career that could possibly be more important than my daughter."

"Really?" Daisy snorted. "Fraser said that when Sacha was a kid, you guys had nannies and didn't usually make it home from work until well after she was asleep. He wants it to be different this time. He wants his real child to know real love."

Martha pulled her briefcase toward her and pulled out her laptop. "Incredible how you can just bring your work with you anywhere these days. I could sit here for hours, and not worry one bit about missing something important."

"Chopper," Daisy said. "That's the friend you want to look at."

"Does Chopper have a last name?" Martha's finger hovered above the power button. She was tempted to get up and pour herself a mug of coffee, but she hoped she'd be leaving too soon to have more than a sip or two — and besides, it was fun to make a point.

"I'm sure he does. But I don't know it. He's a snowboarding instructor and he makes LSD in some remote mountain lab. It sounds really cool, actually. Still, not something I want around my baby."

Martha put her computer into her briefcase and stood up. "Thank you for the coffee."

SIXTEEN
CLARE

Clare shimmied into the shapeless black skirt of her new Avalanche work uniform. The skirt was slightly used, and it fit Clare well — she suspected it had been Sacha's.

On the cheap pine dresser, Clare's phone buzzed with a text. She picked it up.

It's Nate, said the message from a Toronto number. *Call when u can talk privately.*

That was weird. It was clearly Noah. Nate was the cover name he'd been using when Clare had met him, playing in the Canadian Classic Poker Tour on an assignment. But why the Toronto phone number?

Before phoning him, Clare double-checked that Jana had already left the apartment for her shift.

"Hey, Clare." Noah's voice was soft, like he was trying to be quiet.

"Are you alone?" Clare slid her arms through the holes of the black golf shirt with the white mountain that was Avalanche's logo. The shirt was two sizes too big and felt new — if that starchy, never-washed, almost abrasive poly-cotton feel was anything to go by. She popped her head through the top and frowned at herself in Sacha's mirror. There was no way this look would earn her tips. Which technically didn't matter, but Lucy would care. Maybe Clare could shrink the shirt in the dryer before her next shift.

"Yeah, I'm alone," Noah said. "But the night's still young."

"Hilarious. Why are you calling from a Toronto number?"

"In case someone sees your phone. Bert's not taking any chances with your cover."

"Good, because the RCMP is doing their best to blow it."

Clare left Sacha's bedroom and glanced at the front door. Still locked tight. She glanced the other way, toward Jana's room, and walked toward it.

"How's that going?" Noah asked. "You and your old handler?"

"It's not my favorite." Clare opened Jana's bedroom door. A jumble of jeans and snow clothes and thermal gear was piled around Jana's dresser, where three of the four drawers were partially open, a black bra strap hanging out from the top one. The bedsheets looked like they'd been torn around violently, maybe in a nightmare. Or maybe Jana just never made her bed. The chaos reminded Clare of her own tiny East Village apartment.

"Amanda knows what she's doing, though," Clare told Noah. "She was smart to land me Jana as a roommate."

"What's Jana like?" Noah sounded more than casually interested. Clare wondered if he was working the case, too. She hoped not.

"She's obsessed with Sacha." Clare opened Jana's bedside drawer to see a big purple vibrator with rabbit ears. Her eyebrows lifted — that was one thing she'd never tried — but she knew exactly what the KY his-and-hers was for. She grinned, wishing Noah was closer, and closed that drawer.

"So are you, like, high all the time since you got there?"

Clare laughed. She opened the next drawer down, which was filled mainly with loose photographs. "We smoked up last night. Which apparently loosened Jana's tongue. She came right out and told me that Sacha moved to Whistler from New York to chase this mountain LSD."

"We think Sacha was doing more than just using the drug," Noah said.

Clare let the photograph in her hand — of Jana and what looked like her family, a happy, if conventional crew of dirty blonds with their arms around each other at the Grand Canyon — flutter back into its drawer. "Who's we?"

Noah hesitated before saying, "Bert has me on background stuff."

"Sorry," Clare said. "Must be boring as hell."

Clare leafed through for a photo of Jana and Sacha. She found one: Jana had one arm wrapped around Sacha, squeezing tight and grinning. Sacha was smiling, too, but she looked bored.

"I'm digging the office routine," Noah said. "I grab a coffee and a donut on the way in, I get to answer to my own name, which is refreshing . . . Anyway, we're pretty sure Sacha was involved in a smuggling ring to bring the LSD into the States."

Clare's fingers gripped the edges of the photo. She set it down so she wouldn't accidentally tear it. "Does Amanda know?"

"I'm sure she'll tell you if and when you need to know." Noah sounded irritatingly amused. "You have to learn to trust your handlers. They can't have your back unless you let them."

"Noah, stop talking to me like you're fifty and I'm ten." Clare sank onto Jana's bed. "And why are we fighting?"

"You're the only one fighting."

"Yeah, but you're baiting me. Being condescending."

"Sorry." Noah clucked his tongue. "I miss you, and I'm frustrated."

"Why are *you* frustrated?"

"I want you, you want freedom. Kind of a no-win situation."

"You don't think an ideal relationship gives both partners *more* freedom?"

"Yeah, philosophically. Not the freedom to fuck around."

"Whatever." Clare shut the photograph drawer and pulled the bottom drawer open. A Bible, all on its own, like at a hotel. Jana didn't seem religious. Clare opened the top drawer and found the family photo again. She looked closer: everyone in Jana's family was wearing a gold cross. Clare was pretty sure Jana didn't wear one now.

"We've said all this before," she told Noah.

Noah was silent for a moment. Then, "Roberta's been trying to reach you."

"Great." Roberta wasn't family, but she was the closest thing to an aunt or an older sister Clare had known. This would be about Clare's dad. He might be dead, but worse — he might be clinging to life one more fucking time, and Clare would be a cold bitch for not dropping everything — her career included — and rushing to his side. "Did she say why she was calling?"

Noah sighed. "No. But you should call her. What if your dad dies and you haven't made peace with him?"

Clare grabbed a corner of her work shirt and twisted it fiercely around her fingers. She tried to focus on where to look next in Jana's room. Her father always did this — had a health crisis right when she was busy. "I have peace. I accept that my dad wants to die, and I love him too much not to give him that freedom."

"I'm sure he doesn't want to die."

"Nobody with emphysema smokes if they're looking for fifty more years of health."

The closet? Clare opened it to see clothes and shoes. Mostly super-casual, but good names, like Timberland and Burton.

"Addiction's complicated," Noah said. "Hey, you think you could get me a phone number?"

"Whose?" Clare stood on tiptoes to see the top shelf. She reached to pull a shoebox forward and it tumbled down onto the floor. *Shit.* More photos, now spread all over the carpet. And under that, wedged into the bottom of the box, several pieces of white paper.

"Wade Harrison's. He owns the bar where you're working."

"Of course I can get Wade's number." Clare started pulling photos up, placing them back in the box. They were all of Sacha. "What do you want it for?"

"Bert wants me to ask Wade some questions. But he doesn't want you asking, because he doesn't want to threaten your cover."

"Oh, so you're not only doing paperwork."

"No, it's a bit more engaging. Maybe if things go well, I'll end up in *Casino Royale* with you."

Clare snorted. "Because I'll really want someone along to cramp my style. Nice talking to you."

"Clare, I —"

"Don't worry. I'll get you that number you want."

Clare pressed Off on her new phone.

What was wrong with her? She couldn't go to her sick father, she couldn't be nice to the man she was in love with. Her best relationships were phony. Because it was easy to be warm when your time with a person had a shelf life?

Maybe that's why she and Noah had clicked so hard, so fast — they were both undercover when they met, and Clare felt free to be herself behind the shield of a second persona. But a year of real life had been chipping away at that honesty.

Clare gripped her phone tightly, glared at it. She wanted to call Noah back, but she'd wait until she had something to say.

She pried the papers from the bottom of the box. There were three or four documents that Jana clearly wanted hidden, about U.S. drug policy. Clare didn't understand their significance — looked like bureaucratic jargon about being tough on crime — but Martha Westlake's name was all over them.

Clare took pictures with her phone. She made sure the images were clear before emailing them to Amanda. She wanted to delete the photos from her phone — and the sent mail history along with them — but she should make sure they'd been received first.

Clare was still annoyed that Amanda hadn't looped her into the possible smuggling, but she bit her pride and dialed Amanda's number as she replaced the papers in the bottom of the shoebox and began to gather the scattered photos from the floor. Hopefully Jana's slobbery extended to her mementos and she wouldn't notice that the contents of the box were wildly out of place.

"Lucy." Amanda's voice was clipped.

"Can't talk." Clare matched Amanda's short tone — better to pretend she was busy than to let her anger show. "Just sent you some files — can you confirm receipt before I delete them from my phone?"

"Um . . ." A beat while Amanda checked. "Yup. Received. Wait . . . yup, the images are good. Go ahead and delete. Talk tomorrow?"

"Sure." Clare ruffled the comforter so it didn't look like she'd been sitting on the bed, reached on her tiptoes to replace the shoebox in Jana's closet, and left the apartment for work.

SEVENTEEN
RICHIE

Richie sliced his snowboard's edge to a hard stop outside the chalet. He smiled at the neighboring mountains in the Coast range, snow-covered and wild-looking. The air smelled best on powder days. The fresh snow had a sweet, clean scent. Richie could see why so many laundry detergents tried to replicate the outdoors. You couldn't see the village from the peak, but you could feel that it was down there. Down there to be conquered.

Once Richie owned a piece of Whistler — a respectable bar like Avalanche, no less — he'd be that much further from Scarborough. The concrete jungle of apartment blocks and sirens at all hours couldn't reach out and grab him back into its fold.

He waved at Chopper, already on the patio with a pitcher of beer. Richie leaned his board into a holding slot and climbed the outside stairs to join Chopper at his table.

"I'm shocked, man," Richie said as he sat down. "You, riding groomers — must be a powder day."

Chopper leaned back in his chair, cast his glance around at the falling snow, thick and chunky. "Why go to the trouble of climbing into the back country when the lifts can drop me right into this sick shit? It's Monday, all the weekend warriors are gone. It'll take two days for this snow to get skiied out."

"Hey, you don't need to convince me." Richie hated having to skin up a hill. A gondola or chair was so much more civilized. But he wasn't meeting Chopper to talk sports. "We got a real big problem."

"Yeah?" Chopper's eyebrows rose, but his shoulders stayed relaxed.

Richie glanced around to make sure no one was near enough to overhear. "Seattle. They want the Snow tomorrow or they'll only pay half-price."

Chopper laughed. "And I want a time-traveling snowmobile. We'll ship them the batch when the heat clears. Full price."

Richie shook his head. "This is how they roll. And it gets better: after next Monday, they're calling a default."

"What's a default mean?" Chopper wasn't laughing anymore.

"It means we owe them a million bucks — which might sound crazy, but the Snow is worth two mil street value." It still blew Richie's mind that they were dealing with such giant figures, but that was LSD — virtually cost-free production, tiny little squares of paper that were ten bucks a pop at street value. Stuff a travel backpack full of the shit, it added up quick.

"And if we can't pay?" Chopper asked.

"We deliver free product until we work it off."

"Fuck that, I'm not their bitch." Chopper shook his head, blond dreads sticking down straight like pipe cleaners. "This last batch of Mountain Snow tried to kill me."

Richie frowned. "Did it come out bad?"

"Nah. Just had to adjust the cooking temperature by a couple degrees to allow for this sub-zero weather. I was rushing at first. I've been messed up since . . . you know."

Richie knew. "You got everything put away okay? I'm hoping our FBI friend never makes it up your mountain, but *if* he came to your place, would he twig that you're running a factory?"

"Shouldn't," Chopper said. "I dismantled the whole setup. Ingredients are locked away separately from each other — so not suspicious. I scattered the apparati so some of it looks like kitchen gadgets and other stuff like chemistry class nostalgia."

"How'd you manage that?"

"It's packed in a box that says *High School*." Chopper laughed. "With report cards and essays and the pinups of Alyssa Milano I used to keep in my locker."

Richie's eyebrows lifted. "And the batch is good?" The last thing he needed was to risk his freedom bringing drugs across the border only to have the batch rejected on the receiving end.

"Beautiful. I tested the new batch last night; pure as it always is. Had a wicked cool vision of Sacha smiling out from a tree."

"Good." Richie didn't want to hear about it.

Chopper sipped his beer.

"You seen anyone new in town?" Richie asked.

"Just ten zillion tourists. Man, is it me, or is the gaper alert super-high right now?"

"Yeah, rental shops are booming," Richie said. "Anyone asking questions?"

"Nah. But there's a new cutie I gave lessons to. She spent the first half of the lesson telling me how much she hates me, then she asks if I'm available for another lesson tomorrow."

"You say yes?"

"Damn right." Chopper flashed a broad grin. "Gonna take her on some hard runs. Piss her off."

Richie poured himself half a glass of beer from Chopper's pitcher. "We got a second problem, too. Norris wants more money. Ten Gs. Allegedly to find out the name of this FBI agent."

"You don't believe him?"

"I'm not sure." Richie kissed his lips — a long, slow smacking sound that Jana said was ghetto, but felt too good to stop doing. "There's something true and something not."

Chopper pulled a joint from his pocket and lit up. Right on the public patio — man, this town was good for the pot industry. Richie realized — too late — that he should have stuck with the drug that he knew. Or at least stuck to dealing locally. It was Sacha who had stirred up the idea about bringing the Mountain Snow south.

"I think we should pay," Chopper said. "What's five grand each? Hardly painful."

"Hardly painful when we're rolling in it. You forget our money supply is dry at the moment. Or is it because you and Norris are friends, you want to cave to his demands?"

"No, I think Norris is being a douche not to swallow this. But if we don't pay, we could be screwing ourselves out of protection while we need it. We can always punish him later."

Richie could work with that: pay now, punish later. "You're right," he said. "What's five grand?"

EIGHTEEN
CLARE

Clare slammed back a fruity shot and met Jana's eye behind the bar. "You sure we're allowed to do shooters on the job?"

"Chill, Goody Two-Shoes. We're allowed." Jana stuck a sword with three small olives into a murky martini. "Makes the customers way less annoying."

Clare loaded her tray with the martini and two pints of beer. Her body screamed from the abuse she'd put it through on the ski hill — every movement she made shot a different muscle with pain.

"You sure you're fine with that tray? Most people don't use two hands."

"I'm afraid I'll break something."

"Okay, but if you keep holding the tray from its sides, Wade's going to know you lied on your résumé."

"Shit, you're right." Clare flattened her palm like the waitress who'd trained her had shown her. "Wait — how did you know I lied on my résumé?"

Jana grinned. "I know what experience looks like. It's not that."

Clare slid the tray onto her palm even though she was sure it would fall over and launch drinks in every direction. "Hey, do we have a karaoke song book? My customers want to look through it."

Jana reached down the bar for a thick green binder. She peered at Clare's table. "The women are going to choose Madonna or Cyndi Lauper, and the men . . . Metallica."

"Why Metallica?" The group was in their thirties and dressed like they'd just come from Wall Street. Or whatever the BC equivalent of Wall Street was.

"Mainstream, but makes them feel bad-ass. You and I should do a song later." Jana poured a rum and Coke — or rum and cola, because the bar used a generic brand. She popped a straw inside and started sipping.

"Are we allowed to sing? What if our customers want a drink while we're onstage?" Clare felt like a square for asking, but it was important to keep this job.

"You need another waitress to cover your section and I need to ask Wade to work the bar, which is always fine with him — he loves being close to his liquor. You should take those drinks now. Your customers are looking over."

Clare balanced the tray and songbook successfully — all the way to the table with no spills, to her surprise. As she left her customers, she saw Chopper coming in the front door.

"Hey, Lucy." He flashed her a toothy grin. "I want to sit in your section."

"My section is one table, and it's full."

"So I'll sit at the bar. You have to come there for your drinks, right?"

Jana nodded hello at Chopper and started pouring a pint of something dark. "A shot, too?" she asked him.

"If Lucy's having one with me."

"Sure." Clare could come to like this job. "What are we drinking?"

"I like SoCo, but feel free to shoot what you like. On me."

"Southern Comfort works. And I owe you a beer," Clare said. "For all this pain you put me in."

"Pain. That's fitting because you were being a pain on the mountain today. Do you always insult people who are trying to help you learn?"

"Do you always laugh at people who aren't superstars on their first run down the hill?"

Chopper smiled slowly. "Okay, buy me a beer, I'll buy you shots all night."

"Are you trying to get me drunk?"

"'Course I am. A girl like you would never hook up with me sober."

"Oh," Clare said. "So you like sloppy drunks."

"There's always the next morning."

Jana rolled her eyes as Chopper and Clare handed back their empty shot glasses. "Already, MacPherson? Give her, like, a day to look around at her options." She turned to Clare. "You'll find much better guys here than Chopper. You want to rebound from your Toronto ex with someone fabulous."

"Like who?" Clare glanced around the bar. It was half-full, which she thought was pretty good for a Monday night.

"Like me," Chopper said.

"Lucy's not into brainiac freaks."

"Brainiac?" Clare glanced at Chopper and saw the same laid-back snow bum she'd met at her lesson. Maybe brainiac was snowboarder slang for its opposite. "What are you smart in?"

"Thanks a lot." Chopper smirked.

"He's smart in everything. Especially chemistry." Jana pulled a songbook from the pile and started flipping through it on the bar. "We used to sing the Divinyls' 'I Touch Myself.' Me and Sacha. We'd do shooters and look through the list, and we'd always end up picking that. Remember, Chopper?"

Chopper raised his eyebrows, like of course he remembered, he just didn't find it especially cute. "Are those Sacha's bracelets?" He gestured to Jana's wrist where several bands of beads and string and silver charms tangled over top of one another.

"Yeah. They help me remember her." Jana cast her pretty eyes down to the bar for a moment. "Anyway, people thought we were funny. Neither one of us could sing but they liked our dirty gestures. You want to sing it with me, Lucy?"

"No." Clare was starting to wish there was a lock on her bedroom door — or someone else sleeping in the apartment with her and Jana. She thought again of the box of Sacha photos in Jana's closet, wondered if she should study it more closely. "Is that normal, that my customers are waving at me?"

"At least they're not snapping their fingers. You better go see what they want."

Clare found her group ready with its first round of karaoke requests. She returned to the bar and asked Jana what to do with the song selections. Chopper wasn't there but his beer and his coat were, so he couldn't have gone far.

Jana took the papers. "Ha! Cyndi Lauper — what did I say?" .

"You said Cyndi Lauper. What did the guys pick?"

"George Michael. 'One More Try.' God, what a downer. Don't put that sheet in."

"I have to," Clare said. "They'll wonder why their name isn't called."

"Fine; put it in. Depress the whole bar. But if you do, I'm putting your name on 'I Touch Myself.'"

"Jana!"

Jana held the tiny pencil above the tiny paper. "Lucy."

Clare didn't see how she could win. But four angry customers didn't sound as bad as dancing publicly on a dead girl's grave, so she said, "Fine. I'll tell them the DJ can't find the George Michael track. I hope no one else requests it."

"No one will." Jana set down her pencil and continued to flip through the songbook. "And no one cares if you sing Sacha's song. It's not like she owned the patent. But I'll find us something else."

Onstage, a man in a plaid shirt was singing "Friends in Low Places." When Clare turned and looked at his face she saw it was Chopper.

"He's good," Clare said to Jana.

"Chopper? He's annoying."

"He's a really good snowboard instructor." Clare felt something stirring in her, watching Chopper croon the Garth Brooks lyrics with a sexy combination of silly and serious.

Jana snorted. "So you won't sing Sacha's song, but you'll sleep in her bed and work in her job and drool over the guy she used to sleep with."

"You said she was sleeping with Wade."

"She was in love with Wade. But Wade's married."

"So Sacha and Wade weren't having sex?" Fatigue and Southern Comfort fought for the job of clouding Clare's brain.

"Of course they were having sex. But Sacha was afraid of falling too hard for a married man. She slept with Chopper the odd time — and a couple other guys, too — like she was trying to convince herself she could take or leave Wade. Haven't you ever done that?"

Clare looked at Chopper up onstage. The song was almost over, which was a shame — she could listen to him sing all night. She figured him to be in his late thirties — he'd just missed the memo about getting a real job sometime at the end of the last decade. Or maybe he had it figured out better than anyone. Maybe chilling in paradise, getting exercise and fresh air and women when you wanted them was exactly what the world's real geniuses aimed to achieve.

And the way he sang — Clare could climb on top of his tall, muscled body with energy to spare. But as she let her thoughts turn graphic, picturing just what she'd like to do with Chopper, Clare suddenly missed Noah. She wanted to be in New York, eating takeout in his tiny Chelsea apartment, figuring out a way to make their relationship work.

"Yeah," she said to Jana. "Yeah, I have done that."

NINETEEN
WADE

Wade watched Lucy work the floor. He was pretty sure her résumé was fudged. He'd overheard her asking Jana how much rum went in a rum and Coke, which anyone who'd worked anywhere licensed in Canada would know was one ounce unless it was a double. But she looked a lot like Sacha — which Wade found both comforting and unbearable. He'd keep her around until one emotion won over the other.

"Are you listening?" Richie waved a hand back and forth in front of Wade's face. "I want to know when we can get this deal signed. I have a promoter interested in doing gigs here. He says he'll start with Avalanche Nights — and he *never* works with oldie bands — to show us what he can do. If it goes well, he'll take Saturday nights regular."

Wade's eyes panned the room. Ten p.m. on a Monday and the place was buzzing. Not packed like a weekend, but most tables were occupied and the bar was half-full with regulars. It killed him that Avalanche was making no money. Prices were high enough, business was good enough, labor was cheap enough. It was the rent that was too damn high.

"Saturdays are already slammed," Wade said. "Maybe the promoter would like Thursdays."

"Fine, he'll take Thursdays. But he won't lift a finger until I'm officially your partner."

Wade frowned. "Soon, I promise."

"What's the delay, dude? Norris told me that without a cash infusion, this bar will be toast in two weeks." Richie picked up his Heineken and took a long sip, but when he set the bottle back down, Wade saw the level hadn't fallen much.

"Why would Stu say that?" Wade voiced his thoughts aloud.

"He wants to help you. Said he'd give you the money himself but he's tapped."

Wade wondered if this could be true, that Stu Norris was broke. He had expensive taste for a cop, and his wife hadn't worked in years. But Norris was careful. He'd been Avalanche Nights' bookkeeper because he was the only one of the three who even cared about balancing their income with expenses.

Wade said to Richie, "I'm waiting to break this to Georgia. She's . . . well, she was hesitant enough when I went into the bar business. She won't love it if I take on a partner and start running Avalanche like a downtown nightclub."

Richie grinned, exposing his designer grill — one gold tooth on the upper right side of his mouth with a small diamond on either side. Wade liked the look. He could never pull it off personally, but it suited Richie.

Richie said, "We don't have to do club nights. I'm not looking to take over or change the place. Except the waitresses' uniforms — but you gotta admit that any change is a plus in that department."

Wade laughed. "Georgia chose those."

"I bet she did. But seriously, man, you're the businessman — I want to learn from you."

"Learn what?"

"How to run a legit operation." Richie spread his hands and smiled as he glanced around the bar. "You think I want to stay down with the criminals forever? No, thank you. I want to fly in the big leagues."

Wade smirked. "This bar is hardly big leagues."

"One step at a time, man. That's what Billingsley says."

"You read Bob Billingsley?" Wade wondered if he was racist to feel surprised. "The motivational speaker?"

"Dude's a genius," Richie said. "Anyway, I don't need controlling interest — just a deal where I can't get screwed."

The door chime jingled and Georgia walked in. Her long beige coat made her look like a movie star among the Patagonia- and toque-wearing bums in the crowd.

Wade made eye contact and smiled. Georgia took a stool at the bar.

"Okay, let's do this," Wade said to Richie. "We're agreed on terms. I'll draw up a contract. Give me a couple of days so I can get the legalities right. Let's meet again Wednesday night and make this official."

"Sweet." Richie shook Wade's hand, and Wade walked off to join his wife.

He pulled up the stool next to Georgia's. "Long day today?"

Georgia pushed back a long strand of hair, still immaculate after her workday. "This commute is murder."

Wade frowned. "Maybe we should move back to the city. I can be the one to commute."

"We agreed to give Avalanche five years. We're nearly there, right?" She gave him a weary grin.

Wade took Georgia's hand. "I've been offered an amazing deal."

Georgia's hand remained limp in Wade's. "Is that why you were talking with Richie Lebar just now?"

"I know he's not your first choice. And I understand why. But the kid's reading Bob Billingsley. He's trying to make something of himself."

"Billingsley? Are you serious?" Georgia pushed her mouth into something between a smirk and a sneer. "I mean, don't get me wrong — he has impressive *marketing* skills. But he's a quack — he's peddling one plus one equals two and selling it as the great new equation. If Richie buys that shit, it makes me *less* impressed by his intelligence."

Wade tried to remember if Georgia had been such a snob when they'd met. If she had, she'd hidden it well.

"That's kind of what you want in a partner, though," Wade said. "Someone who will work hard, but who won't be able to outsmart you."

Georgia rolled her eyes. "You remind me of a teenager trying to borrow his parents' car. You'll keep coming up with a new argument until I say yes. Except I won't say yes."

"Without Richie, I have to close. It will take even longer for your parents to get their money back."

"Please. My parents have written that money off."

"I haven't. I'm planning to pay them back if I have to write jingles for twenty years to do it."

Georgia's eyes darted to Wade's. "Don't write jingles again. You hated advertising."

"I know, but it pays well. We're only twenty-five grand short of making this payment. Richie's offering fifty thousand for twenty-five percent."

"Twenty-five grand, hmm?" Georgia took a deep breath in. "Seems like such a low number until you can't raise it."

"I *can* raise it. You just won't agree to the terms."

Georgia squeezed Wade's hand tight. "Don't worry if this fails, Wade. I'll support us until you find a job you can feel good about."

"Like what?" Wade knew he sounded morose. He couldn't help it.

"You could teach guitar in high school and play gigs where you can get them. Good things happen when you're at least trying to pursue what you love."

"Can you at least consider Richie? He wants to bring live music into Avalanche. Blues bands, jazz bands. And Avalanche Nights. It's the perfect setting for that."

"Oh, Wade . . . My instincts are screaming no bloody way. But I want to see you thrive again — be the long-haired dude I married." She fingered the hair behind his neck — which was becoming more like a mullet each day. "Not that I liked the long hair. But you were happy then. We'll figure this out."

Man, Wade wished he were in love with her.

TUESDAY / FEBRUARY 14

TWENTY
MARTHA

L aGuardia security waved Martha on. She plied one foot at a time back into brown patent loafers, packed her laptop and iPad into her rolling briefcase, and headed for the lounge.

She felt strange, out in public for the first time in nearly two weeks, eyes on her from all directions. Though she normally passed through this airport several times a week, it felt foreign today, like she was seeing its kiosks and gates, learning its security regulations, all for the first time.

Several of Martha's colleagues resented being herded and scanned through with the masses. Some flew private if they had their own money. Geoff Kearnes, as governor of Georgia, had a jet his constituents paid for. But Martha felt that was hypocritical — using power the people gave you to live in an exalted world beyond their reach.

She smiled bitterly when the thought crossed her mind that she had not been raised to feel so egalitarian but had picked up this way of thinking — accidentally — from Sacha.

Martha saw a Starbucks and rolled her bag up to the counter. Instead of ordering her usual black coffee, she heard herself ask for a chai latte. Sacha's favorite. Martha stared absently as the barista made the drink.

She couldn't get Daisy's allegation out of her head. If Sacha had been smuggling LSD, where the hell was the daughter Martha thought she knew? If the adult Sacha was so far removed from the child Martha remembered, how much of a leap was it that she might in fact have taken her own life?

Daisy must be lying about the drugs.

Martha fished her BlackBerry from her pocket to compose a message to Ted. He was her assistant, but also her liaison to her campaign manager and to pretty much everyone else in her work life. She stopped typing when the chai latte appeared at the end of the counter. She clicked No to *Save Draft?*

Martha took a long sip of the latte. For an instant — less than a second — she was with Sacha six years earlier in the Starbucks on Columbus at Sixty-Seventh, tasting Sacha's new drink of choice — the chai latte — while the young African-American barista grinned at Martha's order of a tall, black bold — the word *coffee* left off as implied. Sacha had caught the double entendre first, met the barista's eyes questioningly, and when it was clear he wasn't offended, all three had cracked up simultaneously.

That was the kind of stupid joke Martha couldn't share with anyone again. For one thing, it was mildly racist. For another, who would care?

Martha left Starbucks and rolled her briefcase down the airport hall. She stopped at the door to the executive lounge. On a regular day, she didn't think twice about waiting for her flight in the more private and comfortable setting. Not to mention more secure. She'd have her iPad or her laptop or sometimes both running, and she'd suffer the lousy coffee they had on offer. But today, Martha hesitated outside the lounge door.

She heard Sacha's voice challenging her to wait in the uncomfortable row seats with the bulk of her constituents, Sacha's laugh mocking Martha's objection that the public seating wasn't as safe, asking *Hasn't everyone here been scanned through high security?*

Martha tilted her case and headed toward the gate.

A young man in ripped blue jeans approached her. He had dark hair that flopped across his face, obscuring his eyes almost completely. His skin was dark, but not dramatically so — Latino maybe, or southern European. Or maybe New York Jewish. "Are you Martha Westlake?" he asked in unaccented English before a Secret Service agent placed his body between the young man and Martha.

The man was craning his neck to meet Martha's eyes behind the guard.

"Are you a reporter?" Martha asked.

"I have a blog."

Another Secret Service guard stepped between the young man and Martha.

"Wow," the man said. "You guys really don't like the Internet revolution, huh?"

Martha didn't know what to think of all the new media. Sacha had seen it as stripping down snobbery, making all viewpoints equally accessible, turning the world into a more casual place that was less hung up on decorum. Martha agreed that the Internet was doing those things; she just wasn't sure the effect was beneficial.

So maybe it was unwise to engage, but it was also unwise to snub the media during an election. Martha was interested enough to say, "Gentlemen, please move aside. I'd like to talk to this young man."

Secret Service patted the man down, which made Martha feel like a heel. But she had to let them do their job.

Finally, she and the young man were face to face. Martha guessed his age to be around thirty, though he slouched like a belligerent teenager.

He said, "Am I right that you'd be interested in an interview?"

Martha's immediate urge was to say of course not. Ted arranged her interviews in conjunction with her publicity team. But today, she said, "An interview would be fine. Would you like to come into the lounge with me or are you comfortable out here?"

"I prefer to be out here, with the people."

Martha resisted an eye-roll. Although the same thought had passed through her head minutes before, spoken aloud it sounded self-righteous. "Let's walk to my gate." She took the lead in that direction. "What would you like to discuss?"

The blogger scrambled to manage his bulging shoulder bag while keeping up with Martha's clipping pace. "My real interest is in your daughter."

Martha felt her heart stop. Just for an instant. She took a deep breath and said, "I'm afraid that's the one topic I wouldn't like to speak about. Politics, anything else — shoot. But my daughter is off limits for now."

"Fair enough," the blogger said — softly, which Martha appreciated. "Politics is fine. I presume you're headed to Detroit for the university talk?"

"Yes." Martha hoped he didn't ask about Reverend Hillier.

"Your first public appearance since . . . I mean, in the past two weeks?"

"Yes."

"Your popularity has risen dramatically in that time."

Martha cringed.

"From a weak fourth to a strong second. Many think you're poised to come out ahead of Kearnes, if you can take Michigan."

"Yes," Martha said. "I've heard that speculation."

"In your time away from the public spotlight, have you changed your stance on any key issues?"

"No."

"Maybe your position on drugs has softened?"

Martha's chest felt heavy, like the frothy milk from the latte was sticking to the walls of her lungs. "I'm afraid I don't follow."

"Perhaps your daughter's activities in Whistler caused a shift in, say, your hard line with end users? Or maybe even with smugglers?"

Martha tightened her grip on her carry-on handle. When they arrived at her gate, she leveled her suitcase and locked eyes with the blogger. "I've asked not to speak about my daughter."

"I'm sorry I've upset you. I guess there was no nice way to ask that question."

"Because the question is groundless. How could Sacha waitressing in Canada impact my position on narcotics in the United States?" This was not the tone Martha was supposed to take with press. She hoped the blogger didn't have a microphone running. The last thing she needed was a sound clip of herself sounding bitchy reaching an audience across the Internet.

The blogger frowned. "You really don't know?"

Martha perched on a hard row seat. She leaned back, which was even more uncomfortable. "Tell me."

The blogger sat, too, leaving one seat empty between them. Martha appreciated the space.

"A source told me that Sacha was smuggling LSD. But not for profit. I heard she had an agenda of her own, with the greater good in mind."

Acid smuggling for the greater good. Martha wondered how she could have missed this. She'd seen Sacha's idealism as intelligence, as compassion, when clearly her daughter should have been in psychiatric care.

"I'm Lorenzo." The blogger reached out a hand, which Martha shook because it was easier, and likely wiser, than avoiding him. "Lorenzo Barilla. And . . . well . . . I promise that if you talk about Sacha — just a friendly piece about her life — I'll keep this information about the drugs out of my blog."

"Fine," Martha said. She knew that name. But why? "We can talk about Sacha."

TWENTY-ONE
CLARE

Clare peeled off the comforter, then immediately pulled it back over her shoulders. Her room was freezing.

She smelled coffee, though. Easily a good enough reason to crawl out of bed and suffer the cold. She chose some thick black sweatpants and a hoodie with the slogan *I Think Therefore I'm Single*. She padded out to the kitchen.

"Coffee's made," Jana said. "I don't know if you had time to get groceries yesterday, but you can have some of my cereal if you want. Just not my Smarties."

"Thanks." Clare pulled a mug down from the cupboard. She was tempted to eat all the hard-shelled chocolates just to see how Jana reacted. But that would definitely be a Clare, not a Lucy, move. Too bad she had to stay in character.

Jana glanced up from her laptop and said, "Nice hair."

"Is it bad?" Clare hadn't looked in a mirror.

"Not bad if you're a strung-out rock star." Jana turned back to her computer. "Holy shit. I just Googled Sacha's name and this blog came up. Dude has an interview with Sacha's mom."

"Didn't you say Sacha's mom was a politician? She must be interviewed all the time." Clare took a long sip of coffee. It tasted pretty good — not too dark, not too bitter, but strong and thick the way Clare liked it. "Is this coffee organic?"

"Yeah," Jana said. "And shade-grown. Sacha used to insist on that — something about bird habitats. This is the first time Martha Westlake has been in public in two weeks."

"Maybe her publicist told her it was time to get back on the campaign trail."

"Right. What do you care? You never knew Sacha." Jana clearly didn't like Clare's dismissive tone.

Clare picked up the bag of Mueslix and pretended to study the ingredients. "Fine, I'm curious."

"Why? Because I said you look like her?"

"Maybe. Chopper said the same thing."

Jana pressed her lips together forcefully, like she was deciding if she wanted to talk to Clare. After a moment, she said, "Did you see the teddy bear in your room?"

Of course Clare had seen it. And picked it up and flipped it over, like she had done with most things in the apartment. But since Lucy wasn't a cop, she wouldn't have been quite so observant. "No."

"His name is Jules. Jules the Bear. I was going to bring him into my room but he only has one eye and that freaks me out. Mrs. Westlake says here . . ." Jana poked at her screen. "'Sacha took Jules everywhere. If she went to her father's weekend home, Jules would go. When she had her interview at NYU, even though it was only a subway ride away, she tucked Jules into her knapsack for good luck. That's how I know my daughter didn't kill herself. If Sacha was going up that mountain to die on purpose, Jules would have been with her."

Clare wanted a cigarette. There was a smoking area out back by the kitchen door. But it was well below freezing, and hard to smoke with gloves. Jana's rule inside was hard and fast: marijuana, not tobacco. So Clare warmed her hands on her coffee. "Sacha's parents didn't want Jules sent home with the rest of her things?"

Jana made a sound like she was sucking on her tongue. "You're pretty inquisitive, Lucy. For someone who allegedly doesn't care."

"I guess I'm more curious than I let on." Clare said. "It's a weird feeling, arriving in a town where this girl who kind of looked like you has just been found dead. Is what her mom says true? You think Sacha would have taken Jules with her, if she was going to . . . you know . . . kill herself?"

"Can you keep a secret?"

"Of course," Clare said.

"Sacha left Jules behind on purpose. She didn't want him to see her in her final, awful moments. She loved him too much."

"Um. How do you know?" Clare tried to keep her voice light — as in, not like an inquisitive cop.

"She left me a note inside Jules."

"Inside?" Clare imagined Jana slicing up the bear, surgically or maybe violently, in order to find this note. If it existed.

"He has a zipper on his back. When Sacha was found dead, and it looked like suicide, that's the first place I looked."

Clare tried her best to act like Lucy would, when the wheels in her head were screeching madly against each other. "That's so sad."

Jana brushed a tear from her face. Real or forced, Clare couldn't tell. "I hate her for leaving, but her mom is so wrong. Sacha killed herself."

Clare pulled out a chair and sat with Jana. She didn't know what to say. She had to get her eyes on that note, and if she could, she had to get the note to Amanda.

"Have you shown the letter to the police?" Clare decided to come right out and ask.

"I gave it to Richie on Sunday to give to the cops. I get it back when the case is closed, though."

"Oh. Good." Clare didn't give a shit who got what once the case was over. She'd be back in New York by then, fighting with Noah.

"Richie thinks the note should get rid of the undercover, once the handwriting analysis comes back and they know it was Sacha's writing."

Clare wondered why Amanda didn't know about this suicide note. Maybe Richie hadn't actually given it to the cops.

"You want to read her mom's interview with me?"

What Clare wanted to read was the suicide note, but she'd have to find a copy first. "Yeah. Why not?"

Jana pushed her computer toward Clare so the screen was halfway between them. She scrolled back up to the beginning.

```
MARTHA WESTLAKE UNPLUGGED

A chance encounter at LaGuardia put me up close and
personal with Martha Westlake, New York's junior
senator in Washington. Did we talk about politics?
No. Foremost on my brain -- and readers' brains, and
Martha's -- is the death not even two weeks ago of
Martha's 23-year-old daughter, Alexandra Westlake --
known to friends and family as Sacha.

"Sacha may have fallen off the beaten path," Senator
Westlake told me, "but she would not have taken her
own life."

I asked the Senator what she meant about the beaten
path.

"I judged Sacha harshly," Westlake said. "For wanting
to take time out in Whistler before she jumped into a
high-impact career. But maybe my generation should
have taken our twenties for self-exploration before
ramming head first into our own adult lives. Maybe
then we wouldn't have presidents who think bombing
other countries is the optimal conflict resolution
technique."

I pointed out that Westlake sounded more like a
radical than a Republican -- that her party has led
the United States into some of the most irrational
```

bombing in history -- and I asked her if she wanted
me to strike that quote from her reply.

"I don't care," she said. "Does anyone even read your
blog?"

"Has anyone commented yet?" Clare asked.

Jana scrolled down to the bottom of the page. "135 people. The
post has only been live for an hour." She scrolled back up so they
could keep reading.

TWENTY-TWO
WADE

Wade pounded his fist beside his keyboard. He hoped that stupid detail — that Sacha had been found without her teddy bear — wasn't enough to convince the undercover that he needed to make himself comfortable in Whistler. Sacha was gone, and Wade needed to make himself some money — fast.

He read the blogger's profile in the sidebar:

My name is Lorenzo Barilla. I am an investigative journalist. I work for myself, because if you call yourself an investigative journalist and you work for a traditional newspaper, you are actually a peon in their system that is designed to control the world.

Wade snorted. Kid must be in his twenties.

His coffee tasted bitter. He reached into the cabinet beside his desk, pulled out a bottle that he'd hidden behind some books, and added a healthy dose of vodka to his mug. It still tasted bitter, but at least it would make him feel better.

Wade closed the blog and opened Facebook. His news feed reminded him that it was Valentine's Day. Georgia had already left for work, but he could buy some flowers for when she got home. Roses, because she was conventional like that. And some chocolates — nice ones, from Rogers or Rocky Mountain. And a bottle of something she liked.

Wade let his fingers take him to Sacha's profile. The past two weeks had turned it macabre. Messages like "Luuuuuvs you OMG u r gone 2 higher place & don't mean high on acid" adorned the page along with pictures of flowers and candles. One idiot had even posted a clip-art tombstone — Wade looked closer and saw that the idiot was Jana.

He clicked through a bunch of party shots until he found a photo of Sacha alone. She was standing in the woods in a dark green ski jacket. Snow covered the ground and trees and there was even some in her hair.

Wade wanted to reach into the photo, to brush the snow from her head, to touch her tiny, upturned nose and magically pull her out of the photograph, into his arms where she would whisper encouraging things to him, let him know he wasn't a fuck-up. He felt like a necrophiliac for the erection that was bulging in his jeans.

He remembered their first night together, in his condo. Georgia had been in Hong Kong trying to sell Schenkers on an ad campaign, and Wade brought Sacha home from work. Sacha said, "Normally I wouldn't be here with an old married guy, but the way you sang 'My Way' at karaoke had me hot all night. It's like, you get it."

"I have a guitar," Wade said, "if you want more."

"I want a lot more." Sacha nodded, a sweet, solemn expression in her eyes. "Can you play the Beatles? My favorite song in the world is 'Revolution.' But you have to sing it like you feel it, like you want to change the world."

"How about 'Fool on the Hill'? I feel like that guy, especially in my marriage."

"Misunderstood?" Sacha laughed. But she got it. Georgia would have given him a confused stare and told him to get a grip.

"Fine." Sacha had shifted toward Wade, taken his hand in hers and squeezed it like they'd known each other for years. "Sing 'Fool on the Hill' and I won't feel so guilty about screwing someone's husband."

TWENTY-THREE
MARTHA

The plane thudded down onto the Michigan tarmac. Martha did not like landings. She'd had a bad experience once in France, and since then, she always imagined the plane careening too far off the runway or smashing into another plane or burning up in a spontaneous explosion. Today, though, despite the ice and snow, she felt relaxed about her fate. She still imagined the fiery death, but for once that thought was peaceful.

Had Sacha shared that feeling — that numb sense of not caring if she lived or died — when she rode up the mountain that last time? Martha closed her eyes and imagined she was sitting beside Sacha on the chairlift, telling her daughter what she needed to hear to stop her from taking her life. Except even in the daydream, Martha couldn't open her mouth. And Sacha couldn't hear her.

Martha waited for the in-flight announcement to give the green light back to cell phone use. When it came on, she immediately powered up her phone and sent Ted a text:

Need you for phone call in 15.

Ted's response came in under a minute.

Here & ready. Hope you're OK.

There was something claustrophobic-making in the *hope you're OK*. Martha wasn't sure what. Probably she was being unfair.

She tugged her briefcase from the overhead container and followed the foot traffic off the plane. When she found a quiet corner where she wouldn't be overheard, she phoned Ted.

He picked up on the first ring. "Are you in Detroit? What can I do for you?"

Again with the claustrophobia — like Ted was trying to baby her.

She said, "I need you to tell the FBI that Sacha was — possibly — transporting LSD across the American border. Two independent sources have confirmed this." Martha decided not to mention that the two sources were a blogger and a floozy.

Ted's end of the phone was silent.

"Are you there?" Martha said.

"Who are your two sources?"

"I'm keeping them private."

"Surely not . . . from me?" Ted's voice had a trace of a tremble, reminding Martha how young he was.

"From everyone," she said, "until I get confirmation. Will you pass this on, or are you too busy?"

"Of course I'm not too busy." The tremble seemed to border on rage. Or maybe she was imagining that. "But I'm not sure the FBI needs to be let in on this."

Martha gave a death glare to a gray-haired man who was coming too close to her. Her security guys stepped between the man and Martha, and the man moved on. "Ted, why don't you sound remotely surprised to hear that my daughter may have been smuggling drugs into our country?"

"Well . . ." Ted paused for several beats. His breathing was shallow and audible. "You know my friend who works for Governor Kearnes . . ."

Martha waited, her knuckles clenched white against her black phone.

"He let it slip, maybe three weeks ago, that their campaign had dirt on Sacha. They weren't planning to leak it unless you climbed high enough in the ratings to be a threat."

Martha's head began to spin. If Kearnes knew about Sacha and the drugs, and the blogger knew, and *Daisy* knew, how was this not in the press? And how did the police not know — on either side of the border? The DEA, in particular, should be on this. "What's going on, Ted?" And then she asked her real question: "How did *I* not know?"

Ted sighed. "I first heard the allegation a week before Sacha died. I was looking into it discreetly, to find out what was true before distressing you. And when Sacha died . . . well, I didn't see the point of adding to your grief. Or of investigating the rumor any further. Kearnes won't release it now — he'd look desperate and cruel."

Martha saw a Starbucks, and the only thing that calmed her enough to not hang up on Ted was the knowledge that once this conversation was over, she could walk up to the kiosk and order another chai latte.

"Should I have told you?" To Ted's credit, he sounded uncertain.

"Yes," Martha said. "Why are you reluctant to share this with the FBI?"

"Because what if we tell them and the press gets wind? It could really hurt your shot at the nomination. Things have been going so well in the past couple of weeks, rating-wise."

"You did not just say that."

"I'm sorry." Ted sighed. "I'm not celebrating the reason behind the surge. But which is more important: finding Sacha's killer or leading the country back to greatness?"

"*Justice* is more important. I want you to give the FBI all the information we have. Including anything you haven't told me. Where are you now?"

"Dulles," Ted said. "My plane to Detroit boards in eight minutes. My plan is to meet you at the tail end of your lunch with Hillier. We can head to the university together. I have a list of talking points we can go over in the car. The team has done some good work on this."

Martha was too enraged with Ted to want to see him. "I can

handle today on my own. Email the notes if you like, but I want you to stay home and work on counter-spin. If this bit about Sacha and the drug smuggling does come out, I'd like us to have our line snug and ready."

"I'm sure the girls in charge of media can work on counter-spin." Ted sounded deflated.

"I want your brain on this. I'm flying straight home from the debate, and I look forward to speaking on the phone first thing tomorrow."

"I look forward to it, too. Um, should I call you, or . . ."

"I'll call you."

Martha hung up and walked slowly to the Starbucks. But as desperately as she gulped at her second chai latte, the flavor was not as consoling as it had been hours earlier at LaGuardia.

Martha really had to wonder if this investigation made sense. Not because it might cost her the presidency, but because she didn't want to learn — not conclusively, anyway — that her daughter had taken her own life.

TWENTY-FOUR
CLARE

Amanda opened the door for Clare. Amanda's townhouse was a vacation rental that looked like it would have been all the rage in the early eighties — sloped ceiling, shag carpets, lacquered blond wood accents. She ushered Clare in quickly. Like she was paying the heating bill.

"How was your snowboarding lesson?" Amanda asked.

"Ugh. Chopper." Clare ripped off her puffy plaid gloves and set them on the radiator in the hallway. "He's all 'Lucy, I think you're ready for a new challenge.' So he takes me on a blue run. But it should have been coded black, it was so steep, and there were these bumps that make it even harder, they're called moguls, covering an entire section of the hill. I took off my snowboard and slid down on the seat of my ski pants."

"Because you were scared?"

"Because I was mad." Clare hung her purple ski parka on the hook by the door. She loved this jacket — it was warm, but sleek-lined, with high-tech thermal design. Lots of pockets, including a few that were hidden unless you looked super closely. She hoped she could keep Lucy's wardrobe at the end of the assignment.

Amanda shifted her tan leather coat over a couple of pegs, away from Clare's wet parka. "Your instructor's name is Chopper?"

"Yeah."

"Good. Chopper's who I asked for, but the ski school is run by such hippies, they said there was no guarantee." Amanda gestured past the foyer, inviting Clare to come into the open living space, where a dining area, kitchenette, and sitting area with a fireplace rolled into one room. It would be a great space for a house party, if anyone other than Amanda were staying here.

Clare took a seat in a plush, plaid armchair. "Why would you care who my snowboarding instructor is? Is it because he used to sleep with Sacha?"

"I didn't know about the sleeping with. But yes, we knew they had an association." Amanda perched on a bar stool by the kitchenette. "Would you like some coffee? I've just brewed a pot."

"Sure, thanks. But why would Lucy request a specific instructor? She's not supposed to have known a thing about Whistler until she got here."

"I told the ski school I was your brother's friend, and your brother wanted to surprise you by having your lessons arranged, and I have a condo here and I've heard good things about Chopper. It works with our cover story if we're ever seen together." Amanda passed Clare a chunky pottery mug.

"Smells good."

"I brewed it with a stick of cinnamon. I called you here because we need to learn more about Chopper."

"Oh," Clare said. "I guess it was wishful thinking that you called to loop me into Sacha Westlake's drug smuggling." Damn, she had to learn to cut the spoiled teenager from her voice. But Amanda always brought out the best in her.

Amanda sighed, took a seat on the couch opposite Clare. "I know you'd like to be included on every level of this investigation, but can you please concentrate on your own job and trust that I'll tell you what you need to know?"

Trust, like Noah had told her to do. Clare wished she could say yes. It just felt so counter-intuitive. She cupped the mug in her hands, warming them.

"Okay." Clare attempted a smile. "There probably isn't even a killer, anyway." She told Amanda what Jana had said about the suicide note.

"We're waiting for handwriting analysis on that."

"Sorry — you already knew about the note and didn't tell me?" Clare shot Amanda a confused glance.

"Yes."

Clare couldn't find words. Which was probably a good thing — if she did speak, it wouldn't be to say something nice.

"Handwriting results are unconfirmed. As with the drug smuggling, we don't feel it's wise to loop an undercover in to every speculation. It could cloud the information you gather."

"I'm not a squirrel collecting nuts." Clare knew her voice was verging on extremely rude, but at least she wasn't sharing how she really felt.

"You're not the detective — you're the probe. A squirrel collecting nuts is actually an excellent metaphor. My job is to get information from you, not share down from above."

Clare wanted to strangle Amanda when she talked about above and below like that. But she couldn't change Amanda's hierarchical mindset any more than she could bring Sacha back to life.

"Whatever," Clare said. "What's the deal with Chopper?"

Amanda pursed her lips. "All right, I will share this: Senator Westlake's office thinks Chopper may be involved with the LSD smuggling."

"They're right. Jana told me. Chopper makes the acid."

"That was easy," Amanda said. "Do you know how old Chopper is? I haven't been able to look him up because no one can find his real name."

"Late thirties? His last name is MacPherson, if that helps. I don't know if it's Mc or Mac — or his real first name."

Amanda pulled her notepad toward her on the table and wrote

McPherson/MacPherson on the lined page. "Can you get to know Chopper better?"

"Yeah. He flirts with me relentlessly. I wouldn't mind sleeping with him — you know, for the cause."

Amanda frowned. "You're an agent, not a prostitute."

Ugh. First Noah, now Amanda. "If a man sleeps around, no one calls him a whore. They assume he's having a good time."

Amanda arched her eyebrows.

"I love this job, and I love getting right into role. Lucy would fuck Chopper in a heartbeat."

Amanda still said nothing.

"Well?" Clare said.

"Well, you'll do what you like, as usual."

"What's that supposed to mean? You're my handler — do you think it's a good idea or not?" Conflict aside, Clare valued Amanda's opinion. She felt like she'd be flying blind without it.

"You know what I think. Chopper is a person of interest, so it's great if you can get close to him, socially. But that doesn't have to involve sex. I think you equate the two too often."

"Fine," Clare said. "I'll only drop acid with him."

"Now that I do forbid. No LSD *at all*, with Chopper or anyone."

"I think I should play that by ear. This peer group you've dropped me into, they're all such acid heads — Jana, Chopper, Sacha when she was alive. I think it might help me understand them."

"Have you ever taken acid?"

"No. Have you?"

Amanda made a face and Clare knew she wouldn't answer from her own experience. When she spoke, her tone was clinical. "It makes you lose touch with reality for approximately eight hours. You'll hallucinate, there's no telling what you might say or do, and if you run into trouble, you won't have the mental capacity to protect yourself."

"Are you stupid?" Clare's contempt bubbled up to the surface. "You tell me to investigate Chopper — a drug smuggler who wants to sleep with me. I suggest sex, you call me a whore. I suggest drugs, you forbid it? Maybe you want me to hold Chopper's hand and skip across the village cobblestones until he confesses that he murdered Sacha on the mountain?"

"No LSD, Clare. It's not safe."

"Sacha died on the ski hill drugged up on Ambien." Clare knew she should tone down her derision if she wanted to change Amanda's mind, but it was too hard to hold back. "Not on LSD at Chopper's house. I think if he had it in for me, he'd find a way to kill me during one of our snowboarding lessons."

"You want me to forbid you to take lessons from him?"

"See, now you're not even being reasonable. Is this because I called you stupid?"

Amanda didn't seem to know that answer.

"So what do you want me to do?"

"Gather information. Anything you can find without putting yourself at risk."

"I'm an undercover FBI agent. I'm not paid to run from risk. Down in the States, they don't childproof the job. It's probably why they get better results." Clare was pleased with herself for making her point without swearing. "I just had a thought. To run a drug operation large scale, do you think Chopper would need the cooperation of the Whistler cops? Or even American cops?"

"It's possible. You got angry last time I said this, but we are very deliberately not sharing your identity with the local RCMP for reasons just like that one. Or with the FBI at large."

"You didn't know Chopper made drugs, though, when you made the decision not to share information with the local cops."

"No," Amanda said. "And I'm sure there's more we don't know. Would you like to stay here and argue with me, or would you like to go out in the field and find out what that is?"

TWENTY-FIVE
MARTHA

The Detroit diner was loud with a blue-collar energy Martha enjoyed. Nothing false in the clanging plates, in the orders being shouted down the line, in the screaming baby two booths over with food dribbling down his chin.

"How's your chicken?" Reverend Hillier said. "Not too greasy, I hope."

"It's greasy." Martha pushed her plate aside. She wanted to finish the drumstick and thigh combo, if only for political reasons, but her stomach was already protesting. "Tasty, though. I can see why this place is your favorite."

"It's my favorite because it's my congregation's favorite." Hillier waved at a man in a neighboring booth, gave him a warm smile. "I never forget the people who gave me my power."

Martha would have thought *influence* or *responsibility* were words more behooving a religious leader, rather than *power*. Or maybe, like the clanging plates, there was no point in pretending.

"My assistant tells me you're thinking of backing Geoff Kearnes. I'm sorry to hear that. I thought I could count on your support."

Hillier pulled grease off his fingers with a wet nap. "I'm keeping my mind open until I make my call publicly."

"Kearnes offered you a cabinet post."

"I'll make the best call for my congregation. Please don't insult me by suggesting otherwise." Hillier opened a second wet nap and dabbed around his mouth, paying special attention to his tidy black mustache.

Martha smiled grimly. "What does your congregation need that you're worried I can't provide?"

"They need a strong leader. You've been absent from public life for nearly two weeks. I want to know that if I throw my weight behind you, it will take you all the way to the White House."

"I'm here to win, Reverend."

Hillier asked the waitress for the pie list and waited while she recited it. He chose lemon meringue. Martha nearly asked for mint tea, but at the last second got sensible — no need to get a reputation for highfalutin' demands in lowfalutin' places — and asked for black coffee.

"My chances of winning have soared since our last conversation," Martha said when the waitress had left. "So statistically, you should have more confidence in me now than ever."

"Statistics." Hillier gave a disgusted snort. "Statistics say my congregation's youth will end up as criminals and dropouts, and still I believe in their potential for success. I see good people dealt a bad hand. I see my job as to improve that hand, to pull them up and help them shine like I know they can."

Martha wanted to vomit from the rhetoric — or maybe it was the chicken. "That's an admirable mandate. One I hope to help you pursue."

"A cabinet position *could* allow me to help them in ways I can't now."

"I'm not setting up my cabinet as a reward box for political favors."

"I admire your ethic," Hillier said. "But I don't want to turn down an opportunity that could help my people rise up."

"I can understand that." Greed was what Martha understood. But she smiled and said, "I think you'll find my new anti-drug policy will do wonders for inner-city congregations like yours."

Hillier's mouth moved in an expression Martha couldn't read. "New policy? You've been head of the senate drug committee for years. I would have thought your position on narcotics was snug by now."

Martha watched the waitress cut the pie behind the counter. When she had transferred the enormous piece onto a dessert plate, the waitress ran two fingers along the pie lifter and licked them off. She was still smacking her lips when she dropped the piece of pie in front of Hillier.

"It's amazing," Martha said, "how two weeks away from work will clear up your vision."

"So what's this new vision?" Hillier asked with an amused look before tucking into his pie.

Martha frowned. "The old model is broken. It's time to put away the hammer and pull out the scalpel — starting with opening our minds to legalization."

Shit. Those were not smart words to say out loud. Especially not without developing the platform, working on the talking points with Ted. Martha leaned back in the booth, hoping she had done no harm. It was an argument she'd had a million times with Sacha — except suddenly Martha had switched sides and taken her daughter's position.

Hillier's second forkful of lemon and meringue hung over his plate, its motion toward his mouth suspended. "You want me to support a bid for legalization?"

Martha smiled, though she felt more like kicking herself — hard. "Not necessarily implementing it — just looking seriously at the legislation Colorado and Washington State are endorsing, and maybe adopting that on a federal level, instead of rejecting the option out of hand like we've been doing for the past forty years. I want this country to be healthy, Reverend. It isn't, at the moment." She pointedly eyed her plate, which the waitress hadn't cleared despite the crumpled paper napkin in the center.

"I knew you didn't like that chicken."

Martha smiled thinly.

"Look, Martha. I'll admit it: I'm a conservative. The mere possibility of legalization makes me want to run screaming. With a cabinet position, of course, I could work on the policy with you — ensure that the changes would be good for my people." He shoved the bite into his mouth, catching some meringue on his mustache. Martha wished she had a camera.

"I'm afraid I can't play this game, Reverend. I believe I'll be an excellent president. My daughter's death did temporarily knock me down. But I'm back. With a fresh perspective that I think this country needs. I plan to look at every issue with clean eyes. And I'm not offering a cabinet post to anyone with religious affiliation."

"That's not very Republican."

Martha resisted a snort. "The separation of church and state is one of the principles our country was founded upon. It's the most Republican of Republican values."

"You'll forgive me, then, if I back Geoffrey Kearnes."

"No." Martha stood up. The noises in the restaurant were jarring now. She wanted to muzzle the screaming baby, clean up his face with a cheap napkin. "I won't forgive you. But I'll understand what that says about your character."

TWENTY-SIX
CLARE

Clare stood at the bar as Jana prepped the drinks for her order. Clare thumbed the plastic bug in her pocket. She needed Jana's back to turn so she could stick it onto the beer glass she was about to serve Chopper. He was talking to Richie and their voices were low. Clare could tell the conversation was significant.

"I don't like these limes." Jana squinted into the dish on the bar. "They look mushy. I think they were cut yesterday."

Okay, Clare said in her head. *So go to the fridge and get more.*

Jana frowned. "No, they'll be okay. It's that guy's third drink. He would have complained by now." Jana added a vodka tonic to Clare's tray and studied the two order chits to see if there was anything left to make.

"Plus a Heineken for Richie," Clare said.

"Oh yeah." Jana smirked. "We always forget the ones we love, huh?"

Clare studied the full pint glass on her tray, the dark ale for Chopper. The logo was probably the best place, where the sticker would be most invisible.

Clare slipped the tiny clear sticker from her back pocket. It wouldn't take long to attach it to the glass, but Jana was weirdly observant. Especially of anything Clare did.

As Jana bent over to pull a Heineken from the fridge, Clare glanced to make sure Chopper and Richie weren't looking her way. She peeled off the backing and pressed the miniscule bug onto the beer glass. While Jana popped the cap off the Heineken bottle, Clare held the sticker firmly for a few seconds so it wouldn't fall off from moisture.

"You're holding that glass pretty tight," Jana said.

"I am?" Clare tried to keep her breathing steady. What had Jana seen?

"You are. You think maybe you have the hots for Chopper?"

"Maybe." Clare gave Jana a weak smile. "He's not my normal type, but maybe that's exactly what I need."

Clare walked slowly through the room. This would be the wrong time to spill her first tray, though she felt wobblier than ever. She set Richie's bottle and Chopper's pint glass on their table.

The receiver was in Clare's bag behind the bar. If all went well, she would leave tonight with an audio recording of Chopper and Richie, deep in conversation.

TWENTY-SEVEN
RICHIE

Richie smiled as he surveyed the bar. The waitresses would look hot in their new uniforms — which should be white, not black, in keeping with the name Avalanche. Drink prices could go up a few cents. But mostly this place was damn decent. He liked the sloped ceilings, the wooden beams, the funky lighting, the view of the mountain. Not bad for an entry-level business. Not bad at all.

But first, Seattle.

"We're officially overdue at midnight," he said to Chopper.

Chopper glanced at his watch. "We'd have to run the batch down ourselves to make it in time. Are you suggesting we . . ."

"No, man. Way too risky. Norris and I already agreed that we should wait this out a few days, eat the hundred grand penalty. And you know how rare it is for Norris and me to agree."

"What about one of your sub-dealers? The kids you wholesale pot and shrooms to."

"Can't trust them," Richie said. "If they make the run successfully, they have shit on me. If they get busted on the drive, I'm the first name they'll sell out."

Chopper checked his watch again. "Seriously, we can hop in my truck now and make it."

"No. We have to play this right. There's always an optimal solution if you look at a problem from the right angle." Richie hoped this was true — the stress buzzing inside him was making him doubt the Bob Billingsley line he'd just quoted.

Chopper tilted back on two legs of his stool. "I paid Norris the ten grand. The wheels are in motion to get the undercover's name."

Richie leaned forward. "You want to talk quieter? Walls have ears. Even Wade's walls."

"Should I use my inside voice?"

"Use your fucking inside a library voice."

Chopper grinned. "I've never fucked inside a library. You think it would be hotter with the librarian while she's on shift, or with another chick, trying not to get caught by the librarian?"

"This is serious." Richie crooked a finger to get Chopper to stop tilting and come closer. "How long did Norris say it will take to get this name?"

"Dunno. I gave him the cash and he couldn't get away fast enough."

"Better be soon, or I'm asking for a refund."

"Chill, Richie. This is going to come together."

"Chill. Yeah. Easy for you to say. You're stoned all the time."

"Not all the time." Chopper smirked, and Richie wanted to punch the expression off his face.

He settled for clenching his fists below the table.

"What about Norris, for the run?" Richie said. "I bet the UC's not looking in his direction."

Chopper nodded slowly. "I like that. Plus it sounds like he could use the cash."

"He's getting docked ten grand off the top," Richie said. "For the money he extorted today."

"We're not docking anything until the case is closed and the undercover has gone home."

"Fine. Where's he spending all his cash, anyway? You think it's for real, that a cello for his kid could cost that much? Must have been nearly two hundred grand we've given him the past ten months."

"Yeah, it's sadly real." Chopper's finger picked at the embossed logo on his pint glass. "Norris wanted a career in music so bad, it's like he's transferred his dream to his kid — like it's okay for him to fail as long as he helps her succeed."

"Norris should grab a guitar and hit the road. He should do it soon." Richie flicked his tongue along the back of his grill. For whatever reason, the gesture calmed him — like the adult version of sucking his thumb.

"We need Norris. You want some RCMP chief who isn't sympathetic to our cause?"

"Might be easier. The guy's going rogue on us. Which makes me wonder who the hell he's working for."

"He's scared," Chopper said, still thumbing the logo on his glass. "Nothing more sinister. I'll ask him about making the run."

"What about Wade?" It killed Richie to suggest it — he wanted to solve Wade's cashflow problems by being his partner, not by giving him a job — but this was way more important.

"No." Chopper was suddenly not chill. He stopped playing with his glass and sat up straight. "I'm sure he'd take the deal. But his boozing is out of control these days. We can't take chances with him being sloppy."

"Anyone else we could trust?"

"Maybe Jana?" Chopper's eyebrows lifted as he looked at Richie. "She'd do it. Twenty grand to drive to Washington for a shopping trip would be right up her alley."

Richie watched Jana pour a draft beer across the room, watched her smile flirtatiously at the man she was serving it to. Damn, she was good at winding men up. Richie could get a boner if he watched her for long enough. To prevent that, he turned back to face Chopper. "Forget that. I'm not tangling my woman up in my business."

"She went with Sacha that one time."

"And I gave Sacha shit for it. Not Jana."

TWENTY-EIGHT
MARTHA

The plane's wheels hit the Queens runway. The pilot braked hard and the airplane skidded in the rain that was gushing down upon the city. But again, Martha wasn't gripping the armrest in fear. She felt like she was floating, almost dreaming — and if the plane blew up, so be it.

As she walked out to the pick-up line where her car was waiting, a microphone plonked itself in front of Martha's face. A camera appeared seconds later, followed by an oversized umbrella that sheltered Martha and the rest of the setup.

"Good evening, Senator Westlake." A ponytailed reporter in a beige raincoat with Burberry trim stood between the camera and the microphone. She looked like she was twelve, but she was probably in her twenties or early thirties. "You've had a busy day in Michigan. Lunch with Reverend Hillier. A talk at the state university. Can you tell me how lunch went?"

Martha was pleased that she still remembered how to smile on cue. "Reverend Hillier took me to a favorite place of his constituents'. Elroy's Fried Chicken. It was lovely."

"Does Reverend Hillier plan to endorse your campaign?"

"To my knowledge, he hasn't made his position public yet."

"So no sneak previews?" The reporter grinned winningly.

"No." Martha returned the grin.

"Governor Kearnes announced earlier that he's confident Hillier's endorsement will go his way."

"Perhaps that's because Kearnes offered Hillier a cabinet post." Martha could imagine Ted cringing in front of his TV at home. She shouldn't have said it, but it felt strangely liberating to speak the plain truth, like she was swimming naked or riding a horse without a helmet.

"Really?" The peppy young newswoman's eyes shot wide open. "And you're not willing to match the offer?"

"Of course not. I'd like to win this election, but I won't buy endorsements with the public purse."

"So will Hillier go with Kearnes? Is that your guess?"

"I'm not sure." Martha put a finger to her chin. She hoped Hillier was watching. "I believe that Reverend Hillier is a man of deep principle. He'll make the choice that will benefit his congregation."

"Can you win the nomination without Hillier?"

"I have no idea. The numbers say no, but numbers are more about pollsters jerking themselves off intellectually than accurate predictions of the future." Martha shouldn't have said that, either.

The woman's eyes danced delightedly. Martha's language had likely given her a viral media clip. "Will you withdraw from the race if Hillier backs Kearnes?"

"Let's see what tomorrow brings, shall we?"

The reporter pursed her lips, most likely searching for a segue into something fresh. "Have you thought of bringing Jules the Bear on your campaign trail? That was an interesting blog interview you gave this morning."

"Thank you." Martha had trouble believing that interview had been only that morning. "And in case that was a serious question: no, Jules will not be joining me."

"I like the new you," the reporter said, as if they were chums. "You seem to have a new voice since your return to the public spotlight. A more honest voice."

Martha wasn't sure what to say, so she borrowed the line Ted wanted her to take. "My priorities have changed since losing my daughter."

"Has your official platform changed?"

"Yes," Martha said and immediately wondered how on earth she was going to back up her affirmative answer. It was one thing to spout off in private, at lunch, and another thing entirely in a nation-wide television interview.

"On which policies, specifically?" The reporter relaxed into a comfortable standing pose. She knew she'd landed the scoop of the week.

Martha wasn't used to scrambling for words. "We're planning a press conference within the next couple of days, when the new plat-form is ready. It's still the same ethic — conservative spending, sepa-ration of church and state — but we're tweaking some of the other issues. Would you like an invitation?"

"I'd rather have a hint tonight. Just a teaser. The nation is dying to know."

The girl had such natural charm — not phony like most of her media colleagues. Martha said, "There's something new in the War on Drugs."

"Is it . . . less hard line than your previous views?"

Martha nodded. The warm car was waiting. She should get the hell inside, let her driver take her home. But it was like she was dreaming — her mouth was moving faster than her brain could con-trol. "I think it's time to decriminalize possession."

The reporter's lips pushed out from her face and curled into a perfect O.

"Details to follow." But Martha knew she'd said too much. Her heart was already thudding down into her stomach.

The reporter regained her poise. "Possession of . . . all drugs? Or just marijuana for the states that independently sanction it?"

"I'll outline specifics in the press conference. And let me be clear: I'm as adamant as ever about removing drugs from our society. But, well, old methods clearly aren't working."

"Who do you think would vote for such a radical new policy? Surely not existing Republicans?"

Martha sighed. "I know it's unrealistic. But I want Republicans to start thinking outside the box."

"So you're hoping to pull votes from the left?"

"From the center," said Martha. "Which is where I believe most Americans draw their beliefs."

As she slipped into the car — smiling and waving at her stunned-looking constituents — the answer became clear to Martha.

She texted Ted:

`Need to talk ASAP. You awake?`

Of course Ted was awake. He phoned in under a minute.

"I'm pulling out," Martha said.

Ted was quiet.

"Of the leadership race. Can you take care of that for me? Get me the papers I need to sign? Whatever else there is to do."

"No," Ted said.

"You work for me, Ted. No isn't one of your options."

"Did you not make headway with Hillier?" Ted's voice was shaking.

"This isn't about Hillier. It's about me speaking without thinking on three separate occasions today — to that blogger, to Hillier, and just now to a reporter. I need to pull out, to regain control of who I am and what I say. I'm sorry. I thought I'd be ready but I'm not."

"You should sleep on this."

"Turn on your television, Ted. You'll understand."

"Whatever you said . . . we can fix it."

"We'll talk in the morning. Maybe you will have come to terms with my decision."

WEDNESDAY / FEBRUARY 15

TWENTY-NINE
CLARE

I t would be six a.m. in Manhattan. Clare imagined Noah tossing under his comforter, maybe with some other girl beside him. She wished she could kick the imaginary girl out of his bed — wished, too, that the image didn't bug her so much — but at the moment all Clare could do was her job. In Whistler, it was three, and her night was going strong.

She followed Chopper down the outside stairs from Avalanche, into the street. It had been raining when Clare arrived at work, but the temperature must have dropped off again, because now, soft flakes of snow were falling.

Chopper pulled out a joint from his ski jacket and sheltered it from the wind so he could light it. "So what's your deal, Lucy? Why'd you come to Whistler? Is it because your brother gave you that snowboard from Sport Chek?"

"My board is not from Sport Chek." Clare knew that was the ultimate insult. "I came because I was miserable in Toronto."

"You weren't the perfect yuppie your parents dreamed you'd be?"

"I didn't want to get stuck in a career that sucks me in and doesn't spit me out until I retire too old to do anything. But I also don't want to screw up and slack off forever. No offense." Clare slipped a bit in her step — the stones were icy under the thin layer of new snow.

Chopper reached to steady Clare with one hand and passed her his joint with the other. "Don't knock the slacker life. It's all about who you choose to live for."

Clare took a drag but was careful not to inhale. Snow trickling past the streetlights made the village look like it was in a work of surreal fiction. If it were a movie, it would be with puppets. Like the Jack Frost Christmas Special. In her head, Clare could hear Kubla Kraus, the evil Jack Frost villain, singing his evil villain song while stomping past the sloped-roofed two-story buildings. Maybe she'd inhaled without realizing it.

"You want to grab some sleep?" Chopper said.

Clare giggled — very out of character; must be the pot. "Good line," she said. "But isn't there a coffee shop open where we could chill and talk?"

"At this time of night? Wouldn't you way rather crawl into a warm bed?"

Clare glanced at Chopper. He looked big and cuddly in his yellow ski jacket and baggy blue jeans. She did want to crawl into a warm bed with him. The question was, would Lucy? "I mean, I like you, but we just met. Shouldn't we, like, go on a date first?"

"This is a date." Chopper spread his arms out to show Clare the town. "Some drinks in the bar followed by a beautiful moonlit walk . . ."

Clare missed this — fun, flirtation. Everything with Noah had become heavy. Clare suddenly wanted to have sex with Chopper then and there, outside in the snow where all of Whistler could watch, just to screw Noah out of her system.

But she wasn't Clare. "It's weird enough sleeping in Sacha's bed, living in her apartment. I don't know if I could sleep with her man on top of all that."

Chopper laughed. "So leave Wade alone — that's who she was in love with. You wouldn't have much choice left if you avoided everyone in town Sacha slept with."

"Was she a slut?" Clare suddenly liked Sacha more. Though the

Wade thing confused her — she couldn't see the attraction to a middle-aged man with a mullet.

"No. She just loved to connect with people. She felt like sex was the ultimate conversation."

"Why Wade?" Clare might as well come right out and ask.

"He was a project," Chopper said. "Sacha thought she could fix him."

"She told you that?" Clare wrinkled her nose. The picture she was forming of Sacha was both really sweet and incredibly manipulative.

Chopper nodded. "She thought if she helped him connect with his dream — with his music — Wade would stop drinking so much; he'd be excited to be alive."

"Seems strange," Clare said, "that a girl who was so into living would kill herself."

Chopper's eyes darted down to meet Clare's. They were freezing cold. "You don't want to go there."

"Um . . . okay." It was easy for Clare to give this timid Lucy response — this side of Chopper scared her.

Luckily, his darkness disappeared as quickly as it had come. His eyes relaxed, and Chopper said, "Look, sorry to be harsh. But we're all sad, we're all confused. We've speculated high and low. It makes even less sense that she died by accident — or by foul play."

Clare privately agreed. The sliced wrists, the note, all the drugs Sacha was using . . . the signs really did point to suicide.

"Personally, I think it must have been temporary depression," Chopper said. "When you get high, you get low afterwards — like really low. You think you suck; you think the world's against you. Makes sense that Sacha would have been bummed on life, the day she . . . died."

Clare felt something move inside her, like a strange shadow passing through. She wanted to reach back in time and pull Sacha back to life.

"She had also just got some news from home. I guess her dad wasn't really her dad, and her stepmom — who she was tight with, until this — wanted Sacha to back out of hanging with the family."

"Shit," Clare said. "That would blow."

"Look, nothing's open until six a.m. for coffee, unless we want to stare at each other in the ugly lights of a Creekside convenience store." Chopper wrinkled his nose and shook his head fiercely. "But you could come to my place. There's coffee in my kitchen."

Clare decided she'd played hard to get for long enough. Chopper was, after all, a person of interest. And she wouldn't have to fake the attraction. "That sounds all right. Do you live in town?"

"Nearby. My truck's in the parking lot."

The cop in Clare wanted to ask Chopper if he was fine to drive with all the booze and pot he'd been consuming. But the Lucy part decided to keep her mouth shut and go along for the ride.

THIRTY
MARTHA

Martha shook her head to wake it up. She could feel her short hair's unruly appearance even before her bathroom mirror confirmed it as a mop of pure mess. She stepped onto her scale — one-eighteen, which was one pound less than the day before. She'd lost ten pounds in two weeks. Which was fine — she'd put on some weight since taking office. But she couldn't afford to lose more.

She slid on fuzzy brown slippers and padded into the kitchen. The moving box was still on the floor, taped up, marked *PRIVATE* in Sacha's forceful, seventeen-year-old lettering.

As Martha's head cleared, she began to feel dread. The previous day — the blogger, the terrible lunch with Hillier, the TV interview at LaGuardia where she had alienated the entire Republican Party by announcing a radical, unformed policy — it was a giant, awful haze.

She'd spent her whole adult life being careful. She even watched what she said to the cleaning lady, lest it be quoted later. What had possessed her to undo all that in one day?

She called Ted.

"Good morning, Martha." His voice was heavy; his syllables lasted longer than usual. "Did you sleep well?"

"Yes, thank you." Martha was surprised to realize this was true. "Did you?"

"No. I've been up all night."

"I haven't changed my mind, Ted. I'm dropping out of the race."

"I guess you saw the news, then."

Martha didn't think there was any news that could shake her, short of finding out that the corpse Fraser had flown to Whistler to identify was not, in fact, Sacha's.

"Hillier announced his endorsement. He's backing Kearnes."

"I see." Martha surprised herself by caring. She wasn't aware until that moment how much she wanted the nomination. Oh well — too late. "If you'd like to work for another campaign, I'd be happy to provide a reference."

"There's no one else I want to see as president."

"That's nice, Ted. Thank you. If you change your mind, the offer's there."

"So you're dropping out." His voice was flat. "I should draw up the paperwork."

"Do I have any other options? Your voice is saying no."

"Of course you have other options. Do you think Hillier controls the state of Michigan?"

"You seemed to think he did a few days ago." Martha glanced at her coffee wall unit in irritation, wondering why it hadn't warmed up yet. Stupid thing had cost a fortune, it should make her day more, not less, efficient. She lifted her eyebrows and pressed the On button.

"It will be hard without Hillier. I'll be honest — we'll probably lose. And this new narcotics position of yours won't help. That's the reason he cites for not endorsing you."

"Please. Hillier wants a cabinet post."

"True. But his official statement says . . . never mind."

"I can take it, Ted. Read me his statement."

Martha heard Ted's fingers fly over his keyboard for a few seconds before he started reading, "He says, 'My original plan was to endorse Martha Westlake. But when I heard her supporting recreational drug use, I knew she had lost touch with her voters — and very likely with herself.

"'I wish the Senator good luck. Grief is so challenging, and the loss of a child is the worst kind of grief. I'm sure she'll return to her senses one day. But she's too much of a wildcard right now. I encourage my congregation to vote for Geoffrey Kearnes in the Michigan Republican primary.'"

When Ted went silent, Martha realized that everything she could clench was clenched — her shoulders, her teeth, her grip around the phone.

"I'm sorry, Martha."

"I'm staying in the race."

"What?" A ray of hope shot through the phone. Martha could hear that Ted wanted this, almost as much as she did.

"Hillier is lying," Martha said. "He wants the cabinet post. He would have grabbed at any straw to get away from backing me."

Ted exhaled audibly. "While I was up last night, I did some researching. It's going to be a hard sell, but I think we can work legalization into your hard-line anti-drug platform."

"Of course we can." Martha willed herself to sound more positive than she felt. Ted was good, but Martha didn't know if he was *this* good. "South and Central American countries have been making intelligent arguments for this for years. And Mexico. I met with Ernesto Zedillo last year at Yale. If it wouldn't have been political suicide, I might have entertained his arguments more seriously."

"Good," Ted said. "We'll play it like you've been a long time mulling. We'll say you took Zedillo's comments seriously but only now are you acting, because you needed intense research and contemplation to satisfy yourself that they're workable."

Martha smiled. She could hear the strain in Ted's voice. This was going to be stretch. "One more chance to leave," she said. "With a glowing letter of recommendation."

"Stop saying that. I told you, I've been up all night for *you*. Do you want to hear your new platform?"

"Sure, but in person. Can you be in New York this afternoon?"

"I'm on the next plane. Can you hold off on leaving your house — or answering your phone — until we have your new platform in order?"

"Unfortunately, no. I have a lunch I agreed to attend several weeks ago."

"Okay. So let me give you some sound bites."

Martha smiled as she pressed the button on her coffee machine. "Don't worry," she said over the whir of the grinder. "I'm back."

THIRTY-ONE
CLARE

Clare liked riding in Chopper's truck. It was a big red Dodge diesel and it bounced up and down with the highway. The radio was tuned to a country station as Chopper navigated the snowy curves with confidence. What had she even seen in Noah, old before his time, preferring jazz to any music recorded in this century? She was glad to be with a real man for a change.

After twenty minutes or so of highway driving, Chopper pulled onto an unpaved side road. He drove a hundred meters or so before stopping.

Clare tried not to show her dismay that there was nowhere in sight that a human could conceivably call home. She tried not to recall the *Sopranos* episode where Silvio took Adriana into the New Jersey woods to whack her. She tried not to picture Adriana crawling away from the truck, screaming "No!" while Silvio popped two bullets into her back.

Chopper cut the engine.

Clare wanted to ask how Chopper knew, how he'd found out she was an undercover. She thought of the memory stick — the conversation she'd recorded in the bar — sealed tight in one of her secret inside pockets. Maybe the answer was on there? Or maybe he'd seen the transmitter on his beer glass at Avalanche. No wonder Chopper wanted her to think Sacha had killed herself — he'd been lulling Clare into a false sense of security.

Clare needed to find a way out of this.

Chopper turned in his seat to face Clare. "You ready for a sled ride?"

Damn. Was a "sled ride" snowboarder slang for bumping someone off? Chopper looked friendly enough asking the question — but Silvio had been upbeat on the car ride with Adriana.

"Sure," Clare said, because she couldn't tip him off that she suspected anything was wrong. She could get out of the truck and run, but where would she go that Chopper wouldn't be able to chase her? And if he caught her, he would win.

Man, Clare must be stoned. Wasn't paranoia one of the side effects?

But not all fear was paranoia — especially not when a killer was in town.

Chopper trudged through deep snow to the back of the truck. Still in the cab, Clare looked back to see Chopper sliding a ramp out and easing his snowmobile to the ground. Clare felt incredibly stupid. A sled ride was a snowmobile ride. She knew that.

Still, where the hell were they? She got out of the truck and slipped through the snow to meet Chopper at the back. "You said we were going to your place."

"We are. I live up Cougar Mountain."

"Why aren't we taking the road?" Clare eyed a wide pathway not far from where Chopper had parked.

"It's a logging road. It isn't plowed beyond that point you can see. Come on. You can have the helmet."

Aargh. How could Clare sound like Lucy and figure out if it was safe to get on the snowmobile? She had to rely on the lying tells she'd learned in agent training in Quantico. She said, "You could have told me you didn't live in civilization before you lured me with promises of coffee."

"Would you have come?" Chopper's grin was symmetrical and

slow to develop — both signs of sincerity. He handed Clare a small knapsack. "Here. Put this on."

"What is it?" Clare slipped the straps around her arms.

"Avalanche pack. Pull the cord if you feel any slippage underfoot — or under the sled skis. The pack will expand into a balloon on your back and keep you above the snow."

Clare's eyes shot open. These woods felt full of risks she hadn't even considered. The moon was bright — nearly full — creating shadows in the trees that seemed to shift, like little animals. Snow created a white blanket that covered the ground. Clare wondered what the blanket was hiding.

"Avalanche danger is extreme," Chopper said. "We're pretty safe in trees, but I'd feel like a jerk if I didn't let you wear the pack instead of me."

Clare found that kind of sweet. Not a detail a murderer was likely to consider. Or was the avalanche pack the first thing Chopper planned to take from Clare's back when he killed her? "How come you live in a place where no roads go?"

Clare studied Chopper's eyes as he said, "I love privacy. I can retreat up there for days on end, if I want to. Plus I built the place myself — in summer, obviously, so I could use the logging road to truck supplies up." Too much information? If so, it was a sign of lying. But no eye-flickering, no looking away. And also not overly intense. Seemed sincere.

"You live in a homemade hut? Is there electricity, or do we have to melt snow to make coffee by candlelight?"

Chopper laughed — easy, relaxed. "Is your mind still on coffee? No worries. I have a generator *and* running water." His hands were steady. He wasn't touching his nose or covering his mouth. His legs weren't shifting or shuffling. All signs of sincerity.

But people could fake that shit. That was the other half of Clare's lying tell training — learning to look truthful under pressure.

Chopper locked his truck and handed Clare the helmet.

Clare fastened the strap. She felt like a kid on a first date — both terrified and thrilled. She sat behind Chopper and was at a loss for what to do with her arms. She looked down to see if there was something she could grip.

"Hold on tight," Chopper said.

Clare shrugged, put her arms around Chopper's waist. He squeezed her gloved hand and said, "You ready?"

Damn, his touch felt good.

Clare felt her stomach jump as he zoomed up the snowbank at a near right angle before settling on terrain that was more trail-like.

"You all right?" Chopper shouted over the engine.

"This is awesome." Clare felt wide awake and amazing. The snowmobile's speed felt as good as her motorcycle — which she missed like crazy in winter. If Chopper was leading her to a wooded death, at least she was getting one last adventure.

Chopper gunned the engine and rode faster. His body felt strong — and oddly warm, though he was covered in layers of snow clothing. The machine hugged the mountain like it was made to climb, like it was a mountain lion grabbing hold and clawing to the top. Despite all the sharp turns and steep inclines and trees right next to the path, Clare felt safe the whole way up. Chopper pulled to a stop outside a log cabin.

As he killed the engine and they climbed off the snowmobile, Clare felt giddy with relief. Seeing an actual home — as opposed to a clearing and a bloodstained ax — meant she was far less likely to be murdered that night.

Chopper unlocked the door, flicked a switch, and lit up the room. The ground floor was open concept. There was a kitchen in one corner with a hodgepodge of appliances that looked like they'd been dragged to the cabin from the 1950s. In another corner, a plush leather couch and two deep matching armchairs surrounded a rugged stone fireplace. In the middle of the room, a winding wooden staircase led up through a hole in the ceiling.

"How can you afford this? It must be way more expensive to build up here than to rent in town." Shit. Maybe Lucy shouldn't be quite so curious.

"Totally more expensive. But worth it. I might not seem like a typical loner, but when I want to be alone, I want to be the hell alone." Chopper grabbed some sticks and a thick log from the wood pile and put them into the fireplace. He crumpled up some newspaper and wedged it in, too. "You sure you want coffee, or would you rather have a beer? You might sleep better with beer. Or did you want me to take you home after the coffee?"

Clare laughed lightly. "A beer would be good."

Chopper pulled a giant beer bottle from the fridge and poured it into two glasses. The bottle was still half-full.

"What kind of beer is that?" Clare tried not to sound suspicious asking.

"Howe Sound Rail Ale. It's local, brewed in Squamish. Come on, let's sit by the fire." Chopper took Clare's hand and led her to one of the couches. "We need to keep each other warm."

Clare let herself be led. The couch was comfortable. Even more comfortable when Chopper grabbed her by the waist and pulled her toward him so they were sitting right against each other. The coffee table was an old sailing trunk with a glass top. Clare set her beer down.

"What's this?" Clare picked up a blue plastic tube from the table. It looked like a cross between a mechanical pencil and an X-acto knife.

"That's a bear banger."

"A what?" Clare was trembling with nervous attraction. She hadn't felt this way in ages — like since a year ago, when she'd met Noah. She wanted Chopper to make his move, but at the same time she wanted to prolong this part, this not-quite-anything where they both knew something was going to happen soon.

"You attach a tube of explosive to the end, shoot it out to make a big sound and scare away bears."

"Where are the bears you have to scare off?"

"They live here. In the mountains."

"They do? Should I be scared?" Like with avalanches, no one had briefed Clare about avoiding wildlife.

Chopper laughed. "It's winter. Bears are sleeping."

"Oh."

In the real world Clare would take action around now, maybe hook her thumbs into the belt loops of Chopper's baggy jeans.

As Lucy, she smiled shyly and was pleased that Chopper tightened his grip around her waist, pulled her closer, and leaned in for a kiss.

THIRTY-TWO
MARTHA

Martha sliced the yellow utility knife through six-year-old moving tape. Is this what surgeons felt like, slicing into someone's stomach? She peeled back the cardboard flaps — or cracked the ribs and separated them — to open the box on which Sacha had written *PRIVATE* before sticking it in storage and leaving for university.

Was it private even now? Sacha would have to forgive her.

There was six years' worth of storage room dust. Martha's hands felt filthy. But she forgot all about hygiene when she saw Lorenzo.

She picked up the photograph: a dirty, dusty road with a skinny ten-year-old boy. The boy was smiling in that brave yet forlorn way the Christian aid photographers liked their poster children to pose. The sun was high and the child's shirt was torn at one shoulder.

Lorenzo Barilla. This was how she knew the name.

When she was eight, Sacha had sponsored a ten-year-old boy in Central America. After watching one of those horrible commercials (the kind that made Martha wish she had a weaker stomach so she could vomit to display her disgust), Sacha asked Martha to sponsor a child "for less than the price of a cup of coffee a day, Mom! You're trying to drink less coffee anyway."

Martha explained that these organizations were corrupt, that only five cents on the dollar really went to the children. Sacha hadn't believed her; she'd committed nearly all of her small weekly allowance to Lorenzo, convinced that her few dollars per week was enough to feed his whole family, buy Lorenzo's clothes, and send him to school.

For two years, Sacha had walked to the post office each Friday to send letters to El Salvador — via the aid organization. Sacha seemed happy enough with the correspondence she got back: quarterly packages with a photo Martha was sure went to a few more sponsors than Sacha, and a letter she was sure had been typed in an office somewhere in Kansas.

Martha had always assumed that Sacha had given Lorenzo up — abandoned him innocently, like her Cabbage Patch Doll and every other childhood toy except Jules. But as she leafed through the papers, Martha was shocked to see that Lorenzo had started writing back real letters — not packaged school photos with the Christian Aid logo in the corner, but letters from a teenager, complete with broken English, discontent, and foul language.

Lorenzo Barilla was the blogger who had interviewed her at LaGuardia. He'd said his name slowly, like it was supposed to mean something to Martha. It meant something now . . . but what?

She studied the photograph. The child looked darker than the man she'd met at the airport. Also, the blogger's accent wasn't nearly as strong as it should be — not like someone who had grown up in Latin America. She'd heard of people hiring voice coaches, practicing hard to eradicate an accent, to blend into a new culture. But why would he want to?

Martha looked at the clock. If she didn't get moving, she'd be late for the Women of Influence luncheon she'd agreed to attend — an educational session where 120 of Manhattan's brightest female high school students were invited to mingle with women in so-called powerful positions. When the invitation had come several months earlier, Martha had deemed it a worthwhile cause. Now, she felt like the privileged princesses — most of whom would no doubt be from private schools — could do without the added insider advice about their futures. It was the youth in Harlem and Alphabet City who needed these sessions.

But she'd agreed to go.

Martha put the letters back into the moving box and closed it, feeling like she was leaving Sacha inside.

THIRTY-THREE
CLARE

Clare woke up and wondered where she was. The green curtains looked familiar. So did the brown plaid comforter. Traveling for work so much, she was used to waking up disoriented. And as Noah would note, being a slut should make that feeling even more familiar.

She wanted Noah's arms around her, if only so she could wrestle them off and tell him what a jerk he was.

Not like Chopper, who was actually nice to her — and whose bedroom Clare slowly realized she was in. Upstairs in his groovy mountain cabin. Man, that sled ride had been fun — once Clare had dropped the illusion that she'd been about to die. She really had to figure out how to not inhale.

Some thermal socks and sweats were folded on a wooden chair beside the bed. A piece of paper on top said *Wear me* in scratchy male handwriting. Clare put on Chopper's clothes, which pretty much drowned her, and descended the twisty staircase down to the main floor.

Chopper was facing the stove, pushing a spatula around in a pan. The smell of vegetables and spice made Clare's stomach growl. "That smells amazing."

"It's a tofu omelette. Didn't know if you were a vegan or not — so many chicks in Whistler are vegans or vegetarians — but I had some tofu in the fridge, so I figured I'd get creative instead of waking you up to find out."

"I'm not a vegan." Clare hoped she never had to go undercover as one, either. "But if their freaky food can smell like that, I'll gladly eat it."

Clare sat at the kitchen table — a long wooden slab that looked both homemade and designer. "Do you make your own furniture?"

"The wooden stuff, yeah."

"You ever sell it?"

"No way. I'm not interested in hearing some yuppie couple ooh and aah then tell me how they want theirs done custom."

Clare wondered if Chopper had already smoked a joint that morning or if the smell still clung to the air from the night before. "Why are you called Chopper?"

"My summer job in high school. I was an arborist, like my dad. Chopping trees down for rich homeowners who want a nicer view."

"What's your real name?"

"You have to sleep with me three times before I tell you."

Clare liked watching him cook. His shoulders were massive; the guy was made of muscle.

He'd been good in bed, too. They'd clicked well. Clare recalled the flick of his tongue as it made her writhe in pleasure while sun had begun to filter through the curtains. She was tempted to get up and lure him back into bed for another round, but her coffee tasted too good. She also felt kind of hollow — like maybe fucking around freely wasn't who she was at heart. She wished Noah were there, so she could squeeze his hand and feel him squeeze hers back.

Clare said as casually as she could, "I feel like getting high today."

Chopper turned quickly. Something green flew off his spatula and onto the counter. "You want to smoke before breakfast?"

"I don't mean pot," Clare said. "I mean something to take me out of my head. Shrooms or X would be awesome. Or are you all earthy Nature Boy — nary an artificial chemical can enter your body?"

Chopper sprinkled a green herb onto his tofu concoction. "I'm not big on X unless I know the source. Shrooms are always fun. But my drug of choice when I have eight hours to spare? Hands down, LSD."

"Seriously?" Clare leaned back in her chair. "Jana said the same thing. Is it still 1970 in Whistler?"

"Pretty much. Yuppies have built this town up into their very own clapboard paradise, but when you have nature as pure as this, it's gonna draw the free loving, free-thinking crowd, too. If that's what you mean by 1970."

Clare rolled her eyes. She couldn't help it.

"You're not into free love or free thought?"

"Of course I am. But I don't need to create a lifestyle around it."

Chopper scratched his chin, which had a couple days' stubble. "The acid I have is beautiful. It will stone you and make you see clear at the same time. You working today?"

"No."

"Let's drop after breakfast. Day-tripping is sick." Chopper checked his watch. "As we're coming down, we can grab the last gondola to the top of Whistler or Blackcomb. We'll be sober enough by then, shredding won't be dangerous — but the drug will still be tingly enough in our system to make for a sick ride."

It did sound fun — in a world where there wasn't a killer. But Clare had to get to Amanda's place so they could listen to the recording from the bar. She eyed her ski jacket on the hook by the door, with the memory stick hidden inside. She couldn't believe she'd made such a stupid move, leaving such a damning piece of evidence unguarded overnight.

Chopper pulled two plates from the cupboard and started dishing his steaming faux-omelette onto them. "Lucy, how come you're not on Facebook?"

Clare's eyes focused on the plate of food Chopper set in front of her. It was a good question. Bert had been talking about creating a database of social media identities to add depth to their cover roles. The problem was that if a suspicious person started to explore the friends and family, they'd quickly find a group of people who only existed in ether. The other option was making all the cover identities friends with each other, but that was even more dangerous — once one identity was made, it would be easy to identify all the rest as bogus. So for now, no Facebook.

"I think social media is stupid," Clare said. "It's for narcissists and people with something to sell. Are you on Facebook?"

Chopper laughed. "Yeah, I am. Enjoy your breakfast."

Clare took a bite. It was delicious, but something about Chopper's question had made her nervous. She pushed her plate away. "Sorry — I'm not really a breakfast person. The coffee's great, though."

THIRTY-FOUR
WADE

W ade pushed his ugly black boots through the fresh snow that had fallen overnight. Tourists were frolicking through the village like it was fabulous, knocking each other over and tossing snowballs like kids. Did they not have real world problems? But no, of course they didn't — they had the money to play in Canada's most expensive outdoor playground.

In his pocket, his phone rang. Wade fished it out and answered.

A young male voice. "Is this Wade Harrison?"

Another collection agent, no doubt. How they kept getting his cell number, Wade had no clue.

"I'm sorry," Wade said. "You must have the wrong number."

"I'm looking for the owner of a bar called Avalanche."

"Definitely the wrong number." Wade ducked to avoid a snowball — which cleared him by several feet, but he glared at the group of kids who threw it, because that wasn't the point.

"Look, I'm sure you've been getting hammered with phone calls since your waitress died. But this isn't like other interviews. I want to know why Sacha died."

"Sacha who?"

"Sacha Westlake. Even if this were a wrong number, you must have heard about her death."

"Right," Wade said. "The Whistler suicide."

"Okay, well, I obviously have the wrong number. I guess I'll go try to find the real Wade Harrison, so I can try to help him save his bar."

Wade pulled the phone away from his ear, glanced at the screen. The caller's number was blocked. "Who are you?"

"Call me an interested party. I got a tip-off that your landlords are about to foreclose."

"From who?"

"Sorry . . . are you or aren't you Wade Harrison?"

Fuck this guy. He was almost definitely a collection agent for one of Wade's maxed-out, unpaid credit cards. There was no low those assholes wouldn't sink to. But what if he was for real? "I'm Wade."

A chuckle. "That's what I thought."

"Who are you?"

"I'm a reporter. But before you hang up, I really do want to help save your bar. And find Sacha's killer."

Wade sighed. "Sacha killed herself."

"Was that because she was in love with you?"

Fuck. "Can you identify yourself please? Who do you write for?"

"It must have been horrible for her. Young girl, away from home, in love with someone she can't have. You had no plans to leave your wife, right? Still don't?"

Wade didn't have anything to say. And yet he couldn't hang up.

"What was Georgia doing, the afternoon Sacha died?"

"She was at work. In Vancouver." Wade at least knew the answer to that.

"Hm. Well, for her sake, I hope she was in meetings. Or somewhere people remember having seen her."

"My wife is not a killer."

"Don't worry, I won't breathe a word. About your affair, I mean."

Before Wade could think of a smart way to deny the charge, he had to scoot around yet another pack of rowdy twentysomethings decked out in the latest Lycra fashions. They were blocking nearly half of the wide cobblestone pathway, with no concern for people who might have to be somewhere.

The caller must have taken Wade's silence for affirmation, because he said, "What I type, on the other hand . . . that depends upon how forthcoming you are about other things."

"Like what?"

"My next article is going to be 'A Day in the Life.' I want to recreate a typical day in Sacha's Whistler experience." The reporter's voice seemed accented — maybe French or Spanish.

Wade arrived at Avalanche. He dug his keys from his pocket with one hand and let himself in. He went to press his alarm code into the pad by the door, and stopped — the monitoring company had canceled his account the previous week for non-payment.

"What was Sacha like in bed?" the reporter asked. "I swear, this is just between you and me."

Wade grabbed a glass from behind the bar and poured himself a thick finger of vodka before taking his coat off. "What do you think? She was phenomenal." He shouldn't be talking like this — and certainly not to the press. But short of seeing Sacha — holding her, feeling her — talking about her was all Wade wanted to do.

"How was she involved in the money you were laundering?"

Shit. "I think someone has been sadly misinforming you."

"Okay. So it's fine for your wife to read that you were sleeping with your waitress?"

"Jesus fucking Christ. Who are you already?"

"My name is Lorenzo Barilla. I have a blog you may be familiar with."

THIRTY-FIVE
MARTHA

Ted smoothed his pressed white shirtsleeve and picked up his pen. The campaign office was buzzing with activity, but the energy was subdued. Which Martha didn't blame anyone for — if she were a staffer on this campaign, she'd be scurrying in dazed confusion, too.

"Is that a Mont Blanc?" Martha couldn't remember having seen the pen in Ted's hand before.

"I didn't think it was very presidential for your assistant to be writing with a Bic."

Martha lowered her voice so she wasn't lambasting Ted in front of the others. "Did that come out of campaign funds?"

"No — constituency funds. Should I spend my own money on office supplies?"

"Change the books. I'll write a personal check and the pen belongs to you. Call it a birthday present."

"My birthday's in September."

"Do you care? It's a free pen."

An intern arrived with coffees. "Chai latte for Senator Westlake … um, was it dark roast with milk for you, Ted?"

Martha thanked the young woman for her coffee and gave her a big smile. She liked this office — an open white space with lots of dark hardwood — in the West Eighties, ten blocks from her brownstone. It felt companionable, working alongside her team.

"It was blond roast with cream." Ted was glaring at the intern.

"Oh." The girl laughed nervously. "Sorry. Same difference, right?"

"Not even close. Did you get your own order right?"

"Um. Yeah, because I was there."

Ted shook his head. "Well, at least you're free labor. You get what you pay for, *right?*"

The girl chewed her lip. "Um. I'm really sorry. I'll listen better next time."

She wandered off, two blond braids trailing behind her.

"Ted, what was that?" Martha hissed. It had taken all of Martha's restraint not to call Ted out in front of the intern. "That girl is volunteering her time to help my campaign. We should treat her with nothing but gratitude."

"Sorry," Ted said. "If you worked here more often, you'd understand."

Martha raised her eyebrows.

"She's just . . . frustrating. Only listens halfway." Ted leaned forward in his chair. "The FBI called. I'm afraid there's some difficult news."

"What difficult news?" Ted should know she loathed preamble.

Ted's knuckles were white around his new pen. "There's a note. From Sacha."

Martha moved her lips but couldn't speak, at first. "A . . . note."

"A suicide note."

Martha set her latte down, afraid it would slip out of her hand. "What does she say?"

"They won't let me read it. But they've analyzed the handwriting. It's hers."

Martha's stomach was churning; she found herself wishing for mint tea. But if she asked for some now, her campaign team would worry — it was way too out of character. Maybe there were some soda crackers around, or some plain white bread . . . She said, "Sacha must have known she was about to be murdered."

Ted reached across and touched Martha's hand. Martha jerked hers away.

She opened her eyes. "She must have known, someone must have forced her to write it, because Sacha didn't kill herself. You agree, right?"

Ted took a long breath in. "Do you want some more time off?"

"If I take any more time off, I might as well hand the nomination to Kearnes. I want to hammer out my platform, as planned." Actually, Martha wanted to crawl into a hole with Jules and every letter Sacha had ever mailed from summer camp, every finger painting she'd created in preschool. "I need to push forward."

Ted slid a piece of paper across the desk. "Here are some more detailed talking points I've been working on. I've taken the research of Zedillo and a few others and Americanized the language so it will hopefully appeal to everyone with a brain. The trouble is . . ." Ted looked around.

"The trouble is, most voters don't have a brain." Martha finished his sentence.

Ted smirked. "Yeah."

"I think I have to get savvy with this new media. I'm going to need the support of the younger generation."

"You mean social media? Facebook and Twitter?"

"And, uh . . . a blog?"

"You have a blog. Christy and Melissa run it."

"Great. Will it work if I start writing posts?"

"All the posts?"

"I don't know. How often do we post?"

"Daily. Sometimes every other day."

"Maybe I could write the post once or twice a week. Can I sign it as me, so voters know when I'm speaking to them directly?"

"Uh, yeah. I think so."

"Good. Make it happen. Something else has been nagging me."

Martha wasn't sure how to broach this, but there had been something in Ted's voice the night before, when he'd refused to accept her resignation. And something in the way he had just spoken to the intern. "What are your goals, Ted?"

"At the moment, to win this election."

"And after that?"

"To work for you in the White House."

"Do you want to be a political assistant forever? Do you want to run for office yourself one day?"

Ted pinged a finger against his white paper cup. He walked a few feet to the small fridge and returned with a Red Bull. "Why are you asking?"

"Because I worry about you."

"You do?" Ted's voice was small, like he didn't quite believe that. He opened his Red Bull and took a long glug.

"Of course. Everything you do, professionally, is for me. And since you work more hours than most people are even awake, I'm guessing most of what you do in your life is for me. That can't be good for you."

"It's what I want."

"Why?"

Ted shuffled his hands. "You'll think I'm lame."

Martha did her best not to groan. "Go ahead."

"You . . . well . . . you remind me of my mom. You know she's gone, right? She died when I was four. When my dad gets drinking, he tells me about how when they were younger, like in their early twenties, my mom used to go to every protest she could find. Sometimes she even helped organize them. He always says that she could have been president."

Martha didn't understand the connection. Her own youth was filled with respectable dresses and trying to act old before her time. Rallies and protests were what the Young Democrats did. "How, uh . . . do you see us as similar?"

"She was idealistic," Ted said, "in this super-practical way."

That sounded more like Sacha than Martha. Martha wished she

hadn't brought the question up, but she could hardly drop it now. "I'm sorry, Ted. How did your mother die?"

Ted glanced around the office and lowered his voice even further. "She was bipolar. She jumped off the Queensborough Bridge after phoning my dad to tell him she knew how to fly."

Ah. Martha hoped she didn't remind Ted *too* much of his mother. "I'm sorry. That must have been horrible."

Ted nodded, glanced down at his pen.

"What are your own goals, though? Separate from mine. It's easier to handle setbacks — like me dropping out of this race, if I choose to — if you have a vision of where you want to go."

"I want to be president," Ted said, with a staccato punch in his voice.

Martha was a bit blown back by his answer. "That's fabulous. Why?"

"Because . . . you know what, screw that. It's stupid."

Martha wasn't sure of the right thing to say, so she said, "If we win this, I'd love to make use of your ambition."

"You would? How?"

"You're excellent at policy." Martha fingered the page of sound bites Ted had given her. "I'd be glad to give you an office, a role of your own. Maybe on this drug committee. Or something else if you prefer."

"For real?"

"Absolutely. For now, though, let's win this election." She glanced around the office, which seemed to have picked up some energy since she'd been sitting there. "Can you point me to someone here who can give me our campaign's Twitter details? I'd like to start doing some of my own tweeting, as well as blogging."

Ted laughed.

"I'm serious."

"I know. I wish Sacha could have seen this new you."

And Martha wished Ted would shut up about Sacha. But she said, "I wish that, too."

THIRTY-SIX
CLARE

Clare had her legs crossed on Amanda's couch, earphones plugged into her laptop. It was strange, listening to Chopper's voice talking to Richie. Strange but interesting.

When the recording was finished, she ripped out her earbuds and looked at Amanda. "This is bad."

"How bad?" Amanda was grating carrots at the kitchen island. "What's on the recording?"

"You want to listen, or you want highlights?"

"Highlights now; I'll listen later."

"Richie and Chopper paid to find the name of the undercover cop." Amanda set her carrots down.

"They seem confident my name is on the way. Though they're still saying *he*, even to each other, so that's something."

"I think your identity's safe." Amanda started grating again. "My strong guess is that they'll run against a dead end."

"Your strong guess? Is that what you'll say at my funeral?"

Amanda smiled. "Clare, don't be dramatic."

"Chopper and Jana have both independently asked me if I'm a cop. Jana directly, Chopper indirectly. He wanted to know why I'm not on Facebook."

"Sure, because you're a newcomer."

"I might be able to deflect their suspicion. I can prove to them I'm not a cop by dropping acid."

"Good one. Because it will be true — if you drop acid, you'll no longer be a cop. At least not on my watch."

"Has the handwriting analysis come back on the suicide note yet?"

"Yes," Amanda said. "It's a match."

"So Sacha killed herself."

"Looks that way."

"Can I read the note?"

Amanda shook her head. "Remember your job is to gather, not analyze."

Clare smiled as sweetly as she could when she said, "So if Sacha killed herself, there's no killer on the prowl. I guess you won't be needing my services."

"Both organizations are extremely interested in the drug smuggling."

"Is that my new assignment, then?"

"It's all part of the same investigation. No need to change the assignment. But yes, please do gather information about the smuggling operation."

"My pleasure. Here's more good news: Norris is for sure dirty."

"How is that good news?" Amanda scraped the carrots into a large salad bowl and started grating a hard, smelly white cheese.

"Norris is the guy Chopper and Richie paid for my name. So now that we know that, we can feed him disinformation — like a false name to answer his query."

"I'll think about that," Amanda said. "But like I've said, it's hardly necessary when only the six people I mentioned know who you are. Six very secure individuals."

"And Noah."

"Noah from poker?"

Clare nodded.

"Are you still dating him?"

"Yeah. And before you jump down my throat about breaching

security, Bert cleared me to talk to Noah about the case. Noah's working on it from the New York end."

"How's that going? The relationship, I mean."

"Fairly fucked up, thanks. How's your love life?"

"Still engaged," Amanda said.

"Same big shot you were dating last year? The corporate lawyer who never has time for dinner?"

"Same one. What's wrong between you and Noah?" Amanda put the smelly cheese into the salad.

"Noah challenges my brain. He knows my quirks and doesn't care — he even kind of likes them."

"But?"

"But he makes me insecure. Like if only I were someone *slightly* different, things could work out so much better." Clare had no idea why she was confiding in Amanda. Probably because she was the only person in Whistler she could talk to about her real life.

"So he's wrong for you."

Clare stared at the orange shag carpet. She poked at some of its hairs with her big toe. "It's not really fair for you to say that. You've never met him."

"No, but I've seen his file."

"Really?" Clare looked up. "What's in his file?"

Amanda glanced away. "I can't tell you that."

"I won't tell anyone if you break one rule. Norris takes bribes and he still has a job."

Amanda laughed. "That's not the professional logic I like to employ."

"Seriously, it's not fair to tease like that. I'll find the information somehow."

"Yes, I'm sure you will. Okay. When you encountered Noah on the poker tour last year, his employment security was tenuous."

Clare sensed that now was not the time to complain about Amanda's gratuitous use of big words. "What do you mean by 'tenuous'?"

"He'd botched up a case massively. The FBI figured Canada was a good place to breathe him while they decided if he was going to stay or go."

"Love it," Clare said. "Canada as exile. Is that why I'm here?"

"No, you're here because you're Canadian *and* FBI; plus your age fit the profile."

"So how did Noah fuck up?"

Amanda rifled through a drawer. She pulled out a small paring knife and peered at it before trading it for another slightly larger one. She pulled a tomato on the counter toward herself and began to slice it into bright, pulpy wedges. She set the knife down on the cutting board with a sigh. "Six months before you met him, Noah killed an innocent person."

Clare felt cold inside, though the gas fire was on full blast. "Man or woman?" was for some reason the question she asked first.

"His cover character's girlfriend. But he was cleared of any charges."

Clare was quiet as she tried to take this in.

"Noah had done a wonderful job befriending and seducing the daughter of a Mafia boss. He'd been dating her for six months when she invited him on a family boat trip. He should never have gone, but the file suggests that he might have actually fallen in love with the woman."

Clare blinked hard.

"I shouldn't have said anything." Amanda looked up from spinning the lettuce.

"It's cool," Clare said. It wasn't cool at all. Who *was* Noah, that he'd killed a girl and kept it secret from her? How could Clare trust someone who would hide such a big part of his past from her?

Amanda smiled sadly. Clare appreciated her silence; it felt kind.

But she needed to know more. "What happened with this girl? Why did he kill her?"

"At some point when the boat was at sea it became clear to Noah's handlers that his girlfriend's father wasn't duped. That Noah had been invited on that weekend so he could have an accident."

"They couldn't get him the message?"

"They got him the message. Noah was lowering the lifeboat when the girlfriend tried to stop him. From his perspective, she was a threat. Turns out, she probably had no clue about Noah's identity. But as Noah testified in court, he couldn't know that her struggling with him to prevent him from escaping wasn't the girlfriend colluding with her father — she was likely just confused herself."

"How . . . how did it happen?" Clare heard herself stuttering. She frowned. She never stuttered.

"He stabbed her. In the chest."

"What?" Clare closed her computer. This was so completely fucked. "Why didn't he just stab her leg? Immobilize her so he could get away?"

"His emotion was involved, most likely. Clouded his brain. On the record, he said he felt betrayed."

Clare went to join Amanda at the kitchen island. If she was honest with herself, it was because she needed to be physically closer to another human being. Apparently Amanda counted. Clare pulled up a stool and sat down. "What's the moral of the story? Should I run from Noah because killing this girl is going to leave him fucked up for a long time? Or should I understand if he's skittish and maybe try to coax him back to feeling okay about women?"

"Yeah," Amanda said with a faraway frown. "One of those, I think."

Amanda took a handful of raisins from a bag and sprinkled them onto the salad. Which was fine — Clare could politely eat this so-called meal and grab a slice of pizza later.

To distract herself from thinking about Noah, Clare said, "The recording also confirms what you suspected: Sacha was smuggling Mountain Snow across the border. They're desperately trying to find a replacement transporter for a new shipment they want to deliver this week."

Amanda glanced up at Clare.

"Should I volunteer?"

"Absolutely not." Amanda pulled some froufrou dressing from the fridge. Ginger soy, or some such yuppie delicacy. "A cop would jump at the chance to play a role in a cross-border drug deal. As soon as you said yes, it would red flag you to the criminals."

Clare wrinkled her mouth. Amanda was right. "Okay," she said, "but by the same token, a cop would never drop acid. I totally get why you think it's too dangerous. And honestly, I'm not keen to try the drug. But if I end up having to drop, and I keep my phone on, you'll know where I am at all times."

"Your phone's GPS wouldn't tell me if you're alive or dead."

"Maybe I could wear a discreet wire?"

"You wouldn't have your faculties, Clare. What if you ended up naked and rolling around with your new boytoy, and he found the wire? Then you haven't only killed the case, you've put your life in jeopardy."

A timer dinged and Amanda opened the oven. She pulled out a baking tray with bread.

"I didn't know you ate carbs." Clare eyed the fresh loaf hungrily, even if it was covered with oats and other extraneous grainy things.

"I don't, normally. But this mountain air makes me famished." Amanda opened the fridge and pulled out a tray of cold cuts. "Did you think I would serve you just salad for lunch?"

"I don't know," Clare said. "I have trouble figuring you out."

THIRTY-SEVEN
RICHIE

Richie looked down the Blackcomb Glacier. He remembered when this run used to scare the shit out of him. Cold and steep, it looked like the jagged edge of the world. Now it gave him power. The metal blade of his snowboard chiseling lines in the glacier made Richie feel like he was slicing edges off his fears and carving his niche in the world at the same time.

Nicki Minaj's "Fly" was in his earbuds. He felt the tune lift him. Though he'd die before admitting it out loud, the song always made him feel okay about shit for three minutes and thirty-two seconds.

Richie took the glacier slowly, grooving halfway down the run before plonking his ass on the hill. It was cold. He imagined all the layers of ice and snow beneath him. It was a wonder this glacier didn't slide off the mountain and take all the skiers and snowboarders with it. Maybe one day it would.

He didn't know the exact spot where Sacha had lain. But Norris had shown him the photo. All that blood — bright red against the white snow.

Why the fuck did Sacha have to breach security? She was so damn proud of herself — smuggling drugs was a lark to her. A fun way to get back at her big shot war-against-drugs mother. Get back at her for what, Richie had no damn clue. He wondered if Sacha even knew what she was doing.

Richie felt his eyes moisten. He growled and willed them to dry up. He missed Sacha, straight up. He used to tell her shit he'd never told a soul — like how he'd bought his first gun at fifteen after watching his father hit his mother one too many times. He never pulled it out at home, but knowing the sleek metal nine millimeter was there in the drawer beside his bed gave Richie the confidence to stand up to his old man. Sacha didn't give him any sentimental girly response. She'd just shaken her head and said, *Parents. They should feed kids and leave them the hell alone. We'd be better off all raised by wolves.*

"Jesus, Sacha," he said aloud, tracing a glove in the snow. "What the hell were you thinking?"

"Oy! Richie!" Richie heard Chopper's shout before the big yellow ski suit skidded to a stop beside him.

Richie quickly pulled his goggles off, wiped his eyes, and replaced the goggles before turning to face Chopper. He was glad he'd worn his tinted pair. "I think I have a leak in these," Richie said. "They were fucking expensive, too — Oakley."

"Are you freaked being up here? It's my first time on Blackcomb since Sacha bailed." Chopper slid his skis back and forth, like he was running in place.

Richie said nothing. He hoped Chopper would get the point and ski away.

"It's like, she's gone, but she's not, you know?"

"No." Richie flicked a chunk of snow off his board. "It's like she's gone. The end. What are you doing on groomers, anyway? Second time I've seen you here this week."

Chopper shrugged. "Avalanche warning's been crazy high. Back country's dangerous with all this new snow. Is this the place? This spot where you stopped to . . . defog your goggles?"

Richie wanted to throttle Chopper. Interrupt his grief and then call him on it? "This is the run."

Chopper nodded, was silent for a moment, and said, "I talked to Norris. He told me we absolutely cannot make this delivery to Washington."

"You tell him about the million bucks if we don't?"

"He doesn't care. Not only will he not make the drive; he says he'll bust us if he catches us trying."

"What?" Richie pooled some saliva and spat at the ground. "Does he understand that he doesn't get to be bent one minute and toe the line the next?"

Chopper shook his head. "This is bad, Rich. There's something going on with Norris. Says it's bigger than we know, bigger than all of us. But he won't elaborate."

"Shit."

"It could be nothing," Chopper said. "Norris is scared for his job, his rep in town. He's always been a worrier. I think the risk of being caught is way exaggerated in his mind."

Caught for what? Richie wanted to ask. He tapped a gloved finger to his mouth. "What if one of the Seattle crew recognized Sacha — figured out who her mom is — one time when she was down in Blaine for the delivery?"

Chopper squinted, pulled his tinted goggles back over his eyes to block the sun. "What are you talking about?"

"I mean, yeah, Sacha's mom's famous. Powerful, even. But for the FBI to go outside their jurisdiction — pretty sure they'd need more than just a murder case. You know?"

"Um . . . no."

"What if someone in the Seattle crew thought he could make a quick buck selling that info, about Martha Westlake's daughter as part of a smuggling ring?"

"Who would they sell it to?"

"Maybe to the DEA? More likely, though . . ." Richie tapped his mouth some more. "More likely they would have sold it to someone who would pay a lot of money. Like one of Westlake's opponents in Washington who could use the information for political leverage."

"Heavy," Chopper said. Which meant he was too stoned to think too hard.

Richie's wheels were spinning. "Sacha Westlake smuggling drugs would be some juicy information in the wrong hands. The question is *whose* hands?"

Chopper's eyes sharpened, like his mind was finally on this. "You think Seattle ratted Sacha out to some politician? And that's how come the FBI's so interested? Not because of her death, but because of the drugs?"

"Yeah," Richie said. "That's exactly what I think."

"Shit. I gotta go see Norris again."

Chopper kicked off and did a few stylish 360s on his trick skis before disappearing around a curve on the hill.

THIRTY-EIGHT
CLARE

Clare strapped on her left binding and pushed off. She tried to keep the fear off her face as Jana glided toward the double black diamond — double black meaning it wasn't just challenging, it was a run that only insane people took.

"You good?" Jana yelled up the hill.

"Are you kidding?" Clare shouted. "I learned how to snowboard two days ago. I am not jumping off a cliff."

"You said Chopper wanted to show you some jumps."

"Yeah, and I told him to get lost."

Jana put a hand on the hip of her baggy snowboard pants. "Please? This was Sacha's favorite run."

Clare rode down and stopped beside Jana so she could talk without shouting. She stared at the trees and the near-empty slope. It was four-forty-five. The last chairlift had just taken them to the top of the Blackcomb Glacier. It was almost dark. Almost exactly like the day Sacha had died.

"I'm not Sacha." Clare peered over the edge. It looked more like a cliff of certain death than a run someone would go down on purpose.

Jana shrugged. "You kind of are the same. You'll totally get it when we trip on Mountain Snow."

When, not if. Clare hadn't felt peer pressure like this since she was thirteen.

"Are you working tonight? I didn't see you on the schedule."

Clare shook her head under her balaclava. It had been a sunny day, but now a bitter wind was picking snow up from the hill and whipping it around like a fresh blizzard. Clare looked forward to being back inside, curled up with a hot chocolate. Or maybe one of those craft beers she was actually coming to like.

"I'll bail on my shift if you drop with me. I have two tabs in my pocket." Jana patted her pink plaid jacket. "It would be so perfect if we take them now. We'll be coming up on the trip by the time we reach the village. We'll have the whole evening to enjoy the natural wonder."

"You sound like an ad for Grand Canyon Travel." Clare's legs ached from how she was leaning, but she didn't know how else to stay upright on her snowboard.

"Good comparison," Jana said. "On this drug you'll go places that will make you contemplate your own insignificance. At the same time, you'll feel beyond empowered."

"Cocaine makes people feel empowered," Clare said, "and yet I have no desire to try that, either."

Jana laughed. "Mountain Snow won't turn you into an asshole. I'm talking real empowerment — the world will open up and you'll see it more clearly. You'll learn to take control of your destiny."

"Is that what Sacha learned?" Clare immediately wished she'd kept that thought to herself.

"Way to bring the mood down. That's totally a question a cop would ask." Jana pushed off and snowboarded away down the easier of the two runs, the one coded blue — not the cliff, which Clare appreciated.

Still, as she followed, Clare got worried. Was Jana accusing her of being a cop?

Halfway down the run, Jana skidded to a stop. Clare stopped beside her.

"Why don't we do LSD some other time?" Clare said. "With Chopper. He wants to drop with me, too."

Jana pulled her gloves off and held them with her teeth. She unzipped her pocket and pulled out two tiny squares of paper. "Now. How else will I know you're not a cop?"

Clare laughed too loudly — she hurt her own ears. "Doesn't a cop have to say they're a cop if you ask them?"

"Yeah," Jana said. "I've heard that, too. Is it true?"

"I don't know. I'm not a cop."

"You'll always be an outsider, though. Until you drop with us, we're not going to trust you. But maybe you don't care. You can find other friends here. I'm sure there's a goody-two-shoes club you can join. Spend evenings baking muffins with the Bible as your guide." Jana put her gloves back on, pushed off, and rode straight down the hill for several feet before stopping and waiting again.

Clare pushed off, too. The hill was getting icier. All the fresh snow had been packed down, and Clare thudded onto her ass the first time she tried to turn. She understood now why powder days were so sought after. She edged down to meet Jana.

She had to react right now as Lucy — it was more important than ever. "This isn't junior high," Clare said when she'd caught up. "I don't care if I'm in the cool group. I'll fit in where I fit in; it's no big deal."

"*If* you fit in. But whatever; you can always move again. Salt Lake City — where I grew up — is excited about people like you."

Clare's impulse was to laugh, but she thought that would annoy Jana. "Look, I'm not going to ruin my brain to make friends. What's next, I have to kill someone to stay in the club?"

Jana's eyes glassed over. "Low blow, Lucy. Aren't you on fire today?"

"Sorry. I didn't mean it like that."

"You have to decide if you're here or you're not. Why did you come to Whistler?" The edge was leaving Jana's voice, being replaced by the level calm of a guidance counselor. Clare wasn't sure which was scarier.

"To figure my life out," Clare said, playing along.

"Mountain Snow will help. You'll get answers to questions you didn't think you could find in this lifetime."

"But I'll forget it all when I'm sober."

"No." Jana's eyes were wide, like she was talking about a cult leader who had sold her hook, line, and sinker. "You don't forget. That's the amazing thing — you remember every millisecond. The wisdom that you gain is yours to keep."

Clare couldn't help laughing. "Now you sound like an infomercial. How many brain cells does it cost?"

"No long-term damage to your brain. There have been tons of studies. Pure LSD — and Mountain Snow is the purest, that's why Sacha was so excited to find it — is one hundred percent safe." Jana pulled off her glove again to show Clare the acid. "You think these tiny pieces of paper can hurt you?"

The tabs *were* tiny.

"I'll show you Sacha's suicide note. *If* you drop with me. The police still have the original, but Richie scored me a photocopy for the meantime."

Clare tried to sound disinterested while her mind fired with excitement. "What does the note say?"

"No sneak previews. Because only on Mountain Snow will I know if you're the real Sacha coming back — if you're even supposed to see the note."

"Are you already high?" Clare hoped so, because the alternative was Jana being insane.

Jana giggled. "No, I said that to freak you out. I *do* think you're Sacha, but not in a ghosty way. Just in a . . . I don't even know . . . I just really want to drop with you."

"I'm afraid," Clare said.

"Of learning something? Having fun?"

Clare thought of Amanda, stomping her little foot and ordering Clare around. Amanda might have the right answer if she were taking a test with a lead pencil in an RCMP classroom, but Clare knew the field. She was going with her gut on this.

Clare grinned — she tried for casually — and said, "Fine. Give me one of those pieces of paper. What do I do? Swallow it?"

"Stick it under your tongue. Here — hold your mouth open."

Jana was quick to close the deal before popping the other tab into her own mouth and pushing off with her snowboard.

Clare followed. Though it would take the drug several minutes to work its way into her bloodstream, she was already trembling with a strange kind of excitement.

THIRTY-NINE
RICHIE

As they shook hands, Richie held Wade's grip firmly. He eyed up Avalanche's cramped office and wondered where his desk would go. They'd have to clear out one of the filing cabinets to make room. But it was a nice problem to have.

Wade clutched the envelope Richie had given him. "Welcome to Avalanche. Looking forward to working together."

"Yeah, man, I'm stoked, too." Richie heard himself talking like a snowboarder. "Especially to get Avalanche Nights back on that stage."

Wade smiled. "You've never heard us play."

"Yeah, but you guys *are* this place. You and Chopper and Norris. You got any CDs kicking around from your glory days? We can sell those at the opening gig. Unless . . . did they even have CDs back when Avalanche Nights was touring?"

"We have CDs. But Norris will never agree."

"Norris will come around. Should we take the check to the landlords together? I'm free now if their office is open." Richie eyed the walls. At least one of the Grateful Dead posters could come down; Jay-Z could go up in its place.

"Oh, you can leave the landlords to me," Wade said. "We don't need to tell them about a new shareholder immediately."

"No?" Richie fixed Wade with a hard stare. "I'm smelling something off here, Wade."

Wade took a gulp from a coffee cup that probably had something stronger in it. "I want to ease this by Georgia first — before I tell my landlords and she finds out from someone else in town."

"You mean our landlords."

"Of course. I mean our landlords."

Richie shook his head. "What's to ease by her? It's your business, ain't it?"

"Of course Avalanche is mine. Do you see my wife pouring draft at one in the morning? But she's not thrilled that I have to take on a partner. She sees it as a sign of failure that I couldn't make it on my own."

Richie's heart was starting to crash and burn. His dreams might not be as close as they seemed. Just like fucking always. "Do you own this business or not?"

Wade frowned. "Technically, Georgia owns the company. It's for tax reasons — in name only. So yes, it's my business."

"So Georgia's my partner." Richie wasn't sure how he felt about being in business with a stuck-up broad like Wade's wife. Like being a slave to the advertising business made her some kind of expert on everything. It was a business full of pretenders. Richie thought his own work was a lot more honest.

"No. I mean, yes, technically. But effectively, the partnership is between you and me."

"Shouldn't she be at this meeting?" Not that Richie relished the patronizing glances Georgia would give him, like she was scared of him pulling out a gun but didn't want to admit that she was racist.

"She's not interested in running the bar. The closest Georgia comes to making management decisions is telling me which sauvignon blanc to stock for when she stops in after work."

Richie kissed his lips. He didn't give a shit if the gesture seemed ghetto — Wade was the one who should be interested in making the good impression. "So it ain't official. Gimme back that envelope for now."

Wade drew the cash closer to himself. "She'll sign off on this. I'm going to take her out for dinner, talk about old times, explain how having a partner would mean I could leave the bar in good hands for a week or two so we could have a life again — *and* be more profitable. It's win-win, and she'll go for it — there's no doubt."

"Great. So there's no doubt I'll pass you that cash back tomorrow. Tell her I want her at the meeting."

"She won't come to a meeting. I'll bring you the documents after she's signed them, though, if that would make you feel better."

"You planning to forge her signature?"

"Of course not."

Richie shook his head. "Call a meeting with all three of us. I can wait until the weekend if she don't want to meet on a work night. Shit, and here I thought we were this close."

"We *are* this close. You wanted to talk about the waitresses' uniforms? Let's talk."

"Not yet. I want to do this in the right order." Richie picked up his envelope and left the room. He wasn't sure if there even was room for a second desk.

FORTY
WADE

otherfucker. Wade watched Richie leave. *That close* to saving Avalanche. He took a large gulp of cheap whiskey and phoned Georgia.

"Hello?" Joni Mitchell was singing in the background and abruptly stopped. "Sorry. I'm driving. Hello?"

"Are you on your way home?" Wade asked. "I thought we could have dinner tonight. Umberto's."

"I love Umberto's. But we're severely strapped for cash."

"I did a deal to save the bar. Fifty grand for twenty-five percent, plus my new partner has promotional plans to get sales up all through the year. Exciting, huh?"

"Very. I can't wait to hear all about it. Not Richie Lebar, then?"

Wade focused on a poster of Mick Jagger making love to his microphone onstage. "It's Richie. But with twenty-five percent, he has no control. He's basically free labor plus a massive cash infusion. Win-win."

"No."

"But you said . . ."

"I said I'd think about it. And I have: my answer's no."

Wade let a moment of silence go by before saying, "I know why you're hesitating. But Richie's decent. He's been wanting to go legit for a couple of years now."

"How nice. Let him go legit for a couple of years first, *then* get into business with him. Even that would be inadvisable, but better than this. I'll stop in Squamish for groceries, since we're not actually loaded."

Wade's phone pinged with a text. He pulled it away from his ear briefly to see that the message was from Jana: *Can't work tonight. Maybe food poisoning or really bad flu. Vomiting every five minutes. Sorry!*

"Lying bitch," Wade said out loud. He put the phone back to his ear.

"Excuse me?"

"My bartender. I can't do dinner tonight — I'm now stuck covering the bar. But I could arrange a meeting between you and Richie — at Avalanche, so I can pop over and join you when it's quiet. He'd really like to meet you."

"I don't think so."

"Give him a chance. You can still say no after the meeting. He looks like a rapper — and he sometimes talks like one — but he's smart. He's also my only option."

"It's not fair to him if we meet. I'd be wasting his time and mine."

"Please? I don't want to lose this place."

"Why? You don't even like running a bar."

"A bunch of reasons . . . your parents' money . . . the music . . . plus I don't know what else I'd do." What Wade didn't say was that as leaky as Avalanche was, it was the only scrap of boat between him and the big stormy sea — without it, he was sure he'd drown.

"You're smart, you're educated, you're under forty. There are jobs out there for guys like you in any economy."

She didn't get it. Sacha got it. That's why she'd been helping Wade write songs — so he could produce them, release them on YouTube and iTunes or even find a record deal, and give his dream one more shot. Even Richie got it.

"With a partner," Wade said, "I'd have time to do other things

— not just wake up and come to work and fall into bed exhausted at four in the morning. You and I could take vacations. We could go back to Morocco."

"Morocco was fun once. I have no desire to go back. Especially not now, with all the troubles in the Middle East."

"There were troubles then, too. I guess you used to be more adventurous."

"I used to be young and stupid."

"Just one meeting? How about if I ask Richie to come by around ten or eleven?"

"That late? I'm working tomorrow."

"He's a late-night guy — another good thing, because it would mean I could do mornings and he could close up nights. More couch time for you and me."

"Right. And while we're curled up watching Leno, Richie could rob you blind by playing with figures at the end of the day."

"He's not that way. He has honor — more than most businessmen I've met." Wade couldn't tell Georgia how he knew this, of course — that he and Richie had already been in business together for several months.

"He's a criminal, Wade. They steal because they think that if they don't, they're wasting an opportunity."

Wade tried not to laugh out loud. "I think you'll find as many businessmen who think that way as criminals."

"I'm nearly in Squamish, so I'm about to pull off. But fine, I'll come meet Richie. Apologies in advance for wasting his time. I can tell you now the answer is going to be no."

FORTY-ONE
CLARE

Snow had started coming down again. The falling snow-flakes looked like individual pieces of wonder, sharp and defined, like they'd jumped out from an illustrated children's book. They also looked terrifying — like they could burn a hole of cold right through your skin if you let one land on you. Clare was starting to feel the acid, she was pretty sure. She was glad she and Jana were arriving at the base in Whistler Village.

Jana skidded to a stop and unbound her boots from her board. Clare pulled up behind her and did the same.

"You tripping?" Jana asked.

"I think so." Clare's mind felt crystal clear, but she was noticing things she didn't normally. "Is the hill always this friendly or does it sometimes get angry?"

Jana laughed. "It stays happy unless you piss it off. You were getting really good, toward the bottom of the slope. Slicing edges like a pro. Did you notice you didn't fall once?"

"Hey, yeah." Clare realized Jana was right. "You want to do another run?"

"No, because I don't feel like walking up. The lifts are closed."

Clare looked at the motionless gondola and said, "Oh yeah."

The sky was beginning to darken. Like the snowflakes, the looming night felt both ominous and beautiful — like it could protect you or ruin you, depending on the tone of your approach.

"The village lights . . ." Clare pointed toward a block of shops — a souvenir store, a café, a rental shop. "They're trying to say something."

"Yeah? Like a message?"

Clare nodded solemnly.

"Is it about Sacha?"

"I don't know. I don't speak light language." Clare realized she would sound ridiculous to a sober person. But at the same time, she was intrigued by what these lights had to say.

"Come on." Jana started walking toward the lights. "Let's drop off our snowboards at home. Can I call you Sacha tonight?"

Clare shook her head so hard she was surprised her helmet didn't burst free of its chinstrap and fly off her head. "No. That freaks me out."

Jana shrugged. "So I'll say it in my head."

In the village, Clare pressed her nose against the window of the Aveda salon. Inside, a woman cut another woman's hair. The hair-dresser's face was delicate and pretty, but as Clare watched, it flattened into a bland pancake — Clare could see she was vapid at her core. Clare switched focus to the woman having her hair cut. Her lips were tight; she looked smug and middle-aged, but the harder Clare stared, the more attractive the woman in the chair became. She began to look warmer — so warm, in fact, that a slight orange glow began to surround the woman's head and then her body. Clare wanted to go inside and meet this woman, have a conversation and learn about why she felt the need to put on a sour face for the world.

Jana tugged at her. "Come on, slowpoke. I know this is all so fascinating, but you can dawdle all you like once we've unloaded these giant boards we're lugging and changed into comfortable boots."

Clare looked back into the salon as Jana dragged her away. "But it won't be the same. When we come back, that scene will be gone forever."

"We'll find magic someplace else. I take it you like the Mountain Snow."

"I love it." Clare wondered what Amanda had been so worried about — what she herself had been so worried about. She wasn't out of her head — she was in it, more deeply than ever. Pot was more dangerous — it made her paranoid, lethargic, out of it — more likely to say things she shouldn't. Clare was excited to share this observation with Amanda — oh, but she couldn't admit she'd been tripping because then she'd lose her job.

Clare wished she could help Amanda out of her shell. She imagined a chisel that she passed to Amanda — a designer chisel, of course, in yuppie pink. *Here*, Clare said in her head. *Use this to free yourself, to see how fun life is outside your invisible box.* Because really, Clare liked Amanda — she just didn't like the bossy bitch on the outside.

It was when they arrived home and walked through the door of their apartment that something went wrong with Jana's face.

"You look freaky," Clare said.

"Really? How?"

"Like a turtle trying to poke out of its shell. But, like, a serpent turtle. A little bit evil. Are you evil? Hey, can you drink beer on acid?"

"You can, but there's no point. You'd be better off with juice. I'm not a serpent turtle, don't worry."

Clare wasn't so sure.

"You want to see the letter from Sacha?"

Clare nodded.

"First, juice." Jana pulled the carton from the fridge. The picture of the orange on the box looked like it had the power to nourish them from the toes up. It took all Clare's patience not to stick her mouth under the stream as Jana poured.

When she finally had the glass in her hand, Clare took a massive gulp of orange and mango awesomeness. She was about to ask Jana for more when she saw that she already had a full glass.

"It's liquid magic," Clare said. "The glass refilled itself as soon as I wished for more."

Jana laughed hard. "You only had a tiny sip. Your senses are heightened; things taste bigger."

Clare swirled another sip around her mouth. She closed her eyes and felt like she was on a tropical island, drinking oranges and mangoes right out of a coconut. There was a man with her — Noah. She smiled at Noah and asked him if he was going to be a prick or if he wanted to stay on her island. He took her coconut and had a long sip of juice. He was about to answer when Jana grabbed Clare's arm, startling her.

"Let's go get Jules!"

"Whoa, I don't have any jewels, though," Clare said before contemplating if Lucy hated jewelry as much as she did. Luckily, Clare realized, Lucy was even lower maintenance than she was.

"*Jules*," Jana said. "Jules the *Bear*."

"Right." Clare held her index finger straight up in the air in front of her. "Wait. Why?"

"Because in Sacha's note, she says the answer is in Jules."

"The answer to what? Hey, you said you'd show me the note."

Jana peered into Clare's eyes like she was appraising her soul. She took Clare's hands and held them a moment before saying, "Okay. You pass the test."

Clare laughed. "What test?"

"You're cool. You're here to help, not to hurt anyone."

"Oh."

Jana grabbed Clare and pulled her into her bedroom. The bed was unmade and clothes were all over the floor — exactly like on Clare's last visit, though she had the presence of mind to pretend she'd never been in the room before.

On the wall, Jana had a framed Picasso print — a ragged blue man slumped over a guitar.

"Where did you get this painting?" Clare said, walking up to the print and peering at it closely. She wanted to be in the room with the man, in Europe all those years ago, but she shuddered when she realized she might not be able to climb back out of the painting — and the world back then seemed bleak and full of social injustices. It would be horrible to be stuck in a less enlightened time. She turned away and looked at Jana's mess again.

"It's Sacha's. But when she started dating Wade she said the man in the picture depressed her, so we moved it to my room."

Jana reached under her pillow and pulled out a folded sheet of lined paper. Clare thought it was funny, why Amanda wouldn't have just shown her a copy. She wasn't angry anymore — she felt like she was watching the situation from above, where no anger could exist because the issue wasn't that important.

Jana handed the note over solemnly. "Read it."

Clare unfolded the page.

```
If you're reading this, pretty sure I'm already gone.
I know I'm probably a danger to myself. But I can't
stop. I'm following the only path that makes sense
to me. I'm so sorry to leave you like this. If people
wonder why I died, you can tell them the answer is
in Jules.
```

"That's it?" Clare said before she could stop herself. Half of her brain was wondering why Jules was with Jana, why Sacha's parents hadn't insisted on having Jules shipped back with her things. The other half answered that Sacha's parents were grieving too hard to think clearly. Jules had slipped through the cracks, and only Jana was vigilant enough to notice.

Jana said, "Sacha was cryptic. This note is probably code. I've been too freaked out to try to decipher it, but tonight — with you here — I feel like I can do it."

"What do you mean by code?" Clare said. She glanced at the page, tried reading every second letter, then every third, but a hidden message didn't emerge.

"I don't know. That's why I need your help."

"Hm . . . I guess the first thing to rule out is the literal meaning. Is there physically an answer inside Jules? Like, hidden in his fur or something. Or inside that zippered pocket where the note was?"

Jana smiled indulgently. "She would hardly need code if her meaning was literal."

"Yeah, but maybe it's not code."

"Fine, we'll look, just to satisfy you," Jana said.

Clare followed Jana into Sacha's old bedroom — Clare's room, for now.

Jana picked Jules up from the dresser and poked him in the missing eye. "Ow! Jules bit me."

"From his eye? Maybe he doesn't like being poked there."

Jana pried back the eye socket just enough to peer inside. She held the small brown bear up to the light. "I think it's a camera."

Clare took Jules and peered inside the eye socket. It could be a camera. It could also be a beady little bear eye, dislodged and pushed back into the stuffing. She squeezed strategically and felt two different hard places — one right behind the eye where the maybe-camera was, and the other in the middle, near the back. She flipped Jules over and saw the zipper. "You think Sacha would mind if I opened him?"

Jana shook her head. "Tonight, you are Sacha."

Clare stuck her hand into Jules' back. Jana was right: he felt empty. As she was about to pull her hand out, though, she felt a small ridge. Could be the seam in the lining, but it felt more like a second zipper. She moved her finger along the seam until she found a zipper tab. She unzipped it, reached further inside the bear, and felt a thin piece of plastic.

She grinned at Jana. "Score, I think."

Jana watched gravely as Clare opened Jules up wide enough to see a memory stick connected into the bear by some kind of wire. Clare wished she was sober so she could know for sure what this was — but a camera or even an audio recorder was looking pretty damn likely.

Clare looked at the alarm clock in her room: seven p.m. They'd dropped just after four. That meant around five more hours of being insanely high.

"Do you have any TUMS?" Clare asked. "Or Pepto Bismol?"

"I don't think so. Why?"

"I want to be sober to crack this bear puzzle."

"What would TUMS do?"

"It's an antacid," Clare said. "It should neutralize the effects of LSD."

"Of course! You're so smart, Lucy. All the times I've dropped and I never figured out the secret. Should we go find a pharmacy? I mean, I don't want the trip to end, but we can always drop again. It would be so cool to find out if that works."

"No." Clare's shoulders slumped. She set Jules down. "It's a stupid theory. I don't know why I even thought that." She felt her veins throbbing inside her, like they were contemplating exploding. She felt her eyelids fall heavily and flutter as they stayed mainly closed. She felt Jana's hand take hers and lead her to the bed to sit down.

"You're okay." Jana's voice was warm, but Clare did not feel safe. "The drug does this sometimes."

Clare opened her eyes to meet Jana's. They looked friendly enough — not like an evil serpent turtle, anyway. More like a turtle fairy god-mother. "Am I having a bad trip?"

"Just a bad patch. You'll be okay."

"How do you know?"

"Mountain Snow is powerful. If you try to fight it, it fights back. It probably didn't like your antacid suggestion. But if you go with it, it will pick you up again. Here — drink your juice."

Clare felt the cold juice glass as Jana placed it in her hand. The juice tasted good — maybe not desert island awesome like before, but strong, nourishing.

But all Clare could think about was how stupid she'd been to swallow that tab, how Amanda had been right — had been trying to protect her — and Clare had thrown all that away by being her stubborn, contrary self.

Clare's mind started spiraling. Down, into the darkest part of her brain, where she asked herself, was she a fatally flawed fuck-up like her father, with no hope of ever rising above that fate? They both loved fixing cars, riding motorcycles, smoking cigarettes . . . maybe they were the same and there was no escape for Clare. Or was she like her mother — wearing blinders to the bleak reality all around her?

Have another cup of tea, dear. Oh, don't be angry — your father's just out for a walk — of course he isn't smoking. You're leaving already? But I've baked these lovely cookies. Clare shuddered to think of the two of them, sequestered in their trailer in their *folie a deux*, her father slowly dying and no one willing to say it out loud, like if they didn't name the disease he could stay alive indefinitely . . .

Jana grabbed Clare's hand and yanked her up. "Come on. We're changing rooms."

"Why?" Clare let herself be led into the living room.

"We all have dark spots in our lives. Don't dwell on them or you'll depress yourself."

Had Clare been talking? Shit. Amanda was so right — she should not have trusted herself to take this drug. She was going to blow her cover in no time. "Um, was I talking?"

Jana laughed. "No. But I know Mountain Snow. Here, sit on the couch; it's the most comfortable place in the room."

Clare sat on the couch. It was blue, like the ocean. She felt kind of seasick, but not bad enough to stand up. She just rode the waves, pretending she was skippering a sailboat, pulling at ropes to keep the sails taut and the course true. Noah was on the boat, but he was being lazy. His feet were up on an overturned bucket as he reclined in a deck chair. Clare wanted to tell him to get up and help but there was no point — he looked like he might even be asleep. She put a hand to her forehead and scanned the horizon. And then she *was* the boat — way more fun — chopping through and feeling salt water lap at her hull. She was carrying Noah — which suddenly felt right — navigating for both of them and leading Noah to a safer place, where he could deal with having killed a girl and forgive himself for it. And then Jana appeared and Clare was Clare again. And Lucy.

Jana put Jules in Clare's hands and bent down to study the stereo. "We need happy music, STAT."

From the speakers, a guitar started strumming, and soon Kermit the Frog began singing "The Rainbow Connection."

The song made Clare smile. The lyrics were sweet and hopeful, making Clare feel like Sacha had written in her note — that wherever she ended up, she was on the only path that made sense to her. She still felt weak, like she was recovering from a vicious virus that had attacked her whole system. But she also felt strong, ready to take on what came next.

"Are you ready to see what's in Jules?" Jana unzipped the bear's back, stuck her hand in, and wiggled it around. She frowned. "This memory stick is lodged in here. I don't want to ruin Jules, but I don't know how to get it out. I wonder if scissors would help."

"We could wait until tomorrow," Clare said. "Or until the acid wears off. I don't want to ruin Jules, either."

"We have to act now."

"Okay." Clare stroked Jules' plush ear, silently telling him she wouldn't let any scissors come near him.

FORTY-TWO
MARTHA

From the midtown fortieth floor, Martha looked out upon nighttime in New York. Below, the East River's murky waters rushed down the length of the city. Part of her wished she could hop onto a working barge, ride it out to sea, and drift indefinitely. But the largest part of Martha was focused on this party.

She smiled at a terrible joke that a man in a well-tailored suit had just told — something about a bear and a beer in a bar. She sipped her gin and tonic. She made an equally lame but friendly reply.

"We're so glad you came out tonight." The Wall Street baron hosting the soiree touched Martha's arm. "When your assistant called to cancel last week, we thought we were going to have to invite Geoff Kearnes."

The man spoke lightly, so Martha laughed — though she felt the serious undercurrent. The host was a friend of Fraser's; Martha had known him socially for years. But it was hardly the time to fall back on familiarity. His endorsement was to New York what Reverend Hillier's was to Michigan. The nomination would likely be clinched before a New York primary happened, but she couldn't afford to lose his support. "Back in full swing," Martha said. "I'll never stop missing Sacha. But I'm pushing forward, fresh each day."

"Good, good. Here, there's someone I'd like you to meet."

As Martha was led away, her phone rang with Ted's distinct ringtone. Ted knew her schedule — he wouldn't interrupt unless it mattered.

"Sorry," Martha said. "I need to take this."

The host frowned. "I hope you're not long."

Ted was breathless. "Remember the blogger who interviewed you at LaGuardia?"

"Yes." Martha hoped this was important enough for her to have snubbed the host.

"He knew Sacha as a kid."

"Yes." Martha, of course, already knew this. Though the photograph in Sacha's box was still nagging her. Could skin color lighten as someone aged? She thought of Michael Jackson and realized that anything was possible.

"The blogger is trying to solve the case through the Internet. He knows about the suicide note, but he doesn't believe Sacha killed herself."

"I'm at a party, Ted. For work. Can we talk about this tomorrow?" But Martha's mind had kicked into gear — how could Lorenzo already know about the suicide note?

"Sure," Ted said. "Sorry. I forgot you were doing that. The soiree still shows as canceled in your calendar. I'll email you the link to this latest blog post. You can check it out whenever."

Whenever might as well be immediately. Martha slipped into the bathroom and pulled out her BlackBerry. She clicked the link Ted had emailed her.

ON THE CASE
by LORENZO BARILLA

Sacha Westlake has been dead for 13 days and Whistler police are nowhere near finding a lead.

Maybe that's because they're not looking.

Yesterday, I interviewed Martha Westlake. She had
the most to gain from Sacha's death. Or is that the
most to lose if Sacha remained alive?

Martha wished she'd brought her drink into the bathroom — she
could use a heavy glug.

Today, I interviewed Wade Harrison, owner of the bar
where Sacha worked.

Here are some facts I learned:

1. Wade and Sacha were sleeping together.
2. Wade is in the middle of a descent into financial
   ruin.
3. Wade's wife is the legal owner of the bar.

Did Wade kill Sacha to keep his wife from finding
out he'd been cheating?

Did Georgia Harrison kill Sacha out of jealousy?

Did Senator Westlake murder her daughter for political gain?

Or is the killer someone whom I have yet to
interview?

If you have information that could help me find
Sacha's killer, please add your comment below.

Because yes, Sacha left a note. But this was no suicide note: she left it because she knew she was about
to be murdered.

Martha held her phone in her hand and stared at it. As if her world wasn't already upside down enough. She drew a long breath, plastered on her cocktail smile, and went out to find the host.

FORTY-THREE
RICHIE

Norris squirmed in his armchair in Chopper's cabin. Richie watched Norris, wondered what was going on inside that small, tightly wound head of his.

Chopper bridged his hands in the air and said, "You need to let us in, Stu. What's this big secret eating you?"

"I'm not cleared to say," Norris said, making Richie want to leap across the coffee table to punch him.

Richie's phone, nestled in the pocket of his raw denim Levi's, was recording this conversation. He couldn't hold back from saying, "I don't think you're cleared to take bribes from drug dealers, either."

"Look, I know that. And I wish I never helped you guys." Norris sounded like a six-year-old who maybe thought magic could erase his past actions, or that pouting would make people care. "I made a mistake taking your money. I should have just turned a blind eye and left it there."

Chopper shrugged. "A blind eye still deserves a piece of the action."

"But the money makes it official — it makes me complicit. And the fucked-up thing . . ." Norris pounded his fist against the soft leather arm of his chair. "The fucked-up thing is I don't even want the money."

Richie wanted to call bullshit on that, but he kept quiet.

He was glad when Chopper said, "If you don't want the money, why did you ask for ten grand for the undercover's name?"

Norris' lip twitched. "Because I didn't have the cash."

"Because of the cello?"

Norris shrugged. "And my wife. I take her to nice restaurants, give her extra money for shopping — she doesn't question it."

Chopper cocked his head, like he was trying to see his friend from a different angle. "But you're the careful one, the guy who always has a reserve fund and another one to back it up."

"I still have my RSPS. But they're the one-year cashable kind. I couldn't exactly wait to wire the money."

Wire the money where? Richie wanted to ask. But Chopper met Richie's eyes and shook his head slightly, and Richie knew he was right: Norris wanted to talk, but he was so skittish. It made more sense for Chopper to take the lead, coax what he could out of his old friend.

"You said this is bigger than us, Stu," Chopper said. "What does that mean?"

Norris pulled out a pack of cigarettes. "Can I smoke in here?"

"Yeah, why not? Normally I say no tobacco, but Lucy's been lighting up like a little chimney."

Norris' hands were trembling so hard that he tore the first cigarette he tried to pull from the pack. He tossed both pieces in the ashtray, pulled out a second cigarette, and fumbled with the lighter until it was lit.

"First," Norris said. "You guys have to know you're protected. Wade, too. I have that in writing. None of you are going down when this is over."

"So who is going down?" Chopper asked.

"Your friends in Seattle."

"That's not a bad thing. How can I be of assistance?" Richie said it like a joke, but he meant it. He had no loyalty left toward Seattle.

"You can help by not even contemplating taking this batch across the border. If the FBI gets wind of this — and I'm sorry to say it,

Chopper, but your name has come up on their red flag list — then the whole operation to bust the Seattle cartel could get blown. The immunity deal I negotiated for the three of you would be off the table."

"Not much good you having a signed agreement then, is it? If they can change the rules whenever they please."

Chopper shot Richie a sharp glance that said, *I'll take it from here.* "Stu, who are you negotiating with? The RCMP, the FBI . . . ?"

Norris' shoulders slumped. His little gut pushed out — Richie hadn't noticed him having one before. "You guys swear this stays right here?"

"Of course." Chopper's tone was warm and level. Richie saw that he could learn a lot from Chopper about how to talk to people in business, how to get them to relax and open up.

"I've been working with the DEA," Norris said.

An electric glance shot between Richie and Chopper.

"You little motherfucker. You sold us out?" Richie said, before he remembered to be nice.

"Of course not." Norris glowered at Richie. "They got in touch with me. They knew everything — Chopper's manufacturing, your dealing, Sacha's drug-running. They wanted — still want — our help in nailing the Seattle cartel. But they can't have the FBI see us, or they're worried the operation will get botched."

"Fucking Sacha," Chopper said. "She could never keep her mouth shut."

Richie wasn't so sure the leak was from Sacha, but he wouldn't say a word until he knew just who it *was* from. Too many people were friends with each other in this strange little town.

Norris' eyes were wide, pleading forgiveness.

"I should have told you guys way sooner, I know. Like as soon as the DEA got in touch. I thought I could keep control of this."

"So they knew about you, too," Richie said. "About your taking bribes. Otherwise, how would they know you'd work for them so willingly?"

"If they don't bust Seattle, they're telling the RCMP everything. My life and career here would be over. I'm thinking seriously of bailing anyway, taking my family and getting out." Norris hauled hard on his cigarette, like the nicotine could somehow protect him.

"The run pays twenty grand," Richie said, more worried about the Seattle cartel than a couple years in prison if Norris happened to be right about the DEA. "You want to get out of town, why not take your family in Chopper's truck and catch a plane out of Bellingham to somewhere sunny — somewhere that doesn't extradite. You can make up for your fuck-up and save your ass at the same time. It's not often life hands you a win-win like that."

Norris' mouth wrinkled. "If the run pays twenty grand under normal conditions, I'd need at least fifty to make it worth my while now."

Fifty? Richie met Chopper's eyes. Chopper nodded.

"But," Richie couldn't help saying, "you just said you don't want the blood money."

"I didn't need it before. Now, it's my ticket to a new beginning."

"Fine," Richie said. "Fifty grand is half the take, and this is all your goddamn fault, but fine." Even if Norris made off with the whole hundred grand, and even if they never got Chopper's truck back, it was saving Richie and Chopper a million in debt. Like Billingsley said, *Cut your losses quick to give your profits room to grow.* He'd followed it up in the book with a tomato plant analogy for readers who were too dumb to get his drift.

Richie's phone beeped with a text from Jana: *Got Lucy 2 drop. Yay me.*

"You know what else is nagging me?" Norris took the tiny end of Chopper's joint and sucked back hard before squishing the butt into the ashtray.

"Your wife?" Richie texted back: *Good 2 know. Still b careful what u say.*

"There's a blogger on the case, so to speak. Interviewing so-called suspects, trying to find out who killed Sacha. He knows things, like that Wade was cheating on Georgia with Sacha. What if he has eyes in town and follows me to the States?"

Richie thought this was taking paranoid to a whole new level, but Chopper said, "Richie or I could follow you as far as Squamish, make sure no one's on your tail."

"Even still . . . Look, if I were single, I wouldn't be this cautious. But if I'm in jail, or if I'm dead, I'm no good to my family."

Richie wished his own dad had had even a fraction of that attitude. He said, "The blogger is nothing to worry about. I've been reading the posts with Jana, and I'm pretty sure the blogger and Sacha were friends back in New York. He's gone all emo about losing her, but it's not some deep mystery why the guy knows she was fucking Wade. It doesn't make him a genius detective with eyes into our living rooms."

"Au contraire, my friend." Chopper reached forward and pulled his open box of marijuana supplies toward himself. He pulled out a Rizla and some pot, and started rolling a new joint. "I've been reading, too, and this blogger is emotionally invested. He might not be here now, but he'll find a way into our living rooms. He'll find eyes here, little spies. He won't rest until the verdict's overturned and Sacha's been cleared of suicide."

"But she *did* kill herself," Norris said. "The suicide note only compounds the evidence."

"So why can't you close the case?" Chopper's eyebrows lifted, challenging.

"RCMP head office says the suicide note isn't clear enough. They're petrified of American scorn if we get it wrong."

Richie looked at Norris. "Can you go the other way? Change the diagnostics and call this a murder case?"

"Why would I do that?" Norris pushed his little chest out. "I truly believe Sacha killed herself."

"I don't. But that's not the point. A murder verdict might make the FBI and the blogger go away quietly. Their objection is to Sacha being labeled a suicide — not that we haven't found a killer."

"They're not going away until Sacha's death has been vindicated."

"You think?" Richie said. "Because even if only one of them leaves, that's one less wolf at our door. We could maybe get away with this one last run before we pack up and find a town with less heat."

"You forget that the DEA is watching, too."

"But they *want* us to make the run. Just not while we're being watched."

Norris wrinkled his small nose. "Even if a murder verdict made the blogger *and* the FBI leave — which I'm not convinced it would — it would attract more press. We'd have just as many eyes on us, if not more." He looked to Chopper. "What do you think?"

"Richie's right," Chopper said. "You should change your official position to murder. You don't have to actually find a killer."

Norris was quiet as his eyes moved back and forth between Richie and Chopper. "I'll change the verdict," he said finally. "But until the DEA gives me the all clear, I'm not helping move those drugs across the border."

FORTY-FOUR
CLARE

The doorbell rang. Clare and Jana jumped.

"Who's there?" Clare asked Jana. She was playing with Jules' ear, which suddenly reminded her of their mission to see what was inside him. For the past hour, she and Jana had been absorbed by the *Muppet Movie* soundtrack, analyzing the lyrics for hidden clues to the secret of the universe. They'd already found several.

"I don't know," Jana said.

"Don't know what?"

"Who's at the door. Should we check, or pretend we're not here?"

Chopper's voice came from outside. "We can hear you guys talking. You can pretend you're not there, but we won't believe you."

Clare and Jana burst out laughing.

"Let's hide," Jana said. "So they won't know where we are."

"How will they get in? Anyway, who's they?"

"Me and Richie," Chopper said. "Come on, you guys. We're freezing."

"Oh, fine." Jana got up and let them in.

The guys took off their outside gear and joined Clare and Jana in the living room. Chopper shared the couch with Clare. With blond hair against a white shirt, he looked like a polar bear. Not the kind that would growl and eat her up, but a big goofy nice one, like the kind from the Coke commercials. She leaned into his body and he wrapped his furry arms around her.

Richie looked like a tiger — or maybe a cheetah — Chester Cheetah — strutting around in designer baggy duds like a man on a mission. He didn't look scary, either. More like he wanted to look scary.

"We found a camera inside Jules," Jana said. "But we don't know how to watch it."

"For realz?" Richie asked as he slid into an armchair.

Jana laughed. "There's no Z on the end of real if you're outside the ghetto."

Richie rolled his eyes and muttered, "Whatever. You're cute when you're high. Too bad you're probably not horny."

"Sex on acid rocks." Chopper picked up Clare's hand and squeezed it. It felt juicy, like he was pumping positive energy into her hand. "We should try some later."

Jana wrinkled her nose. "Don't listen to him. Richie's right. It feels like robot sex."

"That's the beauty," Chopper said, walking his fingers up Clare's arm and giving her an awesome tingly feeling. "It's like two minds merging on this sick astral plane. Which Jana wouldn't know about, because she's never been up there."

Clare met Chopper's eyes and felt a line form, pulsing from her eyes to his and back again. It was blue, like electricity. Like they were shooting thoughts back and forth. She wondered if Chopper could feel it, too.

"Man, I wish I was high with you," Chopper said. "You seem like you're telling me something important, but without the drug, I can't receive the message."

Clare wasn't sure what he meant, but she thought she knew. She nestled into him and felt safer than she'd felt in years.

"So what's with the Jules cam?" Richie asked. "You have it here, or what?"

"Yeah," Jana said. "But me and Sacha — I mean, me and Lucy are way too stoned to figure it out. Lucy, show him Jules."

Clare thought this was a terrible idea, sharing their clue with two more prime suspects. Even if they were a polar bear and a tiger-cheetah, you couldn't rule anyone out until it was over. But she turned back into Lucy, who wouldn't share those concerns. She unzipped Jules and handed him to Chopper. Chopper looked inside and tugged with his free hand. The memory stick came loose and he pulled it from the stuffed bear.

Jana and Clare locked eyes and burst out laughing.

"Does one of you have a computer we can use?" Chopper asked.

"My laptop." Jana got up and retrieved it from the kitchen.

Chopper pulled his arm away from Clare, making her feel like her fire had just gone out and she was sitting alone in the cold. She gave him a look to let him know he'd abandoned her.

"Sorry." Chopper patted her shoulder.

"That's okay. I think you're nice." Clare laughed inside at her own lame words. She would never speak them sober — or if she wasn't being Lucy.

"I think I'm nice, too." Chopper opened the computer on the coffee table and turned it on. "Is this Sacha's laptop?"

"Yeah," Jana said. "I've been using it to remind me of her. Mine's so old and slow."

"Um, yeah. I'm sure she doesn't miss it. But wouldn't this have been, like, evidence?"

"Oh my god." Jana rolled her eyes. "You're not even a real scientist, and you have to be so technical about everything. I gave the police her desktop and her phone. That's all they asked for."

Chopper plugged in the memory stick and clicked the first icon in the folder that popped up on the screen.

A video started playing. Sacha came to life.

FORTY-FIVE
RICHIE

Richie roughed up Jana's hair. She was on the floor in front of his armchair, snuggled against his legs. Maybe if his business plan worked out, he could ask her about moving in together. He knew she didn't want a conventional rich guy who wore a suit to work and pretended to know about wines, but she wasn't going to settle down with a drug dealer, either. Which was a good thing — Richie wanted a good life for her.

On the tape, Sacha was driving Chopper's big red truck. Her hair was messy, like she wore it around the house. She said, "This is my official documentary into the heart of the American drug smuggling trade."

She sounded far away — the microphone wasn't the greatest. But her little lithe movements, that sparkle just behind her eye — it was like she was in the room with them.

"My mother is one of America's biggest fighters in the War on Drugs." Sacha leaned closer to the camera, like she was telling it a secret. Jules must have been sitting on the center console. "Except she isn't fighting. Not really. She's been presented with creative solutions that would reduce the power of the cartels. She met Ernesto Zedillo at Yale. Can you believe that? This guy is a genius, a free thinker who wants to eradicate drugs from the world using methods that might actually work, and she won't listen to him. Instead, my mother keeps playing politics — choosing the policy that will win her the next election over the one that will actually work.

"My goal with this Whistler project is twofold: To show how horrible cartels are by working with one of the worst, based in Seattle. And to open the public mind to legalization."

"I'm worried that I won't be here much longer. I think someone wants me dead." Sacha had clearly done editing work on the film, because dark music played for four beats or so. It was almost hilarious, except Richie was seething that his friend had deceived him so thoroughly.

Sacha — the traitor — continued: "Yesterday, I took Jules along on an acid trip — to show how much fun it is, and how educative it can be if you treat the drug with respect.

"Today, we're on a road trip. Across the border with a knapsack filled with LSD. Street value: two million dollars. But I'm only planning to collect two hundred grand — there are a lot more middlemen who will be paid out before this hits the streets." Sacha's hand came toward the camera and the view shifted so it was facing forward, toward the border station at the Peace Arch. "Stay tuned to see how easy it is to get across."

Chopper paused the recording. "Fucking Sacha. I can't believe she'd sell us out like this."

Richie gritted his teeth. He wanted to tell Chopper to shut the fuck up around Lucy. And really, they shouldn't be watching this video around her at all. What he said was, "I think we should get these girls outside for some fresh air. The best way to come down from Mountain Snow is surrounded by mountain snow."

"So right," Chopper said, maybe getting the point or maybe just wanting to feel his new toy, Lucy, squeezing him from behind. "You girls in the mood for a sled ride?"

Lucy's face lit up. "Always."

Richie took that as a good sign. If Lucy was the cop, she'd want to keep watching the video.

"Yeah," Jana said. "Let's get out of this place. I'm pretty sure Sacha's mad at us."

Richie waited for the other three to head toward their winter coats before slipping the memory stick into his pocket.

"Damn, I forgot I have to meet Wade," he said as Jana locked the door behind them all. "You guys have fun. I'll catch up to you later on your trip."

FORTY-SIX
WADE

Wade tried to remember what ingredients were in a Singapore Sling. He knew it was orange with a red floating liquid . . . he went with orange juice and cherry brandy. There should probably be another liquor involved — rum? Gin? Vodka? Maybe another juice, too. He texted Jana to find out.

She texted back quickly: *Gin. But u can get away with whatever — as long as color is right most customers have no clue.*

If she wasn't so damn good at her job, he'd fire her in five seconds flat.

It was busy for the middle of the week. A young couple was slamming back shooters at the video game machine — pumping lots of coin in, which was good. A recently divorced regular was drinking beer in his suit and tie — he would have three or four more pints before stumbling home to his newly empty condo.

Wade's nerves were on fire as he watched Georgia and Richie, deep in conversation at a high-top table. They were both smiling.

After fifteen minutes or so, they shook hands and Richie walked out the door. Still wearing her office clothes, Georgia sauntered over on her high-heeled snow boots to join Wade at the bar. Watching her movement as she came toward him, he couldn't help but remember the twenty-four-year-old copywriter he'd met at his first advertising job. She'd been intense, sure — she loved her job and was great at the networking that went with it — but the Georgia of the past had also been funny, quirky; she could laugh at herself, and did often. Now everything was so heavy.

"So?" Wade put a new glass of white wine in front of her, as well as the veggie plate she'd ordered.

"So it's a no-go," Georgia said.

"What? Things looked like they were going so well."

"Richie's a smart guy. Charming. Like you said. I told him I'd think about it."

"And you've already finished thinking?"

"He's a drug dealer. I don't want to be in business with him."

"Jesus, Georgia." Wade grabbed the Laphroaig bottle from the top shelf. Might as well drink the good stuff before he had to abandon the bar along with all its liquor. "I thought at least you'd go into the meeting with an open mind."

Georgia eyed Wade's pour, like she was critiquing how full his tumbler was. She sipped her sauvignon blanc — her second glass, so she had no right to be judgy. "My hairdresser told me about this blogger."

Fuck. This was the last thing Wade needed. He seized on the word *hairdresser*. "You had your hair done? It looks great. New color?"

"Highlights. And about three inches shorter. Wade, I didn't want to have this conversation at your work. But I read the post this afternoon, and it's making me crazy."

Wade took a long gulp of Scotch.

"The blog said you were cheating on me."

"Are you serious?"

Georgia nodded. She looked small and sad, like the young woman he'd fallen in love with.

Wade shuffled his feet on the rubber floor mat. "Why would he invent such an awful lie?"

"Is it a lie?"

"Of *course*." Wade reached across the bar to hold Georgia's hand in his.

Georgia pulled her hand away and picked up a carrot stick, which she used to poke a piece of celery. "I can handle the truth. Things have sucked with us lately."

"I know. I've been stressed, a crappy husband. That's why I want a partner in Avalanche — so I can be married to you, not to work."

"Is it true that Sacha had a teddy bear?"

Wade wanted to find that bear and tear him into shreds, starting with his missing eye. Seriously. Fuck Jules. "I don't know. How would I?"

"It's in the blog." Georgia's eyes flickered to life. She reminded Wade of the kids in the *Scream* movies — it was all so exciting until they got killed by a psychopath. "If you cheated, Wade, we'll get past it. I just need to know. I miss that honesty, from the beginning. Remember when we were so excited to tell each other every tiny detail from our days?"

Wade knew it had been there once, but could only remember feeling that way about Sacha. "Of course I remember. And of course I didn't cheat with some scraggly snowboarder waitress." Wade nearly choked to talk about Sacha that way, but he needed Georgia onside. "You know that murderers do sometimes lie?"

"Murderers? I'm talking about a blogger."

"A blogger who cares a bit too much about this death. I don't think we can discount him as the killer."

Georgia looked down at her veggie platter, then up again, her eyes alight like she was caught up in something dark and interesting.

Wade came around the other side of the bar and wrapped his wife in his arms. "Maybe I *will* close this bar, if it's tearing us up like this."

"I'm doing my best to help, Wade. But sometimes you have to cut your losses."

"I know." Wade touched a strand of Georgia's hair and wished it was straighter and darker, like Sacha's.

FORTY-SEVEN
CLARE

Clare dawdled behind Chopper and Jana. The cobblestones seemed to be rotating, singly and together, glistening with snow and colors. "This is amazing," she said. "Like I have a kaleidoscope in my eyes. Whoever invented that toy must have been on acid."

Jana stopped walking. She turned around to look at Clare. "Lucy, are you a cop?"

Clare wrinkled her nose and tried to look serious. She ended up bursting out laughing. "No."

Jana's face started to blend into the kaleidoscope. Clare wished she could get rid of it.

"Are you sure?" Jana said. "You weren't going to drop with me until I said *how will I know you're not a cop* and promised to show you Sacha's suicide note."

"Is that true?" Chopper said. Now his face was in the kaleidoscope, too. He was still a polar bear, but with sharper teeth than before.

Clare wanted to run away, but she forced herself back into Lucy mode. Lucy wouldn't be afraid, because she wouldn't see these two as a threat. "Can you guys keep walking? I was having this awesome visual and now your faces are involved."

"Lucy, we're asking you a serious question." Chopper advanced toward Clare, foam dripping from his polar bear fangs.

Fuck. What would Lucy do? "Stop attacking me," Clare said.

"I haven't touched you."

"I mean with words. You guys are invading my trip with mean thoughts. I'm not a cop. Now please shut up." They'd left the village center, were about to cross the road to the parking lot where Chopper kept his truck. Clare looked around for people who would hear her if she screamed. No one. "I'm not going on your stupid sled ride, either."

"Because now you've seen the Jules footage," Jana said. "I'm not sure how safe it is if we let you live."

Clare gasped, involuntarily. "I wasn't even watching the footage. I was sitting there wishing I was naked with Chopper."

Chopper smirked. "You can get naked with me later. Come on, let's cross the street."

He and Jana started crossing, but Clare stayed rooted to the sidewalk. Jana and Chopper didn't even like each other, but suddenly they were acting like best friends?

Jana was laughing hard. "Come on, silly. I was joking. We're not going to kill you. The sledding will be wicked with all this fresh snow."

Chopper came back to Clare. He took her gloved hand and squeezed. "Even if you are a cop, no one's going to kill you. Not while I'm there. You're way too cute to be a corpse."

His touch, even through padded snow gloves, felt hot. And his eyes were not lying. She let him lead her across the street.

Jana was waiting. "I'm sorry. I thought you knew I was joking. I know you're not a cop because you wouldn't have dropped acid, like, for sure. I checked with my brother-in-law who studied forensics in school, and he said there's no way an undercover would be allowed to take a drug like that. They're even supposed to avoid marijuana, if you can believe that."

Clare laughed, because everyone had some friend like that, who wasn't really a cop but loved to pretend they had inside information. "Wow," she said. "That sounds extreme."

Chopper shrugged. "If I was a cop, I'd still drop. I'd be the law, man. Who could tell me not to?"

Jana rolled her eyes. "Can we please just go on this sled ride? I'm burning for some action."

Clare climbed into the truck, wondering if she should be following her first instinct and staying in the village. But the kaleidoscopes had stopped. She felt clear and in control. "Let's do it."

THURSDAY / FEBRUARY 16

FORTY-EIGHT
MARTHA

Martha liked the dark mornings of winter. She liked the moments to herself before the sun came up. She liked the efficient routine of popping a bagel in the toaster, stretching on her pantyhose, and gulping down a coffee before heading to the car that was waiting outside to take her to the airport. What she did not enjoy was having this purposeful solitude interrupted by her phone ringing.

"I have news." Ted was breathless. "The FBI got a call late last night. I mean really late, as in only a couple of hours ago."

Martha was tempted to tell Ted that there were no undecided voters present; he didn't need to create extra drama or urgency.

"Whistler RCMP thinks Sacha was murdered."

Martha's bagel popped in her toaster. She was glad she hadn't eaten it already. "Yesterday you said they found a suicide note."

"They did. But apparently the note is ambiguous. Isn't there someone we can pressure into showing it to us?"

Martha thought of Paul Worthington at the FBI. She'd been pushing her comfort zone even asking for the first favor. If Paul was keeping her in the dark, it would be for the good of the investigation. "No."

"Come on. Worthington?"

Martha didn't like Ted's tone. "I have to trust that Paul is doing his job."

"Really? This is your daughter we're talking about. You should be entitled to read her last words. You should also *want* to."

Martha wondered if Ted was right, if there was something wrong with her for not wanting to probe further.

"I have a friend with the NYPD," Ted said. "I've asked him to keep his ears open . . . maybe to open them up a bit further than usual . . . to hear what he can about Sacha."

Martha felt her eyebrows lift. "You have a friend with the police? What does he do?"

"He's on the enforcement side in Queens. He's pretty respected."

"You mean he's a street cop." Martha wondered when Ted would learn that he'd be a more interesting guy if he stopped trying to cover up his middle-class background.

"He thinks that the way Sacha was murdered . . . well, if it isn't suicide, then it's most likely a serial killer."

"Why?"

"Because of how she was posed. It wasn't random — not an angry lover. It was deliberate . . . someone who enjoys the kill, on some level."

Martha's stomach wanted to hurl its bile all over her kitchen counter at the thought of a killer taking pleasure in taking Sacha's life.

"Are you going to the University of Michigan talk?" Ted asked. "I know it's bad planning — you were just in Detroit for Hillier — but we need to go hard at the youth vote."

"That was my plan." Martha's head had begun to nod involuntarily. She felt like a bobble toy, which made her woozy feeling ten times worse.

"My friend suggests . . . we maybe need to tighten security. He thinks you might be a target."

"A serial killer would have a pattern, no?" Martha pictured Sacha's wrists being lifted, slashed, gently placed back on the snow for her life to bleed out of her.

"My friend thinks maybe the killer has a vendetta. He thinks it might be the blogger."

"Is your friend working with a team of psychologists on a case he's not even assigned to? Or is this simply conjecture from a street cop?" Martha eyed her bagel. Maybe it would be smart to choke some down — soak up a bit of her nausea. "Look, Ted. It's touching that you're going the extra mile for me on this. Really. But I have Secret Service with me at every turn. If they're good enough to keep presidents from being assassinated, they're good enough to keep me safe from a blogger."

FORTY-NINE
CLARE

Clare woke up to loud metal crashing sounds coming from the kitchen. She felt okay. The world seemed to be moving a little more fluidly than usual — walls didn't seem quite so fixed in place; the bright colors seemed to dance within their patterns on the drapes — but she felt solidly sober, and glad to be in control of her own mind. She threw on some sweats and headed into the kitchen.

Jana had her hands in the sink, cleaning the orange-mango juice glasses from the previous night. God, that had been delicious. She glanced at Clare. "Lucy! Thank god you're awake. I need someone to talk to."

"I figured," Clare said, "by the clanging pots, that you didn't want to be alone."

"Did I wake you up? Sorry."

Clare poured herself a coffee and sat down. "Sorry I got weird about the sled ride last night. I'm glad I went — it was a great way to come down from the trip."

Jana smiled. "My fault, really. I shouldn't have messed with your mind on your virgin excursion."

"Yeah, that was evil. Whoa. Why did a lightning bolt just shoot across the kitchen?"

"Tracers." Jana set the last glass in the drying rack and sat at the table with Clare. "You'll see those for a few days. Maybe even years from now, you'll see one."

"What? You said there were no harmful effects."

"Tracers aren't harmful. They're fun. They remind you that life isn't only three dimensions."

Clare hated the thought of her brain being permanently altered. But she had no one to complain to but herself. She was just glad she hadn't blown her cover — and that she hadn't run into Amanda anywhere in the cobblestone labyrinth that was the town.

"Have you watched the rest of the footage from Jules?" Clare asked.

"No. I can't find the memory stick. But we can look for it later. That blogger posted again."

Clare was way more interested in finding the memory stick and downloading the video so she could share that with Amanda. But as Lucy, she said, "For real? Who did he interview this time?"

Jana pointed to herself. She was grinning broadly.

"You?" Clare's shock was genuine. "Did you know you were talking to him?" She was bursting to grab Jana's phone and trace her call log, find out the area code and hopefully other details of the caller.

"He said he was a *New York Times* reporter. But this is so much cooler, don't you think?"

Clare could think of other words, like *scarier.* She leaned in to read.

THE BEST FRIEND
by LORENZO BARILLA

Jana Riley knew Sacha better than anyone.

Or so she says.

According to Jana, they were best friends in college and moved to Whistler together, to have one last year of freedom before springing into their careers.

But when I interviewed Senator Westlake earlier this week, she said Jana was more of an acquaintance than a friend to her daughter -- someone fun to pass the time with, nothing more.

This angered Jana.

"I know the Senator hates me," Jana said. "She couldn't understand my friendship with Sacha because she never understood her daughter in the first place. She wanted Sacha to be someone else -- someone more Republican. Which is funny, because my family's been Republican for generations, and they hate Martha Westlake. They say they'll vote Democarat if she wins the nomination because they can't abide her separating church and state."

I asked if she wanted to elaborate on her family and their politics -- or their religion.

"No," Jana said. "Politics are boring and religion is hypocritical. Which is why I left home."

I asked Jana why she thought Sacha left home -- by which I meant the comforts of her East Coast world -- to be a small-town waitress.

"Sacha thought her mother would be a better person -- happier, more fulfilled, better able to make a real contribution to the world -- if she was out of politics. So she came to Whistler on a mission to destroy her mother politically. It seems to have worked -- though I wish she didn't have to die to win the battle."

When I asked about this mission, Jana said no comment.

I asked Jana if the mission involved drugs. A certain kind of LSD I keep hearing about that's manufactured in the Whistler woods.

"That's just a rumor," Jana told me. "Sacha dropped acid with her stepmother in New York -- a tab called Mountain Snow -- and I guess someone told her it was made up here. I haven't seen it."

A shame that we couldn't trace the drug and close one piece of this nebulous puzzle. Interesting about the stepmother, though. I asked if Jana could tell me more.

"Daisy and Sacha used to be friends. Daisy was cool -- she came skiing with us, she was fun. She was halfway between Sacha's age and her father's, and she didn't try to pretend she was anything else. But things went bad a week or two before Sacha died."

Interesting timing. "Bad how?"

"Daisy told Sacha that her father wasn't really her father, and with a new baby on the way, Daisy was cleaning up her own life. She wanted to cut ties to anyone she'd done drugs with -- and since Sacha wasn't family anymore, that included her."

I asked how Sacha took the news.

"She was gutted, obviously. She tried not to show
it, but you could tell it made her feel homeless
and lonely. She hated her mother, and now she had
no father. And her stepmother -- her one so-called
friend in her family, was hanging her out to dry.
I know Sacha was an adult, but we all need roots. I
think that's why she killed herself."

Clare stared at the screen, blankly trying to take it all in.

"That was cool," she said finally, "the way you gave the blogger just enough truth to make him not suspect you were lying about the Mountain Snow."

"Right?" Jana said. "If there's one thing I learned from Sacha, it was how to make a lie seem like the truth."

"The stepmother seems like a bitch," Clare said. "Were she and Sacha really friends?"

Jana shrugged. "Personally, though, I think Sacha only told Daisy about the smuggling so it would get back to her mom."

"Sacha *told* Daisy?"

Jana nodded. "They thought I was asleep, I guess. But I was in my room. I heard everything."

Clare wanted to ask if anyone else knew Sacha had a leaky mouth. Like, did Jana tell Richie or Chopper that Daisy knew about the smuggling? But since Jana wasn't exactly a supermodel of secret keeping, Clare was pretty sure the interested parties had been told.

At least Clare was starting to develop a credible list of suspects: Jana was insane. Wade was married and seemed to want to stay that way. His wife — Clare should find out more about her. Richie and Chopper had a business to protect. And Norris . . . Clare wished there were a way for her to get closer to him, to talk to him and feel him out. But she couldn't — not as Lucy.

FIFTY
MARTHA

Martha banged on Fraser's apartment door. Yes, she could use the buzzer, but banging felt better. She would need to be rushed through security to make her flight to Michigan on time, but this stop could not be postponed.

Was it true that Sacha thought Martha wanted her to be someone else? If so, she could not have been more wrong. God, what Martha wouldn't give for one more conversation.

Fraser answered the door in his housecoat. Red velvet, like he thought he was some British lord in another decade — or century. Maybe he and Daisy were playing twisted sex games. Martha remembered Fraser liking to get twisted — but that had been years ago.

"I need to speak with your wife." Martha pushed past Fraser and went inside the apartment.

Fraser lifted his eyebrows. "I'll get Daisy."

"Hurry, please. I'm on my way to the airport."

Fraser tossed her an odd grin. To his credit, he walked quickly toward the bedroom.

Martha helped herself to Fraser's coffee and sat at the round kitchen table. While she waited for Daisy to change out of her chambermaid costume, or whatever, Martha looked out the window onto the typical New York scene: more apartments. The Upper East Side wasn't too different, visually, from the Upper West — through various windows, two girls doing lines of cocaine, a naked man walking around his apartment while talking on the phone, a brunette in her forties screaming at her husband. Though she'd grown up in the city, it never failed to baffle Martha how little people in Manhattan cared for privacy. Like having an audience of ten million somehow equaled anonymity.

Martha pulled her iPad from her purse and loaded Lorenzo's latest post.

Daisy shuffled into the kitchen, pouting like a teenager who'd been woken early on a weekend. Fraser was close behind. He'd changed into his work clothes — a suit and a striped green tie.

Martha slid the iPad in front of Daisy.

"What?" Daisy wrinkled her nose, as if she found the device distasteful.

"I'd like you to read this. If you come to any long words, feel free to ask for help."

"Fraser, why did you let her in?" But Daisy picked up the tablet. Her eyes flickered briefly as she read. After a couple of minutes, Daisy shoved Martha's iPad back across the table. "The bitch is obviously lying."

"I don't think so."

"You think I dropped acid with your daughter?"

Martha tilted her head in the briefest of nods.

"This is ridiculous. You believe some random blogger and one of Sacha's drug friends over me? Fraser, talk sense into her."

"This is not some random blogger," Martha said. "This is Lorenzo Barilla."

Fraser looked startled. "The kid Sacha sponsored?"

"Yes. And now he's keen to find Sacha's killer. Unless, of course, he is the killer — a theory one police officer has presented."

Fraser shook his head. "Martha, when are you going to give this up? Sacha killed herself. Even her best friend thinks so."

"Not according to the police. Whistler RCMP issued a press release this morning."

Fraser had obviously not turned on his TV. Which made sense, given his and Daisy's appearances.

"New evidence," Martha said, "points definitively to murder."

Fraser's mouth opened and shut a couple of times. He looked like he didn't know what to address first. He turned to Daisy. "Did you do LSD with Sacha?"

"What do you care?" Daisy said. "She wasn't your daughter."

"Which Daisy also told Sacha." Martha lifted her eyebrows and watched Fraser's eyes grow dark. She remembered that look from the few times he'd taken a stand in their marriage.

Fraser said to Martha, "What if the blogger isn't *actually* Lorenzo?"

"Of course it is. Lorenzo and Sacha maintained correspondence throughout her high school years."

"That wasn't Lorenzo."

Martha froze. "What are you talking about?"

"I don't know if I was right or wrong, but I hated watching Sacha pour her soul into those letters, hearing nothing back from that ungrateful kid she was supporting. After two years — I think Sacha was ten — I told her I'd mail her letters from work to save her the hassle and postage. Only instead of mailing them, I gave them to one of the girls in the secretary pool — nice kid, wanted to be a writer. She read Sacha's letters and responded as Lorenzo."

"But — when Sacha left for university . . . ?"

"'Lorenzo' wrote to say that his address was changing. Sacha began mailing the letters herself, to a post office box I intercepted."

"That's a lot of work, Fraser."

"I helped," Daisy said. "I was Lorenzo through her university years."

"You . . ." Martha hated the thought of Daisy knowing a part of Sacha that Martha never had. It was bad enough that Sacha had confided in Daisy about the drugs. But this . . . this was worse. It was part of Sacha's childhood.

"I asked her for help," Fraser said. "The secretary changed firms, and Daisy's studying psychology — I thought she'd be able to get behind Lorenzo's eyes to write convincing letters. Plus she knows Sacha."

Martha was too angry to comment, or to correct Fraser's verb tense.

Fraser chuckled. "I didn't think they'd keep it up for so long. Do you know they were still corresponding when Sacha was in Whistler?"

"It was good for Sacha," Daisy said. "Even though she went off the rails a bit, and I didn't want her around my baby, I would have continued to write the letters, to keep Sacha connected to her childhood."

Martha ignored Daisy and addressed Fraser. "What about the real Lorenzo? Did he never get Sacha's letters?"

"He got them for the first two years," Fraser said. "If he existed. But since he never wrote back, I don't feel bad for him."

"I'm going to have to tell the FBI. So they know Lorenzo and Sacha weren't truly in contact. And I'm going to mention Daisy's involvement." Martha shot Daisy a dagger-filled look.

"Mention away." Daisy shrugged.

Martha said to Fraser, "God, I hope that awful blogger isn't involved in Sacha's death. I can't believe I sat with him in the airport, confided about Jules."

"Don't shoot yourself, Martha. You loved her. You haven't done anything wrong."

Martha needed to leave. Her car was idling outside. Or maybe driving around the block, by now.

"I miss her," Fraser said. "I miss her sitting at this table telling me I'm a shallow sellout for working on Wall Street and not using my intellect to effect change in a positive way."

Martha snorted. "I miss her telling me I'm a self-interested Republican who wants to rule the world by maintaining the status quo instead of using my influence to change it for good."

"I miss Sacha, too," Daisy said. "She was really fun to party with."

Fraser and Martha cracked up simultaneously.

"Well, she was."

They laughed harder.

"You two don't make any sense." Daisy touched Fraser's arm. "Are you okay, babe?"

Fraser shook off her touch. He said to Martha, "I'm sorry I doubted you about the suicide."

FIFTY-ONE
CLARE

Amanda handed Clare a chunky pottery mug from her vacation rental kitchen. "What part of 'Don't do LSD' was unclear?"

"Um." Clare took the mug. She had no idea how Amanda knew, or if she was only guessing. Maybe the little pink chisel Clare sent had reached Amanda. Clare nearly laughed out loud at that thought — there was no way Amanda was attuned to psychic messaging. Clare nearly laughed again, because at least part of her own brain must still be high to be thinking that way. Thankfully, she kept a straight face through this entire thought process.

"You texted Chopper last night. Would you like me to read you what you said?"

Clare swallowed. Of course Lucy's phone was being monitored.

"Your message was surprisingly coherent."

Clare could lie and say she'd faked the trip, but why? "It's a surprisingly coherent drug. In fact, I'd say LSD is safer than smoking pot."

Amanda perched on an armchair, like she wasn't planning to stay long. "The RCMP is unimpressed, Clare. I'm recommending that you be sent home immediately."

"That's extreme," Clare said, as a tracer shot past the fireplace. "I didn't drop acid for fun — I did it for work."

"Clearly, you didn't. The directive you were given was to *not* drop acid."

"Why are you being so uptight?" Clare realized the question was rude, so she softened her tone. "I took your suggestion to avoid the drug seriously."

"Suggestion."

"Yeah." Clare wasn't going to budge on the issue of who she was working for. She would be friendly and professional — when she remembered to be — but not a drone. "I know it was dangerous, but I assessed things carefully. I thought — still think — that the benefits of dropping Snow were worth it."

Amanda's eyelashes fluttered. "Just because you're dressed like a snowboarder and you smoke pot on your assignment doesn't mean the chain of police command doesn't apply to you. And it certainly doesn't give you creative license with direct orders."

"What police command? I work for the FBI — that's who I take orders from."

"I made it clear that I was your direct liaison on this case. That means you take orders from me."

"Not in my books." Both friendly and professional seemed to have fallen out the window. Clare tried again. "I value your input; you're smart, and I appreciate the ins you created for me. But this whole assignment is creative license — on everyone's part."

"That's not how this works and you know it." Amanda's straight blond hair was dank — because she hadn't washed it yet, or because she was hormonal? Clare decided not to ask.

Clare took a deep breath in and said, "I understand why you said no — and you were right, if this case existed in a test tube, dropping acid would be a mistake. But I'm in, now — they trust me. No one thinks I'm a cop anymore."

Amanda strode over to the fireplace and turned the gas up a setting. Even with dank hair and in yoga pants, she looked more put together than most women Clare knew. "Same old Clare, huh?"

"What does that mean?"

"It means you do what you like, regardless of orders. I can't work like this."

Clare wrinkled her mouth, shifted the conversation to what would hopefully be safer ground. "I see you guys overturned the suicide verdict."

"Yes." Amanda perched again on her chair opposite Clare.

"Why?"

"Inspector Norris came to his senses and agreed with the rest of us that this is looking more like foul play."

The news pinged in Clare's brain in an odd way. "You're not suspicious about his timing? A suicide note gets found, and suddenly he's calling the case murder?"

"Head office is officially accepting the new verdict."

"Sacha was making a documentary," Clare said. "About the drug trade. I watched footage of her crossing the border with a knapsack filled with LSD."

Amanda's eyes narrowed. "Why haven't you told me this before?"

"It's what I came over to tell you. And guess what — I learned it because I dropped acid." Okay, the smug tone wasn't needed — Clare made a self-edit note for the future.

"Really? This isn't some last-ditch attempt to save your job?"

"All I can do is my best. If the RCMP prefers a drone, they should hire one." Maybe not the most conciliatory words Clare could have chosen. "I think it has something to do with those papers I found in Jana's closet. The ones I emailed you. Do you know anything more about those?"

"Tell me about the documentary."

Clare warmed her hands on the mug. She liked the way its lines grooved in her skin, almost like a massage stone. "I could look in Jana's closet again — I was just hoping not to have to, because why take an unnecessary risk?"

"This won't be your case in a few hours, most likely. Those papers mean nothing to you."

Clare breathed. In and out, willing herself to wait a few beats before speaking. "Look, I learned shit last night — and I don't mean transcendental shit, though that was cool, too."

Amanda laughed — bitterly, but Clare thought she heard some mirth mixed in. "What did you learn? About the case, not the universe."

"Can you please just tell me what the papers were?"

"Irrelevant minutes from a classified meeting about the U.S. drug trade."

"Who was meeting?"

Amanda sighed. "Martha Westlake and some South and Central American political leaders. It was just a conversation, Clare. The Latin leaders wanted the U.S. to soften their policy on narcotics — some suggested legalization — and Martha Westlake said no way."

"Why is that classified?"

"I have no idea. Our best guess is that Sacha liberated the pages from her mother's office. We don't know why."

"Well, I can guess." Clare met Amanda's gaze levelly. "Sacha's documentary about the LSD ring was designed to take down her mother."

Amanda pursed her lips. "I'll need you to send me the footage you found."

Clare shook her head. "I think someone lifted the memory stick from our place last night. Either Chopper or Richie."

"Maybe if you hadn't been high, you might have seen who took it. Or even better — you might have taken the memory stick yourself."

Clare set down her coffee and met Amanda's eyes. She couldn't believe she was being dropped from the case because of one bad decision — a decision that had yielded good results. "No wonder the rest of the world laughs at the RCMP. You prefer to dwell on protocol, rather than clues. I'll go pack."

"Your dismissal is not official yet. You're still expected to perform until you're formally let go."

"Fuck off, Amanda. And then take a look at yourself — you'll see that you're ridiculous." Clare regretted the words immediately.

Amanda's calm face didn't crack even an inch. "Why do you hate authority so much?"

Clare stood up. "Because it always lets me down."

FIFTY-TWO
RICHIE

"Step right up," Richie said to Norris inside his pristine white condo. "I have the deal of a lifetime, a one-of-a-kind offer. And the price is right. A mere ten thousand dollars."

Richie didn't like this part of his job, but when someone had to be pushed around, you couldn't shy away from it. In his pocket, Richie's phone was recording.

"Would you like to see what's on this TV? Would you like to know what can be yours for this low, low price?"

Norris' voice was calmer than his trembling body betrayed. "Why the hell are you talking like a carnie?"

Richie didn't know. His best guess was nerves. He continued his patter: "I have exclusive video footage taken from inside a teddy bear. That's right, never-been-seen-before footage from a bear. And this can be yours for a mere ten thousand dollars."

"I don't have ten thousand dollars."

"Of course you do." Richie dropped the act. "Me and Chopper gave you exactly ten grand two days ago."

"I wired that money to a colleague in exchange for the FBI agent's name."

Richie's hand brushed the outside of the pocket where his phone was. Norris' last line was choice material for the recording.

"Show me what you have, Lebar."

"Nah," Richie said. "I think I'll sell this footage to someone else. Or maybe just donate it. The RCMP might be interested. Or the FBI." Richie put a finger on his chin. "Maybe even the DEA."

Norris stomped across Richie's white carpet. At the club chair, he turned to face Richie with more distance. "We both know you're not climbing into bed with any of those organizations. Why are you making this a fight?"

Richie shrugged. "I'm pissed off. I didn't like the way you extorted my cash the other day. Chopper said to go along with it, but I don't think it's cool."

"I agree," Norris said. "It wasn't cool. I'm sorry."

"Come again." Richie wasn't ready for that one.

Norris' top lip was quivering. "Can you just show me the footage? I'm assuming this is Sacha's documentary. Chopper told me. I'll get you your money back somehow."

Fuck, Richie actually felt bad for him. He frowned gently at Norris. "How about you don't owe me the money, and I take it out in trade?"

Norris sank down on Richie's couch, his body seeming to shrink into the big white cushions. "What kind of trade?"

"Make this run to the States."

Norris eyed Richie pleadingly. "Anything but that."

Richie kissed his lips. Maybe Norris would change his tune once he saw the first clip Richie had selected.

Richie pressed a button on his computer and Sacha's face came alive on the fifty-four-inch screen.

Sacha looked at the camera, lifted one corner of her mouth. "Hi, Jules. You ready for a boring few hours? We're going into my boss's office. We're going to listen to some conversations. Actually, *you're going to listen. I'm going to drop you off and make myself scarce for the night.*"

Richie pressed fast-forward for about a minute. Sacha left, and

Wade came in, followed by Norris. Richie could see the offscreen Norris biting his lip as he turned the recording back to regular play speed.

Onscreen, Wade pulled an envelope from his top drawer. "This is for you. Eight grand this week."

Norris smirked. "I could quit my day job on the cash we're pulling. Too bad it's my day job that makes it all possible."

"Drink?" Wade pulled a whiskey bottle from his bottom drawer, along with two tumblers. "This is nicer than what I have out there on the shelf."

Richie froze the frame on Wade and Norris clinking glasses. "You want me to keep going? Or you get the gist?"

On Richie's couch, Norris seemed frozen in place — frozen and shaking.

Richie was going in harder. "What I also have — now, this is just for posterity, I don't expect to have to use it — is the three of us on tape in Chopper's cabin. I had my phone recording the whole time we were talking."

"Why?" Norris' mouth hung open. "Aren't we . . . on the same side?"

"We are." Fuck, Richie hated strong-arming. "But you haven't been playing your end so nice. I need you to take the Snow across the border. You do that for me, I'll not only forget about the ten grand and pay you the fifty we talked about, I'll give you all of Sacha's recordings. As far as I know, I have the sole, exclusive footage. I'm assuming you've gone through her computer."

"We have. It's clean."

"You also might want to check out Sacha's laptop. Currently in use as Jana's laptop. That information is free, but please don't tell Jana I told you."

Norris stood and walked over to Richie. He kicked the white carpet with his shoe, leaving a gray mark. "I'm going to need to confiscate your phone."

Richie chuckled. He was mad about the gray mark. "Yeah."

FIFTY-THREE
CLARE

"Where are you?" Clare asked Noah. She was sitting against a tree with her snowboard on just off a ski run. "I'm at home."

"What's that banging sound?" Clare watched a family skiing by. The father leading the way, kind of dweebishly. Two little kids with earnest looks on their faces — the taller one confident, the smaller one snowplowing and frowning. The mother, in all the right gear including a perky ponytail poking out from under her helmet, keeping up the rear.

"Huh?" Noah said. "Oh, that's Stacy. She's making popcorn. On the stove — retro, huh?"

Retro wasn't the word that leapt to Clare's mind. "Who's Stacy?"

"My ex."

"Oh." Clare had heard about Stacy. She was one of those Upper East Side girls who'd been going for pedicures with girlfriends since junior high. Noah said he didn't dig manicured princesses, that he found them too high-maintenance. But Clare wasn't sure she could trust a word Noah said anymore.

"She's bummed because her boyfriend dumped her. I invited her over to watch chick flicks."

"You never watch chick flicks with me."

"Because you hate romantic comedy. Rambo is too soft for you."

That didn't feel like a compliment. Clare wondered if Noah would prefer to be dating Tiffany, the girly cover role she'd been playing when they'd met on the poker tour.

"I guess you can't talk, then, about your end of the job." Clare looked out onto the snow-capped panorama and wished she could stay in Whistler longer. It was a clear day, which sucked for the snow because it made the hill hard and kind of icy, but the glistening sun made the mountains in the distance dance with a beauty Clare wanted to reach out and touch. She suddenly didn't miss New York at all. The buildings were too gray and the pace was too hurried. How could anyone even catch their breath in a place like that?

"I could take a walk," Noah said. "You okay?"

"I'm fine," Clare said. "I mean, no, I'm not fine at all, but what do you care?"

"You are such hard work." Noah sighed. "Hey, Stacy, I've got to take this work call. I'll be back in, like, ten minutes. Don't start the movie without me."

A female voice said something, and Clare heard Noah's thin apartment door shut behind him.

"Okay, I'm in my stairwell, walking down to street level so the elevator doesn't cut off the call. You going to tell me what's up?"

Clare slid her snowboard edge back and forth across a patch of snow. "I dropped acid last night and I'm probably being sent home."

Noah laughed. "Are you serious?"

"Yes, and before you get all judgy, the situation called for it."

"I'm sure it did. It's just — you won't even smoke a joint with me."

"Because it messes up my head. Acid's different, though. It's like . . . you can see so much more of the world."

"Oh yeah? Are you Timothy Leary now? You planning to come home and drop every weekend?"

Clare smirked. "Once was enough. It's, like, such a downer the next day. I feel like slitting my wrists."

"Like Sacha."

"Shit. Yeah. Bad metaphor."

Through the phone, Clare heard a car horn honking — most likely an impatient cab — and suddenly she missed New York again.

Noah was quiet for a few seconds before saying, "You think it could have been suicide, then?"

"No." Clare told Noah about the video she'd seen. "Sacha thought someone wanted to kill her."

"She say who?"

"No. But honestly, it could be anyone here. She told her stepmother she was smuggling drugs — and her friends here knew she'd opened her mouth. Chopper, Richie, or Norris might have wanted to silence her permanently. That blogger could release a new suspect interview every day for a week, and they'd all be good candidates in my eye."

"So the blog's hit Whistler, huh?"

"Um, yeah." Clare found the segue strange, but answered anyway. "Everyone reads it. Have you thought about finding this Lorenzo guy? Or do we already know where he lives?"

"We already know," Noah said.

"He must have really hated Sacha."

"Lorenzo? Why?"

"Wouldn't you?" Clare thought the dynamic was obvious. "Some rich kid decides your life is so flawed she needs to send you her allowance?"

"Sacha didn't decide Lorenzo needed help. It was some Christian foundation."

Clare pushed a strand of hair back under her helmet. It came loose again immediately. "You wouldn't get it. You went to private school, your dad's a surgeon — no one ever saw you as a charity case."

"People saw you that way?" Noah sounded surprised.

"At school, they looked at us trailer kids like we were plotting to steal their lunch money."

"So did you?"

"Fuck off."

Noah laughed. "What's the big deal? You came out of the experience strong enough."

"Exactly. And if a little rich girl had come along and tried to rescue me from my so-called poverty, pretty sure I would have punched her in the mouth before I took her charity."

"Yeah, I can see you doing that. But Sacha's money wasn't buying Lorenzo new toys. It was for food, health care, education — things you Canadians take for granted as your god-given rights."

"Most first-world countries consider those rights." But Clare didn't feel like arguing politics.

"What's wrong, Clare?" As in, Noah didn't have all day; he had to go watch chick flicks with Stacy.

"I don't know. I'm feeling kind of lost."

"Why?" Noah's voice became gentler.

"I guess I screwed up. Amanda hates me."

"Do you care? I thought you didn't like Amanda."

"I don't. Well, not really. I don't know why I feel lost. Maybe it's just drug aftermath."

"Hey — did Amanda tell you, or maybe this came in after you talked to her — some interesting news on Norris."

"I already know he's dirty." Clare glanced at the trees to make sure no one was hiding there listening.

"But what if he isn't?"

"Huh?"

"Norris contacted the RCMP about half an hour ago with a detailed list of the criminal activity in town. The acid manufacturer, the drug dealer, the bar owner who's been laundering the cash. He detailed Sacha's involvement."

"So? We already know all that. All this means is he's decided to sell out his friends."

"He says he's been playing both sides. He forwarded correspondence he's been having with the DEA."

Clare felt her shoulders sink. All this information made her feel like she was underwater, and her arms were too tired to swim. Maybe Amanda was right — maybe they shouldn't give her too much information. Still, she said, "If Norris had been playing both sides, someone else in the RCMP would have known about it."

"Maybe," Noah said. "There's a drug run on Monday that he's planning to make. He's looping in authorities because he thinks this will bust people from both sides of the border."

"So can we talk to the DEA? Find out if he's for real?"

"Paul Worthington is on it now."

"Big guns," Clare said.

"Big case."

"Hm. Well, you better get back to Stacy, I guess."

"I wish I could be there with you. You sound like you need a hug."

"Don't worry. I have someone here to take care of that." *Damn.* Why did Clare ruin a good phone call with a single low blow? She missed Noah. But she was freaked out by what Amanda had told her, about the girl on the boat.

"You want me to say I'm happy for you?"

"No," Clare said.

They were both quiet. Noah broke the silence, kind of. "Okay, well . . ."

"Yeah. Bye."

Clare hung up and rode down the hill. She was awkward on her board. She fell a lot. The hard snow didn't help — it made falling much more painful. She started becoming afraid every time it got a little bit steep, so she stuck with the green runs and edged down as slowly as she could. She felt alone, abandoned, like if she were to ride off one of Whistler's many cliffs, no one on Earth would really miss her.

If Sacha had done enough of this drug, had enough LSD lingering in her system, maybe she felt an amplified version of this emotion that was gnawing at Clare. With all the real shit going on in Sacha's life, maybe the world did look bleak enough for her to want to leave it.

Maybe the killer Sacha feared, in her note and in her video, was herself.

FIFTY-FOUR
MARTHA

Ted rushed up to Martha as she was about to walk onto the Battle Creek town hall meeting stage. His voice was tinnier than usual. Maybe he'd been ingesting aluminum shavings from his Red Bull cans. "The FBI called with a change of plans."

"Again?" Martha felt chai-flavored milk froth on her upper lip and dabbed it off with her finger. She slipped off her microphone and made sure the switch was turned off.

"They're pulling the Whistler operative."

What? Martha would get on the phone with Paul Worthington as soon as this production was over. If his favor had expired, so had her need to politely let him do his job.

"It's good news, I think." Ted had the decency to soften his voice, to take the tin out. "Now that the RCMP is treating this as a murder investigation, the FBI is confident Sacha's killer will be caught. So their efforts would be superfluous, even invasive."

That didn't sound like any FBI Martha had ever worked with. They loved invasive. She double-checked her microphone before saying, "Did they say if their operative had found anything while he was in place?"

"No. They're being irritatingly tight-lipped."

"Better than loose. Has your . . . other friend learned anything?" She disconnected the microphone from the wire, just in case. "The cop?"

"He's not sure."

"So there's something."

Ted frowned. "Maybe we should ignore the investigation, now that it seems to be proceeding in a good direction."

Martha's head throbbed. She could take an Advil, but there was no point. The headache would just be there waiting in four to six hours.

"You're on in five minutes," Ted said.

"So I have four to talk. What did your source say?"

Ted smoothed his suit jacket. "He thinks maybe Kearnes was involved."

"Geoffrey?" Martha said Kearnes' first name in full without thinking. God, it would be brutal irony if he had anything to do with Sacha's murder. "Involved how?"

Ted looked at her, like *Do I have to say it out loud?* "Involved in arranging the murder."

Martha nodded to the interviewer who was waiting for her onstage. She returned the woman's smile and removed the smile to face Ted. "Is this more speculation, or does your friend have any facts?"

"He found some phone calls from Kearnes' campaign office to Whistler and Washington State. Where the, um, drugs were being smuggled into."

"Washington State is hardly a surprise — the caucus is two weeks away. But Whistler? Have you told the FBI?"

"I will," Ted said. "You want that, right?"

"Of course I want that. Maybe this will make them think it's worth their precious resources to keep their man in Whistler."

"Okay."

"I have to get onstage. Was there anything else?"

Ted nodded. "You've fallen to last in the Michigan polls. The legalization platform seems to be having purely negative impact. I think we should blow open the story about Sacha and the smuggling — make it clear that you're not pro-drug, not at all. That your desire to get creative with policy is actually you fighting harder for the eradication of drugs from our society."

"We need to talk about this now?" Martha lifted her eyebrows once more at the host, who was standing onstage tapping her wrist.

"Christy and Melissa wrote a blog post that's ready to take it live. All it needs is your final edit, so when we post it will be in your voice. The angle will be a mother's remorse for not knowing what was going on in her daughter's life."

Martha's neck and shoulders joined her head with their tension pain. "Look, I understand that Washington culture forces people barely out of college to think faster than you're emotionally capable of. But please don't turn my daughter into political leverage."

Ted was silent.

"You're a smart kid," Martha said, one foot on the stairs to the stage. "Hell, when I was your age, I had to fight sexism *and* ageism, and I'm sure I was twice the brat you are."

Ted's small voice exploded out of him. "Your career is my life. I wake up at five-thirty every morning and I've often fallen asleep with my head on my keyboard because I'm that devoted to your success."

Shit. Martha had been way too harsh. Just like she'd been too harsh with Sacha all her life. She didn't mean to be unkind; it was the way things came out of her mouth, like she was missing the softening filter that everyone else seemed to have been given at birth. Which was strange, because on camera, she found it easy to turn on the charm.

"Send me the blog post," she said. "I'll read it, but my strong guess is that I won't agree to publish. Okay? I'm on." Martha climbed the stairs to join the event host onstage.

FIFTY-FIVE
WADE

I n his claustrophobic office, Wade shook his head at Norris, then at his computer screen. Today's blog post was odd.

```
CHARITY AND RESENTMENT
by LORENZO BARILLA

I spent my childhood hating Sacha Westlake. I needed
her money. I did not need colorful letters filled
with stories about Central Park and snobby school-
girls and Jules the Bear.

For two years, she wrote me. I was learning English
so I could write back with intelligence, to tell her
I was not a charity case. I need not have bothered
-- her letters stopped coming two weeks after my
twelfth birthday. The money still came, but Sacha's
heart had moved on to more interesting causes than
poor Lorenzo Barilla.

I came to America to get my revenge. I planned to
```

become so wealthy in this Land of Opportunity that I
could squish Sacha Westlake with my power, then give
her a helping hand up. Show her how that felt.

But when I arrived in New York, she was dead.

I instantly hated myself for all those years of rage.
Sacha had been kind to me, and I was so self-obsessed
I could not see it.

I wanted to turn back time, to write back even in
imperfect English, to say thank you to this sweet
little girl who shared her allowance and her world
with me, in letters.

But I could not -- cannot -- because some senseless
idiot killed her.

My penance is to find Sacha Westlake's killer and
bring that person to justice.

"This make any sense to you?" Wade asked Norris, who was still staring blankly at the screen.

Norris shook his head, sipped coffee from the ceramic mug Wade had given him. "The kid was right the first time. People like Sacha think they can fix the world's problems by patting their heads and throwing money at them. They consider themselves the ruling class. Like we commoners couldn't possibly know what's good for us."

Wade poured some brandy into his coffee, held the bottle for Norris, who lifted one shoulder and said, "Why the fuck not?" before setting his cup down on Wade's desk. "God, this is bad."

"I know. Sorry. I had to switch to a cheaper coffee. Want some more brandy?"

"I don't give a shit about the coffee. I'm swimming in fucking chaos, if you haven't noticed. Actually, fuck swimming. I'm drowning in chaos."

Norris wasn't usually metaphorical, not at all. It worried Wade.

"Did you . . ." Wade wasn't sure how to say this. For better or worse, the booze eased the question out of him. "Did you have something to do with Sacha's murder?"

Norris' eyes shot wide open. "God, no!"

Wade relaxed. "Okay. Then it really can't be that bad."

Norris said, "I'm going to run the Snow down to Seattle. I don't feel like I owe Chopper that — and I certainly don't owe Richie that, like he keeps trying to tell me I do — but I know I screwed this up. If I leave them with their shit sorted, I'll feel okay about things."

"Leave them?" Wade peered at his friend.

"I'm taking my family out of here. Permanently. Will you be okay?"

Wade didn't know why the thought of Norris leaving Whistler made him feel orphaned. "Of course," Wade said. "I'll be fine."

FIFTY-SIX
CLARE

Amanda sat across from Clare, staring her down like they were strangers on opposite teams. Across the playing field of the orange shag carpet, the blond wood coffee table sat between them like a referee. It wasn't even three hours since their previous meeting, but apparently all had been decided.

"You're officially being sent home." Amanda closed her sentence with a brief nod.

"Cool. I'll go pack." Clare matched her even tone, tried to replicated the nod.

"Cool?" Amanda's eyebrows lifted. "Does your job mean so little to you?"

"My job means everything to me. But I'll take this up with Bert, or someone reasonable, once I'm back in New York."

"What makes you think that your job in New York will be waiting for you?"

"Because Bert will hear my side before he makes a rash decision. And by hear, I mean he'll listen to it and process it like an intelligent human, not a robot who needs a rule book to get out of bed each morning."

"I don't . . ."

"And when he hears my reasoning," Clare said, "he might agree or disagree — he might be damn mad, who knows? — but he'll be more interested in why I dropped LSD than in the fact that it went against the bylaws of the job."

"This isn't about . . ." Amanda's jaw was moving wildly, like her words were stuck in there, trying to escape.

"What *is* it about, Amanda? What did I do that's so unforgivable?"

Amanda shook her head. "You could be so good at this job — so good — if you just opened your mind and saw that the rules are here to help you."

"Oh wow, that's funny. You telling me to open my mind. Are you saying you wish I hadn't found Sacha's documentary?"

"Of course not." Amanda folded her hands gently in her lap. "I'm saying I'm not equipped to handle you."

Clare wanted to tell Amanda that she was a human, not a horse. Instead she said, "I think we work together well. We closed the poker case together, and we've made great progress here." Clare couldn't believe she'd just pleaded a case *for* working with Amanda.

"It's not you, Clare. It's me."

Clare did her best not to laugh at the line that made her feel like she was in a teenage sitcom.

"You're right," Amanda said. "I need rules, I need order. That's why I'm an excellent administrator, an okay handler, and I could never be an operative like you — you dive into a world where it's all so muddy, and you have to make it clear."

Clare wrinkled her mouth.

"So no hard feelings?" Amanda said.

"You're still dropping me?"

"Look, maybe one day, when you've matured and I've mellowed, we'll find some common ground on a case. But right now . . . we'll just be at cross-purposes. Conflicts like this will arise again and again."

"But . . . this is going to mess up my career big time. Paul Worthington is watching the case. I know in a way it's my fault if I'm leaving, but can't you just give me one more chance?"

"Right. I said you're officially being sent home. In fact — and unofficially — you're staying."

"What?" A tracer went by, as if to remind Clare that everything was fucked.

"The recording you took from the bar impressed my colleagues. They've decided that — gross negligence aside — you're still an asset to the case because of all the inroads you've made." Amanda's jaw clenched and unclenched as she spoke, like she couldn't decide if she was still angry. "We're not sure why Inspector Norris has suddenly changed his verdict from suicide to murder, but the timing works perfectly for us to make a strategic shift."

Clare leaned forward in her comfortable plaid armchair. "What's the shift?"

"We've told Norris that the FBI is pleased with his changing the investigation to murder and no longer feels the need for their agent to be here — which Norris will believe, because I'll be back in Ottawa instead of here in a handler capacity." Amanda brushed a strand of her straight blond hair behind her ear. It was fuller now; she must have washed it in the three hours since Clare had seen her. "Clare ... I ..."

"What?"

"I've liked a lot about working with you. I wish this could have gone differently."

"I liked you, too, sometimes." Clare stood up, trying not to let Amanda see how shaken she was by what was really only a professional parting of ways. "I should get back to work."

FIFTY-SEVEN
RICHIE

Chopper exhaled slowly and passed Richie the last of the joint. Richie hadn't been smoking lately — too damn paranoid — but he felt chill in Chopper's cabin. He liked the way nighttime folded itself around the place, like some blanket he could reach out and hold onto while sucking his thumb.

He'd been dumb to confront Norris. No matter how Richie played it back for himself in his head, he couldn't get a version where his carnival act wasn't a mistake. Still, Norris had agreed to make the run — so technically Richie had achieved a good result.

"You're *sure* Norris said yes." Chopper leaned into his coffee table, more intense than usual.

"Yeah," Richie said. "But the thing is . . . I kind of had to threaten him."

Chopper looked half-amused and half-alarmed. "With what?"

"I played a clip from Sacha's documentary. Scared him into thinking he better be on our side until the end."

"Must have freaked him right out."

"I also told him I have some conversations recorded — him and us in the cabin last night, to be specific."

Chopper shook his head. "I don't like blackmail, Rich. Yeah, we're up to our waists in this shit, we have to scramble for any shovel we can find. But Stu Norris is my friend."

"Here." Richie reached in his jeans pocket and pulled out the memory stick. "I've downloaded Sacha's videos onto my computer. You should do the same — and password-protect it, in case one of our places gets raided. Then store the stick somewhere good."

Chopper waved the small black and red memory stick in the air. "Anything here that could put us away? You and me, I mean."

"Yup."

"So why do we want this info around? My vote is to stomp the shit out of the memory stick and bury its remains deep on Cougar Mountain."

"I think Norris could turn on us," Richie said. "We need ammo if that happens."

"I've known him over twenty years, man. He won't fuck us over." Chopper stubbed out the joint in a clay ashtray that was shaped like a bear claw. "He's being weird because he's paranoid. Thinks his bosses know his every move. He should have never got bent — his mind is too weak for this shit."

"I should email the audio recordings to you, too. In case something happens to my phone. Norris tried to confiscate it today. Like I was going to hand it over because he told me to." Richie fished in his jacket pocket for his phone. "Fuck."

"Already gone?"

Richie walked over to his parka hanging by Chopper's front door. He unzipped every pocket and came up dry. "Little fucker must have picked my pocket. I knew he was slippery, but I never thought he was a street thief."

"You did kind of threaten his career."

Richie felt in his jeans pockets again. "*Damn.* I should have watched that chihuahua like a hawk."

"Not to mix animal metaphors."

"A hawk could kill a chihuahua." Richie spread his arms and came down for the kill on one of Chopper's couch cushions, which he held up and started shaking fast so it looked like Norris. "Gimme your phone; I'm gonna make that fucker pay."

Chopper grabbed his phone off the coffee table and clutched it tightly. "What are you going to say?"

"I'm gonna tell him I already emailed you a recording."

"Fuck off. Then he'll steal my phone, too. You want to antagonize Norris, or you want him eating out of your hand?"

Chopper leaned back on his couch and basked like a cat in the moonlight. His phone beeped. He looked at it and smiled broadly.

"Booty call?" Richie tried to grin, but his heart was beating overtime. What else was on his phone? At least it had an unlock password. But Norris had a cop shop at his disposal. He probably knew how to crack a stupid four-digit code.

"I'm starting to dig this chick." Chopper's smile spread wider.

"Not Lucy again. You've known her four days."

"Maybe that's why I still like her. I'm gonna hit the trail, go pick her up in town."

Richie looked out the window at the black night. He felt a sudden urge to get back to the village where the action was. This isolation could eat your brain, if you let it. "I'll ride down with you."

FRIDAY / FEBRUARY 17

FIFTY-EIGHT
WADE

"Georgia, I have to level with you." Wade had played out various scenarios and this had won out.

"Now? I'm leaving for work in less than five minutes." Georgia froze where she had finished putting in one earring. The other gold hoop lay on the kitchen counter next to her purse and car keys. "Wait, is this about your affair?"

"I wish it was as simple as an affair."

Wade noticed Georgia eying the clock on the microwave. Five to seven. She reached out for her half-finished coffee and took a slow swallow.

He reached for the pot and refilled the cup for her.

"If I don't take Richie's deal — if I have to close Avalanche — I'm worried that I'll end up in jail."

"Jail?" Georgia's eyes bugged. She patted her smooth wavy hair, as if feeling for flyaways that weren't there. "What have you done?"

"I feel like an idiot." *Lie with the truth*, Sacha had once said. "Chopper asked me for a favor a year ago. He's been my buddy forever. I felt like I couldn't say no."

"Oh god." Georgia pulled out a stool from the counter. "Tell me you haven't been laundering money for Chopper's drug deals."

Wade hung his head. He was also kind of shocked. "How did you guess?"

"It's only the most obvious crime for a bar owner with drug dealer friends. I'm surprised the cops haven't figured it out, if it took me three seconds."

"The cops — well, Norris — he's involved, too."

"Does his wife know?"

"No, and please don't tell her. He didn't want to get involved, it's just that Chopper's so persuasive . . . Look, I know I should have let Avalanche go long ago, before your parents invested, when it was clear it would never be profitable."

"But . . ."

"But I guess I was clinging to the stupid dream of turning it into a music haven, reviving Avalanche Nights and getting other local musicians playing there."

"You never took one step in that direction."

"I let the stress get to me." Wade wondered if she'd recognize these as the lines she'd been spouting to him, the little criticisms she'd worked into her sentences every day for the past few years. "I made some colossally bad decisions. And I've been drinking too much."

"You can say that again." But she did seem relieved to hear him say the words.

Wade smiled thinly. "Here's the thing: Revenue Canada is suspicious now. They've just told me they're going to audit."

"And they'll find this?"

"Richie's been on the books as a manager. If he buys in as a partner, that legitimizes his role."

"And Chopper? And Norris?"

"Chopper's getting paid, too. He'll have to come in and do a few shifts to prove he works there. No big deal. Norris has been off the books — cash only."

"I don't like this."

"I don't either. I've been careful with the accounting software — justifying everything as well as I could."

"So why is Revenue Canada suspicious?"

"I don't know." Wade was starting to worry himself, until he remembered the audit was a lie. "Maybe the same reason you were."

"I don't like this, Wade. It makes things worse, not better. I'd rather close the bar than let Richie in as a partner, especially if he's been complicit in all this . . . activity."

"If we close now, it looks really suspicious. Avalanche turns a profit, gets told it's being audited, then suddenly closes? Auditors are pencil-pushing rule junkies. Their biggest thrill in life is busting someone who's been breaking the rules. Their eagle eyes would be on me in five seconds."

"I guess I see what you mean." Georgia gave Wade a lopsided smile. It was actually pretty cute. "If I sign with Richie, will you go to rehab?"

"Rehab? For what?"

"For your drinking."

Wade sighed. Georgia had never understood the bar owner's life-style. "I can stop anytime. With Richie working nights, I won't drink half as much."

"That's my offer," said Georgia. "My signature for AA. I'm frankly petrified to be in business with a criminal, but if it will get you back to me in one sober piece — and keep you out of jail — it's a risk I'm willing to take."

"Fine," Wade said. He could go to a few meetings and stop. "Deal."

FIFTY-NINE
CLARE

Clare knocked on the door of the room where Amanda told her Bert would be staying. Seemed like a nice hotel — not too ritzy, a clean alpine look, smack in the heart of Whistler Village. Clare would love to be staying so close to the lifts, not to have to drag her snowboard on a fifteen-minute walk each morning.

But instead of Bert opening the door, Noah answered.

Clare did her best to control the violence inside her. She wasn't ready to see Noah. She hadn't decided how she felt about him killing that girl, and she certainly wasn't ready to address it. Plus — and she hated this part of herself — she was jealous. She wanted the case to herself. Noah was a better cop than her, in all the traditional ways. If they solved this together, Bert would think it was more to his credit than Clare's.

"Seriously?" Clare heard herself say. She was on autopilot; she didn't bother wishing she was being nicer. "Bert brought you with him? Are you his new little acolyte?"

"Come in, it's great to see you." Noah shut the door behind Clare. "Where's Bert?"

"No hug?" Noah reached for Clare, pulled her close against his body.

Clare returned the hug limply. "Where's Bert?" she said into his shoulder.

"New York."

"No." Clare's body slackened even more against Noah's. "You cannot be my handler. There's, like, no chance I'll answer to you."

"We're still equals, don't worry." Noah pulled away, his eyes moist and present.

"Is Bert okay?" Clare realized this should have been her first question.

"He's fantastic. He thought it made more sense for your contact here to be a studly young guy than a middle-aged man. So we can hang out in public if we have to. Or you could spend the night here." Noah's voice was flat, like he now knew Clare wasn't going to jump at that chance.

"I already have a studly guy here I spend nights with," Clare said, to confirm it for him.

"Is there a business connection, or are you with this guy for pure pleasure?"

"Did you bring your ex-girlfriend, or did her chick flicks not fit in your suitcase?"

Noah sighed. "For someone who gets along so well with subjects on assignments, you can be a real prickly bitch to your friends in real life."

"Is that why you liked Tiffany better?"

Noah walked toward his kitchenette — because of course he was staying somewhere great while Clare was stuck with a slob psycho roommate. "Would you like a beer? A Coke? I can make tea or coffee."

"Coke."

Noah took two red cans from the fridge. "Why would you say I liked Tiffany better?"

"Because my Tiffany costume included makeup and designer jeans."

"If I liked you better then, it's because you were nicer to me, not because of what you were wearing."

Clare took a long glug of soda. The sugary bubbles felt great against her throat. "You know how horrible it is to be with someone who always talks about your relationship like it could end any day?"

Noah sat on the brown fabric sofa. "As horrible as being in love with a woman who gets pleasure from sleeping around in her land of make-believe."

"You're not in love with me." Clare pulled out a dinette chair and sat, too.

Noah met her eye hard. All Clare wanted was for him to contradict her. Instead he said, "We're here to work. You can tell people I'm your ex-boyfriend who's followed you to town to torture you."

"They couldn't come up with a cover story?"

"They did. I'm Lucy's ex. From Toronto."

"Oh, good one. You think you can pretend to come from somewhere so backwater? If you're talking to anyone, Toronto does have the Internet now. Running water, too."

Noah grabbed a handful of popcorn from a bowl on the coffee table. "Bert's worried that you're not safe."

"Of course I'm not safe. There's a killer in town. And you know there are probably GMOs in that popcorn you're eating, which is almost as scary." Clare had clearly been spending too much time with Jana — she was actually beginning to care about this natural food stuff. "Why is Bert extra worried?"

"I guess because the RCMP can't keep their damn mouths shut. My opinion is they should pull you, your cover's so precarious. But I don't call the shots."

"Anyway," Clare said. "I guess it's good you're here. You can get better interviews for your blog."

"What?" Noah's eyes shot wide open. "How did you figure out I was the blogger?"

"I recognize your cocky style." Clare rolled her eyes and held them upward. The ceiling had ugly yellow water stains.

"Shit. I tried to add stilted grammar here and there — so it would look like English was my second language."

"The real tell was when you wrote the piece on charity and resentment — you know, right after our conversation on the same topic. What if the real Lorenzo comes forward?"

"Can't. He died in a gang fight when he was thirteen."

"And the foundation kept taking Sacha's money?" Clare wasn't sure why she was outraged — or even surprised.

"They say it's not their policy to turn down donations. They redirected Sacha's money to the administration of other children's accounts."

"I'd like to go undercover in that organization one day. I'd love to expose their hypocrisy."

Noah smiled. "Don't like to choose your battles, do you? Just want to fight them all."

Clare wanted to cross the living room floor to sit beside Noah on the couch, to lean into that smile and return one of her own. Instead, she said, "What are you blogging for? Are you trying to get leads through the site, or unsettle the criminals?"

"Both," Noah said. "Bert said this method sometimes works — like a tip hotline, kind of, but for the younger crowd. People Sacha's age."

"Have you been given lots of leads?"

"A lot of random oddballs, like *Maybe Jules is made of* LSD and *I met Sacha once, in another life in Mexico.*"

"Why Lorenzo? Why not some guy no one's heard of?"

"We want Sacha's parents following this. They're both still suspects. Even if they know Lorenzo died, they'll wonder about someone blogging under his name."

"You think the blog could work against you? Spook the killer into bailing the country or killing again?"

"It could if we're not careful," Noah said. "Bert's vetting each post and so is Paul Worthington. Worthington's actually a really smart guy."

"You're working directly with Worthington?" Clare was annoyed to find she was even more jealous.

"You want to blog with me? Help me unsettle these people into showing us their colors?"

"Really?" Clare felt herself smiling for the first time since she'd arrived at Noah's hotel.

"Yeah. I think it would be fun to do this together. Maybe even stop us fighting."

Clare exhaled. "I'd love to."

"Good. Who should we interview next?"

"I think Richie."

"You like him for the killer?"

Clare tapped a finger against her lip. "No. I'm liking Jana, Chopper, Wade — maybe Norris, but I haven't figured out a way to be in contact with him. Ditto for Georgia — I've seen her at my work, but it would look weird if I got too chatty with the boss's wife."

"So why Richie?" Noah asked.

"I like Richie for the guy who stole the memory stick from Jules."

SIXTY
RICHIE

Richie pushed off from the top of the hill. The madness in town couldn't touch the magic of the mountaintop. He looked out at the neighboring peaks of windswept snow and felt like he was on top of the world. "Gangsta's Paradise" was on his iPod — since his phone had been stolen, Richie was stuck with his playlist from a few years back. But it was cool; he could groove out to this until Chopper got his phone back from Norris.

He kicked off with his snowboard. Man, nothing felt as good as looking down an empty run and feeling the hill with his legs, with his whole damn body. Conditions were crap — gray sky, and the snow packed hard like a bullet. But it was the right kind of snow for riding hard. Richie carved some tight edges and before he knew it, he was more than halfway down the hill at the Mid-Station.

He hooked onto Lower Fantastic — an easy blue run — and smiled at the whole damn world.

Fuck, and all at once Richie knew he must be drugged — his head was lagging and the view looked very foggy.

But what had he taken? And when? Suddenly Richie was sitting on the hill, staring at the snow and the trees, wondering why it wasn't cold.

He laid his head on the snow. Still not cold; just damn comfortable. Why had he never slept outdoors before? The wind felt like a blanket, fluttering over him. The sky was getting dark and he had the wide open run to himself.

Richie felt his arm being gently lifted. It felt nice, so he kept staring at the sky. The lingering rays of sun made him feel like he was melting into the hill.

Ouch; then he felt a sharp pain, like something had sliced against his wrist. Sharp, or cold — maybe it was snow. With all the energy that remained in him, Richie lifted his head to see — and feel — a familiar figure slicing his other wrist.

Motherfucker. But he couldn't even say the word, could only watch his own life being taken. It was late — well after the last gondola had stopped taking passengers. He doubted he'd be found before morning.

SIXTY-ONE
CLARE

"Ugh." Clare slammed her tray onto the bar and started loading it up with drinks. "My stupid ex followed me to Whistler."

"Really?" Jana wrinkled her nose, like she didn't approve of this development. She glanced at her phone. "Where the hell is Richie? I've texted him, like, seventeen times."

"Maybe his phone's off."

"It's never off. It's his lifeline to his business. So where's your ex staying? Does he want to crash with you?" Jana's eyes said she hoped not.

"Don't worry. He might want to, but I'm not letting him. He's staying in some hotel in the village. Close to the hill, he says, so we can go snowboarding together."

"Is he rich?"

"No, he just spends his money like an idiot."

"Are you happy to see him?"

"Do I sound happy?"

Jana laughed. "No."

Clare shook her head. "He's here for a two-week holiday. He thinks that's all it's going to take to win me back. Asshole even bought me a return ticket to Toronto."

"He sounds like he's really into you."

"Only when I'm living a better life without him. I hope Chopper comes by tonight. If Nate shows up, I'd really like to be in the arms of some other hot guy."

"So your ex is hot?"

"Extremely. But in the exact opposite way from Chopper. Nate has short dark hair that always falls into his face. Man, all I want to do is brush it away, but it's so cute the way it sits there, you know?"

"Yeah," Jana said. "Because you're still in love with him."

"Fuck off. I'm not."

Jana grinned. "It's fine. Fuck Chopper instead. So when do I get to meet Nate?"

"He's probably coming by the bar tonight. Ugh." Clare saw Noah push through the entrance door. "There he is."

"Lucy!" Noah grinned and waved, like this was all so fun for him.

Clare rolled her eyes — this part of the acting was easy, at least — she was genuinely not pleased to see Noah. "Nate, meet Jana."

"You're one of Lucy's new friends? Great to meet you."

"He *is* hot," Jana said to Clare. "You should jump back into his arms before someone else takes him."

"Oh my god, you can have him. Have each other. Have a blast."

Noah wrapped his arm around Clare's waist and gave her a long kiss that she wished she didn't like so much. "I came to win you back. I've been an asshole back home — I mean that for real. You leaving made me see that."

Clare glowered at Noah. She wished she knew which part of his lines — if any — were sincere.

SIXTY-TWO
MARTHA

Martha closed her eyes and leaned her head against the back of the campaign bus seat.

"You were great tonight," Ted said from across the aisle. "You were the strong Martha we all remember, plus the newer, more enlightened Martha that's the face of your new campaign."

"Thanks, kid. I have a good team propping me up. Shame the ratings aren't supporting that. We still in fourth?"

"Hovering between third and fourth. Social media seems to be pulling some youth vote that's previously belonged to the Democrats."

"Are we in danger of funds drying up?" Martha asked.

Ted pursed his lips. "Borderline."

"Shit. Suggestions?"

"We go harder after the youth vote. They don't donate as much — a college student put a dollar on his Visa this afternoon. Said he had no money to spare but he wanted you to know you have his vote."

"That's very nice," Martha said.

"Yeah, and in the meantime three heavy Wall Streeters have pulled out to back Kearnes."

"Ah."

"We can get by on the funds we have until the Michigan and

Arizona results. If we lose either one — which I have to say looks very likely — we'll have to reassess."

"So there's no harm in my going all-out radical."

Ted shot her a glance. "What do you mean?"

"Why don't I fly economy for a while? Be so accessible it hurts."

Ted's eyebrows lifted.

"Bad idea? I have the Secret Service for security."

"Could be a great idea." Ted walked to the back of the bus and helped himself to a Red Bull from the fridge. Apparently he planned to get no sleep that night. "You want something? A Scotch?"

"Pellegrino," Martha said. "Thank you."

Ted brought back a couple bags of mini-pretzels with their drinks. Martha noticed that he was so used to the rocking of these tour buses the kid didn't even falter as he navigated the aisle. "My friend found something interesting. About Sacha."

"Your police officer friend?"

"Kearnes' assistant. They found hard proof of Sacha's drug smuggling. Video evidence."

Martha felt numb. "Video from what? Border security?"

"Sacha was making a documentary about the LSD importing trade."

Martha smiled. For the first time in two weeks, a real smile. Of course Sacha wasn't a degenerate smuggler, trying to make a quick buck at the expense of the public good. She had larger goals. But Martha darkened again quickly. "So we know, now, why she was killed."

"I guess." Ted reached across the aisle to put a hand on Martha's shoulder. She didn't like it there, but she let it rest; she knew Ted was trying to be sweet. "Kearnes is contemplating how and when they want to break it open."

"I don't follow. Why would they break this open now?"

"They won't unless you start climbing back to a competitive position in the polls. But since that's clearly still our goal, we have to be prepared."

Martha exhaled. "So what do we do?"

"I really think the blog post is the way to go. The one where you write about Sacha from a mother's perspective, outing her activities up in Whistler as if you're trying to make sense of them. I forwarded you the draft."

Martha turned on her laptop. "How is this going to help?"

"Mainly, it steals Kearnes' thunder. He doesn't have much of a story if you've already told it — he certainly can't spin it like it's a scandal. Second, we paint you as someone people would want in their homes — compassionate, willing to listen and change. Third, if we make sure it's written right — Christy and Melissa will go over it again after you've put your spin on it — we strengthen your new platform by showing where it came from."

"I don't want Sacha to look like a common criminal."

"She won't," Ted said, "because she wasn't."

Martha hoped like hell that was true.

SIXTY-THREE
CLARE

Clare stretched her legs out on Noah's hotel suite's plain brown sofa. The kiss Noah had given her at work several hours ago still lingered on her lips, but she didn't want to ask if it was real or he'd been acting.

Noah glanced at her sideways. He'd been looking at her strangely all night, since Clare had arrived at the end of her shift. Outside, drunk party sounds continued in a steady, raucous stream.

"Has it been like this all night?" Clare asked.

"So far," Noah said. "It's like being back in college."

Clare realized with a start that Noah and Sacha had both gone to NYU. And Jana. "You didn't know Sacha or Jana at school, did you?"

"No," Noah said with a smirk. "You don't know John Smith from Canada, do you?"

Clare rolled her eyes. "I meant, I hope Jana doesn't recognize you. But I guess you were a few years ahead of her. And why are you looking at me funny?" she asked.

"How am I looking at you?"

"Like you're worried I'm going to pull out a gun and start shooting up the walls of your hotel."

"I, uh . . . I don't want to say the wrong thing. In case I piss you off."

Clare set her beer down on the plain wooden coffee table. Noah had invited her to spend the night, but she still wasn't sure if she wanted to. "We're fine as long as you don't call me a slut."

Noah laughed tentatively. "Okay, noted. So what's your take on Wade, working for him?"

Clare grabbed a handful of pretzels and chomped on them while she contemplated. "He's not an idiot, and he's a pretty good boss. He was probably cool before booze got him."

"Can you see what Sacha saw in him?"

"Chopper said he was a project. Sacha figured she could help Wade get clean and sober. Not sure where his wife was going to figure in, long term. But I don't get the sense that Sacha thought through her do-gooder master plans all that carefully."

Noah groaned. "Women always think they can help a man."

"I don't," Clare said, and wondered which other women Noah meant. His mother? His ex-girlfriends? Clare was dying to ask him about the girl on the boat, but it was better to let him bring that up in his own time. If he ever decided he could trust her with it.

"You think Wade could have posed Sacha on the hill?"

"Sure," Clare said. "He doesn't snowboard, though, or ski. So I can't see Wade choosing that location. People who know him would find his being there odd."

"Jana likes the hill, though," Noah said.

"Loves it." Clare picked up her beer. Noah had stocked his place with Bud for her, but for some reason tonight it didn't taste like it had much flavor. She was surprised that she wished she had one of those darker craft beers Jana and Chopper preferred. Clare asked, "Did you learn anything from your interview with Jana?"

"Yeah. One of Jana's church group friends from Salt Lake City sent an email to the account we set up in Lorenzo's name. Said back in the day, Jana went kind of Single White Female on her."

Clare felt her eyebrows lift.

"The friend said Jana had a problem with reality."

"Anyone who reads the Bible has a problem with reality," Clare said.

"That's not *totally* fair." Noah had gone to Hebrew school, taken

Judaism as far as his Bar Mitzvah, where he'd made a bunch of money from his relatives then decided the religion wasn't for him. "A lot of people study religion for metaphorical truth. Doesn't mean they believe the magical stories."

"Whatever." Clare thought of her father, dying in some hospital bed because he preferred to lie about his problems than to try to fix them, and on the flip side, the lengths Clare went to to forget that he even existed. "We all tweak our reality to help us live in the world. Jana just makes more adjustments than most people."

"Any idea what Sacha saw in her? They were best friends, right?"

Clare had been thinking about this a lot. Externally, it seemed like a terrible match — Sacha thought of others, Jana of herself. But hearing about Sacha's home life, Clare was starting to put shape to the friendship. "Jana loved her. No conditions, no logic, just dog-like devotion."

"And Sacha liked that?" Noah fiddled with his Bud label, frowning. "Personally I'd find it oppressive."

"Because your mother was oppressive. Sacha's parents ignored her, put their own lives first. She would have craved Jana's unconditional adoration."

Noah stood up and paced to the window and back again, twice. He stopped and looked at Clare. "So who's next? Who's your top suspect of the people we haven't blogged about? Richie? He likes to snowboard."

"Yeah." Clare wasn't sure how she felt about Richie as a suspect, though. He made sense intellectually — the drug dealer, the fact he probably knew Sacha had ratted them out to Daisy. But he didn't feel right. "What do you think of Chopper?"

Noah's eyes narrowed. "Is he the one you're sleeping with?"

"Yeah."

"Then you can probably guess what I think."

Clare saw the pain Noah was in, and for a moment she felt terrible for causing it. She wanted to cross the room and touch him, make it better. But she remembered that he was the one who wouldn't make their relationship exclusive, and she scowled.

"Would you feel weird helping me write a post about Chopper?"

"No." Clare was annoyed by the question. "I'm investigating Chopper like I'm investigating everyone else. The fact that we have good chemistry is a bonus." She supposed she could have left the chemistry part out, but she wanted Noah to be jealous, to realize that they *should* be exclusive, outside of work.

"Clare . . ." Noah's forehead creased. He sank into one of the arm-chairs across the coffee table from her.

Clare barreled forward. "But I think we should write about Norris."

"Fuck, I'd love that." Noah's mouth corners shot up, like the thought of exposing a dirty cop excited him. "Before I wrote Wade's post, my suggestion was the Band of Brothers — a look at Wade, Chopper, and Norris, and how their friendship turned to crime."

"That's actually good," Clare said. "Especially since they were in an actual band together. Why didn't you write it?"

"Worthington and Bert want to leave Norris alone for a while. He's losing his job at the end of all this, obviously, but they think it would be too disruptive — all the suspects would scatter — if he gets exposed too soon."

"Fair enough. So we're writing about Chopper?"

"Yeah," Noah said. "You have his phone number?"

"Um. You want to call him?"

"Yeah. That's how the posts work."

Right. Of course it was. "What are you going to ask him?"

Noah shrugged. "That's where you come in. What do you think I should ask him?"

Clare took her lower lip between three fingers and started playing with it, strumming it like a guitar. She pulled her fingers away to say, "You want to expose his drug manufacturing, right?"

"If you think it will lead to good comments. You want me to grab you a T-shirt or something? You can't be comfortable in that awful work uniform."

"Thanks," Clare said. "I don't think I'll stay overnight, though."

"Why not? We've got it covered so it looks natural." Noah's eyes flickered down to his hands and stayed there.

"Because." Clare tried hard not to notice how sad he was. "I need you to be in love with me — to want a real relationship. Otherwise we're just going to keep fighting."

"You know I want a real relationship."

"Yeah," Clare said. "But you want it with someone I'm not. Come on, let's work on this post. Let's nail Chopper." She managed a small grin. "You know you want to take him down."

Noah gave her an even smaller grin back.

"Make sure you block your number. I think we should lie with the truth."

SIXTY-FOUR
WADE

M an, it was late. Wade's eyes were glazing over while looking at the poster of Jim Morrison on his office wall. For a minute he thought Jim was coming out of the poster to pour him another drink. But when Wade looked into his Scotch glass, it was empty.

"You heard from Richie?" Wade asked Chopper.

"No. Norris has his phone."

Wade found that odd. "What? Why?"

Chopper laughed and stopped twisting his dreads long enough to wave a hand dismissively. "They have some weird power play going on. It'll work itself out."

"I don't get it." Wade pulled a whiskey bottle from his desk drawer. Empty.

"It's stress, man. We're all stressed." Chopper reached into his banana-yellow ski jacket and pulled out a memory stick. "I came to loop you in to what the girls found in Jules."

Wade's eyebrows popped. "Sacha's teddy bear, Jules?"

Chopper nodded. "Sacha was — get this — only friends with us so she could make a documentary. There's a whackload of footage.

I've been watching it all day, and I haven't even scratched the surface. I'm thinking we should split it up, see what's incriminating. And then destroy it."

Wade wondered if he was implicated.

"And yes," Chopper said. "Jules was sitting in your office for a few of our meetings. We'd all go to jail if this got out. Even you. Fucking Sacha." He shook his head. "She really knew how to fool a guy into letting her in."

Wade didn't like Chopper's implication, like Wade had been played for a fool. Even if Sacha had seduced him with an ulterior motive, the relationship had been real — you couldn't fake that shit. Wade checked his other drawer and found a bottle of CC with a couple of ounces left. He poured it into his tumbler before Chopper could ask for a swig.

Chopper smirked — at what, Wade wasn't sure. "So can I use your computer? Give you some files?"

"I guess." Wade shuffled some papers aside and stood up to trade places with Chopper.

Chopper slid the stick into the USB drive and clicked the mouse a couple of times. "Okay, I've given you clips sixty-nine through one hundred. I can't find a pattern for what order they're in. They're not chronological. And they're not grouped by location or people in them or anything I can identify."

Wade smiled. "She's telling a story."

"Huh?"

"Sacha was putting it in the order she wanted it watched. Telling a story out of sequence because she thinks it tells better that way. It's how I write my music — we had long conversations about it." *See,* Wade felt like saying, *I wasn't trivial to her. Maybe you were, but not me.*

"Okay, that's really sweet, Wade. But unless you want to contemplate story sequence in jail, we're gonna need to get serious."

Chopper lecturing Wade about getting serious? That was a good one. Wade reached over and shifted the computer screen so they could both see.

Chopper looked at Wade. "You ready to see her? It's freaky, seeing her moving again, like she's alive."

Wade swallowed hard. He would never be ready. And he craved seeing Sacha in action more than anything. "Just play it."

Chopper clicked the mouse again and Sacha came to life.

She was in a wood-paneled office, very old world traditional. The room was decorated with red ribbons and twinkling white strings of lights — a tasteful non-denominational holiday scene.

A young man — thin, eager — was seated behind the desk. He looked like he was playing make-believe, pretending he was somebody important.

"Why are you always in my mother's chair?" Sacha asked him.

The young man leaned forward, his elbows resting on the wide black desk mat. He looked at Sacha and said, "You have to stop what you're doing."

Sacha laughed. "Ted, you're adorable. When you look in the mirror, do you see yourself as a fifty-year-old man?"

Ted frowned. "The drugs, Sacha. The LSD. This could ruin your mother's career."

Sacha smirked, like she was well aware and fine with that.

"The game's up, Sacha. I know about your smuggling. I'm afraid that after the holidays, you can't return to Whistler."

"Good one, Ted. That's like the housekeeper telling her boss's kid where she's going to school in the fall."

"I'm not the help." Ted's jaw tightened. "You're the one breaking the law. I should report you, get you thrown in jail."

"But you won't." Sacha laughed again. "It would ruin your chances of riding my mother's coattails into the White House. Here, I got you something."

Sacha pulled a wrapped gift from her shoulder bag.

"For Christmas?" Ted wrinkled his nose.

"Don't worry. I don't expect a gift from you."

Ted took the small box and looked at it suspiciously.

"You don't have to be miserable about the whole holiday season just because your family doesn't celebrate it and you have to eat turkey with us. You've worked for my mom for three years — you, like, *are* family."

Ted tugged at the red ribbon until it came off. He peeled off the silver wrapping — carefully, like he planned to use it again — and pulled out a tie.

"Goofy?" he sneered at the cartoon image on the material.

Sacha grinned. "Because you take yourself too seriously."

"You're making fun of me because I'm not frolicking off in the world on my trust fund, ruining their careers in my wake?"

"I'm not spending my trust fund. That's gathering interest — it's going to be my philanthropy fund when I figure out how to use it best. For now, I'm earning my own way."

"Whatever." Ted put the tie back in the box, pinching it with two fingers like it was a smelly old fish. "I don't aspire to be less serious."

"You'd live longer," Sacha said. "Hell, you'd live, period."

"What you call living, I call wasting a life. You're smuggling drugs, Sacha. Surely you're not suggesting I do the same."

"No, the stress would kill you. Just wear the tie for Christmas dinner. Goofy's dressed up as Rudolf, see?"

"I'm not wearing it. You can have it back, if you saved the receipt."

The footage stopped abruptly. Wade downed his drink and stood up to get more from the bar. On his way out of the office, Chopper's phone beeped.

"Jesus!" Chopper said before Wade was out the door. His eyes scanned his screen for a moment before he said, "That fucking blogger is talking about my mountain lab."

Wade reluctantly sat back down. He wanted a shot of booze before reading or listening to anything, but if he prioritized drink, he'd look like an alcoholic.

"I should have known that fucking guy who called tonight wasn't FBI. Why would FBI call me? They might bust me, but they're not going to fucking phone first. Honestly, I'm such a moron."

"You're not a moron," Wade said. "The blogger fooled me, too." He followed Chopper's eyes and read:

THE FOOL ON THE HILL
by LORENZO BARILLA

I got Chopper MacPherson on the phone. This one was good.

I said I was FBI.

I said I was interested in his mountain lair -- the one where he makes LSD. I told him I knew he'd been in business with Sacha, that if he answered a few choice questions he'd have an easier time when it all got blown open later.

Chopper was cool. He was clearly stoned, but he's no dummy. Until I said I knew he was trying to pay for my name.

"What are you talking about?" MacPherson said.

"You heard me. I'm here undercover in Whistler. I've seen you at Avalanche. We've ridden together in the Blackcomb gondola."

"You what? Who are you? What do you look like?"

"My boss got a phone call. Someone offered him ten grand for my name. Said the money had been put up by Chopper MacPherson and Richie Lebar."

MacPherson was quiet. I mean, what could he say?

I said, "You sure you don't want to help me? Your friends are going down. From our point of view -- the American side -- what you did personally isn't really that bad. You made some drugs you only intended for local Canadian consumption. It's the importers we're after. Now do you want to help, or do you want to hinder your own shot at freedom?"

Chopper's breathing got heavy. "What do you want to know?"

"First," I said, "I want to know who you think murdered Sacha Westlake."

"That's easy," Chopper said. "I think she murdered herself."

"Okay," I said. "Second: who runs the transport operation?"

"Come again."

"Which of your cohorts is connected to the Seattle crew, across the border?"

"That was Sacha," Chopper said. Too quickly? Not sure.

Because I don't think it was Sacha at all. I think Sacha wanted to expose this drug running just like I want to expose her killer.

Did Chopper chop up Sacha's wrists to silence her?

Wade met Chopper's eye.

"This blogger is trying to mind-fuck us." Chopper held his matted blond head in his hands and rocked it back and forth slowly. "You think the Whistler undercover has been the blogger all along?"

Wade nodded. "Yeah, that actually makes sense."

"I guess that's a good thing." Chopper let go of his head. His eyes, which normally looked on the verge of laughing, were dark and serious. "It means we have one enemy, not two. But if the cop's still in town, does that mean Norris lied?"

Wade shook his head. "We can't even start thinking that way."

"But I can't believe — do you really think Norris gave my name when he offered the bribe?"

"Of course not." Wade was firm. "They're trying to divide us. Divide and conquer."

"You got any booze in this place? I could use another beer, and a stiff whiskey to go with it."

"Let's move to the bar." Wade stood up, shut down his computer. He and Chopper would need several stiff drinks each to get to sleep that night.

SATURDAY / FEBRUARY 18

SIXTY-FIVE
CLARE

lare saw the police activity just below the Mid-Station. She had a gondola to herself, which was fairly luxurious considering that later in the day this same ride would be crowded with tourists. She pulled off her gloves and fished her phone from her pocket. She saw a missed call from Noah.

"Hey," Clare said when she reached Noah. "What's going on?"

"Richard Lebar has been murdered."

"Shit — Richie?"

"Sorry. Forgot these are your friends now."

Clare's grip on her phone all but slipped away. She glanced down at the receding police scene. "Why haven't they closed the hill?"

"I'm sure they will, but I don't think anyone's thinking clearly."

"When was he found?" Clare asked.

"An hour ago. Looks like he's been dead all night. His family in Toronto has only known for fifteen minutes."

"Is anyone flying out here?"

"His mom asked for plane fare."

"They could probably take that from his pocket," Clare said. "Or is that not officially allowed?"

Clare remembered Jana the night before, cursing because Richie wouldn't return her texts. Wade, too — he kept asking Jana where Richie was, for some meeting they had arranged. Had one of them been pretending? Had they both? "I'm nearly at the peak of Whistler. You think I should ride down to the body?"

"Yeah. I just got off the phone with Bert. He asked me to tell you to go to the scene. He wants you to study faces and reactions."

"Our blog last night," Clare said. "Do you think . . . could it have anything to do with . . ."

"Don't think about that," Noah said. "We're not the guilty ones here."

"Still . . ."

Though Clare was well wrapped in long underwear and snow clothes, the gondola felt a lot colder than it had a few minutes earlier. She found herself wishing there were tourists crammed in there with her. Or that Noah was.

SIXTY-SIX
MARTHA

Another airport. Another chai latte. And another death in Whistler.

Martha sat on the hard row seat near her gate, longing for the privacy of the first-class lounge — where even if she was recognized, she was unlikely to be bothered. But she'd already launched her new brand: accessibility. A camera catching her entering one airport lounge would throw all that off.

So instead of reclining into a massage chair with a bad cappuccino and a great view of the runway, she was staring into a big fuzzy microphone that had materialized in front of her face.

"I'm intrigued by your blog, Senator Westlake," a gray-haired woman said. "Particularly your post this morning about your daughter smuggling drugs into Washington State from Canada. Was that difficult to write?"

"Astonishingly, no." Martha stood to meet the woman's eyes; she couldn't decide if she liked what she got back.

"Were you responding to the other blogger — the one who hinted at Sacha's activity up in Whistler?"

"No," Martha said. "My team and I have been working on my post for two full days."

"In your post, you imply that Sacha was smuggling for a higher cause than money. Can you elaborate?"

"No. At the moment, there's too much conjecture, not enough proof. We'll share everything with the public once we've made sense of all the pieces."

"Of course you will." The woman's eyebrows lifted. "I've heard that Geoffrey Kearnes has been known to resort to dirty politics. Do you think he might be implicated in the murders?"

Martha laughed mirthlessly. "Are you asking if I think my political opponent murdered my daughter?"

"No. I'm asking if you think your ex-boyfriend did."

"Which news station did you say you worked for?"

"WKCR."

"The Columbia University radio station?" Martha couldn't keep the surprise from her voice. The woman seemed old for such a gig.

"A television station upstate." She named a town Martha had never heard of.

"Ah. Well, to answer your insightful and sensitive query, I highly doubt Geoff Kearnes or any of my other opponents — or ex-boyfriends; god, that was so long ago — were involved in either murder."

"Could the killer have been someone from your own campaign? Maybe someone who knew about Sacha's smuggling and wanted to make sure that it didn't hurt your campaign?"

Martha smiled blandly and said, "I'm no detective, of course, but my office has been buzzing dawn to dusk. There's not a member of my team who has had a decent sleep in weeks. Not only would they have no reason to murder my daughter if they care about me winning this election, but they have not had time to skip off on a ski trip to Canada for any reason."

The woman took two small steps backward. "I'm sorry if the question was too forthcoming."

"No worries." Martha continued to smile winningly in case anything she said got pulled for a news bite. "Now why don't you go interview Geoff Kearnes? Ask him the same question."

SIXTY-SEVEN
CLARE

Clare shoved off from the top of Whistler Mountain. Next stop: Richie's body.

In her earbuds, her phone rang. She touched the tab on her earpiece to answer. "Hello?"

"You sitting down?" her friend Roberta back in Ontario asked. "Noah gave me this number. Sorry to bug you at work."

"It's fine," Clare said. "I've been meaning to call you back; I just never remember at a time when it's convenient."

"'Course you don't. You're avoiding me." Roberta had known Clare since she was twelve. The downside was she could read Clare like a book.

"I'm not avoiding you."

"No? What's different?"

Clare gave a small laugh. "Fine; I'm avoiding you."

"I forget if you said if you're sitting down."

"Did my dad die?"

"No."

"Then I'm fine standing up. I'm snowboarding, actually."

"Snowboarding? That for work or pleasure?"

"Work. And I don't have much time." Clare felt a bit bad being short with her, but she had a dead body to ride down to.

"You never have time for your dad."

"So it is about my dad."

"His new lung is failing."

"Why doesn't he call me himself?" Clare knew that was mildly unfair — it would be hard to talk without a lung.

"Because you don't answer his calls."

"Because he lies. He told me once, when I was about to take a job with the Thunder Bay police, that he had cancer of the everything — that it had invaded his entire body and he had, like, a month to live. So I turned down the job and, lo and behold, his diagnosis was reversed the next week. A real medical miracle."

"And thus you ended up with the job in Toronto that has taken your career to places you never dreamed it could."

Clare adored Roberta, but sometimes she could severely miss the mark. "How's the shop?"

"Business is good," Roberta said. "Though I could have used your nimble hands this morning. I had the most finicky carburetor to clean."

Clare laughed. "You know I like more complicated problems."

"Yeah? You should be pleased to come home and see your dad, then."

"So his new lung is failing. Maybe that's because he's smoking it black like his first pair. How long does he claim he has to live?"

"A week or two."

Clare edged harder into the snow. "He's lying, though, right?"

"I wish he was, kid. He's in Barrie on a respirator. I've spoken with his doctors. He needs a new lung to survive outside the hospital, and he's not being considered for a transplant because they know he's still smoking. Or was, until he got admitted last week."

Clare was nearing the Mid-Station. "I have to go. I'll be there as soon as I can."

Always when she was busy. Her father had a knack for creating massive drama right when Clare had no time to come running. And what would she do with her mother if he died? Would Clare have to visit more, pretend that they had shit in common?

It felt like a test — one she had no hope of passing.

SIXTY-EIGHT
WADE

Wade sipped brandy from his metal flask, but it didn't warm him. A crowd had gathered — snowboarders gaping at the body because this was all so fucking interesting. They were smoking cigarettes and joints, littering the hill, and ski patrol wasn't stopping them. Wade had ridden up on the first lift he could after Norris phoned with the news. He didn't know why he was there, but really, where else would he be?

He watched Norris unzip Richie's inner jacket pocket and pass one of the crime scene workers a cell phone and some earbuds. From another pocket, he pulled a thin wad of cash.

"That's it?" Norris said as he passed the bills to one of his evidence crew. "You'd think a drug dealer would carry more money around."

Wade agreed. Richie's wad was normally three times as thick.

"There are still more pockets," a young cop said. "Snowboard gear is made with hidden zippers everywhere. Maybe check the pants."

Norris put his gloved hands into Richie's baggy nylon pant pockets, passed the team more items to bag — keys and coins and a couple of gum wrappers. "You know what I'm thinking? This killer probably liberated some cash for himself."

Once the pocket search was exhausted, Norris walked over to join Wade.

"You want a cigarette?" Norris held his pack open to Wade.

"You bought a pack?" Wade took one.

"Can you believe I didn't smoke for ten years, and this pack I bought yesterday is nearly gone? Here, walk with me. I have to stay where I can see the scene, but let's head over to those trees where we can talk in relative privacy."

Wade followed.

"I wasn't made for this job," Norris said, once he'd found them some seclusion.

Wade smiled sadly. "You're a good cop. You just need a town where you're not friends with all the criminals."

"If I was a good cop, I'd be thriving now — called to action like this. All I can think about is keeping my wife and kids from suffering this same fate."

"What's wrong with you, man?" Wade peered at Norris, like maybe squinting would help him see inside his friend. "You're a ball of fucked-up nerves ever since the FBI came to town. So the DEA's involved. Big deal — that's probably what's going to save your ass in the end."

Norris sighed. "It's the pressure. I've never felt anything like this. Man, I wish I could have a long sip from your flask right now."

Wade took a sip himself, then extended his flask to Norris.

Norris waved the flask away. "No, I have to look professional. Can you keep a secret?"

"Of course." Wade was great at keeping secrets. He had a secret stash of booze in every room of his life.

"I think . . . I might have been tricked."

"Tricked." Wade's tongue flicked at the word. He liked the feeling in his mouth, warm booze mixed with cool air.

"I'm not convinced anymore that it was the DEA I was talking to. Anyone can make up an email address, right? Even if it ends in 'DEA dot com.'"

Wade didn't know what a real DEA email address would look like. "I guess."

Norris looked like he had more he wanted to say, but wasn't. "This is bigger than us. It's invisible and I don't know what's behind it."

"You keep saying that, Stu. But if it's not DEA — then who the hell wanted —"

Norris threw his cigarette into the snow and stomped it out. "Look, I have a death investigation to get back to."

"Stu, I know you. You need to get this out, whatever secret you're keeping, or you'll make yourself insane."

Norris pushed his lips together and out, like he always did when he had something big to mull over. "You gotta keep this super quiet," he said finally. "I haven't decided how to handle this, professionally. Which organization to tell first."

"Okay."

Norris pulled his pack from his pocket, lit himself a new cigarette. He glanced at Wade, but he was only halfway through his first one. "Geoffrey Kearnes is involved. At least, his campaign is. That's who's been giving me orders — not the DEA."

"Shit." Wade didn't know what else to say.

"Yeah, shit is right. Someone slipped up, forgot to block a phone call. So I traced it — a cell phone paid for by the Kearnes campaign."

Wade knew U.S. campaigns could get dirty, but something about Norris' theory didn't jive. "You think this is connected to the murders?"

"I have absolutely no idea."

Wade put a hand on Norris' shaking shoulder. He was surprised when Norris relaxed into the gesture. "I've written some new songs. I was hoping you and Chopper and I could record them."

"For what? Our grandchildren to throw away when they're clearing out our attics?"

"You don't need a big label anymore. Anyone can put a song up on YouTube or iTunes. If people like it, maybe the band could get going again — I mean commercially, not just gigs here and there for free beer."

"We're all a bit old to think we're Justin Bieber."

"We're not even forty. Chopper's up for it."

"It's a nice fantasy, Wade. Fill that flask up a couple more times."

SIXTY-NINE
CLARE

Clare spotted Jana behind the police tape. Jana's body was heaving; tears were streaming down her face. Clare made her way through the crowd to her and put her arm around Jana's bulky shoulders. She felt awkward, but she guessed this was what she was supposed to do.

Clare looked over at the Mid-Station and saw Chopper waving. She hoped her text to him, *Feeling fucked up, come hang with me*, hadn't been too wussy. She'd played the needy card to get him there, because Bert was right: Clare should see as many reactions to Richie's death as possible.

Inspector Norris was standing apart from the investigating crew. He was with Wade. Their conversation looked heavy, and they were passing a flask back and forth. It was hardly professional, but then Clare wasn't one to judge.

Chopper arrived at Clare's side and squeezed her hand. It felt good. Really good. If she'd asked Noah to be there, he would just grunt and watch the action, maybe make a few snide comments like *I forgot these guys were your friends*. She looked up at Chopper. "Thanks for coming."

He ruffled his other hand against Clare's toque, looked at Jana, and frowned. He leaned into Clare's ear. "She stoned or sober?"

"Um, sober, I think." Clare hadn't thought to wonder.

Chopper left Clare and moved around to Jana's other side. He said something to Jana that Clare couldn't hear. Jana nodded, still sobbing, and allowed Chopper to lead her away toward the lift. He looked back at Clare and beckoned with his head for her to join them.

She wasn't sure where her energy was better spent — watching the crime scene, studying Norris and Wade and the others who had gathered around the body, or following Chopper and Jana back to wherever they were going.

What would Lucy do?

That made things simple. She'd go with Chopper and Jana. Clare picked up her snowboard and followed them to the Mid-Station to ride the gondola down to the village.

SEVENTY
MARTHA

Martha felt her stomach twist as she saw her opponent approaching in the large Flagstaff convention hall. "Geoffrey." She did not extend her hand.

"Ah, Martha." Kearnes' suit was so slick it looked oily. His styled gray hair matched his silver voice. "Riding economy. Legalizing marijuana. Have you thought about crossing party lines, maybe seeing if the Democrats will have you? Actually, you might be too far left for them."

"Now why would I look for another party?" Martha felt like a child at a playground. She had a big smile on her face that was only half phony. "You know you're the one I want to beat."

Kearnes leaned in close. Martha thought she smelled sausage on his breath. Or maybe that was sauerkraut. "We should have a conversation later. I have an attractive offer if you'd like to pull out of the race."

"Let's have the conversation now. The answer is no."

"My offer could save your family a lot of embarrassment."

Martha laughed. "My family? You mean me?"

"And, posthumously, your daughter."

"This morning, I revealed that my daughter was smuggling drugs into America. Which I understand you were about to leak to the press yourself. I don't think I can do much more damage to her reputation."

"Why would I leak that?" Kearnes frowned. "You think I knew about your daughter's smuggling before I read about it on your blog?"

"Don't give me that, Geoffrey. Your game has always been dirty — since you were twenty years old working on your father's campaign. You'd prefer to dig up dirt on your opponents than try to win votes on your own steam."

"My own steam has me on top of the polls right now."

"Well, have fun up there. Just don't fall."

"Back out, Westlake. Before you force my hand."

"Jesus, Geoffrey. What do you have?"

"You want to hear this here, where prying ears might be listening? Or would you like a discreet meeting later?"

"I would like to hear now."

Kearnes shrugged. Still, he lowered his voice before saying, "I know Fraser Westlake is not Sacha's father."

Martha raised her eyebrows. Did her best to look fearful. The stupid thing was, in no other country would this be a big enough scandal to cost someone the presidency. But America loved both its Bible-thumping ethics and its Schadenfreude — watching a political figure go down for less than perfect family values was almost as fun as a good football game. Unless Martha spun it correctly.

"Is that a yes to a discussion?" Kearnes gave a toothless smile.

Martha chewed her lip. "Your office or mine?"

"Oh, I'll come to you," Kearnes said. "I'll have to do some glad-handing in New York, now that it's winnable territory. Plus I wouldn't want to put you out. Traveling coach isn't such a wonderful experience."

"You'd be surprised," Martha said. "It's led to some excellent conversations with constituents."

"I'll stick with private. But I'm glad you're having fun."

When Kearnes had wandered off to smirk at some more voters, Martha whipped out her phone and sent Ted a text: *Go public with the affair.*

SEVENTY-ONE
CLARE

"You guys, this is mental." Jana was curled into Chopper's big fuzzy armchair, scrolling quickly on the screen of her phone. Her tears had dried, but she seemed to still be frantic, looking for distraction in whatever form she could find.

"What's mental?" Clare asked.

"Did you know Sacha's mom had a blog?"

Of course Clare knew. But she was more interested in why Jana still cared after what had happened that morning with Richie. "What kind of blog? American politics?"

"Maybe normally. But in this one, she admits that Sacha's dad isn't her dad. You want to hear?"

When neither Clare nor Chopper responded, maybe because there were about ten zillion more pressing issues at the moment, Jana started reading:

```
You know what I hate about politics? It's never about
the issues. You don't hear candidates saying "Vote
for me because I'll make education more accessible,"
nearly as often as you hear "Don't vote for that guy.
He cheated on his wife. And definitely not that other
```

guy. He got caught having sex in a rubber fetish suit."

As in many areas of this campaign, I'd like to do things differently.

Rather than wait for an opponent to find this and cast a sinister spin on my entire political platform as a result, I'd like to reach into my closet and drag out the one secret that would be gold to my opponents. You can forgive me or not, but at least you'll hear it in my words -- and know that I am honest with constituents.

Twenty-four years ago, I dated Geoffrey Kearnes. We were working on his father's campaign. He was running it, I was an intern. It was a high-strung campaign -- hard work, hard play.

We had fun. Our minds worked well together and the heat of the campaign kept things sizzling. We dated for several months until I overheard him asking another intern to dig up dirt on the candidates who were in second, third, and fourth place so we could use it to secure his father's lead. This happens all the time -- I wasn't naive about that -- but somehow I'd believed that Geoffrey was above the dirt. I stormed off the campaign with the righteous indignation of a 22-year-old.

What I didn't know when we split was that I was pregnant.

I had a rebound relationship with Fraser Westlake. When I found out I was pregnant, I assumed

```
-- perhaps because I wanted to -- that the father was
Fraser. We were married shortly thereafter, shared
twenty lovely years together, and until last week I
believed he was Sacha's biological father.

Since I now know that he isn't -- I'll spare you the
science, but trust me: I know -- the only possible
father Sacha could have had is Geoffrey Kearnes.
```

As Jana finished reading the blog post aloud, her voice wobbled. Tears were falling from her eyes again. They were quieter tears than earlier, on the hill. Clare wished she could go over, make it better somehow. But she didn't have the first clue what she'd do.

In the kitchen, Chopper cracked one of his giant craft beers and poured it evenly into three glasses. Clare checked her phone for messages and was shocked to see it was already two p.m. The day had been such a strange haze, her father's health and Richie's death fighting for top spot in her mind.

"I think you two should stay here for a while," Chopper said. "Overnight, and maybe longer. I don't like the thought of two women alone in an apartment."

No — much better to be alone with two prime suspects.

"We'll lock our doors," Clare said. "We won't do any midnight skiing."

"Lucy, trust me on this. Stay here tonight."

Clare met Chopper's gaze and tried to figure out what lay behind it. "You're scaring me."

"You're scaring me, too," Jana said.

"Good. Listen, I have a suspicion that doesn't make me happy, but if I'm right, you could both be targets if you're in town."

Clare didn't like the guessing game. "A target for who?"

"I'm not saying more until I have proof. I'm worried it's a friend." Norris or Wade.

"I need to take my contacts out," Jana said. "And get a pair of glasses. I can't stay up here overnight without them."

Chopper nodded. "That's cool. We can mix up some saline with boiling water and salt. I did that for a girl once."

"I can only wear contacts for five or six hours. My eyes are already starting to sting."

"So be blind for one night. You don't need eyes up here."

"I'm not staying without my glasses, Chopper. You're the one with the whack theory that we're safer up here. If you're wrong, I'd like to have my vision in good working order."

Chopper's forehead wrinkled. Clare watched his eyes glance in a few different directions before saying, "Okay. I'll take you back into town. Lucy, you want to follow on my extra sled? I think that's safer than three of us taking the one."

The three of them had come up the hill on one snowmobile — not a three-seater, but an ad-hoc arrangement that had only sort of worked.

What Clare really wanted was the chance to scope out Chopper's place alone. Maybe even poke in his woodshed if she could get in. But she had to play that cautiously. "I'm baked from that joint. Not sure I should be driving anything."

"Jana, you want to ride the extra?"

"Yeah — but I've never driven a sled *and* I'm baked. So Lucy's a way safer option."

"I'll crash on your couch," Clare said. "I could deal with listening to music and staring at the falling snow right about now." Clare was sober. She'd figured out how to *actually* not inhale, unlike her first couple of attempts. Either that or she was getting used to being stoned.

Chopper hesitated. Clare wasn't sure if the pause was for her security or his own. "Yeah," he said. "I'm sure you'll be all right. Just lock the doors. And call me if anything happens."

"What could happen? You said all the bears are asleep."

"Please, Lucy. Take me seriously. Keep your phone close to you. We'll all be fine if we look after each other."

Clare hoped that was true. She liked Chopper. She didn't want him to be guilty. Jana, she could go either way on. The police had questioned Jana at length that morning before Clare had arrived at Richie's body — Clare would go over the transcripts with Noah later.

Clare waited until Chopper's snowmobile had zoomed off into the distance and she could no longer hear its engine.

She was about to light a cigarette when she thought about her father, clinging to life in some stupid hospital bed. Was she horrible for not wanting to go running to his side? She didn't want to end up like him — rasping and gasping and all his own stupid fault.

Clare grabbed her cigarette pack from the coffee table, wet them from the tap so they couldn't tempt her later, and tossed the pack into the garbage can.

Then she eyed the coffee table — the pirate-style treasure chest with the piece of glass on top. The chest was locked. Didn't people realize that a lock was the best way to tell someone where to look? Clare planned to find her way inside.

SEVENTY-TWO
MARTHA

Martha caught Ted's eye across the convention hall floor. He was deep in conversation with a pretty young blond whom Martha recognized as the assistant to one of her less awful opponents. She hated to interrupt budding romance, but she crooked her head to let Ted know she wanted to speak with him.

Within seconds, he was at her side.

"That was nice work, kid." Martha felt strangely giddy, like she wanted to give Ted a high five. "Great idea, prepping that post in advance. I'm glad you're on my team."

"I could never replace Sacha."

"Of course not."

Ted's face flushed bright red. He gave a small laugh. "I don't mean in your life. I mean, Sacha's been the best influence on this campaign."

Martha didn't want to speak to that.

"I got the name of the undercover, if you're interested," Ted said.

"The FBI agent? I guess it's not as highly kept a secret, now that he's off the case."

"He's a she — and she's still in Whistler."

"Do I want to know how you know this?"

"Probably not. Her name's Clare Vengel. Twenty-four-year-old

Canadian, moved to New York less than a year ago. I only saw a head shot, but she looks a lot like Sacha."

"Why would the FBI tell us they'd pulled their man out?"

"I don't think it was us they were trying to misinform. Looks like the village cop is dirty. Stu Norris."

"Is the village cop a suspect?"

Ted wrinkled his mouth. "Don't think so. I'll let you know when I know more. My NYPD friend is risking his job to stay on top of this case. I'm going to owe him big time."

"Thank you, Ted." Martha reached over and gripped Ted's hand. It felt odd, so she pulled her hand away. "I wish Sacha could be here today."

"We all do." Ted glanced at his brightly polished loafers. Martha remembered Ted and Sacha together. They'd squabbled like brother and sister, bantered about politics with affectionate confrontation. He must miss her, too.

"No," Martha said. "I wish she could be here to see the look on Kearnes' face at this very second. One guess what he's reading on his phone."

SEVENTY-THREE
CLARE

Clare's chest felt hollow, like it needed a cigarette. She'd been dumb to ruin her pack, especially when she needed to focus on the task at hand. She thought about pulling the wet smokes from the trash, drying the tobacco by the fire. She could re-roll the dried tobacco with Chopper's Zig-Zags. Might not be delicious, but it would kill the craving.

But she thought of her father, gasping for breath in a hospital ward with her mother stressing beside him, and she didn't want to be anything like that pathetic man.

Still, the craving was brutal. It was grabbing at her lungs and her hands and her mouth, telling them they were missing something, they were empty without nicotine. And her agitation wasn't helping her pick this damn lock.

Her tools at home would have made short work of this trunk. But of course when you traveled undercover, you didn't get to bring your cop kit with you. Clare was working with her tiny purple Swiss Army knife — the most complex tool that could conceivably belong to Lucy.

Shit. A snowmobile was coming. Clare scrambled to put the glass top back onto the trunk with all its things in place. As she set down a dish of keys and other random items, she saw the memory stick from Jules. At least she was pretty sure it was the same stick — black with a red stripe. Clare slipped the memory stick into her pocket and tried to guess which way the January *Snowboarder Magazine* had been facing.

She heard the motor stop outside the cabin. She couldn't remember the magazine's orientation, so she flopped onto the couch and pretended to be engrossed in an article about some Australian half-pipe superstar.

There was a loud knock at the door.

Which was weird, because Chopper had a key.

Clare tiptoed to the door in her socked feet and wished like hell that Chopper had built in a peephole.

She peered out the window to where Chopper parked his sleds. The spare snowmobile had been joined by a black-and-green sled — not Chopper's. Clare moved silently toward the kitchen and picked up the key to the spare from the counter. She stuffed it into her pocket with the memory stick.

On her way back to the door, she saw a small, thin man walking around outside. Inspector Norris. He was looking in the window at her.

Fuck, fuck, fuck. Chopper had told her to call him if anything happened. But Norris looked friendly enough. He smiled at Clare, motioned to the door.

Clare picked up her phone and dialed Chopper. Norris was still staring at her. He pulled something from his pocket — his police badge — and held it open so she could see it. He pointed again to the door. Still smiling. Shit, maybe he was nice.

Clare pointed to the phone in her hand and held one finger up, to say she'd be with Norris in a minute. But Chopper wasn't picking up. She called Noah.

Norris was getting visibly annoyed. He pointed a third time to the door then started walking toward it. He pounded three times, hard.

Clare had no idea whether she should answer it or find a way to run. She had one eye on the door as she heard Noah answer his phone.

"Hey, Lucy." It felt weird, Noah addressing her by her cover name when they were alone. But of course it was protocol.

"I can't talk. I'm at Chopper's. Just listen, okay?"

Clare slipped the phone into her pocket and hoped like hell Noah would be able to help her if she needed him.

She opened the door for Inspector Norris.

SEVENTY-FOUR
WADE

Avalanche was packed. The tables were full and the bar was three people deep. Wade was pulling pints and mixing cocktails as fast as he could to help his staff keep up with demand. As Jana had said, no one knew what was in a Singapore Sling as long as it was the right color. Wade hoped the same was true of a Dark and Stormy. Cheap rum and ginger ale would have to do.

Chopper sat across the bar, sipping a pint of dark ale. "It's like New Year's Eve in this place."

"Nothing like a murder to make people want to congregate," Wade said. "You know how many tourists today have asked me, *Is this the bar? Is this where Sacha Westlake used to work?*"

"What do you tell them?" Chopper asked.

"I say yes. Even though I know the next question is going to be, *Are you Wade Harrison? Sacha's boss she used to sleep with?* I say no to that one, naturally."

"Tourists asking about Richie?"

"A few," Wade said. "One weekend warrior asked where he was supposed to score his drugs now. Like I'm the tourist information booth."

Chopper grinned. "Have you seen Norris? He's not answering his cell, and his wife says he's not at home."

"Probably still at the crime scene," Wade said. "He's kicking himself hard for Richie's death. Thinks he sucks as a cop."

"He kind of does," Chopper said.

"Seriously, I think he's on the verge of suicide, or something."

"I think he's on the verge of murder."

"What?" Wade glanced around to make sure no one was close enough to hear them.

"You heard me. Jana better get back here soon. I left Lucy alone at the cabin. I'm not too thrilled about that."

Wade poured six shots of Jägermeister for one of the waitresses' orders. He poured two extra shots for himself and Chopper. "Are you worried she'll poke around your things?"

"Nah, everything's locked away tight. I'm more worried for her safety." Chopper frowned. "You know Norris stole Richie's phone. Richie did pull a Sacha — recorded the three of us talking, which is completely whack when we're all in this together — but still. It's weird to just pickpocket someone's phone."

Wade could feel his forehead furrow as he dragged his memory for details. "Did Richie's phone have a black case with a sparkly skull on the back?"

"Yeah." Chopper smirked. "I told him it was girly; he said he didn't care."

"Norris pulled that phone from Richie's pocket." Wade hesitated, wondering if he should have said so. Then he felt the bloom of the liquor unfold in his chest, and he plunged ahead: "This morning. Stuck it in an evidence bag and gave it to his guys."

Chopper's forehead creased. "Is there any way Norris could have been palming the phone — making it look like he was pulling it from Richie's pocket but really it was in his hand to begin with?"

"I don't know," Wade said.

Another guy entered the bar. Floppy dark hair, ripped jeans, and a scowl on his face. He walked straight up to Chopper and said, "You the guy who's been banging Lucy?"

Chopper's eyebrows lifted. "Who are you?"

"Her boyfriend." The newcomer cocked his head to beckon Chopper away from the bar. "I want to talk to you alone."

Chopper followed the guy to the wall by the hot peanut machine. Wade watched them exchange a few urgent-looking words before Chopper returned to the bar.

He picked up his truck key, phone, and gloves from the bar, and dropped ten bucks on the counter for his beer.

Wade wanted to tell him to keep his money — friends bought friends beers, after all, especially on bad days, especially when they owned the goddamn bar — but he let the bill rest there. "What's up?"

"If you see Jana, tell her I couldn't wait."

"And if I see Norris?"

"Text me. And don't let him out of your sight."

SEVENTY-FIVE
CLARE

Clare smiled awkwardly at Inspector Norris.

"Who was on the phone?" Norris' eyelids fluttered, like he had dirt inside one of his contacts.

"My aunt. Is there something in your eye?"

"Sure it wasn't your handler?"

Clare froze in place. "What?"

"I think you should hand me your phone, *Clare*."

Clare's mind raced ahead of her nerves, checking her options. Denying it would be pointless, since he clearly knew her real name. Getting angry would be stupid. It could jeopardize her chance of working together — if there was a chance. Cooperation seemed like her only bet. And mollification, because Norris looked damn mad. Come to think of it, he looked a lot like Clare would look if the situation were reversed. She said, "You're Inspector Norris, right? I've been hoping to meet you."

"Why?" Norris peered at her. "So you can feel important because you're looped in on a higher level than me?"

"Not at all," Clare said. "You're in charge of this case. You're probably the only one who knows anything useful. I wanted to pool notes from day one, but I wasn't allowed."

Norris shook his head like he was shaking off Clare's stupidity. "What would we pool notes about? Your whole job is make-believe. Dropping acid with your new buds. Shredding the pow and calling that a work day." Norris pulled a pack of cigarettes from his pocket and lit one.

Clare nearly asked for a cigarette, too, but she was eyeballing the front door — she wanted to get the hell out of there. It was strange, Norris coming here. He hadn't even asked if Chopper was home. She felt the sled key in her pocket and contemplated the smoothest escape route.

"The FBI doesn't value you," Norris said. "You're a chess piece they move around so the important players can get to where they want to go."

"I know." Clare tried to sound agreeably irate. "It's what sucks about the job."

"And if you're hoping that one day you'll be one of the chess players, you haven't got a prayer. I looked you up — you have no education except Orillia OPP training and twenty weeks in Quantico. Without at least one academic degree, you're not destined for any brass on your lapel."

Clare wrinkled her nose at the thought of working in an office. "Good. I'm happy in the field."

"I hate the field." Norris cringed. "They've been promising me a management job in a big city. But now they're yanking that promise away. All because of little Alexandra the Great. You figure out who killed her yet?"

Clare was about to ask who Alexandra was, then remembered it was Sacha's given name. "Honestly, until Richie's body was found, I thought Sacha had probably killed herself."

"So you are as dumb as you look."

Clare frowned.

"Sacha Westlake didn't kill herself. The body was an obvious pose. I only called it suicide to lull the killer into thinking he'd gotten away. To keep him in town."

"You know the killer is a he?" Clare said.

"I do now. No thanks to the FBI's interference."

"Who is it?"

Norris shook his head. "Why would I tell you? So you can go running to your boss and take credit? Save yourself the years and leave the bureau now. You're a mediocre cop at best, and that's all you'll ever be."

Clare tried not to show Norris that his words cut. She thought she was getting better at her job, but if Norris had already solved the case, clearly she wasn't good enough. Maybe she *should* pack it in, ask Roberta for her job back in the auto shop. Fixing cars might not be the most thrilling job in the world, but Clare was good at it. She wouldn't spend so many hours suffering from self-doubt.

Yeah. And maybe she should crawl backward in time into a life with absolutely no excitement.

"How did you find my name?" Clare asked.

"A contact I have. He's been keeping me informed."

"A contact in the FBI or the RCMP?"

"Neither," Norris said. "Not that it's your business."

"You think you're a sheriff in the Wild West?" Clare wanted Chopper to come back — or to know for sure that Noah was listening. "Inventing your own laws, taking envelopes from criminals. Oh wait — maybe you mixed up *The Dukes of Hazzard* with *The Sopranos*."

"As opposed to you, thinking you're Charlie's next Angel?" Norris snorted. "Look at you. A man has just died, and you're holed up in your new boyfriend's cabin, miles away from the crime scene and any of the suspects."

Norris advanced toward Clare, handcuffs dangling from his belt. Clare noticed that the belt end of the cuffs was open — he could slide them off and restrain her in seconds.

Clare thought about the possible reasons Norris might want her in handcuffs. She felt the snowmobile key on its puffy orange keychain in her pocket.

Norris was blocking Clare's route to the door. Maybe intentionally, maybe not.

Clare didn't know what Norris wanted, but she needed to buy time until she could figure it out. "Can we stop acting like we're on opposite sides? I know our organizations both suck, but that doesn't mean you and I have to be enemies. We're after the same killer, right?"

Norris' puffed chest seemed to deflate a bit. "Look, kid, this makes me sad. Chopper and I have been friends since we were teenagers. But I'm pretty sure he's behind both of these murders."

Clare felt her stomach sink. "Why?"

Norris held up three fingers on one hand. "Three people are involved in a drug export operation." He pushed two fingers down. "Two are dead." He waved his remaining index finger. "One is left standing. Pretty easy to spot the killer."

Clare wondered if it really was that simple. She didn't see anything to be gained by Chopper wiping out his partners.

"Listen," Norris said. "I have an idea. You want to help me out?"

Clare had no idea if she wanted to help. How could she, until she heard the idea? Still, she nodded.

"Okay. Get into these handcuffs. I want to stage an arrest, trick Chopper into a confession when he comes back."

Clare backed a step away. Norris still hadn't asked if Chopper was home — which meant he came to the cabin knowing full well he wasn't. "How will that trick him?"

"Get in the cuffs and I'll explain it. We don't want to miss our window while Chopper's away."

"I'll hear him coming from literally a mile away. Have you heard his sled? It's louder than a helicopter. Plus, I mean, you're a cop, you'll understand this: I need to know more before I let myself become immobilized."

"I shouldn't be saying anything." Norris shook his little head. "But okay, I'll give you this: the DEA's involved now, too. They're actually the ones who suggested this experiment."

"Experiment?"

"To get a confession. I'm wired up to their offices right now." Norris patted his chest, implying wires under his shirt.

"The DEA," Clare said. "Is that who gave you my name?"

Norris frowned, nodded slightly.

Clare would ask to see the wires, but she was pretty sure they weren't there. "Okay," she said. "I'll play your game. Stage the arrest."

"Excellent." Norris advanced toward Clare with the handcuffs.

"But first, I want to show you these papers I found."

"Papers can wait," Norris said. "Chopper will be back any minute."

Clare wanted to ask how he knew that — if it was even true. "These are significant. I don't know how, but maybe you'll be able to help make sense of them. The DEA is mentioned a lot. I think Chopper might have immunity."

"Chopper . . ." Norris' jaw fell.

Clare hated this part — creating doubt in strong friendships — because what if neither one was guilty?

"Where are these documents?" Norris glanced around the room, like maybe they were pinned to the walls.

"In that trunk." Clare pointed. "The one that's doubling as a coffee table. I picked the lock and took photos of all the documents inside. It burned me to do it, because Chopper's a really cool guy. In another circumstance I could really have gotten to like him." Clare was rambling; she was nervous as hell.

Norris took a step toward Clare. She tried not to flinch. "Show me on your phone, if you took photos."

Clare shook her head. "I deleted them after I emailed everything to my boss. It's probably overcautious, but I don't like to leave evidence on my phone, even with an unlock password."

Norris squinted at Clare, like he couldn't decide if she was smart or stupid.

Clare nodded at the coffee table. "It took me a while to pick the lock — all I had was this lame Swiss Army knife — and I've already closed it back up again. But since I've done it once, the second time should be faster. Or maybe you have better tools?"

Norris brushed past Clare to study the coffee table.

"The lock's on the side by the fireplace," Clare said. "Under the glass — you need to crouch down to see it. You want help moving the table top?"

"I'm fine. Thanks."

When Norris was as far from the door as possible, in as awkward a position as possible, Clare bolted. Outside, she grabbed the key from her pocket, threw her leg over the spare snowmobile, and pressed the electric start button.

Which would have been perfect, but the sled gave back no juice. The engine coughed, sputtered, and stalled. Clare opened the choke and tried again. Same thing. Once more and the same. And now she'd likely flooded it.

Of course Norris was close behind. He pushed out the door and headed straight for Clare. She rammed the throttle all the way open, willing the carburetor to open up quick so the engine would start.

"What's wrong with you?" His voice hovered between frantic and reasonable. "Five seconds ago you were showing me evidence. Now you're running like I'm something to be afraid of. Did I spook you? Come back inside and work with me."

Clare pressed the ignition one more time and got power. She hadn't ridden a snowmobile in a few years, and even Chopper's "old" machine was newer than the sleds she'd ridden around Muskoka with her friends. But she gave it as much throttle as she could and bolted the hell away.

The wind was cold and Norris was right behind her. Clare couldn't hear what he was shouting over the roar of the two machines, but she could see his mouth moving in her side mirror.

She had no idea where to drive in these woods. The only route that made sense was back down to the highway. Problem was, she had already started to go the other way — up into mountainous no-man's-land — and Norris was behind her. Turning around was impossible. Clare realized too late that she should have stayed in the cabin, kept Norris talking longer. Even if he'd gotten her in handcuffs, someone would have arrived, eventually, to rescue her.

Or maybe she would have already been dead.

Clare zoomed along, knocking branches away and smoothing the ground, which unfortunately blazed a path for Norris to easily keep pace. She looked for something she could throw, something to catch in Norris' sled skis or even block his vision. A scarf would be ideal. Or a chunk of something hard. But she'd bolted so fast from the cabin that she wasn't even wearing a winter coat.

She could see her hands getting red with no gloves on. They'd have frostbite soon, for sure. But Clare could only feel the pain vaguely.

The trees cleared and Clare arrived at a logging road covered with snow. She had no time to think, so she turned right to head downhill, figuring — hoping — this road would eventually connect to the highway. The problem with a wide road: Norris' sled was more powerful. It took him no time to zoom up ahead of her and block her from passing.

Norris skidded to a stop in front of Clare. She slowed her machine and turned the steering as far as it would go to the right, to avoid crashing into him. Off the sleds, she would stand no chance. Norris had grown up here — he knew the woods and the mountain. Clare didn't even have her Swiss Army knife as a weapon — that was back in Chopper's warm, cozy cabin.

Clare's machine banked nicely — it gave her the angle she needed to avoid crashing into Norris. But just before she was clear, Norris reached out — probably to grab her arm, but he caught the left side mirror instead. Clare's front end tilted onto one ski as she gunned the throttle to full.

Fuck. Clare's machine jerked forward hard and Clare saw she'd lost the mirror. She leveled her sled and zoomed back uphill, because Norris was still blocking the downhill direction. In her remaining mirror she saw Norris toss the mirror away and gun his own throttle. He didn't lose too many seconds getting back on her tail.

The sky was getting dark. It was that weird time of twilight when you couldn't tell what was real and what was shadow. It was even darker in the trees, but Clare banked a sharp left to get back onto the trail they'd blazed from Chopper's cabin. Norris was only seconds behind, but at least this path was narrow and he couldn't head her off again.

Clare felt the front end of Norris' sled skis bump the back edge of her machine. *Motherfucker.* He was nearly close enough to reach out and knock her off her sled. Alone in the woods, with frostbitten hands, Clare would not stand a chance of survival. She had to stay on her sled — and keep it in motion — until they came across another person. A great plan, in the middle of nowhere.

She felt a solid bump. His machine connecting with hers. Which was fine in theory — the engines were in the front; he was more likely to damage his machine than hers. But Clare's frozen hands were having trouble holding on. She looked at her hands, imagined them enveloped in a warm protective orb — two orbs, one for each hand. And in the same thought, she knew that her mind was losing focus — the scene felt a bit like a dream.

Chopper's cabin was in sight, but an empty cabin wouldn't help if he and Jana weren't back from town.

Another bump from Norris. Man, Clare wished she had her gun on her. She was surprised Norris wasn't using his, but then that would be a dead giveaway, if Clare was found dead with a cop's bullets in her. She had to give him credit for a brain.

What could she throw at him? Could she rip off her other side mirror? Not likely, while she was trying to steer. Clare felt like the Road Runner. She needed a cliff to trick Norris into zooming over. Or was it the coyote who always won? Shit, her brain was getting wonky. Clare pulled her left, non-throttle hand in and warmed it on her skin under her shirt.

Pain sliced through her hand at its first contact with body heat, but Clare kept it there. She'd have to ride cross-handed soon, to warm up her right hand the same way.

At the cabin, Clare saw no sign of anyone else — no other snowmobiles parked — so she made a hard left, down the hill toward the highway. She knew this route better, having zoomed up and down with Chopper a few times, but she was still no pro. She couldn't dance with the curves like a local.

Norris lost a bit of ground, not being ready for Clare's sharp turn, but it didn't take him long to find his spot right on her ass again. Another bump of the sleds and Clare nearly lost her balance.

What Clare couldn't figure out was why Norris? Why would he

have murdered Sacha and Richie? Was it as simple as them threatening to expose his dirty ways? Or was there someone else involved — the someone who had given Norris Clare's name? Someone in the FBI or RCMP? Someone pulling the purse strings from New York or Washington? For a split second, she thought of Noah — but that was crazy. She and Noah were working together; he wasn't working with Norris.

She thought again about the girl on the boat.

Clare saw a flash of yellow coming up through the trees below. A third engine's noise joined the chorus and Clare realized with a loud thump in her chest that this was Chopper coming home. She couldn't see if Jana was with him; she just pulled to one side of the trail so he didn't smash into her as he barreled up the hill. Norris seemed to take a couple of seconds to realize what was happening. He slowed, looked like he was about to follow Clare, then zoomed back onto the trail and rode fast down the mountain. The trail was wide enough for two sleds, barely, and Clare watched with nerves on fire as Chopper's sled cleared Norris' by a hair.

Norris was getting away.

Chopper — without Jana — pulled over to the side and stopped by Clare.

"My god; your hands." Chopper pulled off his gloves and gently fit them on Clare. "We need to get you warm. Leave this sled here for now."

"But . . . Norris." Clare pointed downhill. Her teeth were chattering. She was surprised how hard it was to speak.

Chopper put his big yellow jacket on Clare and sat her in front of him as he rode up the mountain. Slowly.

She thought vaguely that she should be going down the mountain, back to the village, but Clare's mind was all over the place — mostly somewhere delirious. And a warm cabin sounded just right for right now. As she daydreamed, feeling Chopper's arms and gloves and jacket surrounding her, she wondered why Noah wasn't as cool or as kind to her as Chopper.

And as she drifted in this space, with Chopper carrying her

into the cabin and talking to her in a low, gentle voice, Clare realized maybe it wasn't Noah's job to look after her. Maybe Noah was the one who had been in the cold too long and Clare needed to be there for him, to put her magic jacket around him and make him feel warm again.

SEVENTY-SIX
MARTHA

Martha swirled the single malt around her glass. She couldn't peel herself out of Fraser's flaming red armchair to have her driver take her home to bed. "I think this is the ugliest chair I've ever sat in."

"It's art," Daisy said. "I thought you were supposed to be the sophisticated one."

"And there, Daisy, is your fallacy. Contemporary art is nothing but narcissistic crap." Martha had never voiced this particular opinion before, even internally. Half of her was pretty sure she sounded like a drunken fool; the other half thought she sounded brilliant. She raised her index finger and turned toward Fraser. "You and Daisy, letting Sacha drink underage at your parties . . . Daisy even giving her drugs . . . how could you *not* see you were confusing her?"

Daisy snorted. "Why don't you write a blog post exposing our laissez-faire parenting? Bore your remaining two followers into leaving."

"I'm sht-still in the race." Martha heard herself slur. Or was that stutter? "Unlike where my opponent is heading."

"Yeah," Daisy said, "and all the other contestants are having a field day. Have you even read the comment section of your post exposing

Kearnes? People are divided into three camps: Those who were never going to vote for you, those who supported you until you alienated the religious vote, and those who liked your progressive new platform until you started playing dirty yourself. Everyone sees through your so-called confession as openly slinging mud at Kearnes. It worked — no one likes him now, either. But how can you even think you're still in the race?"

"I never knew you followed politics."

"I do when it's fun."

Martha pursed her lips. "How many drinks have you had?"

"I don't actually drink at all, at the moment." Daisy patted her belly with a very amused look on her face.

Fraser grinned up at Martha in a way that she wished she didn't find even partially adorable. "Come on, let's get you into your car and home. Last thing we need is paparazzi snapping a photo of you stumbling out of here."

"The press can kiss my ass." Martha saw Daisy and said, "It's not as nice an ass as Daisy's, so maybe they won't want to. But at least I never gave our daughter drugs."

Daisy rolled her eyes. "At least I was Sacha's friend. She hated you."

Martha sprang back an inch in her chair. "What I'd really like to know, though, Daisy, is why did Sacha like you? What was the mysterious bond you shared to make her tell you about the drugs she was smuggling?" Martha was sober enough to know that she needed to be drunk to ask these questions.

"Really?" Daisy rolled her eyes. "You want to know why Sacha and I clicked?"

Martha arched her eyebrows.

"It's because I listen."

Martha's eyebrows fell back down. "Fine. Don't tell me."

"I only met her in her final year of high school, but if Sacha came home with a problem — if she was pissed off because she got a B on an essay she'd worked hard on, or if she was shut out of a social clique because she didn't care about idle gossip — you and Fraser had no time to listen. You were off dealing with your own problems — bigger problems, was how you made Sacha feel."

Martha swallowed hard.

Daisy continued. "I didn't have bigger problems. And if I did, I still made time for Sacha's. I know I'm not some crazy intellectual like you — or some savvy businessman like Fraser. But if you want someone to feel close to you, all you really have to do is listen."

For a moment, Martha believed Daisy. Then she remembered: "You gave her drugs, Daisy. Then you used those drugs against her — to push her out of the family. What was that?"

Daisy frowned, like she was trying to come up with an answer that didn't make her look like a gold-digger.

Martha didn't wait. "Is it because Fraser loved Sacha more? You didn't like having to share?"

Fraser held a hand in the air, as if pretending to be a crossing guard might stop Martha and Daisy from arguing. "We've all had one drink too many. Well, not Daisy, but hormones can make us say things we don't mean. Come on, Martha. Time to let your driver take you home."

Daisy smirked. "You know the bitter irony? It was you who motivated her to import the drugs in the first place."

Martha blinked a few times. She should have stopped with one drink. Or two. Because now she couldn't tell if Daisy was lying.

"Remember the summer before Sacha graduated? You had a meeting at your brownstone. Sacha overheard something that made her damn mad. Sacha and Jules." Daisy smiled a private little smile. "After that, Sacha knew you didn't give a shit about the public good. It was your career here." Daisy held up a hand above her head. "And the public good here." She held a second hand at chest level.

Martha closed her eyes and felt her lids flutter against her eyeballs. It was an odd thing to concentrate on, but it was better than listening to Daisy.

"Let's leave this one alone, Daisy," Fraser said. "Martha's had a long day and I'm sure the same is true for tomorrow."

"No, I won't leave this alone. Martha should know that she drove her daughter to her snowy grave."

"Daisy!" Fraser's voice was sharper than Martha had ever heard it. Martha said, "I want to hear."

Daisy tittered. "Jules was a camera. A video camera. With sound. Sacha left him in your office often."

Too much Scotch — the room was spinning. When would Martha remember that more than three drinks made her stomach turn over? "What did Jules see?"

"A very intelligent Mexican man giving you advice about narcotics. And you dismissing him saying, *I could never implement this. Well, I could, but I'd be out of a job at the next election. Shame, because I think it could work.*" Daisy shook her head and smiled sadly. "I can't believe anyone would contemplate electing you president. You can't even raise your own daughter successfully."

SEVENTY-SEVEN
CLARE

Clare tugged the blanket up around her chin and nestled deeper into the couch cushion. The stew Chopper was stirring smelled amazing — meaty and spicy and not remotely vegan. Though it was probably organic, or at least hormone- and antibiotic-free, which she oddly now felt glad about. But ultimately she shouldn't be here — not at all.

"Are you taking me back to the village soon?" Clare asked. "Or should I get someone to pick me up?"

Chopper was on the phone. He took it from his ear for a moment and said to Clare, "I'll take you after you eat something. Your hands need to warm up; you should get some hot food in you, too."

Clare looked at her hands and saw that she was wearing red fleece mittens — female. Another girl must have left these at the cabin. She was annoyed to find herself jealous of the girl — some ski bunny or rad snowboarding chick who was probably insanely hot. Something was definitely wrong with Clare — she never felt jealous, and recently the feeling was creeping around inside her like it was the new normal. It was one thing to feel it with Noah, but her relationship with Chopper was fake, so why would she care?

Chopper got off his phone and said to Clare. "They got him."

"Got who?"

"Norris. I still can't believe he's the killer. He was my best friend, all through school."

Clare flexed her fingers inside the gloves. Still painful. "Thanks for saving me from him. I'm so sorry I put you in that position, me against your friend."

"Saving you? Shit, I feel bad I left you up here all alone. You ready to eat?"

Clare joined Chopper at the wooden table where he had set down two steaming bowls. "This looks amazing."

"Should warm you up."

Clare spooned the thick broth into her mouth. Nothing could warm her hands, but with every chunk of beef, Clare felt her strength return.

"How come you came back without Jana?" Clare had wondered a few times but her brain wasn't at its quickest.

"Couldn't wait. When your boyfriend came into Avalanche and told me what was up —"

"He what?" The thought of Noah going to her rescue warmed Clare even faster than the stew.

"He said you left your phone on — that Norris had broken into my place and was trying to attack you. He really digs you. You should give him a chance, when you go back to New York."

Clare looked up and saw Chopper smiling at her.

"Norris told me. He texted me, actually — when I was waiting for Jana to get her damn glasses. Said you're the undercover."

"And you told Norris where to find me?" Clare felt her blood pump faster.

Chopper nodded.

"So why did you come rushing to my rescue?" Clare let one hand slide below the table, where she pressed two buttons from outside her jeans. She hoped she'd guessed their location correctly to speed-dial Noah. She just might need saving again.

"I didn't know Norris was the killer until your boyfriend came into the bar, told me what you and Norris were talking about. I was pissed at you, I'll admit that, but I couldn't leave you up here to die."

Clare set down her spoon, which suddenly felt heavy in her hand. "Why am I feeling weird? Did you drug me?"

"Yeah," Chopper said.

"Why?" Clare wondered why she didn't feel much more than vague panic.

"I need a head start, babe."

"For what? Is this the same drug Richie and Sacha were on when they died?"

"Don't know." Chopper grinned. "Didn't kill them."

"That's not funny."

"I know. Sorry. Anyway, if you can give me the memory stick from Jules, I'll be leaving now."

"I don't have it. Norris found the stick before I did." Clare's brain was still working, but her body felt like mush. She got up from the table and staggered to the couch, where she lay down.

"Shit," Chopper said. "That stick is going to bust me."

"Doubt it. Norris dropped it into the snow when he was chasing me. I seriously doubt, if the memory stick is ever found, that the bear cam footage will be readable on any device."

Chopper tapped his spoon lightly against a piece of beef before rising to join Clare in the living room. "Where on the mountain was it?"

"Not far from the logging road. If I was guessing I'd say, like, three trees away. You seriously going to try to find it?"

"The evidence would get me locked up for years. I can't risk someone else resurrecting the data."

Clare couldn't get Norris' accusation out of her head, about Chopper being the only one left standing, the only possible candidate for the killer. Not that she could do much about it, half-comatose on his couch. "Am I going to die?"

"Yes. But hopefully not for many years. If I guessed your weight right — around one-ten? — you won't even lose consciousness. Your body will be numb for the next several hours. You better give me your phone just in case, though."

Clare started to object but realized there was no point. She lifted her arm to her jeans and it flopped back down to her side.

"Good," Chopper said, moving toward Clare. "The drug's working. Where's the phone?"

"Why would I tell you? How come I can talk fine even though I can't move?"

"The drug stones your body, not your brain." Chopper patted Clare down, then reached under her and fished the phone from her back pocket. His touch still felt nice. "There's food in the fridge for when you wake up. No sedatives in anything, don't worry. But maybe don't help yourself to more stew."

Chopper let his hand linger under Clare. She was shocked that he still turned her on, but when he pulled up his hand — with the phone and the memory stick together — she knew he hadn't been feeling around affectionately.

"You're a good liar. I believed you about Norris and the snow. You know your phone's on." He lifted it to his ear. "Hello? Hm. They must have hung up."

Clare felt her eyes grow wide with fear.

Chopper smirked. "I'm not going to kill you. Norris would have, so you made a good call, to your boyfriend. Even knowing you were a cop, I rushed back here to save your life."

Clare watched Chopper pack a knapsack. He did this mechanically, like he'd mapped out his escape long ago, just in case.

"Oh, and if this helps: Norris said his contact — the one who gave him your name — is someone in Governor Kearnes' office. Who for some reason is claiming to be DEA."

Chopper picked up the keys to both snowmobiles and waved at Clare as he shut the cabin door behind him.

SEVENTY-EIGHT
MARTHA

"It's over," Ted's voice screeched through the phone.

Martha rubbed her eyes. She should have taken an Advil — or twelve — before bed. "What's over?"

"Sacha's killer has been caught. It was Inspector Norris, Whistler RCMP."

Sobriety hit fast. But her headache remained. "Why are you talking like your voice got caught in a bicycle chain?"

Ted laughed. "Are you drunk?"

"No. Asleep. Thanks for calling, Ted."

"My pleasure. And have you seen the ratings? Kearnes is falling fast. You were right to leave out the part about his being a newlywed at the time of your affair. The press has done the math themselves and they're loving every minute of this story."

"Forgive me if I'm not feeling quite as celebratory as you are just now."

"Oh, sorry. Of course . . . what this arrest means . . . can I help in any way?"

Martha shook her head — both a wasted gesture and a painful one. The clock on her bedside table read one a.m. She must have only been out for a couple hours after coming home from Fraser's and rolling onto the bed. "You're doing a great job, Ted. Just give me the night to sleep on the news. I'll be gung ho to keep fighting in the morning."

SEVENTY-NINE
CLARE

Clare opened her eyes, though her lids wanted to stay shut. She saw the pastel walls, the steaming plastic mug on the tray beside her bed, the fir trees out the window, where the sky was dark.

With effort, she turned her head to see Noah sitting on the other side of the bed, closest to the door.

"Are we still in the hospital?" Clare asked.

"It's a clinic. But yeah. How are you feeling?"

"What time is it? Is it still Saturday?"

Noah nodded. "Ten-thirty. Are you groggy, or do you feel okay?"

Clare remembered the sound of the helicopter landing just out-side Chopper's house. In her fugue, she had even laughed out loud at the play on words — a chopper to save her from Chopper. She remembered paramedics rushing through the front door, followed by Noah close behind. And the ride down from the mountain to the village health care center.

"I've always wanted to ride in a helicopter," Clare said. "Actually, I'd like to fly one, but I guess I should take lessons first. Why is this tube in my wrist? I don't remember them putting that in." Clare pushed at the edge of the tape that was holding her iv tube in place. She would have peeled it off, but her hands were covered in bandages.

Noah pulled her hand away gently. "The nurses will pull it out when it's time. Does your head hurt? Or feel weird?"

Clare sighed. "My head's fine. I could use a coffee, though. Why are my hands covered with gauze?"

"Frostbite," Noah said. "God, I feel terrible. I should have come with Chopper up the hill to rescue you. I wanted to, but he pointed out it would be awkward if he had to put you on his sled and drop me halfway up the mountain."

"I'm fine." Clare looked at her hands. They felt tingly, but not painful. "What you did was great. Coffee?"

"Yeah. Okay. I'll ask the nurse. Clare, I would have walked the other halfway up — I didn't care about that. I only stayed down so I could confront Norris, make sure his boys didn't conveniently let him slip arrest. Fuck, I hate them both so much right now." Noah shook his head. "Look what they did to you."

Clare lifted her arms — they moved slower than she told them to, but she was regaining control fairly steadily. "I'm really fine. And can I not have hospital coffee? It's so weak, it's like tea, but more awful."

Noah stood up and walked toward the window. Clare liked the sight of his ass in his dark denim jeans. Toned and cute. He leaned a shoulder against the sill and gazed out for a moment before turning back to Clare. He said, "You need to learn to take action, not just let stuff happen to you. You got Norris by fluke — you wouldn't have known he was the killer if he hadn't been trying to kill you."

Clare's impulse was to tell Noah to fuck off and do his own job. But she could see he was worried about her. "I can see why it looks like a fluke to someone who doesn't get my strategy."

Noah shook his head. "Strategy involves planning. What you do involves . . . waiting for something to happen. It's dangerous. You nearly died tonight. Twice."

Clare sighed. "Look, I'm not knocking *your* style, even if I do find it way too forced sometimes."

"Forced?"

"You go in with a plan," Clare said. "You don't give yourself room to roll with things."

"*Roll* with things? No, you're right, I do prefer a plan. It's why I get results."

"I get results, too," Clare said. "Norris is in jail, yes?"

"You only got lucky that he came after you." Noah smacked his forehead. "Sorry, maybe lucky was the wrong word."

Since Noah didn't seem to be moving to get her that coffee, Clare moved to reach for the tea beside her bed. She tried to move her shoulder, though, and couldn't. "God, this is annoying. I can't wait until I can move again. Do they know what Chopper drugged me with?"

"No."

"Is it the same drug Sacha and Richie were on when they were killed?"

"No, pretty sure that was Ambien. Norris' wife has a heavy prescription."

Clare frowned. "I still don't like Norris as the killer."

"No? I don't like the Ambien and pocketknife Norris had when we arrested him. He was going after you to kill you."

Clare swallowed hard. "Someone in Kearnes' camp was egging him on. And pretending to be DEA. Or something. I don't have the whole story."

Noah laughed. "Strong drugs you've been taking."

"Chopper and Norris both told me parts of this. I think Norris' mystery contact told him to kill Sacha. If my brain was working better, I think I could solve this right now."

"Norris was grasping at straws to get you to swallow the Ambien. He would have slipped it into a drink."

"No, he wanted me in handcuffs."

"Handcuffs? Rest, Clare. The killer is caught. It's a solid close on a high-profile case and the credit will be largely yours. Sorry I knocked your skills. It's just . . . I was scared shitless that I'd never see you alive again. Scared enough to trust Chopper." He shook his head. "You should never trust the other guy your girlfriend is sleeping with."

Clare gave him a faint smile. She liked the sound of *girlfriend.* "I'll take credit when the case is over. *Shared* credit. I wish I still had that bear cam footage. I'm sure it could have helped us put this together."

"You mean Sacha's documentary?"

Clare nodded.

"We have that. Well, the RCMP does. Richie Lebar saved every file to his home computer."

"Have you watched it?"

"No. It was password-protected, but our guys cracked it easily in the lab. I hear it's enough to put most of these people in jail. If only we can find that bastard Chopper."

"He's not a bastard."

"He drugged you and abandoned you in the middle of nowhere. In my books, he's a bastard."

"He saved my life today. I hope they never catch him."

"They?" Noah's eyebrows lifted.

"Fine. We."

Noah snorted. "You should worry about developing Stockholm Syndrome."

"At least I don't get so caught up in my cover role that I murder people because I'm in love with them." Clare tried to clap a hand to her mouth, but her arm moved too slowly to make that work. "I did not mean for that to come out."

Noah's brow lowered. "How do you know about that? Bert said it was in the vault."

"Amanda told me. I'm so sorry, Noah. I have to learn to think before I talk. Are you okay?"

"I'm fine."

"You don't look fine."

"Clare, leave it."

Clare felt tears form behind her eyes. Man, this was fucked — all these chemicals in her body were seriously messing with her emotions.

"Norris had something else that nails his coffin: three plane tickets, one-way to Buenos Aires."

"Three?"

"Him, his wife, and his kid. Leaving Monday morning."

"Wow. If he hadn't tried to kill me, he probably would have made it."

"Who knows? The important thing is, Norris is safely behind bars."

Right. Where Clare could visit him, to talk further. She wanted that DEA/Kearnes story.

"I'm going for a cigarette," Noah said. "You mind? If you want, I can ask a nurse if we can get you outside for one, too."

Clare looked up at Noah, surprised. She hadn't had a cigarette since she'd thrown her pack away in Chopper's place, and she'd forgotten to be edgy about it. "I think I might have quit."

Noah gave her a look like the world must have turned upside down.

"I have to stop in Toronto on my way back to New York. You want to come?"

"You talked to Roberta?" Noah lifted a corner of the sheet and started playing with Clare's foot, rubbing it. He pulled up a chair and sat down — apparently the cigarette could wait.

Clare smiled at his touch. "It's not going to be a fun trip. I understand if you say no."

"Of course I'll go."

Clare felt a tiny piece of ice melt inside her. "You will?"

Noah pressed Clare's middle toe mound right where it always gathered stress. "Bert wants us back in New York for official debriefing, but I'll clear a stop in Toronto with him. Then maybe we can go back up for a longer visit."

"Why don't I stop in alone on the way to New York?" Clare said. "A quick stopover to see my dad in the hospital. In case . . . you know. Then maybe we can drive up together, so I can have a real visit with my mom. Not that I want one, but . . ."

"Trust me," Noah said. "I understand guilt. Jewish mother, remember? I think you've met her once or twice."

Clare laughed. She actually liked Noah's mom — she was smart and she served fabulous takeout from their local Upper West Side delis. But Clare knew why she drove Noah crazy. "You don't have to stay the whole time."

"I'll stay for as long as you need."

Clare wanted to punch him, for being so damn nice. Couldn't he just pick a personality and run with it? "Thanks."

EIGHTY
WADE

W ade clutched his phone to his ear. "What?" he said to Chopper. "Seriously, you're breaking up. Where the hell are you?"

He stepped away from the bar. Surprisingly, Jana had shown up for work, as scheduled. She said she needed the distraction, and he could sure use the help — the place was still packed with tourists and locals alike.

"Chopper, did you say Lucy is the undercover?"

"Yeah. I would have told you this afternoon but I was too busy freaking about finding Norris. Look, you're going to be fine. Norris is in jail and I'm bailing. They got nothing on you. If they accuse you of anything, deny it."

"Are you not coming back?"

"Not for a bit. I'll be in touch to keep tabs on the investigation. If they can indict me, I'd rather be in the back country than in jail. If they don't have anything, I'll come hang in civilization."

"I guess I understand."

"Also — listen, I wasn't going to give this to you, because I thought you were better off without that bar. But I have cash — you can take what you need to save Avalanche. If that's what you want."

Wade laughed mirthlessly. "This place has no value without the possibility of the band reviving. That's the whole reason I opened . . . you know, *if you build it . . .*"

"You're the creative genius, Wade — you always were." It was harder and harder to hear Chopper. The signal was fading into nothing. "Screw the bar and play your music. What will it take? Just money?"

"Yeah." Of course it was just money, separating Wade from living his dream. Wasn't that always the case?

"So here's my prescription: Go to rehab first. Go somewhere nice — there's more than enough cash for a month in one of those celebrity havens in Malibu — because trust me, your life will look better with no booze in it. Then, take the rest of the cash that you need to make your music."

"Why are you being so generous?"

"Because if your friends aren't there when you need them, then what the fuck's the point? My cash is in . . ."

Of course the phone cut out. Story of Wade's fucking life. Whatever. He didn't need it that night. Chopper would call again soon.

SUNDAY / FEBRUARY 19

EIGHTY-ONE
CLARE

Clare sat across the metal-legged table from Stu Norris. She was still addressing him as Inspector, though it was mildly ironic on her part. He'd been silent for the last five minutes, refusing to answer Clare's questions.

"I know you hate me," Clare said. "But I think I can help."

"*You* cannot possibly help me."

Outside in the parking lot, an RCMP officer was waiting to take her to the airport. On the drive down from Whistler, Clare had gazed out the passenger window at the water and the mountains and the tall pine trees along the Sea-to-Sky highway, piecing together the broken facts. She had arrived at an answer.

"You're scared to talk about the man who paid you," Clare said. "For your family, I'm guessing, since your own life's shot to shit."

Norris' eyes rolled upward, as if to say, *My, how ingenious.*

"The man who said he was DEA. Chopper said you think he was lying, that he's not DEA, but someone with the Kearnes campaign?"

"Chopper thinks with his dick," Norris muttered. "He wasn't supposed to tell you that."

"He said it for your sake."

"How is that for my sake?"

"Are you thick?" Clare tapped the side of her head. "If we catch this person who manipulated you into *murder*, your sentence could be reduced dramatically. If you help us, it could probably even go down to manslaughter."

Norris shrugged. "Like you said, my life is shot to shit. I'll take protecting my family over helping the organization that never gave me a damn chance to shine."

Clare gave him a blank look.

"Are *you* thick?" Norris tapped his head, imitating Clare's gesture of a moment earlier. "The RCMP has been treating me like crap for nearly twenty years. Why would I care if they catch their man?"

"Have you been threatened?" Clare asked. "By this so-called DEA?"

"What do you think?"

Clare sighed. The threat was probably empty, but she wouldn't be able to convince Norris of that. "I know why you thought you had to kill Sacha."

"I never confessed to killing Sacha."

"You should." Lucy's baggy sleeves were bugging Clare. She rolled them up and leaned into the table. "For Zoe's sake."

Norris's eyes darted to Clare and away again quickly. "Don't you ever talk about my daughter. Her name on your lips is vile. And it's Zoe I'm protecting with my silence."

Wow, it felt great to be hated so much. Clare said, "Zoe loves you right now. She's going to grow up, though, with you in jail for murder. Maybe she'll get past you murdering a drug dealer. You were a cop; these things do happen. But I doubt she'll find a way to forgive you for killing a twenty-three-year-old girl."

"Shut *up*. You think I don't know that?"

"If you help us find the truth, you can tell your story — how you were led to believe you were working for the DEA, how you thought you were acting for the greater good. You trusted the law, and the law let you down." This was drivel. Norris had been acting in self-interest the whole damn time. But it was sellable — his family would believe it. Hell, Norris might even believe it.

Norris held his eyes closed for a long moment before opening them again. "I was an idiot."

"So what happened?" Clare kept her voice as soft and as conversational as she could. "Someone phoned you, said they knew you were on the drug dealers' payroll . . . They said they didn't want to bust you — they actually wanted to pay you to keep on as you were — and report to them?"

Clare hadn't been sure about the payment part, so she was glad when Norris nodded.

"Some time goes by, everybody's profiting, you're reporting to this voice on the phone with some kind of regularity, when suddenly you get the call. He wants you to kill Sacha."

Norris shut his eyes again, leaned his head into his hands, his elbows resting on the table.

Clare wasn't sure why the Kearnes campaign could have wanted Sacha dead. But she didn't think Norris knew, either, so she said, "When you killed Sacha, did you still think you were working for the DEA?"

One short nod. Not an official confession, but Clare didn't officially care.

"And your mysterious contact said if you didn't kill her, they would let you go down as a dirty cop, let the RCMP drag your name through the mud for your family and friends to see, and maybe you'd even do jail time."

Norris nodded.

"Jesus," Clare said. She couldn't help herself. "When did you realize you weren't working with the DEA?"

Norris squinted at Clare like he was deciding what to say. "A few days ago," he said finally, "I got a phone call that I traced back to Geoffrey Kearnes' campaign headquarters. The calls were usually blocked, but this one wasn't."

Clare wasn't sure such a savvy puppetmaster would make such a pedestrian mistake. "Is this the source who gave you my name?"

Norris nodded.

"So why did you have to pay for my name? You'd think they would have given that freely. Or taken it out of your next payment."

"The money had to be sent to a third party. My source didn't want the risk of sending it himself, so I had to raise the cash and wire it."

"To where? Which bank? Which city?"

"To a numbered account, obviously. Sorry I can't give you branch details and the recipient's home phone number."

"Where did your money go? The funds you received from your mystery contact." Canadian banks had no records of Norris receiving large cash transfers. "Maybe a different numbered offshore account?"

Norris gave a gesture that was part shrug, part nod. Clare took it as assent.

"Do you have any cigarettes? We're not allowed to smoke in here so the tuck shop doesn't carry them."

"I'm sorry," Clare said. She meant it. She still hadn't smoked since the previous afternoon, but riding the cravings that morning had been hard. In jail, she wouldn't bother trying to resist. "Can I ask you about Richie?"

Norris nodded. His shoulders had relaxed and his tremble had all but gone away. He would soon confess officially. Clare was glad for his sake.

EIGHTY-TWO
MARTHA

"You're Martha Westlake, right?" A young girl, maybe ten years old, in jeans and a messy ponytail was sitting across the aisle, an in-flight magazine open in her lap, pictures of vacation hotspots bright beneath her small thumbs.

"That's right."

"What you're doing — it's horrible." The girl rolled her R's as if imitating someone else saying the word. "Mom joined the Republicans so she can vote for Geoffrey Kearnes. We live in Michigan."

"I see." Martha was taken with this girl. Maybe because the kid was polite, even while saying she hated Martha's guts. "Would you like to discuss any of the issues?"

"No," the little girl said. "We just really hope you lose."

The girl's mother, beside her, leaned over to apologize. "I'm so sorry, Senator. It's not personal." To her daughter, she said, "You need to remember that politicians are people. Their feelings get hurt, like yours and mine."

"But she's trying to hurt the country. You said . . ." The girl's voice trailed off with the silencing glare her mother was giving her.

"Really," Martha said. "It's okay. I wish discussions like this could happen more often. This country would function better if it worked as one giant think tank instead of pockets of elitists making decisions on behalf of the entire population. Is it the drug policy you don't like? The separation of church and state?"

The girl seemed not to understand Martha, but the mother — the voter — softened her gaze.

"My older brother is a drug addict," the girl said. "He ran away, and we think he's in Detroit but we're not sure."

"Not an addict — just having problems," the mother cut in, but the anxious look in her eyes said she didn't believe her own words.

Martha inhaled deeply.

"My mom says your new policy would make it easier for kids like him to score their drugs. That's why we hate you."

Martha still could not get over how confident this kid was. It was refreshing.

"Oh, please," said the man in the seat in front of Martha. "Drug reform is long overdue. Colombia and Mexico have been pushing for reform like this for years. And it's not because they like the cartels or the street violence, I'll tell you that."

"Thank you," Martha said to the man.

"For what? I'm not voting for you. You had years to listen to those guys — Zedillo, Gaviria, Cardoso — and you didn't. Now suddenly your daughter dies and you're a champion for intelligent thought? You should do the right thing because it comes naturally to you, not because you've been pushed so hard you can't justify the wrong thing anymore."

Martha lifted her eyebrows.

"You might as well make prostitution legal," said a white-haired woman across the aisle. "It's no worse than drugs. You'd get the pimps off the streets and collect taxes to boot."

Martha wasn't sure if the woman was joking or serious, so she asked.

"Oh, a bit of both," the old woman said, before shouting at the flight attendant for another gin. "But your campaign is a bit of a joke, too, isn't it?"

Martha focused on the girl, because she felt her mother's vote was winnable. "Do you know that my daughter has recently died? And police think it's drug-related?"

The girl nodded. "Mom thinks you're angry. You lost your own daughter, so what do you care about the kids in America?"

"Oh." Martha searched for the simplest language she could find, the kind that would make sense to a ten-year-old. "The opposite is true. I don't want anyone else to ever go through this. The man up ahead is right — it took my daughter dying for me to realize what the right thing was."

The man grunted. "You're not going to flatter my vote out of me."

"Nor will I try," Martha said. "But I will try to help this young girl's brother."

The girl wrinkled her mouth. "How would legalizing drugs make the problem better? Doesn't that mean that everyone will have them?"

"Everyone already does," Martha said. "Right now, America is suffering more than it ever has from gang violence. Drug cartels — those are the people who bring the drugs into the country — and gangs who sell on the streets are powerful, mean organizations. To legalize the drug is to take away their power. Does this make sense?"

The girl shook her head.

"Okay, take your brother. You love him, right? But he's doing drugs, and he's run away."

The girl nodded.

"If drugs were legal, they wouldn't be associated with crime, right?"

"I don't know. They'd still be bad."

"Right. But they'd be bad like alcohol, or tobacco, or Krispy Kremes — they'd hurt your health, but they wouldn't make you a criminal."

"I guess."

"You wouldn't be segregated from polite society — to the point where you had to run away and hang out with criminals. And the gangs would not be able to pull young people into their fold — people like your brother — to act as dealers or prostitutes to fund their addictions."

The girl's mother wrapped her arm around her daughter. Her eyes had hardened again. "That's enough, please, Senator," she said to Martha. "I'm worried sick about my son. You're making it worse."

"I'm so sorry. I don't mean to scare you. But I think plain talk will get us to the solution faster than anything else."

"Okay. But not around my daughter."

Martha understood. "How about if I talk to your son myself?"

"We don't know where he is."

"You say you think he's in Detroit. Finding him should not present a challenge if we get enough manpower on it."

"How would you . . . ?"

"I'd use my blog," said Martha. "I'd post your son's picture and ask for help. And when we find him, in addition to making sure he gets the counseling he needs, I would fly to Detroit — or wherever — and talk to him."

The woman's jaw fell. "You'd do that?"

"Of course. To solve America's drug problem, we need to start by helping one child at a time."

And, said the politician inside Martha, *it would be incredible* PR.

EIGHTY-THREE
CLARE

Outside of Arrivals at Toronto's Pearson International Airport, Clare spotted Roberta's blue pickup immediately. She climbed up into the cab and slammed the passenger door shut.

"I got you a coffee." Roberta nodded to the two extra large Tim Hortons cups in the center console.

Clare picked up the one closest to her. "Thanks."

Roberta pulled out of the snowy airport driveway onto the highway that would take them north. Clare sipped her coffee and wondered why she felt so homesick.

"I hope my dad finally kicks it this time," Clare said.

"Really?" Roberta shot Clare a quick glance. Her thick red ponytail had more flecks of gray than the last time Clare had seen her.

"Really," Clare said. "If he's not going to choose to live, I wish he would go ahead and die."

"He *is* dying. Not much will save him except the impossible."

"Good."

"You're fooling yourself, kid. You'll be gutted when he goes."

Clare blinked to keep the tears behind her eyes distinctly hidden. "We'd kill a horse if he was in less pain than my dad's in."

"Don't tell your mother that."

"Don't worry — I'm not interested in watching a waterfall cascade down her face."

"Hey, my own eyes haven't been dry through all this, either." Roberta shifted into four-wheel drive to account for the terrible weather. "When I was a single mother, your dad gave me a job I was no good at — purely so I could pay my bills by working daylight hours. He taught me how to troubleshoot car problems with the right combination of logic and intuition until I was not only competent, but great at the job. Without him, I'd probably still be on overnights at Pauly's Diner."

"You would have found another job. And just because my father used to be soulful doesn't mean he gets to manipulate me now." Clare remembered being a little kid — four or five — peering into an old Chevy engine with her father. He explained how all the parts worked separately, how they needed each other to work together so the car would run. But that man had died a long time ago.

"Okay, at least you're here. How's work going?"

Clare frowned. "I just got off a case. I guess it went well."

"You nab your man?"

"Yeah. And as of half an hour ago, we have a confession."

"So what's still nagging?" Roberta eased off the gas slightly.

Snow had begun to fall almost to whiteout proportions. They could barely see three car lengths in front of them, even with the wipers on full blast. Roberta turned north onto Highway 400.

"The killer was following instructions — but we don't know whose. I told my boss what I know, and he'll get the right people to pursue it. But it's frustrating not being the detective. I don't get to wrap it all up, tie the loose ends."

"Would you rather be a detective?"

"No. I like what I do. I should probably just not get so invested, so I can let the case go when my part is finished."

As Roberta drove past Canada's Wonderland, the landmark that unofficially meant they were leaving urban sprawl and entering their northern home territory, Clare felt her body tense. She wasn't sure she was ready to see what was waiting in the hospital.

EIGHTY-FOUR
WADE

Wade sat across from Norris. Lucy — Clare — had called from the Toronto airport to say that Norris had confessed to both murders. She asked Wade to get more information, if he could. In exchange for Wade's money laundering being forgiven, she said. Wade doubted Clare had jurisdiction to offer that kind of deal, but he trusted that she'd try.

"We done?" Norris said. Like he wanted to get back to his cell or somewhere more exciting. They'd been sitting silently for two full minutes. "I can feel your hate burning a hole through my skin. But thanks for coming."

"Was murder your only fucking option?"

"At the time, I clearly thought it was." Norris' eyebrows flickered. "You bring me anything? Cigarettes? Booze?"

Wade handed over his travel mug full of vodka, which he'd snuck past the guards without incident. "You can share my coffee."

Norris gulped. He didn't pass the mug back.

"How come you rolled over so fast, confessed to the murders?" Wade wanted to shake his friend, make the truth fall out.

"Because I didn't do anything wrong." Norris' shoulders slumped. "I would never have killed Sacha if . . ."

"If what?" Part of Wade wanted to strangle Norris, to kick him in the balls, to tie him to his car and drive down the highway with Norris screaming as the road burned through his clothes and eroded his flesh. But another part saw the guy who had kept the band's finances on track when Chopper and Wade had been too drunk or too stoned — or too busy with women — to care. Norris hadn't complained — he was happy to take the responsible role. To keep things in order.

"If I hadn't have been lured by the so-called DEA's promise to make me a hero. I believed them when they told me that once our operation was over — once they told the RCMP how helpful I'd been, nailing a big-time criminal enterprise — I'd be able to write my own career ticket on either side of the border." Norris grabbed at his short hair and tugged. He looked like he was enjoying the pain. "I wanted to see Zoe grow up. To watch her play in a big American Philharmonic one day."

"You haven't been sentenced yet." Wade was amazed that Norris hadn't once expressed remorse about Sacha's death — about Wade's loss, and Martha Westlake's. And Richie's family. But Wade was here for his own selfish reasons, too: to get the information for Clare, to maybe save his own ass. He said gently, "I think there's a good chance you'll see Zoe play cello one day."

"She won't want me there. I'll be her fuck-up dad, the mercenary murderer."

"Even if she knows you thought you were acting on the side of the law?"

Norris shrugged. "I guess I kind of knew it wasn't DEA, by that time. They wouldn't have had Sacha killed — maybe just warned, or relocated."

Several beats passed as the two men stared at each other. Amazing how a friendship that took years to build could disintegrate so damn quickly.

"I lied to Clare," Norris said.

"About what?"

"I didn't actually lie, but I gave her incomplete information."

"Why?"

"To screw her up. Make her look like an idiot when she got back to New York and started pursuing a false lead. I wanted her to lose her job, lose face."

"Why bother?"

"Because she's responsible for my new home." Norris spread his arms around the suburban Vancouver holding center. "If Clare had never come to Whistler, I'd be leaving for Argentina in the morning."

"But you're not."

"No. I'm not." They sat quietly for a moment before Norris spoke again. "I told her I traced a phone call back to Governor Kearnes' campaign. Which was true. But when I called the number back the next day, I got a confused response from a guy I'd never spoken to."

"I'm missing something," Wade said.

"Whoever pretended to be calling from the DEA also falsified their caller ID, I think to frame Geoffrey Kearnes."

Wade had no idea what to make of this. Or why it mattered.

"Just tell Clare," Norris said. "My lawyer says it will be easier to get my charges reduced if we can find out who was pulling the strings."

Wade looked covetously at his coffee cup in Norris' hand. He wanted to reach for it, but didn't. Maybe he should take Chopper's and Georgia's advice, go to rehab.

Maybe there was no fucking point.

EIGHTY-FIVE
CLARE

Clare's father lay in the hospital bed. His arms were blotchy, sticking out like twigs from his pale green hospital gown. Tubes and wires connected his wrists and chest to an IV machine and monitors above his bed. Clare wished she could turn around, have Roberta drive her straight back to the airport, but the nurse had already announced Clare's arrival — in a chipper voice like she thought it was a good thing.

Her dad lifted his head and winced. His face was thinner than before. His dark brown hair was almost entirely gray. People used to say they looked alike, Clare and her dad. She hoped that wasn't still true.

"I'm alone," Clare said. "There's no one here who believes your martyr act."

He frowned. "I understand your anger."

"You say that whenever I get mad at you."

"You get mad for good reasons."

Clare felt her shoulders trembling. "You're only saying that to make me less angry." *To make me weak*, Clare didn't say.

"I'm glad you came."

"I came because Roberta says you're dying." Clare stared at the heart rate monitor. Eighty-six, whatever that meant.

Her dad wheezed. "Well, I appreciate that. I know you're busy."

Clare waited for the next line, the inevitable guilt trip. Or maybe that was supposed to have been implied.

"How are you enjoying Brooklyn?"

"Manhattan. I haven't been home for a few weeks."

"Clarissa the Brave." Her dad rolled over and faced the window. "Why don't you move your chair to this side? It's brighter."

Clare moved her chair, but slowly. Her mind had fired on something her dad had said.

"You look deep in thought."

"I am." Clare couldn't look at the hospital bed, so she stood up and looked out the window, at the flat parking lot she knew so well from so many other visits there. None, though, had had this finality.

Clarissa the Brave . . . the name played over in her head. Norris had called Sacha "Alexandra the Great." Was that her real childhood nickname? And if so, how did Norris know it?

"You used to get that look when you were a kid. Watching something, learning something new."

The soft sound of air whooshing filled the room. Clare turned back around to see the blood pressure machine pumping itself up around her father's skinny arm. She was almost worried that it would snap his arm off, but then the pressure abated, the arm bands deflated. Clare looked at the monitor, which showed that his heart rate was higher than on the last measure. No doubt that was her fault. She met her father's eye. "I think you've twigged something for me — for the case I've just finished."

Her dad's eyebrows lifted — slowly, like even that was so damn painful.

It didn't work, though, if her hunch was right — it didn't work that the person pulling strings could be someone from the Kearnes campaign. Or did it? Sacha had grown up around politics — someone from the Kearnes camp could have known her as a kid. And Geoffrey

Kearnes *was* Sacha's biological father — though a posthumous paternity test had yet to confirm it.

Alexandra the Great. Could have been Norris' own nickname for her. But if it was also her childhood nickname, if Norris had heard it from the voice on the phone, Clare would put money on the person prodding Norris being someone who knew Sacha very, very well.

But there was still nothing Clare could do — just pass the idea to Bert and let him do what he liked with it.

In her pocket, Clare felt her phone vibrate. She pulled it out and saw that the call was from Wade.

"I have to take this," she told her dad. He grumbled, so Clare said, "It's work, Dad. It's important."

Clare moved to the window as she pressed Accept to the call. In the parking lot, she saw Roberta in her blue truck, drinking coffee and moving her head to some music — probably country. It made Clare homesick — she was glad she was coming back soon for a real visit.

As Wade ran through his conversation with Norris, Clare felt a small laugh bubble up to her surface.

"What's so funny?" Wade said.

"That Norris lied to me. It's awesome."

"Oh."

"It throws the possibilities wide open, unfortunately, but it helps because what he said wasn't sitting right. Thanks, Wade. I'll make sure I let my bosses know you dug that out for me. Seriously hope it can help you in return."

Clare hung up with Wade and turned back to face her father. He looked even more shriveled now, like he was shrinking into death with each passing moment. Which Clare supposed everyone was doing, every second of their life, but maybe not quite this visibly.

"I have to go," she said.

"You just got here."

"There's a lead I have to follow."

"Another agent can't do that? I'm dying, Clare. You could at least stay the night."

Clare pictured the trailer: heaters blasting, her mom drinking and crying with one or more neighbors there drinking, too, all of them trying to rope Clare into the whole stupid sad cycle of grief. If she stayed, she would be pulled back into the headspace of an angry adolescent, raging against the futility — the banality — of the life her parents chose to live. She would also start smoking again.

She would come back, but with Noah beside her for strength.

"I need to make a phone call, fast. I need a friend to ask a suspect a question. And I can't afford to miss my plane back to New York. But really, Dad, thanks for your help. You totally got my mind working in a new direction. I'll come back up north as soon as I can."

"Don't trouble yourself."

Clare rolled her eyes.

"Can I at least have a hug? I might not be here when you get back. Though I'm sure your mother will appreciate the company with the funeral arrangements."

Clare cringed. She hated touching her father. He smelled — and felt — like disease.

"Am I that bad?"

She pulled at the thin, tattered blanket that covered her father's legs. "Are you cold?"

"No."

Clare chewed her lower lip. "I'll be back in a few days. Don't die without me."

"You put on these airs," her dad said. "Like you're too good for us now. We made you. You can never escape us."

"I love Orillia. What I hate is watching you cut off all your lifelines just to feed your addiction for one more fucking day."

"Clare. Language."

"I could say worse."

Her father sighed. "Have you ever tried to quit smoking?"

"I quit yesterday."

"Yeah." Her father snorted. "I can tell by your mood. Good luck staying quit."

EIGHTY-SIX
MARTHA

Martha felt like she was walking in one of those dreams where you can only go extremely slowly, like the air is really water, or maybe Jell-O, but only for you — everyone else can move at their regular, air-walking pace.

She walked like this the entire half block to Broadway, where she turned north to go to Starbucks. A man with a microphone approached, but her Secret Service guys said something to him and he backed off. Martha flashed a smile to the reporter to be on the safe side, but she was glad the guards had snubbed him; she didn't trust herself to talk to the press through Jell-O.

As she waited in Starbucks for the chai latte that she didn't even know if she wanted, she saw the blogger from the airport push open the door.

Martha pointed at him and his eyes shot wide open. He didn't bolt, though, like she would have expected. He froze in place and stared back at her.

"You," she said, feeling for her voice, like she wasn't sure where she'd left it. "You are not Lorenzo."

The blogger moved toward her but he was blocked by Secret Service, who patted him down.

Martha picked up her latte at the end of the counter. She peered around her protectors and said to the blogger, "I guess we could sit down."

The blogger typed something into his phone and followed Martha to a corner table, as far from the windows as possible. The Secret Service guys said something to a man with a computer on the adjacent table. The man nodded at Martha in recognition before picking up his computer and taking a window counter seat. The guards took his table.

"So who the hell are you?" Martha said.

The blogger pointed to his phone. "I'm waiting for permission to tell you."

Martha's eyebrows arched. Sacha used to tell her she looked like the Queen of Hearts when she did that — smug and mean.

"In the meantime, though, I have a question."

"Shoot."

"Did Sacha have a nickname as a kid? Something only you or your husband might have called her?"

Martha took a sip of the latte, as if maybe the answer was somewhere in the foam. "Alexandra the Great," she said finally.

The blogger's phone chimed. He glanced at his new message and said, "My name is Noah. I'm with the FBI."

Martha didn't know why this made her feel let down. Maybe she'd liked the idea that some righteous blogger was out tilting at windmills to vindicate Sacha's murder. Even if she'd known it wasn't really Lorenzo.

Noah met her eyes kindly. In another life, she would have thought that she'd like to introduce the young man to Sacha.

"I'm confused," Martha said. "The case is closed, right?"

"The murder is solved — we have a confession and a man in jail. But the killer wasn't acting alone. Are you flying anywhere tonight or tomorrow morning?"

"Am I under arrest?"

"No. But we might need your help."

"I fly to Phoenix in the morning, and L.A. in the afternoon to tape Bill Maher."

"Can you postpone Phoenix?"

"I can postpone both, if you'll tell me why." Martha's chai latte tasted off. Not like the milk was curdled, but like the chai itself was different. Not a pleasant taste at all.

"I'll get you more information as soon as I can. Thanks for your cooperation."

Martha stood up, walked to the counter, and ordered her usual: a tall, black bold. As she moved toward the trash and held the nearly full chai latte over the hole to dump it in, she felt closer to tears than she had in two weeks. They wouldn't come yet, but at least they were on the way.

She sipped the black coffee. Delicious.

EIGHTY-SEVEN
CLARE

Clare's computer cast a blue glow around the kitchen. Her sink still had dirty dishes from before she'd left town. These four hundred square feet ate up most of Clare's salary, but it was worth every penny to live alone in the East Village.

Her brain was beginning to melt from not enough sleep, but the pot of coffee that she was midway through was keeping her eyes open and her fingers alert on her keyboard.

She was going through the video clips from the bear camera. There were other agents watching them officially — both in the FBI and the RCMP — but Clare had asked to see the footage, too, and though her role was officially over, no one had objected to her slogging through footage for answers.

Sacha had brought Jules into Chopper's woodshed, which he'd decked out as a pretty awesome chemistry lair. Sacha would have made an excellent investigative reporter. Her questions had Chopper basically guiding viewers through the how-to-make-LSD process.

Sacha and Jules had visited Richie at his apartment, hung out on his couch and watched some local dealers come and go. Richie seemed to be the town wholesaler. The young kids seemed to fear him, though he never raised his voice or even threatened them.

Jules had witnessed the border crossing, the knapsack filled with LSD changing hands. Jules caught the faces of the guys who collected the knapsack. *They* looked scary. Clare hoped this tape helped take them down.

Norris was caught in a few different clips — with Richie, with Chopper, in Wade's office at Avalanche where Sacha had left Jules sitting through some of her shifts. This video would have busted him for several years on corruption charges alone.

And Wade — Jules had seen Wade taking cash from Chopper and Richie, cutting them paychecks for some of that money and passing Norris' end to him at separate meetings. Unfortunately for him, the conversations Jules recorded made the transactions clear to anyone: he was laundering for Chopper and Richie, and delivering Norris hush money.

Only Jana seemed immune. She was caught on tape using drugs of all kinds, but in Canada that was barely a misdemeanor. She could maybe get done for complicity — knowing about the crimes and not saying anything — but only a real prick of a prosecutor would go after her. More likely she'd be bullied into testifying against her friends.

What Clare hadn't found was any way Norris might be connected to one of Sacha's parents, a way that he might know — and use — her childhood nickname.

Irrationally, she glanced at her apartment door to make sure it was locked and chained. It was.

On her lined notepad, she wrote the names of her four top suspects:

Martha Westlake
Ted Mitchell
Fraser Westlake
Daisy Westlake

She just couldn't see murder.
But a nickname didn't have to be confined to a parent. It could be

an aunt, a grandmother, a close friend. Maybe Kearnes had known he was the father — maybe Sacha knew, and had confronted him, and he wanted her out of the way so his campaign could be scandal-free. Maybe it was someone in Whistler? It would have to be someone who knew Sacha well.

> *Jana Riley*
> *Wade Harrison*
> *Chopper MacPherson*
> *Geoffrey Kearnes*

Fuck, there were way too many suspects. Clare gulped her coffee. She had to take them one by one.

Martha had gained politically, but anyone could see she was grieving horrendously. Yes, a killer could have remorse. But Clare didn't see a killer when she looked at the senator on TV.

Ted Mitchell — the assistant — was a young hotshot idiot, according to Noah, who had stopped by Martha's campaign office and met him. But Noah could be a hotshot idiot himself; Clare could see their personalities clashing. It wouldn't make sense to murder someone's daughter if you wanted them to win an election. A lot of people in Martha's position would have dropped out of the race, not stayed to fight it.

Fraser? Clare didn't see Sacha's father as the motivating force behind the murder. From his press interviews, he seemed kind and bland — strangely perfect for a killer. But why would he want her dead? Clare didn't know enough about him, so she put a question mark beside his name.

Daisy had been clear about wanting Sacha out of the family, out of the will — out of the way. Chopper and Jana had both told Clare that. But still — people who were clear about their intentions weren't likely to be backhanded as well. People normally played on one level — on the surface, or below it. It took intelligence to play both levels. Daisy didn't seem quite that clever, but maybe she was just that good.

Jana knew Sacha well. She was mildly deranged — probably

because of all the drugs she did. If she had killed Sacha, it would have likely been spontaneous and drug-induced — not an elaborate scheme to set Norris up to do the deed. Also, Norris was paid. Jana did not seem to have money beyond the tips she made slinging drinks after singing provocative karaoke tunes at Avalanche.

Wade's motivation would have been to prevent his wife from finding out about their affair. But again, the elaborate scheme involving Norris made no sense. Wade was a drunk — meaning sloppy. There would have been holes in his plan that would have exposed him long before this. Clare was confident Wade was not to blame.

Georgia? Clare wished she'd gotten to know her, somehow, in Whistler. But she added her name to the list.

Chopper. Easily smart enough. He sure knew Norris well enough to know what would get under his skin, what would compel him to commit murder. Could he have disguised his voice on the phone so his friends wouldn't have recognized him? Maybe he used voice-changing technology. Clare wasn't sure how he would have made a phone call look like it came from Kearnes' campaign, but if anyone could do that, she'd give Chopper the credit.

Maybe it wasn't such a good thing that he'd ridden into obscurity.

But if it had been Chopper, why had he let Clare live?

Kearnes. Too far-fetched? It didn't feel right to Clare, but she couldn't scratch him off yet.

Clare stared at her list and felt like she was still at square one.

She felt dull at the thought of the perpetrator being one of Sacha's parents, possibly because she herself hadn't gotten close to them in this investigation, but she knew that was the most likely scenario. Family killed far more often than strangers did.

She pressed play on the next video in her queue.

Sacha walked into her mom's office and set Jules on the bookshelf. Ted was seated, working at the desk.

"Ted," Sacha said. "How come you're in my mom's chair?"

"I need something on her computer."

"Does she know?"

Ted threw Sacha a smirk. "I set up her password. Pretty sure she's cool with me having access."

"Whatever. I'm going out. Tell my mom I'll do my own thing for dinner."

"I'm not your messenger. If you'd like, you can write it down and put the note in her inbox."

"God, Ted. You're going to see her, right? Can you just tell her for me?"

"Fine. But it's a favor, not my job."

"Yes, it's a favor. I'm so very grateful. If I can ever return it — you know, give my mom a message for you — I'd be thrilled to even things out."

"I said fine."

"What's up with you lately?" Sacha said. "You're acting like the annoying older brother I luckily never had."

A strange smile crept onto Ted's face. "I guess I'm going to miss you. When you go to Whistler."

"Yeah? That's kind of sweet."

"Why don't you stay here? Marry me instead."

Sacha laughed.

"I'm not joking. We'd be the perfect couple. I'll go into politics and that will leverage you to do all that community service you love, but with a super-high profile. The nation will love us."

"But we won't love each other."

"We get along well in bed," Ted said.

Sacha wrinkled her nose.

"You don't think so?" Ted didn't seem hurt, just curious.

"Yeah. I mean, we have a good groove together. Especially that time in Georgetown at your condo with all those confidential files spread out. I felt like we were in a spy movie."

Ted seemed to twig. "You were fucking me for files."

Sacha shrugged. "We both had fun. Who cares?"

"I mean it. Marry me."

"I have to go to Whistler. Maybe after. We'll see."

"What's in Whistler? Some orphans to rescue? Some children you need to teach literacy to?"

"You're right that it's community service," Sacha said. "But its more like the unconventional kind."

"Tell me."

"Not a chance. But the whole world will know soon. I'll only be gone for a year. Two at the most."

"You have to tell me what you're doing. I run your mom's career."

"Yeah. My *mom's* career. Not *my* life."

"She's planning to run for president next year. Everything you do is public — and that's only going to be more true as the campaign gets underway."

"Anyway, you don't run my mom's career." Sacha laughed. "You work for her. You're an employee."

"Is that why you won't marry me? You don't think I'm important enough?"

"I won't marry you because we're not in love."

"You'll sleep with me for files, but you won't marry someone unless you're in love with them?"

"Yeah," Sacha said. "And I slept with you for fun. I could have gotten those files another way if I'd wanted to."

"Do you even like me?"

"You're like a brother to me. Like I said, the annoying kind. But the kind I love anyway."

Sacha walked toward Jules, gave him a little wave, and left the room.

Clare stared at her computer. She watched the conversation a few more times. She'd need more proof — or Bert would, before making an arrest — but she was pretty sure she had her answer.

She grabbed her phone and called the number Norris had traced back to Kearnes' campaign. A male voice answered, scratchy from sleep, but professional even at four-fifteen in the morning. "Geoffrey Kearnes campaign headquarters. How can I help you?"

"Sorry to wake you. I have some questions that can't wait," Clare said.

"Who's calling?"

"I'm calling from the FBI. Is Ted Mitchell a friend of yours?"

"Ted's one of my best friends. Is something wrong?"

"Not necessarily. Have you seen him recently?"

"We were out for a drink maybe a week ago."

"Where?"

"You sure you're FBI?"

Clare frowned. "I can give you a callback number if you like. You can verify that you can trust me."

"No, that's fine. This isn't secret. We were at the King Cole Bar. Fifty-fifth and Fifth."

Clare had had a drink there once with Noah; she'd found it pompous beyond belief. "Do you remember what night that was?"

"I could look it up in my calendar."

"Yes, please."

"My calendar's in my phone. One sec." In less than a minute, he said, "It was Thursday, February 16. We met at ten, stayed maybe two hours. Maybe three."

"Business or pleasure?" Clare asked.

"A bit of both. Pleasure mainly, but we're both married to our jobs and it's a hot time in both of our careers, with our bosses both running for the Republican nomination."

"Indeed," Clare said. "You'd think you wouldn't meet at all, in the heat of such opposition."

"Okay."

Clare realized she'd sounded more confrontational than she wanted to. "Did you, at any point in the evening, lend your phone to Ted so he could make a call?"

"Um . . . yeah. Yeah, I did. He was checking his email all night. I mean, he's normally glued to his phone, but this night more than ever. Then his battery died. He asked to borrow my phone. He apologized — said it was a long-distance call. Like I gave a shit — I have unlimited North American minutes and my job pays for it, anyway."

"Thank you," Clare said.

"That's all?"

"That's all."

She called Bert. His voice was, naturally, groggy.

"Vengel, you need to change your clock back to New York time."

"I know who arranged Sacha's murder. Can you hook me up with one of our hackers? I need to get into the banks and other security footage — if possible, I'd like to get evidence before Westlake leaves for Phoenix in the morning."

"Just give me what you have," Bert said. "I'll figure out how to deal with it."

"Please?" Clare said. "Hook me up with one of the computer gurus on the team — they're up all night anyway; they live for this kind of shit. In the morning I'll pass you everything I know."

"We can't just hack, Clare. We'd need a warrant."

"I'm only asking for a phone number. Forget I said anything else. I want to call these tech guys socially."

Bert laughed. "Yeah, fine."

MONDAY / FEBRUARY 20

EIGHTY-EIGHT
MARTHA

Martha held her office door open for two uniformed FBI officers and a tall man in a gray suit. She motioned to some chairs, which they opted not to take. For lack of a better idea about where to place herself, she returned to her desk chair, opposite Ted.

The two uniformed officers — one male, one female, both around five-foot-six — stood on either side of the door, like the cement dogs she and Fraser once had at their country home. They had expressionless eyes, which Martha was used to now, with Secret Service following her all around.

The tall, sturdy man pulled up a seat beside Ted and said, "Edward Mitchell?" Martha was pretty sure this was Bert — she recognized his calm, low voice from the phone.

Ted twisted his neck to stare at Bert. "That's me."

Martha inhaled slowly. This was real; this was happening.

"You're under arrest for solicitation of murder for the death of Alexandra Westlake." Bert nodded toward the female officer.

In a rough, robotic voice, the uniformed woman recited the Miranda rights Martha had only heard on TV and in movies. Nothing else about this moment felt like television.

Ted's eyes shot wide open. "That makes no sense. Why would I want Sacha dead?"

"Do you understand your rights?" Bert asked Ted. "You can say whatever you like, but we can use it against you in court."

"I understood the first time." Ted thrust his chin forward. "And I'm not worried. I have a friend with the NYPD. Maybe we can call him, he can help sort this out."

Bert chuckled like a patient grandfather. His graying hair made him look gentle, too. "This the same friend who introduced you to Inspector Norris?"

Ted's face whitened a shade or two.

"Same friend who paid high-tech geeks ten thousand dollars to hack the FBI computers, find the name of my undercover agent?"

Ted stayed quiet, and Martha focused on her breathing. She had a role to play, it was coming up, and she hoped like hell she didn't botch it.

"You don't wonder how we know this?" Bert's brow furrowed, like he was pretending to look puzzled.

"You don't know anything. Everything you've just said is a lie."

"Hm." Bert wrinkled his mouth. "Your friend on the Kearnes campaign, Lester Banks, has been brought in for questioning. Says he has nothing to do with this."

"Oh, good. And you can trust him, because most murderers raise their hand and say *I did it* to the first cop who comes around asking."

"So you think Les is a murderer?"

"No — in fact I thought you had your man. That bent cop in Whistler."

"Stu Norris." Bert nodded. "He's the reason I'm here, actually."

"Really." Ted smoothed his notepad on the large mahogany desk. He picked up a pen and tapped at the page, as if he were reading his notes.

"Yes. It was Norris who figured out you'd been framing the Kearnes campaign — that they, in fact, are free and clear of any wrongdoing."

"Right," Ted said, tapping his pen and looking at Martha, like they really should be getting back to work. "Like I said, it's good to trust a killer when they tell you something. They almost never lie."

In a fluid, gentle movement, Bert reached forward and plucked the Mont Blanc from Ted's hand. He placed it in his jacket pocket.

"You can't steal my pen," Ted said. "That cost more than you make in a week."

"I doubt that," Bert said, taking the pen out of his pocket and scrutinizing its matte black finish. "Nice, though." He set it down on the desk, but out of Ted's reach. "Lester Banks is happy to testify about you borrowing his phone the other night."

"Awesome. Throw me in jail for stealing minutes. Oh wait — he lent me his phone, so I guess even that's not a crime."

"Your cop friend in Queens — he's been arrested. Asked for immunity right away. We gave it to him — he's talking pretty freely."

Martha breathed. In, out. She could do this.

"Why would you arrest a lousy street cop?" Ted said. "What could he have to do with such a high-profile case?"

"He had friends in high places," Bert said, "like the office of a future U.S. president."

Ted's chest pushed forward. "I'm sorry if my buddy was involved in Sacha's death. He's been jealous of me ever since I got into Georgetown. I guess he thought I'd stay in Queens, maybe join a trade, keep playing ball with him forever. My strong recommendation is that you find a way to reverse his immunity."

"Thanks for that," Bert said. "Your recommendation means a lot to us."

Ted's brow lowered as he studied Bert. "Are you FBI?"

Bert nodded.

"You'd do well to be less smug. Your organization has messed this case up massively."

"Mistakes have been made," Bert surprised Martha by saying. "But the biggest one by far was made by you."

Ted laughed — nervously, like a schoolboy unsure if he'd been caught pulling the fire alarm.

"Something funny, Mr. Mitchell?"

"I'm curious what you see as my alleged huge m-mistake." Ted's stutter on *mistake* was nearly imperceptible, but Martha was listening closely.

"Several wire transfers were made from the Westlake campaign's bank account to a numbered account in Switzerland. Seventy-five thousand dollars in total."

"Are you saying there's corruption in the campaign? That surprises me — we have good people working for us — but it wouldn't be an American first." Ted was smooth again, his polish back in place.

"On Saturday morning, this money was transferred out of Switzerland to an HSBC account in Argentina."

"Your point?"

"HSBC doesn't allow numbered accounts," Bert said. "The Argentina account had a name attached — Stuart Norris."

"Stuart Norris . . ." Ted tapped a finger to his mouth. "Oh! The cop in Whistler. So he's your man. Convenient, since he's already arrested."

"Yes. And he was paid by you."

"That's ridiculous." Ted met Martha's eye. She did her best to keep her return gaze steady. "Martha, can you tell them this is ridiculous? Even if the funds left our campaign, everyone with access to the bank account has a unique login ID. Are you saying whoever sent Norris the money used *my* ID?"

"No, actually. You used Senator Westlake's password."

"Come on. I tried to frame Martha for murder? Her campaign was everything to me. Still is — because I refuse to go down for this murder. And I refuse to allow her to be framed, too." He turned to Martha again. "Don't worry — I'll grill every member of our campaign, figure out who could have used your password to try to throw you under the bus like this. If it's not the Kearnes campaign — which I still think is way more likely — it means we have a traitor in our midst."

It was killing Martha, watching Ted. Washington put so much pressure on youth — to conform, to compete, to win. Would Ted have become a killer if he'd never worked in politics? Martha doubted that, highly.

Bert said, "When you made the money transfers, you used the computer in the senator's constituency office — which has timed security footage. The undercover you found and exposed to Whistler police — she's been up overnight figuring out your game."

"Wow." Ted's face was blank. "You guys need to go back to cop school, work on those deductive reasoning skills. I have some Sherlock Holmes books I can lend you, if you like. I read them as a child, of course, but they're probably around your level."

Martha suppressed a laugh. Her part was coming soon, and she was nervous as hell.

"We're impressed, Ted. You successfully convinced Inspector Norris that he was working with the DEA."

A slow grin spread across Ted's face.

"Is that funny?" Bert said.

"A little," Ted said. "It's from left field, that's for sure."

"You were smart. You had him convinced he needed to read and destroy all correspondence — emails, voice call logs from his cell phone. Of course, he did start saving things once he realized you weren't DEA. Plus, we went to the cell phone company and retrieved records, and of course we can retrieve deleted messages from his computer. But if everything had gone as planned — and it nearly did, until the senator here asked for further investigation — it would have worked. You would be walking free."

Ted snorted. "Have you been listening to me at all? Or do you just have this predetermined notion of what happened, and you're sticking to it no matter what?"

"Will you stand up, please? We'd like to put you in handcuffs."

"No, I won't stand up and be handcuffed. You can't treat me like a common criminal."

The man in the suit frowned.

"Tell them, Martha. I'm like a son to you. I'm like Sacha — not a common criminal."

Bert locked eyes with Martha, her cue to pick up as he'd coached her to.

"Ted, can I ask you something?" Martha's voice came out more softly than she'd realized it would. Which was a good thing — her true emotion was fiery rage.

Ted shrugged one skinny shoulder.

"Did you think killing Sacha — staging her suicide — would help my shot at the presidency?"

Martha watched Ted's jaw clench.

"You've always stunned me with your brightness. I just think — if we were in a moral vacuum — it was a really intelligent move. My popularity went through the roof." Martha nearly choked on the words she'd been told to say. "We've had to build this campaign up from the ground three times now — it's been a roller coaster. The lows are my fault, and you've just kept on going, building me back up without complaining. I don't think I've ever worked with someone quite as smart as you, quite as devoted."

Ted's mouth was doing funny things. The corners were jerking involuntarily.

"But we're not in a moral vacuum. What you've done has made me very sad." Martha spoke as if to a five-year-old child, as per Bert's instructions when it came to the emotional parts.

Ted's eyes went wide. Martha hoped she was getting through to him.

"They know you had Sacha killed," Martha said gently. "It will be much easier for you if you come clean, let them help you." Considering the times Ted had spoken about his own mother and about his replacing Sacha — the FBI believed this was part of his pathology — it seemed he had a true belief that he belonged in higher circumstances, that he should have been born to a more elite family. "Let *me* help you," Martha finished.

And then Ted's face turned sour. He gave Martha the most disdainful look she'd ever seen — even more disdainful than Sacha arguing politics.

"Who the hell wants to help some dirty kid from Queens?" He

was practically shouting. "Not you. You were just using me for my brain. Telling me, 'Ted, go here. No Ted, we don't need you here — stay home with your computer and be my slave.' Who's looking out for me? Only me. Man, you're worse than my real mother. She never pretended she was anything but selfish."

My real mother. Martha realized that the FBI was right. She said, "The cleaner you are with us now, the better your chance for surviving the system. I'd be devastated to see you done in by the death penalty. It would be like losing both my children." Martha choked back bile — playing into the alleged mental illness made her feel physically ill.

"Why would I care if they electrocute me? If I go down for this murder, my life is over anyway. I'll never be president. Hell, I'll never even be a lowly senator."

Martha used the next line the FBI had fed her: "Ted, there are psychiatric facilities that can take care of you. They can help you sort this out, return to society afterward and thrive."

"Why would you care?" Mixed with Ted's scorn, Martha thought she detected hope.

"Sometimes we do things that aren't really who we are — things we think we have to do because we're temporarily misguided, but when we come back to our senses, we're filled with regret." *Things like raising your child with a string of nannies, saying no to the circus, to DisneyWorld — to almost every fun thing Sacha had suggested because it would have taken Martha's time away from her career.* "But if you want your life to have meaning — and I know that's what you want for yourself — you're *so* bright, you have so much to offer — then you have to take control now. Confess to what you did, and we'll get you psychological help."

Ted shook his head a few times quickly. It was more a spasmodic movement than a deliberate negation of what Martha had said. "These men set you up; they've prepped you in advance," Ted said, his tone even. "If you were learning about all this now — I killed your *daughter*, for Christ's sake — you'd be raging."

Martha was silent. She'd elicited the confession. The FBI could take it from there.

But Ted kept going. "You're just so clueless. You're nothing like my mother. You don't deserve to be president."

"Was it my constituents' money? I don't think you have any of your own. I'll need to know so I can repay it on your behalf."

Ted actually spat at Martha. It shocked her — again, she'd seen it in movies, but it had never happened to her in real life. The spit landed on her shoes. "Of course it was their money. It was your constituents I was protecting. You're not even grateful at all, are you?"

Martha's eyes felt like they popped out of her head. It was only because she could still see that she knew they were still in their sockets.

"Sacha was trying to take you down," Ted continued. "She was in Whistler filming an exposé of your hypocritical drug war. It's only because I was on your side, because I got rid of the obstacles that were standing in the way of the White House, that you're probably going to get there. You know you're in first, now? That kid you're trying to save — the addict in Detroit? Michigan loves you for that."

"Wow."

"Yeah, wow is right. Didn't know your daughter was a traitor, huh? Whereas I was true to the end. Too bad you made the wrong choice."

"No, I was thinking wow, it's a good thing your mother's dead. It would be horrible for her to see who her son grew up to become." Martha snatched a tissue from the box on the desk and bent to wipe the gob of saliva from her Louboutins.

EIGHTY-NINE
CLARE

The phone rang and Clare jumped. She hoped it wasn't Roberta, calling to say her dad had died.

"Hello?" Clare heard her voice come out small and tentative.

"What's wrong with you?" It was Bert. "Pick it up, Vengel."

"Sorry." Clare was relieved. "Did everything go okay with the arrest?"

"Yup. Even got a confession."

Clare felt a grin spread across her face. She'd maybe gotten two hours of sleep, but it was worth it.

"Meet me at the Coffee Shop in twenty," Bert said.

"Is it bad?" Clare knew she'd fucked up with that acid hit. They'd left her in place for the assignment, but she could still lose her job over a bad decision.

"Just be there. And don't dress like a slob."

If she were losing her job, Clare wanted to wear ripped sweatpants and a sleeveless heavy metal band T-shirt. But maybe this wasn't going to be that. She chose some jeans that were fairly clean from the pile of clothes on her hardwood floor, and she rode the rickety elevator down to street level.

She walked six blocks north to Union Square and sat in a window booth to wait. The Coffee Shop was way too trendy for its own good, but Clare ignored the sullen service and ordered a black coffee. She itched for a cigarette but had managed without one so far — even when pulling the all-nighter.

In less than five minutes, she spotted Bert lumbering along the street in his trench coat. At over six feet tall, with a build that was somehow thick and lean at the same time, he looked like a Russian mobster's bodyguard. He was with a shorter man — maybe five-eight or five-ten — who looked quiet and smart, like a professor.

The two men entered the diner.

"This is Alistair Patko," Bert said.

Clare reached a hand across the table, where Patko had slid into the booth. His grip was good — firm, but not bone-crushing.

Bert slid in beside Clare. "Alistair works with the CIA. He's been following your career with some interest."

"He has?" Clare's career was short and spotty — this didn't make a lot of sense.

"You're not conventional," Patko said. "Which works well for the team I'm trying to assemble."

"I'm already on a team like that." Clare glanced at Bert. "A team I like."

"I'm looking for undercover operatives to do pretty much what Bert here has been doing with his team internally. Except my domain is international. So you'd be going to different countries on assignment. Sometimes for months on end."

Clare wasn't sure if this was an offer or just a discussion. She tried to keep her hopes down as she continued to listen.

"Assignments would be riskier. You would need to spend time learning new languages, being trained with different weapons, different martial arts. There are a lot of academics, which I'm not sure is your strong suit."

Clare swallowed.

"The pay would be good. Double your current base salary plus a hefty stipend when you're in the field."

Clare didn't care about salary, but she knew enough not to say so in a job negotiation.

Bert poked Clare in the ribs. "You going to say something, Vengel?"

"Why me?"

Bert snorted. "That's a damn good question."

Patko smiled. "I know that several of your superiors have questioned your decision-making skills. Including Amanda Payne on this assignment — she wrote a scathing report, actually. But then she added a paragraph, an addendum highlighting your intelligence and adaptability. And you did some nice work at the end, getting evidence on the Westlake murder. That combination happens to be what I'm looking for. I don't like working with people who take authority too seriously. Their minds tend to be creatively closed."

"Don't tell her that," Bert said.

"I want resistance, not defiance. She'll learn the difference."

Clare met Patko's eye with a small grin.

"Have you ever had formal undercover training?"

"For, like, three days in the police academy." Clare mentally kicked herself for sounding like a valley girl.

"So you've been fighting uphill. Are you interested in learning more about the craft?"

"Of course. Like what, specifically?"

"Like clear decision-making skills. So you won't be playing guessing games about whether you should drop LSD with suspects — you'll know with more clarity that you most definitely should *not*."

Clare groaned, and Bert chuckled.

"You would learn how to palm that tab of acid and act the whole trip. Do you have shooting experience?"

"I was trained as a cop. I was the second-best shot in my class."

"Well, if you're the second-best on our team, my hat will go off to you. I'd be happy with second worst."

"Is everyone on your team some kind of superstar?"

"That's the idea. But superstars aren't born — they're created through years of hard work. I see that potential in you, too, or I wouldn't be making you this offer."

Clare gulped. "So this is an offer? I can accept it, then I'd have this new job?"

Patko slid out of the booth and stood up. "I'll leave Bert to go over particulars. I'll need an answer by Friday, if that works for you."

"Sure," Clare said. "I'll think it over."

NINETY
MARTHA

Martha sat back in her chair across the desk from Bill Maher. It wasn't even a pose — she felt relaxed and comfortable. Cameras were rolling. Polite introductory lines were out of the way.

"How do you run a campaign while grieving for your daughter?" Maher asked.

"With help," Martha said. "My team has worked their asses off — you can swear on this network, yes?"

The crowd tittered, and Martha remembered how great it felt to have a live audience laughing for her. It was a smaller crowd than usual, since they were taping on an off day. The rest of the show — the political panel — would be taped on Friday.

"Yes," Maher said. "You can fucking swear on this network. We're not Fox. Sorry if Fox is your best supporter — I know they love their Republicans."

"They like Republicans like Geoffrey Kearnes. You know, the kind who like to fly private on their constituents' dime."

"I like to fly private," Maher said. "Why do you think I invite all these celebrities on my show? I want invites on their planes, man. But

I'm interrupting you — your staff have been working their mother-fucking asses off . . ."

Martha smirked. "Yes — they've even taught me to be savvy with social media. I'm lucky with the team I have working for me. Except, of course . . ." Martha let the sentence trail, temporarily, then grabbed back her strength and said, "Ted Mitchell aside."

Maher's eyebrows lifted. "How do you feel about Ted Mitchell now?"

"Sad," Martha said. "He was smart. So much potential. But his mental illness has taken him over."

"Do you know what that illness was?"

"The best guess is Narcissistic Personality Disorder."

"Is there a high success rate, curing narcissism? If there is, we should send the cure to Hollywood."

Martha smiled along with the laughter from the audience. "No, there's very little success curing NPD," Martha said. "But talk therapy occasionally works. Which is maybe why people in Hollywood talk so much." Martha was pleased when the audience roared even harder. It was off the cuff — none of her assistants had written that line and she felt like she was in her element.

"Are you angry with yourself for trusting Ted? You two worked closely together — there must be signs you see, in retrospect. Are there any that are eating at you now?"

"Dozens," Martha said. "But evil isn't something that most of us can see. We shut that part of our brain off because it's too scary, or we don't want to indulge our own evil. Ha — can you tell I went to my first therapy session today?"

Maher laughed, maybe too politely. Maybe Martha should leave the therapy part out of her transparency platform.

"So you're staying in this race?"

"I'm in it more than ever."

"Good. Because if you win the ticket, I'm voting Republican for the first time in I can't even remember how long."

Martha felt a tear form in her right eye — her first in the eighteen days since Sacha had died. She brushed it away, but not before Maher saw her.

"Sorry. Does my vote make you sad?"

"This was Sacha's favorite TV show. Your vote would make me happier than you know."

NINETY-ONE
CLARE

C lare looked at Noah. She moved a pawn forward on the chessboard. "I should grab my toothbrush before I go."

"You don't have to leave." Noah moved his rook to leave his queen unprotected.

"Are you playing stupidly on purpose?"

"Shit. Didn't see that. No, just dumb today I guess."

Clare took the queen.

"I thought things were going well," Noah said. "You wanted me to go with you to see your family."

Clare was tempted to reach for one of Noah's cigarettes, but didn't. "I thought so, too. I changed my mind."

"Why? Because you bail whenever things get tricky? That's fine when you're a teenager. But if you keep running, you'll end up alone with no one to love you back."

"If I'm still single when I'm thirty, I'll get a cat."

"You hate cats."

"So I'll get a dog."

"Dogs need love. You'll think it's being needy when it wants to curl up and cuddle." Noah studied the board before moving his bishop.

Clare moved her knight so it put his king and rook in double jeopardy. "Check."

Noah wrinkled his mouth and moved his king.

"I'm not quitting work," Clare said. "So I guess that means I'm still a whore, still unworthy of your full-time affection."

"You're not unworthy. You're amazing."

"Noah, *fuck off.*" Clare couldn't take his nice guy act — the one that lured her back every single time, because it wasn't so much an act as it was the best side of himself.

Noah leaned back on the couch. "I can't believe you got a job offer from the CIA. You haven't even been back in town twenty-four hours."

"I haven't said yes yet."

"But you will. And you'll get sent off on really cool assignments. To Barcelona, or Hong Kong."

"I'm looking forward to my first Latin lover." Clare took the rook with her knight. It maybe wasn't the kindest thing to say, so Clare tossed Noah a small grin to let him know she was joking.

"Okay," Noah said finally. "I can live with it. With who you are. With what you do."

Clare looked up at him again and held his gaze longer.

"I made a playlist for later," Noah said. "One hundred percent Depeche Mode and Leonard Cohen."

"So make a move. I can checkmate you on the next turn and I'm hungry for dinner." Clare still wished he would say he was in love with her, but this was close.

"Glad your game is back, at least." Noah pushed a pawn forward, though it was futile. "Where do you want to eat?"

"La Palapa. I have to start practicing foreign languages."

"Going home with a Latin waiter doesn't count as research," Noah said, "in case you thought our relationship was that loose."

"What — so now you want to be exclusive?" Clare moved her queen to seal the win. She met his eyes and held them. She liked what she got back.

Noah nodded, keeping her gaze. "Yeah. Assignments excluded. Think you can handle that?"

"I can." Clare chewed her lower lip. "But let's talk about the Latin waiter."

ACKNOWLEDGMENTS

Death's Last Run nearly died on the operating table. It was impossible to write, late for almost every deadline, and eventually turned into my favorite book in the series. To get there, I needed tons of help.

Jack David at ECW Press read an early draft and told me not to throw it out.

Emily Schultz worked magic on this manuscript as an editor. I learn from her each time we work together. Cat London's keen copy-edit eye sharpened and tightened things even further.

I call her Simon Cowell, but actually Sally Harding's incisive honesty is the best kind of feedback there is. Her Cooke Agency team is a supportive, savvy bunch I feel lucky to have on my side.

Keith Whybrow, my husband, built my office using salvaged wood from our reno project. "Because I know you don't care if the wood matches," he said. "You just need a space that's creative and you."

Cover art is done by Cyanotype. I love their style, and they're generous with art clips for my website.

The ECW crew — Sarah Dunn, Crissy Boylan, Jen Knoch, Erin Creasey, David Caron, Jenna Illies, Rachel Ironstone, Troy Cunningham (and probably more) are smart and awesome.

I am massively grateful for pre-readers. My sister Erin Kawalecki dissects each word like it's her own, with encouragement and a sharp eye for making the story as strong as it can be; my cousin Chloe Dirksen cracks me up as I read her warm and witty margin commentary (like "the BJ image is heavy here . . . you might want to change *dick* to *douche*"); my cousin Christie Nash is brilliant at showing me what's missing from character relationships; my friend Scott Hicks has finally realized I am not, nor never will be a literary short story writer like his hero Alice Munro, still he pores over my words in coffee shops, helping me hone them; my friend Christine Cheng worked hard with me on Martha's politics, and ultimately she found the research article that saved the day; my mom Dona Matthews, reads with *just* the right balance of glowing praise and a (helpfully) critical eye; my aunt Shelley Peterson helps me separate and define the characters, not let one slip into another's dialogue; my aunt Carole Matthews helped me flesh out the Whistler setting to bring out its character; my grandmother Joyce Matthews hasn't read the book at the time of these acknowledgments but ·plans to pore over the proofread and catch mistakes. (So if there are issues with the final draft, I'll give you her email address, not mine.)

Huge thanks for the time commitment from my colleagues Angie Abdou, Deryn Collier, Ian Hamilton, Owen Laukkanen, and Dorothy McIntosh for reading and endorsing *Death's Last Run*.

Fellow writers Steph VanderMeulen and Deryn Collier read trouble segments and gave me excellent specific feedback on demand.

Angie Abdou and Commit Snow & Skate in Fernie hooked me up with the raddest snowboarder slang. Angie mailed me her terrific book, *The Canterbury Trail*, so I could groove with mountain culture.

Chevy Stevens was hugely generous with writing tips that helped me hone my writing skills for this book. She made me name a plant after her for her troubles. The plant died, so we named a tree for her instead.

Pam Gross Barnsley gave me Whistler details from a local's perspective, including making Chopper a home on Cougar Mountain.

Shaun Luciano (a.k.a. Domino King) is a cop in California who

I met playing iPhone chess. He answers my U.S. law enforcement questions between moves in our games.

Mark and Elizabeth Sullivan welcomed me into the extreme snow culture that is Tailgate Alaska, where I learned about heli-skiing, sledding, and avalanche safety while having a raucously good time.

And from social media:

Hilary Davidson is my publicity role model — on Twitter and in real life. Jana Benincasa named the bar Avalanche. Kim Moritsugu is the evil genius behind the teddy cam. J.J. Lee is my go-to fashion guru — he can dress anyone from gangstas to politicians. Judy Hudson gave me Zoe's cello brand. Scott Chantler clarified the difference between the iPhone and BlackBerry user. Natalie Stover Miele and Ilonka Halsband hooked up airport Starbucks intel. Kelvin Kong has strong opinions on everything, some of which are surprisingly useful. I could go on forever: I had so much help with title brainstorming and cover art feedback and morale boosts from every corner of the internet.

If I've forgotten you, send me a nasty email. I'll make sure I don't forget you twice.

R obin Spano grew up in downtown Toronto and now lives
in rural B.C. She studied physics at university but dropped
out to travel North America on her motorcycle, waitressing
in various cities and towns while trying to write her first novel.
When she's not lost in fiction, she loves to get outside snowboarding,
hiking, boating, and riding the curves of the local highways in her
big, black pick-up truck. She is married to a man who hates reading.

THE CLARE VENGEL
UNDERCOVER SERIES

ROBINSPANO.COM

At ECW Press, we want you to enjoy this book in whatever format you like, whenever you like. Leave your print book at home and take the eBook to go! Purchase the print edition and receive the eBook free. Just send an email to ebook@ecwpress.com and include:

• the book title
• the name of the store where you purchased it
• your receipt number
• your preference of file type: PDF or ePub?

A real person will respond to your email with your eBook attached. And thanks for supporting an independently owned Canadian publisher with your purchase!

GET THE eBOOK FREE
PROOF OF PURCHASE REQUIRED

DEATH'S LAST RUN

A CLARE VENGEL UNDERCOVER NOVEL